DARCY'S
ULTIMATUM

BY
DAY LECLAIRE

Published in Great Britain 2011
by Mills & Boon, an imprint of Harlequin (UK) Limited,
Eton House, 18-24 Paradise Road, Richmond, Surrey TW9 1SR

© Day Totton Smith 2010

ISBN: 978 0 263 88221 6

51-0611

Harlequin (UK) policy is to use papers that are natural, renewable and recyclable products and made from wood grown in sustainable forests. The logging and manufacturing processes conform to the legal environmental regulations of the country of origin.

Printed and bound in Spain
by Blackprint CPI, Barcelona

To Mom, whose encouragement is unwavering
and who has always believed in me.

USA TODAY bestselling author **Day Leclaire** is a three-time winner of both a Colorado Award of Excellence and a Golden Quill Award. She's won *RT Book Reviews* Career Achievement and Love and Laughter Awards, a Holt Medallion and a Booksellers Best Award. She has also received an impressive ten nominations for the prestigious Romance Writers of America RITA® Award. Day's romances touch the heart and make you care about her characters as much as she does. In Day's own words, "I adore writing romances, and can't think of a better way to spend each day." For more information, visit Day on her website, www.dayleclaire.com.

Dear Reader,

I'm delighted to have the opportunity to share with you four new books that revisit one of my favorite families—the Dantes. I'm also pleased to reintroduce the legendary Inferno, the family legend that claims that a Dante male can recognize his soul mate the first time he touches the woman meant to be his.

In my previous series, we met the patriarch and matriarch of the Dante clan, Primo and Nonna. They had two sons, Dominic and Alessandro. Dominic and his wife, Laura, offered us four fabulous Dante sons—Sev, Marco, Lazz and Nicolò—and their individual love stories, which comprised The Dante Legacy.

Now we have the sons and daughter of Alessandro and Elia. Meet Luc, Rafe, Draco and the one daughter in several generations—Gianna. Resistance is pointless since The Inferno is intent on joining each of these Dantes with their soul mates.

It doesn't matter if you're new to the Dantes or have read all the previous books, these stories stand on their own. Welcome to the warmth of family, the passion inherent in Desire books, strong alpha heroes, and the women—the only women—meant to share a once-in-a-lifetime love affair. Welcome back to the Dantes and their overpowering Inferno. I hope you enjoy!

All the best,

Day Leclaire

Prologue

"I need your help."

If it had been anyone other than his grandmother uttering those words, Luc Dante would have walked away. But coming from a woman he loved with all his heart, he found himself replying, "What can I do?"

Beautiful hazel eyes, wise from the weight of her years, held a wealth of compassion. There was also a twinkling of the irrepressible humor that was so much a part of her character. She hesitated just long enough for a faint warning bell to sound, an internal alarm he'd long-ago learned to listen for…and respond to with all due haste. "The truth is, it is a friend of mine who needs your help," she admitted.

"Nonna—"

"Hear me out, Luciano." In her own way, his grandmother could be as autocratic as his grandfather, Primo. At his nod, she continued. "You remember my dear friend Marietta de Luca, do you not? We all vacationed together one summer at the cabin when you were a boy. You children all called her Madam. Even her grandchildren address her by that name."

It took a moment to summon the memory from his childhood. Then it popped into crisp focus. The Dante family summer home. The lake. His three brothers, sister and four cousins all running rampant. And three little girls—Madam de Luca's grandchildren—with frizzy black hair and pitch eyes whom they'd secretly dubbed the three witches.

There'd been a fourth girl, he recalled, with bright red hair, white, white skin and intense eyes, who'd drifted from shadow to shadow and rarely spoke. Most of the time, she had a nose in a book. Showing stunning originality, they'd dubbed her Red.

Even more oddly, she made him…itch. It was the only way he could describe it, that vague jittery reaction he had whenever she came too close. It made him want to poke at her, to try to elicit a reaction. But she'd shied away from all of them, vanishing like a ghost whenever they approached, showing up at mealtimes long enough to nibble at her food before slipping away again. For some reason, her behavior had irritated him. He might have done something about it if not for the watchful eye of his grandparents.

Luc shook off the memory. "I remember Madam," he admitted. He also remembered thinking that it would make the perfect name for a dog, but decided—even at such a tender age—that it might be wise to keep that particular tidbit to himself. A brief image flashed through his head of an elegant, aristocratic woman with coloring to match her dark-haired grandchildren, a woman who could command obedience with a single black look. "What about her?"

"Her eldest granddaughter, Téa, needs your assistance for a few weeks."

He wondered briefly which of the witches was Téa, but the bell inside his head sounded another warning, this one louder than before and he focused on that, instead. "What sort of assistance?" he asked suspiciously.

"Well…" Nonna released her breath in a sigh. "To be honest, she needs a bodyguard."

Luc shot to his feet, his knee screaming in protest at the unexpected jolt. Damn it to hell! "No."

"Now, Luciano—"

He limped to the bank of windows of Dantes conference room where his grandmother had cornered him and stared out at the city of San Francisco. Any other day, he'd have admired the crystal clear spring morning that offered a stunning view of San Francisco Bay and the startling backwash from a crisp blue sky. Not today. Not this moment. Not when memories tried to crowd their way into his thoughts and heart.

"I can't." The words came out far harsher than he'd intended. "Don't ask me to go through that again."

"It was not your fault," Nonna said quietly.

He pivoted on his good leg, struggling to hold the nightmare at bay. But flashes crept through, no matter how hard he worked to keep them compartmentalized. The urgent rush to escape their pursuers. The SUV coming out of nowhere. The car crash. The child. Oh, God, the child. The husband, gone. The wife, broken. The sound of her weeping. Her pathetic pleas. "Let me die! Just let me die so I can be with them!"

He closed his eyes and forced the memories into the

furthest recesses of his mind. "I can't do it, Nonna. I won't."

"It is not that sort of job," she said with such gentleness that it threatened to overwhelm him.

He waited until he regained his self-control. "It is that sort of job if I need to guard her," he corrected with amazing calm.

"Attend to me, *cucciolo mio*. Téa is to receive a large inheritance when she turns twenty-five." Nonna raised her eyes to the heavens in clear benediction. "*If* she turns twenty-five."

Facts first. Refuse later. "Someone wants to prevent that from happening?"

"No, no. Nothing like that. Téa is…oblivious." Nonna made a tsking sound with her tongue and then switched to Italian. "The girl is highly focused."

Luc lifted an eyebrow and followed suit, switching to Italian. "Which is it? Oblivious or focused?"

Nonna gave a speaking shrug. "Both. She is very organized and focused on that which holds her attention. Such organization and attention to detail causes her to be somewhat oblivious to all else. It has gotten to the point where she has become seriously accident prone."

"So, lock her up in a room somewhere for—" He tilted his head to one side. "How long?"

"Six weeks."

"For six weeks."

"First, the de Lucas would have to get her to agree, which she will not. Secondly, she is the main support of her family. She cannot afford to take a six-week leave of absence. They are in serious financial straits."

"Why does that change when…Téa?" He lifted an eyebrow and at his grandmother's nod, he continued. "When Téa turns twenty-five?"

"On her next birthday, she receives a huge trust fund and ownership in a business which will support the entire family for the rest of their lives. If she does not…" Nonna shrugged again. "The money does not."

"I already have a job."

And he did. Sort of. As head of security for Dantes Courier Service, the branch of the business which handled the day-to-day operations of safely transporting Dantes fabulous fire diamonds, gemstones and jewelry, he wouldn't normally have time for this. But there had been a recent robbery of one of the shipments and while the police and insurance company were investigating, DCS had been temporarily shut down.

Nonna's eyes flashed with hazel fire. "Do not insult my intelligence."

Luc sighed, hearing the painful snap of the trap closing around him. "Let me get this straight. You want me to safeguard a klutz so she makes it to her twenty-fifth birthday? That's it? No danger. No actual bodyguarding. You just want a… What? A babysitter?"

Nonna smiled in relief. "Exactly. Téa de Luca needs a babysitter for the next six weeks and I promised Madam that you would sit on her baby."

One

Luc lounged—as best as a six foot three inch man could lounge—in the dainty chair at the small bistro table outside a trendy downtown San Francisco restaurant. He struggled to control his impatience. Beside him Nonna and Madam chatted happily in Italian while they awaited the arrival of Téa de Luca, or Witch Girl #1 as Luc had privately dubbed her. Because she was late, a trait that—quite literally—drove him out of his mind, he was in hurry up and wait mode, one of his least favorite memories of his military service.

It was rude. It was self-indulgent. And it gave the underlying message, "It's all about *me*." He despised women who adopted that sort of attitude and avoided them like the proverbial plague.

He reached for a breadstick and pulverized it between his teeth. Where the *hell* was she? It wasn't like he had all day to sit around waiting on Her Witchiness.

Well, actually, he supposed he did now that he was temporarily out of a job while the cops and insurance company looked into the fire diamond heist. But there were plenty of other things he'd rather do. Like drive a spike between his ears, or tie himself to a railroad track in front of an oncoming freight train, or swim with a pack of voracious Great White sharks.

He cleared his throat and leaned toward Madam. "Where the he—" He broke off beneath the withering glare emanating from his grandmother and rethought his choice of words. "Would you mind trying Téa's cell again, Madam?"

"Do you have another appointment, Luciano?" Nonna asked. Her tone came across sweet enough, but a hint of hazel fire flashed through her eyes. A warning message he pretended not to notice.

"As a matter of fact, I do," he lied without remorse.

Madam picked up the pretty lavender cell phone she'd set on the table as gingerly as if it were a landmine. Peering through a pair of reading glasses hanging from a crystal beaded necklace around her neck, she carefully punched in a number. "No, no. That's not right," she murmured, her brow furrowing.

"I think if you just hit send several times it dials the last number," Nonna explained helpfully.

"Would you like me to take care of it?" Luc offered.

Madam passed him the cell with an amusing combination of relief and hauteur, reminding him again why she'd been given her particular moniker. "If you wouldn't mind, I would appreciate it."

"Happy to help."

He pushed the speed dial and waited for the call to connect. While it rang he automatically scanned the busy sidewalk just past the frilly wrought iron fence that separated the outdoor section of the café from the rest of humanity. It was an occupational hazard he'd developed first during his military career, and then when he'd opened his own personal security business. And it had spilled over into his current—he grimaced—or rather *former* job as head of security for Dantes Courier Service. With luck, the case would soon be resolved and he'd be back doing something useful instead of babysitting Witch Girl #1.

Pedestrians scurried across the intersection adjacent to the café. All except one lone woman who paused dead center in the crosswalk, juggling a briefcase and a voluminous shoulder bag from which she extracted three cell phones. Without quite knowing why, Luc shoved back his chair and stood, the phone still pressed to his ear.

The pedestrian warning signal guarding the intersection began to blink, indicating that the light would soon change. To his concern, the redhead remained oblivious as she sorted through the cell phones she'd unearthed before selecting one that, even from the distance separating them, he could see was a distinctive lavender. A distinctive lavender matching the one in his hand. She flipped it open.

A breathless greeting sounded in his ear. "Hello? Madam?"

Alarm bells clamored with painful intensity. He dropped the cell to the table, took a single step toward the waist-high wrought iron gate separating the outdoor portion of the café from the sidewalk and vaulted over it, careful to land on his good leg. He forced himself to attempt a swift jog, ignoring the red-hot stab of pain that shot from knee to hip. The light changed just then and cars began to move forward.

Get the woman!

The urgent demand roared through him, deafening him to everything else. He remembered his cousin, Nicolò, describing how his wife had been hit by a cab shortly after they'd first met. The driver had changed lanes to avoid a slow-moving vehicle and sped into the intersection, hitting Kiley. Even now, her past remained a blank as a result of the accident, although she and Nicolò were busy building new memories and creating a new life together—which included a baby due sometime in the next few weeks.

Get the woman now!

Luc watched helplessly as history decided to repeat itself. A cab swerved around a delivery truck who'd unexpectedly double parked outside a mom-and-pop market. With a blare of its horn, the cab accelerated directly toward the intersection. Clearly the driver didn't realize the woman was there, probably because he was intent on cursing at the truck driver, while the woman remained oblivious to her danger as she pressed buttons on her cell.

Get the woman now before you lose her forever!

Luc thought he shouted a warning and forced himself into a limping run, cursing a leg that would prevent him from reaching her before the cab. The driver didn't spot the hazard until the very last instant. He slammed on the brakes with an ear-splitting scream of metal and rubber. Luc forced himself to move even faster, praying his leg would hold him, but he knew he'd never be in time.

A split second before the cab hit the woman, it swerved a few precious feet. It was enough. Just enough. Luc snatched her clear and dove toward the safety of the sidewalk. He twisted so he'd absorb most of the impact, landing hard on his bad hip. Raw pain exploded through him.

"Son of a *bitch!*"

The woman shoved against his chest, surfacing in a tangle of deep auburn curls, lean ivory arms and legs and countless files and papers. Three cell phones rained down around them. A pair of rimless reading glasses dangled from one ear while teal-blue eyes regarded him in open outrage.

"Did you just call me a bitch?"

"Not exactly." Wincing, he grasped the woman around the waist and levered her to one side. Cautiously he sat up. His hip screamed in protest. Aw, hell. Not broken, but not in good shape, either. "Do you always stand in the middle of an intersection daring cars to hit you?" His injury gave the question more of a bite than he intended.

She wrapped herself in indignation while straightening her glasses. One of the fragile bits of wire connecting the two lenses across the bridge of her nose was severely bent, causing the lenses to sit cockeyed on her face. "I was answering a call from my grandmother." As though the explanation reminded her, she scrambled through the paraphernalia littered around them until she unearthed a lavender cell phone identical to Madam's. "Hello? Madam, are you still there?"

"Téa! Oh, my dear. Are you all right?"

The voice didn't come from the phone, but from a few feet away. Madam and Nonna hurried down the sidewalk toward them. Groaning, Luc cautiously climbed to his feet, then offered Téa a hand. And that's when it hit. A powerful spark, followed by a bone-deep burn shot from her palm to his. It flew through his veins, sinking into him, absorbed on the deepest level.

His internal alarm bells went berserk, clamoring and clashing and shrieking so loudly it destroyed all sensation but one—a desire so strong and powerful he literally shook from the desperate need to snatch this woman into his arms and carry her off. Sweep her away to someplace private where he could put his mark on her. Claim her in every way that a man claims a woman.

She stared at him in open shock and he had to assume she'd felt it, as well. Her lips parted, as though begging for his kiss, and her eyes seemed to smolder with blue-green fire. Every scrap of color drained from her face leaving behind a tiny pinprick smattering of freckles dusting her elegant nose. The foam of deep red curls tumbled down her back in bewitching disarray and provided a blazing frame for her upturned face—a face that mirrored every single emotion from bewilderment to disbelief.

She tore her gaze from his and looked at their joined hands. "What… What was that?" she whispered.

Deep down he knew, though he couldn't quite give it credence. Not yet. Not when it defied logic and understanding. Not when every fiber of his being resisted admitting the possibility of its existence. And yet… It was exactly as his grandfather had described. Exactly as his parents had told him. Exactly as what his cousins claimed happened to them. And exactly what he'd hoped would never happen to him.

"*That* was impossible," he answered.

"Téa?" Madam's apprehensive voice cut through the wash of desire. "Téa, I asked if you were all right."

Jerking her hand free of Luc's grasp, she turned to her

grandmother. "I'm fine," she assured. "A little shaken and manhandled, but otherwise unhurt."

Luc's brows gathered into a scowl. Manhandled? *Manhandled?* How about snatched from the jaws of death? How about saved by the generosity of a stranger? How about rescued from a metal dragon by a poor battered knight who could have used some freaking shining armor to protect himself from injury?

Before he could argue the point, pedestrians paused to help gather up Téa's belongings which she carefully organized, tucking everything away into her briefcase and voluminous purse. The desire that had overwhelmed him minutes before eased, at least enough for him to recover her cell phones. One of them was chirping at great volume, urging, "Answer me. Answer me. Answer me, me, *me!*" over and over. Even these had individual slots in her handbag.

By the time she finished, reaction set in. Madam appeared on the verge of tears. Nonna's brow was lined in worry. Only Téa seemed blissfully unconcerned.

Luc, on the other hand, found it difficult to even think straight, other than to resent like hell the events of the past several moments. Pain radiated from every muscle in his body. Between his banged up knee and hip, Téa's apparent obliviousness to her near-death experience, and that undeniable sizzle of physical attraction when they'd first touched flesh-to-flesh, he was *not* a happy man. And the fact that Téa was ignoring the significance of each and every part of all that, only made it worse.

Luc was a man of action. Someone who took charge. Granted, he had finely tuned instincts. But he backed them with logic and split-second decisiveness that had saved his hide countless times in the past. It had also saved Téa's, though she didn't seem to quite get that fact.

Whatever had just happened had done a number on him and he resented it like hell.

Determined to revert to type, he regained control by gathering up the three women and urging them toward the café. After seeing them seated, he went in search of their waiter and ordered a new round of drinks, adding a black ale for himself. If they'd had anything stronger, he'd have chosen that instead, but until he could down a dozen anti-inflammatories chased by a stiff couple of fingers of whiskey, the beer would have to do.

"Thank goodness you were there to rescue Téa from that crazed cab driver," Madam said the minute he returned to the table.

Luc took a seat and fixed Téa with a hard gaze. "Perhaps if your granddaughter wouldn't answer her cell phone in the middle of the intersection, she wouldn't have to worry about being mowed down by crazed cab drivers."

Téa smiled sweetly. "My grandmother tells me that *you* were the one who phoned me. I believe that means this is *your* fault."

"*My* fault?" The waiter appeared with their drinks, but froze at Luc's tone, one he used when dressing down some gomer over his latest FUBAR. "How is it my fault that you chose to answer your phone in the middle of a busy intersection?"

"If you hadn't called—"

"Which I wouldn't have needed to do if you'd been on time—"

"—I wouldn't have answered my cell in the middle of the intersection."

"—I wouldn't have had to call you. But you're welcome."

He glanced at the waiter and gave an impatient jerk

of his head toward the table. Scrambling, the waiter deposited the drinks, scribbled down their orders and made a hasty retreat.

"You're welcome?" Téa repeated.

She blinked, her eyes huge from behind the bent lenses of her reading glasses. As though suddenly aware she had them on, she shoved them into the curls on top of her head. Then her expression blossomed into a wide smile, completely transforming her face. What had been pretty before became stunning.

Heat exploded low in his gut. The urge to carry her off grew stronger, more compelling than before. He snatched up his lager and took a long swallow, praying it would douse the flames. Instead it seemed to make them more intense. All he could think about was finding a way to extract her from this ridiculous meeting and take her off someplace private. To explain in a manner as physically graphic as possible that whatever was happening between them needed to be completed. Several times, if necessary. Whatever it took until the rage of fire and need cooled and he could think rationally again.

"I'm sorry," she said. "Maybe we could start over? Thank you for saving me from being run down. I'm sorry I was late for our lunch meeting. I assure you, it was unavoidable. I don't usually answer my cell phones in the middle of a busy intersection, but it was Madam's and I *always* take her call, regardless of time and place."

She'd ticked off her points with the speed and precision of a drill sergeant. Where before he'd considered her scattered, now he saw what Nonna had meant by her description of Téa de Luca. It would appear she was a woman who existed in organized chaos and operated in focused oblivion.

Luc inclined his head. "Fair enough."

"That said," she continued, "I don't see the point in this meeting." She spared her grandmother a warm smile. "I appreciate your concern, but I don't need a bodyguard."

"Funny," Luc muttered. "Considering what happened just five minutes ago, I'd say that was precisely what you need."

She waved that aside. "It could have happened to anyone. Besides, he would have missed me."

It took Luc a split second to find his voice. "Have you lost your mind?"

She patted his arm, then snatched her hand away. Maybe it had something to do with the arc of electricity that flashed between them. Or the throb that shot through the palm of his hand and quite probably her own. With each new touch, whatever existed between them grew stronger, the tendrils binding tighter and more completely. It gave him some measure of satisfaction to see that it took her several seconds to recover her poise sufficiently to speak. During the few moments of silence the waiter approached and deposited their luncheon choices. He didn't linger.

"You played the hero quite well and I appreciate your efforts on my behalf," Téa said in a stilted voice. She splashed some oil and vinegar on her salad. "But the cab swerved at the last second."

He leaned in, emphasizing each word with a steak fry. "Which gave me just the extra time and room I needed to keep you from getting clipped by his bumper and turned into roadkill." He popped the fry into his mouth. "He would have hit you if I hadn't pulled you clear."

"Luciano…" Nonna murmured.

He glanced first at his grandmother and then at Madam. They both wore identical expressions, a wrenching combination of fear and shock. Not cool, he realized. He'd way overplayed his hand. He pulled back and gathered Madam's hand within his own.

"She's safe and I promise I'll keep her that way."

"Thank you." Tears flooded her dark eyes. "I can't tell you how much this means to me."

"Wait a minute," Téa interrupted. "I haven't agreed to anything."

He shot her a quelling look. Not that she quelled, which amused almost as much as it frustrated him. He excelled at quell. Any of the men who served beneath him or currently worked with him could attest to that simple fact. "Not even for your grandmother's peace of mind?" he asked.

It was her turn to be both amused and frustrated. "Oh, very good," she murmured. "Very clever."

"You will agree, won't you, Téa?" Madam's request sounded more like a demand. "It will make all of us feel so much better. Juliann can concentrate on her wedding. Davida can focus on her studies. And Katrina can…" She hesitated, clearly at a loss.

"Can continue getting into trouble?" Téa inserted dryly.

"She means well," Madam said with a sigh. "She's just a magnet for disaster."

As though to underscore the comment, Téa's handbag began to chirp again. A youthful, feminine voice demanded, "Answer me. Answer me. Answer me, me, *me!*" Téa smiled blandly. "Speak of the devil."

"So we agree." Luc struggled to be heard over the shrill tones of another ringtone as it added its personalized demand to the first. "I'm your baby—" He cleared his throat. "Your bodyguard for the next six weeks?"

She wanted to argue some more. He suspected the trait was as much a part of her as her red hair. He lifted an eyebrow in Madam's direction and waited, not a bit surprised when Téa caved. "Fine." She lowered her voice so only he could hear. "And don't think I missed that babysitter slip."

He kept his expression unreadable. "I have no idea what you're talking about."

Reaching into the bag, she went through each of her three phones and set them on vibrate. Lunch proceeded at a leisurely pace after that and he noticed with some amusement that everyone went out of their way to stick to innocuous topics. Schooling himself to patience, he guided the women through the conversation and the meal, before he could finally pick up the check and pay for their lunch. All the while he watched Téa.

Although she chatted with the grandmothers, Luc could tell that her thoughts were elsewhere. He could practically see the wheels spinning away, analyzing her problem—*him*—while searching for a satisfactory solution.

"Figured it out, yet?" he asked in an amused undertone.

She stared blankly. "Figured what out?"

"What you're going to do about me."

"Not quite." Then she hesitated and a hint of relief caused her eyes to glitter like gemstones. He didn't need the blazing light bulb that flashed over her head to tell him that she'd come up with a plan to escape her predicament. "Madam, quick question…"

"Yes, dear?"

"How are we compensating Mr. Dante for his time and expertise?" She actually smiled at Madam's small inhalation of alarm. "Bodyguards don't come cheap. And you know we're under serious budgetary constraints for the next six weeks."

"Well, I—"

"Didn't Nonna explain?" Luc offered smoothly. "Consider it your twenty-fifth birthday present from all the Dantes."

"How generous." He could hear the grit through the politeness. "But I couldn't possibly accept such an expensive gift."

He allowed irony to slide through his words. "No, no. Don't thank us. It's our pleasure. Besides, babysitters charge far less than bodyguards. Even if you were to refuse, it wouldn't cost you much at all to hire me." He pushed back his chair and stood. "I'll tell you what. Why don't we continue this meeting in private in order to settle the particulars?"

"Excellent suggestion," she replied crisply and gathered up her briefcase and shoulder bag. "My office?"

Not private enough for what he had in mind. Not nearly private enough. "I have an apartment close by."

"I'm not sure that's such a good idea."

Ignoring her, he gave Nonna and Madam each a kiss. Then draping a powerful arm around Téa's shoulders, he swept her from the restaurant. A cab lingered just outside the door and he bundled her inside, protesting all the way. He gave the driver the address to his apartment complex and settled back against the seat.

All the while, Téa bristled with feminine outrage. With her rioting red curls and flashing eyes she looked like a cat who'd been rubbed the wrong way. He couldn't quite help taking a certain pleasure in having upset her tidy little world. Considering the ease with which she'd upended his, it seemed only fair.

The cab had barely pulled away from the curb before she started protesting. "I have to get back to work. I don't have time for this. I don't know what sort of game you're playing, Luciano Dante, but I'm not in the mood for it."

"I'm giving our grandmothers what they asked for. If I can spare six weeks out of my life to make sure you reach twenty-five, you can put up with having me around."

"Well, shoot."

He'd clearly gotten her with that one. She took a moment to call the office and inform them of her change in schedule before turning her jumble of cell phones from vibrate to ring, meticulously checking each for messages before stowing it away. Not that she was through arguing. Not this one.

The minute she finished fussing with her phones, she pushed a tumble of curls from her eyes and glared at him. "And another thing… What was that weird zap you gave to me when we first shook hands?"

He gave an "I'm clueless" shrug, hoping it would satisfy. It didn't.

"Don't give me that. I've heard that you Dantes have some bizarre touch thing you use on women. It knocks them right off their feet and into your bed." A sudden thought struck and her eyes widened. "Is that what you have planned with me?"

Two

"Do you want me to zap you into my bed?" Luc pretended not to notice the cab driver's shocked gaze darting to the rearview mirror.

"No! Of course not."

"Too bad. I'd give it a try even though…" He allowed a hint of bewilderment to drift across his face and lied through his teeth. "To be honest, Téa, I have no idea what sort of bizarre touch thing you're talking about."

"Don't give me that." She brushed his denial aside with a graceful sweep of her hand. "Rumors have been flying all over the city about your cousins and how they acquired their wives."

Luc's eyes narrowed. Heaven help him. The woman was like a dog with a bone. He wasn't accustomed to people arguing with him. Damn it. Didn't she know she should be intimidated? That when he spoke others leaped to obey? Why the hell wasn't she leaping? "I would have thought you too intelligent to give credence to a bunch of lurid gossip magazines, like *The Snitch*."

A hint of telltale color underscored the delicate arch of her cheekbones. "It wasn't just the rags. I believe that whole Dante thing was demonstrated on television with Marco's wife."

He dismissed that with a shrug. "Easily explained."

"I'm listening. Explain away," she challenged.

Son of a— "A publicity stunt. Marco and Caitlyn were married. Of course she'd recognize her husband, even blindfolded."

He didn't need to see Téa's skeptical expression to know she wasn't buying it. "And that weird electrical shock we experienced? Or do you try that with every woman just to see how she'll react?"

"That's never happened to me," he admitted.

She honed in and Luc began to understand what Nonna had meant about her being focused, though he'd call it borderline obsessive. "What was it? What caused it?"

"Static electricity."

"That was *not* static electricity."

As far as Luc was concerned, they'd given their driver more than enough entertainment. "We'll discuss it when we get to my place," he said, hoping that would put an end to the conversation.

It didn't.

"I'd like to know now," she insisted.

"We'll wait." He inclined his head in the direction of the cabbie and gave her a pointed look. "Until then, tell me what you do for a living."

She turned her gaze toward the front seat, blinked, then smoothly switched gears. "I work for Bling." It was a nickname for Billings, who supplied the Dantes

Jewelry empire with their gold and silver needs. "Actually, I sort of own it."

Interesting. "Sort of?" he prompted.

"My grandfather, Daniel Billings, left it to me when he died a few months ago."

"That's your mother's father?" he hazarded a guess.

"No. Mom was married to Danny Billings—Daniel's son—who was killed in a plane wreck when I was a baby. Then, when I turned nine she married my father—my stepfather," Téa clarified. "That's when we were at the lake with Madam. Mom and Dad were on their honeymoon. We de Lucas are a blended family. My sisters are his and I'm hers, but we became theirs and us and ours. All de Lucas in the end with a bit of Billings thrown in for good measure."

The pieces came together. "Got it. Téa seems a rather unusual name for a Billings. Actually it sounds more Italian."

"It comes from a Billings ancestor from way back when. Téadora. It became tradition that the first daughter of the eldest son be given that name."

He tilted his head to one side. "It suits. Or at least, the shortened version does."

"Thanks."

"And you take control of your Billings inheritance in six weeks."

She nodded. "Until then I'm learning the ropes."

A soft bell rang in the back of his head, just the vaguest of alarms. "Who's running the show while you learn the ropes?"

"My second cousin, Conway Billings."

"And if something happens to you before you turn twenty-five?"

She turned her megawatt smile on him again, nearly blowing his circuits offline. "You think my cousin's out to do me in?" she teased.

He took the question seriously. "You'd be amazed what people will do for money. Trust me. I've seen it all."

"Not Connie."

"Connie?"

Téa lifted a shoulder in a careless shrug. "That's what everyone calls Conway. As a bodyguard, you're probably used to looking for trouble, even where it doesn't exist. But that's not the case with me."

She patted his arm in a reassuring manner, the same as she had at the restaurant, then once again whipped back her hand. He found the idea of anyone attempting to reassure *him* disconcerting. It had always been the other way around. She rubbed the surface of her palm as though it itched or tingled, and he wondered if she even noticed her actions. It took every ounce of self-control not to imitate her gesture. Snatching a quick breath, she glanced out the window.

"Are we almost there?"

"Almost." And it wouldn't be a minute too soon. "Tell me about these accidents you're experiencing."

"I'm not experiencing any accidents." That brilliant smile flashed again. "I'm experiencing a failure to walk and talk at the same time."

It wouldn't be the first time he'd come across a recruit with that problem. He'd get her straightened out soon enough. "You're a klutz."

Her breath escaped in a sigh. "I wish I could deny it. But that's pretty close to the truth. I guess I'm distracted."

"Because of your financial problems?" he hazarded a guess.

"That's part of it. I'm also struggling to learn everything I possibly can before I take over Bling. I never expected to inherit the place, so it hasn't been easy," she confessed. "There's a lot to learn that wasn't covered in my business degree at Stanford."

"And you're certain that Connie doesn't have a hidden agenda to ensure you don't make it to twenty-five?"

No hesitation. "I'm positive. He's actually planning to start his own business as soon as I'm able to take over the reins. He can't wait to get out from under his responsibilities."

The cab pulled up just then and Luc handed over the fare. Then he led the way up the front steps of the apartment complex to the door. He swept his keycard across the lock and gestured her in. They crossed the foyer and he rang for the elevator. The doors slid open almost immediately and he used his card again to access the top floor. The instant they were enclosed within the suffocating confines of the car, Téa returned to their earlier topic of conversation.

"So now we're alone," she began.

"We are."

Ignoring proper elevator etiquette, she turned to confront him. "Tell me why we keep getting zapped every time we touch. What's going on?"

He watched the digital numbers tick off one by one. After all, *someone* had to follow proper protocol, especially if it helped him keep his hands to himself. "Magnetic attraction?"

"Not a chance."

"My electric personality?"

She dismissed the suggestion with a delicate snort.

He allowed the silence to consume them while the elevator finished its ascent. The doors slid open directly into the foyer of his suite and she stepped out of the car before freezing. "Good Lord, is all this yours?"

"Yes."

To his relief, her interest in his living accommodations sidelined her questions about The Inferno. "You live here alone?"

"I'm a bit of a hermit." At least, these days he was.

She took her time looking around, examining the Spartan interior, the over-the-top electronics, and the smattering of photos from family gatherings on his walls that offered a few reluctant peeks into his past. She studied each in turn. First the ones of his Dante-filled childhood and those carefree years of raw emotion and puppylike wildness. Then the group shot of his unit revealing his transition to manhood—as evidenced by his uniform and military bearing—with its loss of innocence and rendering of character and spirit until all that remained was sheer grit and the drive to survive. Where life ended or continued based on a confusing combination of fate and experience. And finally, the professional man and the men who'd worked with him, the lone wolf standing ever so slightly apart from the others, who still carried the taint and scars of what had gone before, closed now to the emotional openness of youth. Innocence twisted to cynicism. Joy and hope tempered by reality. Normal, everyday dreams for the future layered beneath caution.

She took it all in, absorbed it without a word, then moved on. And yet, he saw the comprehension in her gaze and realized she understood what so few others had when they'd looked at all those group shots. She'd seen the emotions that existed behind the two-dimensional photos, seen his pain, as well as his determination. She wandered deeper into his sanctuary, forcing him to regard it with fresh eyes. The place would have come across as too austere if not for the warm redwood trim that accented the twenty-five-foot ceilings and the parts of the floor not covered by carpet. She paused in front of the floor-to-ceiling windows and the spectacular view of the bay they afforded with a deeply appreciative expression. Apparently she approved of the uncluttered look. Somehow that didn't surprise him.

Nor did it surprise him when she gathered herself up and transitioned back to business. "Okay, time for answers," she announced, swiveling to face him. "Before we discuss this bodyguard business, I want to know one thing."

"Funny. So do I."

He approached, impressed that she simply stood and waited for him. Allowed him to reach for her. To take her hands in his while desire exploded around them and through them.

"What is that?" she whispered, dazed.

"*That* is Dante's Inferno. Which, if I'm not mistaken, means we're both condemned to hell."

Not giving her time to react, he swept her into his arms and kissed her.

Violent heat flashed through Téa, mercurial swift and burning with white-hot need, making her forget her responsibility to her family—something that hadn't happened since she was sixteen. Her reaction to him was identical to when he'd first taken her hand, igniting where their lips melded, the fit sheer perfection. It flashed downward to the pit of her stomach and lower still until the feminine core of her throbbed with the urge to join with this man. It raced through her, tripping over sense and emotion, instinct and logic, turning every part of her inside out and upside down. And still it didn't stop.

The desperation grew so intense that if he stretched her out on the floor of his foyer, she would have allowed him to strip away her clothing and lose himself in her. Just the thought of having him on her, in her, over and around her, joined with her in the most intimate way possible… She shuddered.

"Luc…" His name escaped on a sigh, became part of the kiss, greedily consumed.

His mouth slipped from hers, following the line of her throat, scalding the sensitive skin as he drifted relentlessly downward. Somehow the buttons of her blouse had escaped their holes. The edges of the crisp material separated, giving him access to explore the gentle swells rising above the lacy cups of her bra.

"I don't think I've ever seen skin like yours before. So pale." He trailed a string of kisses along the demarcation line of silken skin and protective lace. "It seems such a cliché to say it's like cream."

She laughed softly. "Not magnolia blossoms?"

He spared her a swift grin, though his eyes remained a shocking molten gold, flaming with a passion unlike anything she'd seen before. "Definitely magnolia blossoms. Only softer."

She didn't know what had gotten into her. This wasn't like her at all. Not the joking. Certainly not the lovemaking. But one touch from Luciano Dante and she tumbled. Her cell phones began to ring and chirp and plead, and with an exclamation of impatience, Luc opened one of the doors leading off the foyer—a coat closet—and shoved her handbag and briefcase inside.

It gave her just enough time for her head to clear.

"Wait, Luc." Those cell phones were her lifeline. They were a vital link that kept her grounded and connected to her family. Besides, she owed them. She couldn't allow this sort of selfish distraction. "Those calls could be important."

"There's nothing more important than this…"

He pulled her close and all coherent thought vanished. How did he manage to do that, when she'd always been so careful with her priorities? Maybe it was because she'd never known real desire before. Not like this. In fact, she'd gone out of her way to avoid it.

Family always came first. Duty and responsibility had been her obsession ever since the death of her parents. She didn't dare let down her guard and surrender to her baser desires. Not since that one hideous occasion when she'd done just that and her world had come crashing down around her.

She'd learned her lesson well that night. From that moment on, taking care of her family was her life. Her obligation. Nothing else came ahead of that one crucial demand. Nothing. At least… Nothing until Luciano Dante exploded into her world and—with a single touch, palm against palm—short-circuited every last rational thought but one.

She wanted this man. Needed him. For so many years she'd been the one in control. The steady one. The one who looked after her family and protected them. She couldn't and wouldn't indulge her own selfish interest until she'd accomplished that. Once she received her inheritance, she'd be in an even better position to care for her family, instead of constantly scrambling to make ends meet.

But with that one shocking touch, Luc took that burden from her. It vanished from thought and awareness, replaced by a passion she'd never experienced, never even knew existed until he'd shown her the stunning possibilities.

His mouth covered hers again, inhaling her, and she simply tumbled. Duty and responsibility floated away, as did reason and intellect. All that remained was a shattering. Intense. Unspeakable. All consuming.

Without breaking the kiss, Luc swept Téa into his arms. She had the sensation of movement from living room to bedroom—a light floating, then a gentle descent, the softest of cushions at her back when they sank into the mattress and a blazing heat that blanketed her. It settled over her, pressing into her, molding hard, powerful angles against the soft, willing give of her body.

She stared up into his face, at the hard, uncompromising features, examining them one by one. He had chiseled cheekbones coupled with a tough, squared jaw. His mouth was wide and sensuous, bracketed by deep grooves that could convey both humor and displeasure depending on his mood. His hair, cut almost military short, was the darkest shade of ebony and showed a tendency to wave, a tendency he kept under ruthless control. But it was his eyes that dominated his face. He possessed the deep, ancient golden eyes of a predator. Eyes that could cut straight through to the soul and lay bare what she most wanted to keep hidden.

He could never be called handsome. Powerful, certainly. Bold. Aggressive. Blatantly masculine. His face had been carved to intimidate, yet had those elements that—despite lacking prettiness—were wildly appealing to women.

Heaven help her, but he was an impressive male specimen. Tough. A body both strong and muscular. And yet, his touch showed infinite control and tenderness. How was it possible that a man so clearly cut from the cloth of a warrior could also be so gentle?

"What are we doing?" she managed to ask. "What's happening to us?"

"Dante's Inferno."

She shook her head in confusion. "I know it's an inferno. But why is it so intense?"

She caught the smile he couldn't suppress and it dazzled her. "No, that's what it's called. What we're experiencing. Or so the legend claims." He trailed his hand, harshly callused, in a fiery path from throat to breast. She shuddered beneath the dichotomy of rough and soothing. "We call it Dante's Inferno. It happens to the men in our family when they first meet certain women."

She managed a laugh. "How did I get so lucky?"

"I have no idea."

"How long will it last?"

He lowered his head and replaced his hand with his mouth in a leisurely exploration. "I have no idea."

"If we…" She inhaled sharply, shuddering beneath his roving lips and tongue. Her thoughts scattered for an instant before she gathered them up again. "If we make love, will it go away?"

"I hope so." He shook his head with a groan. "Or maybe not. Maybe it'll continue for a while. I wouldn't mind so long as it's not permanent. We could work it out of our systems over the next six weeks."

Relief flooded through her. "But it will go away?"

He reared back, hovering above her like some pagan god. "It better. I'm not like my cousins. They ended up married when it struck. I'm not after the fairy tale or commitment, or even love. You understand that, don't you?"

"I don't understand any of this," she confessed.

He shook his head as though to clear it. "This isn't permanent." The words were filled with grit and honesty. "This is a temporary affair. It's sex. That's all. If you're expecting a fairy tale ending—"

She allowed a hint of the darkness that had shadowed her over the years to reflect in her gaze. "Don't worry. I don't believe in fairy tales. And I definitely don't believe in happily-ever-after endings."

"But you believe in this." He released the front clasp of her bra and cupped her breasts. Sunshine splashed and rippled across her skin, chasing away the darkness. He traced his thumbs across the sensitive tips, eliciting a soft moan. "You believe in the physical, the same as I do. What we can touch. Desire. Sating that desire. You believe in that, don't you?"

"It wouldn't be hard to make a believer of me," she confessed.

His mouth curved to one side and his eyes glittered like sunrays, threatening to blind her with their intensity. "Trust me. By the time I'm finished, you'll believe."

She found herself laughing, a sound free and light-hearted and utterly alien to her. She cupped his face and tugged him down, covering that wonderful mouth with her own. His taste intoxicated her and she rejoiced in the dizzying explosion of pleasure. For long minutes they kissed, slow and sultry. Deep and wet. Learning. Testing. Discovering. But it wasn't enough. Not nearly enough.

Téa tugged at Luc's shirt, struggling to find the buttons and holes and get one through the other. They resisted all efforts and impatient with her own lack of skill, she simply ripped at the edges until buttons pinged all around them. To her delight the edges of his shirt parted and she swept her hands across a broad chest, sharply delineated by gorgeous dips and ridges of toned muscle and sinew.

She'd never felt so free with a man before and she took her time, exploring this one to her heart's content. She rubbed the flat discs of his nipples and bit into his golden flesh, soothing the small mark with her tongue. A soft groan rumbled through his chest, caught within the palms of her hands, and she rejoiced in having provoked the reaction. She'd never wielded so much feminine power. It was a heady sensation.

She took a circuitous route in a southern direction, exploring all the side roads and byways of what she bared, until she hit a roadblock. She made short work of it, her fingers coordinated for a change. The belt parted, the zip of his trousers rasped downward and she slid her hands to the very heart of all that heat and masculinity.

He was hard and swollen, sliding into her hands with greedy urgency. She'd never done this before, either. Never given full rein to her curiosity and her own need to explore. But she couldn't help herself. Not this time. Not with Luc. He didn't stop her or attempt to take charge. Instead he encouraged her with soft, biting kisses and velvety, rough words.

She sensed the effort it took to control himself, could see the iron grip he maintained in order to hold himself back. Instead he devoted himself to stripping away her barriers. Bit by bit her clothes drifted away, her blouse and bra, her skirt and stockings, until all that remained was a scrap of triangular silk guarding her core. She was so caught up in her own exploration that she barely noticed.

Until he turned the tables on her.

Just as she familiarized herself with his body, he began to map hers. First her mouth and throat. Then her breasts and abdomen. Degree by degree he turned up the heat, catching her unaware until desire swamped her in great crashing waves, turning her mindless with need. She stared up at him in utter confusion.

"What are you doing?"

The laughter gleamed again. "Can't you tell?"

"We're making love. I…" Her eyes fluttered closed and she fought to draw breath, to gather her wits long enough to speak. "I don't remember this part."

"This part?" He spread her thighs and feathered a line of kisses from the curve of her knee to her inner thigh.

"No," she quavered. "Not that part."

Before she could even draw breath, he stripped away her panties. "What about this part?"

And then he kissed her, a kiss more intimate than she'd ever known before. A climax ripped through her, unexpected and violent and utterly spectacular. The sound that escaped her was part scream and part denial. She'd never…! Not ever. Pieces of her lay scattered all over the bed and it was several long minutes before she could gather them up and paste them together well enough to speak again.

"Not that part," she said. "I definitely don't remember that part."

"We'll have to do it again, just to keep your memory refreshed." He fumbled in the drawer beside him. An instant later she heard the distinctive crinkle of foil. "But not right now. Now we have other refreshing to do."

She lay beneath him, stretched in more ways than she could count. Stretched to the edge by a desire that still hadn't been quite sated. Stretched by muscles still quivering and clenching from the aftermath of her climax. Stretched emotionally by a man she'd just met. A man she'd allowed to touch her in ways she'd never before allowed. A man she'd allowed in, or who had forced his way in. She was too overwhelmed to figure out which.

Before she could analyze it further, he came down on top of her. His hands—such tender, powerful hands—slid deep into her hair, anchoring her. Their gazes locked and held, and she felt herself sink into him just as his body sank into hers, mating them together in a perfect fit. She felt herself join with him in ways that were more than just physical. Ways that upended her tidy little world.

And she gave herself to him, totally and unconditionally.

He moved within her and all thought slipped away, replaced by something far more primitive and elemental. A driving need consumed her, an urge to become one. To complete the connection that hovered so close. She strained for it. Reached for it. Grasped it eagerly.

Then the strangest thing happened. Téa felt the powerful current from their first meeting complete its circuit. Felt the undeniable melding of man to woman. Knew on some level that this moment had changed her on some irrevocable, fundamental level. Part of her shrank from that knowledge, while another part rejoiced.

She wrapped Luc up in a tight embrace, arms and legs entwined. Each thrust came more forcefully, branding her, possessing her. She rode with him while the wildness stirred. It whipped through her, tearing her apart into shiny fragments of desperate desire. She heard him call to her on the whirlwind, centering her. And with each moment that passed, each driving movement, they roared toward the center of the storm.

It was an exploding. A shattering. A freefall into the most delicious waves of pleasure she'd ever experienced. Together they soared and plummeted. Rode the wild wind. Together they clung one to the other, joined.

Melded.

Mated.

One.

Téa had no idea how long she lay there, lost in the aftermath of passion. Somewhere along the line every scrap of intelligent thought had fled, leaving behind utter confusion. But it was a delightful confusion, one that had her body glowing with pleasure and her practically purring in satisfaction.

The oddest part was that she couldn't seem to get her brain back online. Every time she tried, her thoughts would slip and slide in Luc's direction and all she could think about was how he'd taken her. Possessed her. Thrust her into a realm of sensation that had stripped her down to the bare essence of herself and then imprinted what remained with his personal brand. It was as though they'd mixed and mingled to the point where they could never truly separate out their own unique bits and pieces.

"Dear God," Luc rumbled beside her. "I don't think I'll ever be able to move again."

"At least you can talk," she managed to say.

"Okay. I'll talk. You move."

"Can't."

"'Kay. Come here." He wrapped a heavy arm around her waist and scooped her closer. "Aw, hell. It's still there."

She didn't have to ask what. She could feel it. He spooned the hard sweep of his angles against her soft curves. The press of his body cleaving to hers caused the embers to spark to life in renewed need. Every inch of her skin burned with it. Heat blazed along the contact points and she trembled beneath the onslaught.

"Yeah, it's still there." She shuddered in reaction. "Was it supposed to go away?"

"Thought so."

Or was it that he hoped so? The thought flitted in and out of her head as she turned to face him. He opened his eyes, slumberous, yet still hungry. With a soft growl, his mouth came down on hers again, blotting out thought and reason and words. Her arms slid around him just as his slid around her and their legs intertwined once again. They kissed, soft and gentle, then more urgently. An irrepressible need replaced exhaustion, one that couldn't be denied.

Téa wriggled against him. "Luc, please. I want—"

She couldn't even express what she wanted. Just him. More of him. He didn't need the words. He knew. Knew, and responded with a passion that shredded her world into bright glittering starbursts of pleasure. It was as though all the silver and gold from her company somehow melded with the unique fire diamonds from his and encircled them like a ring, creating a bond neither of them were prepared for, nor wanted.

A bond from which they couldn't easily escape.

Three

Téa awoke with a start and unlike last time, her brain came screaming online, flooding her with frantic messages and warnings. "Oh. My. God."

Luc surfaced from beneath her, rumpled and gorgeous and sexier than any man had a right to be. "Is that a please-do-it-again-even-if-it-kills-us version of oh-my-God? Or have we switched over to what-have-I-done-get-me-the-hell-out-of-here?"

"Um." She carefully untangled male parts from female and put a few precious inches of breathing space between them. It didn't help. Heat and want still pulsated across the breach, threatening to suck her back in. "The get-me-the-hell-out-of-here one."

"Thought so."

With a groan, he levered himself off the bed and limped nude in what she assumed was the direction of the bathroom. Her small gasp stopped him dead in his tracks.

"Oh, Luc. Your hip." Hugging the sheet to her, she crouched in the center of the bed, her gaze riveted on his side. "And your knee! Dear heaven, what did you do?"

His mouth twisted. "I rescued a damsel in distress. Foolish of me, I know."

It took her an instant to understand. "This is *my* fault?" Her misery increased as she took in the huge vibrant bruise that covered his entire hip and edged down his thigh toward his knee. "Why didn't you say something? You must be in pain. Maybe you should see a doctor. Have it X-rayed."

"It's not broken or I wouldn't be walking. I planned to take something for it." A swift, ravening grin came and went. "But I got distracted."

"I'm so sorry. I had no idea you were that badly hurt."

"Trust me, this isn't bad."

She recalled the photos taken of him during his military service and suspected he spoke the unvarnished truth. "And your knee?" She started off the bed, but the change in his expression glued her in place. In an instant he transformed from lover to warrior. To someone she didn't recognize. Someone tough and dangerous, who'd seen and done things she couldn't even imagine.

"Old injury. It has nothing to do with you or what happened earlier."

"But today must have made your knee worse," she said softly.

"It didn't help," he conceded. "My choice, though. And I chose to keep you from becoming cab fodder."

"Thank you." She grimaced as she considered how

blasé she'd been about it at lunch. More than blasé. As she recalled, she'd blamed him for the incident. "Seriously, thank you. When I think of how I behaved at lunch—" She broke off with a shake of her head.

"You weren't very grateful."

Ouch. No doubt she deserved that. "I didn't realize. I was distracted." She straightened her shoulders. "Not that that's any excuse. I can't thank you enough for what you did and I'm sorry I made it necessary."

It was only then that she caught the flash of amusement and realized he was deliberately provoking her as payback for her earlier behavior. And she'd fallen for it.

"No problem," he said. "Next time I'll let the cab have you."

She simply laughed. "No, you won't." If she'd learned nothing else about him in these past few hours, it was that. The words "knight in shining armor" were probably engraved on his soul.

He shook his head with a sigh. "I think it's more a matter of, no, I can't."

He didn't linger, but disappeared through the doorway. The sound of running water confirmed her guess about it being the bathroom. It also gave her an opportunity to escape the bed and gather up her clothing. She winced as she examined the garments. Well, the good news was that most of them could be worn again. Unfortunately some of the more fragile bits and pieces of silk were beyond use or repair.

Tiptoeing and not quite sure why she bothered, she disappeared into the depths of his apartment, relieved to discover that there was a second full bath adjoining his spare bedroom. She took possession of the shower and the various toiletries lined up on the counter.

Definitely a woman's touch and she couldn't help but wonder who had left her mark and whether or not she was still in Luc's life. After toweling off, Téa pulled on the salvageable pieces of her clothing and escaped the bathroom. She could hear Luc rummaging through the bureau drawers in his bedroom and paused.

She caught her lower lip between her teeth and briefly debated. She could either sneak out of the apartment, like a thief in the night. Or she could face him and deal with the situation. Since there was a real chance they would be stuck together for the next six weeks, addressing what had just happened, and doing it now, seemed the wisest course of action. Plus, she'd never been one to run from a problem. She'd learned long ago to take responsibility for her mistakes. Learned it in the worst possible manner. This one today with Luc had been a huge one.

With a sigh, she made her way to the living room. A quick glance toward the windows warned that day paused in those breathless few moments between dusk and true night. Lights from various boats dotted the bay, sweeping straight across the water to Marin County. Off to the left, the Golden Gate Bridge glittered, the suspension cables looking like glowing strands of pearls connecting the city to the northern peninsula. Directly in front of her hovered Alcatraz Island, perched like some mythical land while wisps of fog gathered in a protective mantle about its shores.

Where had the time gone? She shook her head in exasperation. Idiot. She knew full well where it had gone. She'd lost the hours in Luc's bed. No doubt if she went in there and rummaged between the sheets she'd find all those minutes just sitting there laughing at her.

Luc chose that moment to join her. The fullness of his personality exploded into the room, overwhelming it. "You hungry or should we move straight on to getting drunk and pretending none of this happened?"

She couldn't quite tell if he was serious or not, and suspected a combination of both. She swung around to face him. "I really should go. But before I do I thought we should discuss things."

"Discuss things," he repeated. He gave her an aggrieved look, one men had patented back in caveman days. Clearly the last thing he wanted was a discussion. "That definitely calls for a drink. You sure you don't want something?"

"No, thank you."

He crossed to a wet bar and pulled out ice and a cut glass tumbler. Tossing in a handful of cubes that caused the crystal to sing, he splashed a healthy finger of whiskey over the cubes. He swirled the liquor in the glass for a moment and then downed it in a single swallow before facing her. She noticed that when he pivoted he was careful to plant and twist with his left leg so he wouldn't cause any unnecessary trauma to the injury on his right.

He gestured with his glass, causing the ice cubes to chatter. "Okay. Start discussing. I assume this is the part where you say this can never happen again. That we have to work together for the next six weeks and it would be more professional if we kept things on a business footing. We'll just pretend what happened, didn't. Does that about sum things up?"

He hit too close to home. More than anything she wanted to claim he was wrong. That she was hoping for a torrid affair for the next six weeks and would be quite happy to spend every night in his bed, exploring every possible position and variation of their activities over the past few hours.

"I think I'd like a drink, after all," she announced.

"Smart choice."

"Do you have any wine?"

"Red, white or somewhere in between?"

"Red."

He poured her a glass of something dry and deliciously biting that carried the label from a Sonoma vineyard. She sipped it while considering her options and organizing her points. While he waited, he poured himself a second drink, but didn't down this one. Instead he swirled the combination of liquor and cubes. It took every ounce of effort to yank her gaze from his hand and those long, clever fingers, fingers which had done shocking and delicious things to every part of her body.

She cleared her throat, suddenly aware she'd somehow sipped her way through most of the glass of wine. "Here's the problem," she announced. "The reason we've been forced to work together is because I'm so distracted trying to juggle the pressures of my job and family life. We can't afford to have both of us distracted by this…" She lifted an eyebrow. "What did you call it? An inferno?"

"*The* Inferno," he corrected. "With a capital 'T,' capital 'I' and a whole lot of fire and brimstone in between."

She smiled at the name. Clever. "You said earlier that The Inferno, capital 'T,' capital 'I,' fire and brimstone, etcetera, is a family legend?"

"Yes," he replied, making it clear by tone and attitude that he didn't want to discuss it. "Or at least, that's the claim. Never having experienced it before—"

"Until today," she inserted smoothly.

It was like prodding a panther. Those incredible gold eyes narrowed in warning and if he could have snarled, he would have. As it was, he came close. "Hell, Téa. If it makes everything tidier to call a bad case of lust by a more acceptable name like The Inferno, go right ahead. It sure as hell makes it more acceptable to me."

"Lust." She chewed on the word for a moment and decided she didn't care for the flavor. "I thought you said your cousins all married because of The Inferno."

"They did." He threw a lot of emphasis on the word "they." Underscore. Italics. Highlight. Red flashing lights. The works.

She gestured with her glass. "I gather you don't intend to."

"I'm not very good husband material. Too much commitment for my taste." The panther sheathed its claws and he flashed her a smile that practically had her clothing melting off her body. If they could have stripped themselves, they'd be puddled on the floor at her feet. "But, I do make a terrific lover."

It was the unvarnished truth, spoken simply and without pretension or bravado. And one she readily conceded. Considering she'd been the most recent recipient, there was no point in denying facts. Unfortunately there was also no denying the fact that she would have loved to have him prove his words all over again. It took a moment, but she managed to pull herself together again, though she did spare a quick downward glance to make certain all her buttons were still safely in their holes.

Reassured, she couldn't resist provoking him one final time. "Just out of curiosity, how do you plan to avoid The Inferno when none of your other relatives have?"

She could see he'd never even considered the question before. She could also see he didn't care for her asking it…or for the fact that he didn't have a ready answer. To her amusement, it only took a moment for him to come up with one.

"I'm thirty years old and I've had extensive military training, as well as the skills I picked up running my own security business. We'll either satisfy whatever urges we're experiencing and move on, or…" He shrugged. "It's a simple matter of intellect over inclination."

She couldn't decide whether to be amused or insulted. "I believe that brings us back to our main problem. I have to confess, I can't decide which will be more distracting, indulging in an affair with you or trying *not* to indulge in an affair with you."

"Just out of curiosity. Do I get a vote?"

"Just out of curiosity. Which way would you vote?"

He approached, graceful despite the limp. He took the wine glass from her hand and set it on a nearby table along with his whiskey. Then he caught hold of her and pulled her into his arms.

"I vote to end things right now," he told her. And then he kissed her.

Want blew him apart. Heaven help him, she tasted every bit as delicious as before. Soft and sweet and yet potently female. He liked the way she attacked his mouth, like a succulent piece of fruit that she couldn't quite get enough of. And then she would sink into him, savoring him the way he'd seen some women savor a piece of rich, dark chocolate.

Everything about her appealed, from the light, crisp scent of her to the subtle silken curves that had so recently graced his bed, to the wit and intelligence that gave strength to her face and brilliance to the unusual teal shade of her eyes. He almost lost control again, almost swept her up into his arms and carried her back to his bedroom. Maybe he would have if the echo of his last words to her didn't still linger in the air. With a final hungry kiss, he put her from him.

It took her an instant to recover her equilibrium. She stared at him in fuzzy bemusement before snapping back into focus with a soft cry of outrage. "You…!" Anger sparked to life, flaming in her gaze and giving her cheeks a rosy bloom. "Why did you kiss me after what you said?"

He shrugged. "I didn't think I'd get the chance again."

He didn't give her an opportunity to reply. Didn't dare. It didn't pay to give women like Téa too much room to fully exercise their vocabulary. Not when they wielded each word with the precision of a marksman and could slice and dice a man with the skill of a master chef.

"I have some associates who can help with our problem. They can take over as your temporary bodyguard."

He couldn't have shocked her more if he'd slapped her. "And us? What about The Inferno?"

"As I mentioned, I have four cousins who described the sort of instant lust that we experienced and every last one of them ended up married. That's not going to happen to me. I don't do commitment. And I sure as hell don't do marriage."

"Neither do I," she retorted. "I have more important priorities."

"Excellent. Then we end this before it has a chance to get out of hand. Agreed?"

She opened her mouth to reply, when a muffled voice began to call, "Answer me. Answer me. Answer me, me, *me!*" Her eyes widened in horror and without a word she darted to the foyer and dove into his closet. She emerged a bit more tousled, but with her briefcase and shoulder bag in hand.

She took up residence on his couch and pulled out her cell phones, lining them up with military precision on his coffee table. The ring tone on the first phone—a shiny black one covered in neon pink kisses—switched to "Here Comes the Bride."

Téa flipped it open. "Hel— Yes, Jules. Yes, I know. I was in a meeting and couldn't be interrupted." She actually blushed at the lie, then listened for a moment. "Did you check out Divinity for your wedding gown? It won't? Why—" She listened silently for several more seconds. "No, no. I understand. It's just that I arranged for the owner... Okay. If it won't work, it won't. I'll get back to you with an alternative. I've got to speak to Vida now. No, she's not more urgent than you. But there's nothing else I can do about your wedding gown until tomorrow. I'm sorry, but that's the best I can do."

She pushed a button with smooth precision and started a new conversation. "Davida, what—" Pause. "Listen up. If you fail that course, you'll be on academic probation. No, I can't get you off again. You'll have to go in and speak to your professor. Well, why did you miss the exam? Oh, for— Yes, that was exasperation you heard in my voice. Recovering from a frat party is not an acceptable excuse for... I don't intend to argue the point. If you can't work it out with your professor, you know the consequences." A fraction of a pause this time.

"Oh, really? Well, let me spell it out for you. Colleges no longer offer BS degrees in Flirting. If you get kicked out, there's a job waiting for you in the mailroom at Bling. Why, Vida, that's brilliant. I don't know why it didn't occur to me to suggest you speak to your professor and throw yourself on his mercy."

She flipped the phone closed. It immediately began its "Answer me!" chirp.

"Téa—" Luc began.

She held up a preemptory Wait-A-Minute finger which he would have found amusing if it had been aimed at anyone other than him. "What did you do this time, Kat?" Téa asked the instant she answered the shrill summons. "Again? That's the third time you've been in detention this month. It's also the third time I've had to speak to the principal this month. Listen, I have to go. Madam needs me. I'll see you later tonight and we'll discuss it then."

Luc winced at the way she said "discuss." He didn't envy Kat that particular conversation. Téa hesitated, her hand hovering over the lavender phone that had caused them so much trouble earlier in the day. She caught her lower lip between her teeth, but didn't pick it up.

"Well?" Luc prompted. "I thought you said you took her call anytime, no matter when or where."

"Yes," she confessed. "But I really don't want to answer this time."

Amusement filled him. "Afraid she'll know what you've been up to?"

She fixed her startling blue-green eyes on him and nodded. "She can read minds," Téa answered, perfectly serious. "There's no point in trying to lie to Madam. She knows."

"She won't know."

"Yes, she will. You'll see." The response came out in a "we're doomed" tone of voice. Bracing herself, she picked up the lavender phone and flipped it open. "Hi, Madam. What's up?" she asked, sounding a shade too casual.

"It's not that she can read minds," Luc offered helpfully. "It's that you don't know how to lie."

She scowled at him over the phone and mouthed, "Shut up," gesturing to give the demand added emphasis. Then she froze, her eyes huge. Guilt stormed across her face like an invading army. "Nothing. No one."

Luc snorted. "Give it up." Crossing to her side, he snatched the phone out of her hand. "Hello, Madam. It's Luc."

There was a brief pause and then Madam said, "Luc? Are you and Téa still together?"

"Just ironing out the final details over dinner."

An almost girlish laugh came across the airwaves. "I'm so relieved you agreed to do this. Nonna was just saying she wouldn't trust anyone else with my granddaughter's welfare, and neither would I."

"Nonna's with you?" So much for palming the job off on his associates. Even if he could get Madam to agree, Nonna would put a swift end to that particular dodge.

"She's right here. The two of us made a day of it. We've been shopping. Visiting. You know…" He could almost see her airy wave. "Right now, we're sitting in Primo's garden, enjoying the night air over a glass of wine. Do you want to speak to your grandmother?"

He froze, hoping guilt didn't decide to invade his face now that it was done with Téa's. "No, no. That's not necessary."

"It's been hours since lunch. And no one's been able

to reach Téa all this time. That's so unlike her. We were starting to worry."

Luc couldn't help himself. It must have been the alcohol that gave the devil access to his tongue while preventing his guardian angel from curbing it. "She insisted on turning off her cell phones while we put our differences to bed," he explained in a bland voice.

Téa made a choking noise.

"Very wise," Madam approved. "I'm just surprised it's taken you so long to settle everything."

"You know your granddaughter," Luc replied smoothly. He fixed Téa with a hot, hungry gaze. "She's very thorough. Likes to examine every inch of whatever you put in front of her and make sure she's intimately familiar with each and every detail."

Téa closed her eyes with a groan and sank back against the couch cushions.

"She is a bit of a perfectionist," Madam conceded.

"I noticed that. And then the minute you think you're finished, she wants to start at the beginning and go over it all again."

"Well the two of you keep at it until you have it just right."

"I'll be sure to tell her you said so."

With that the connection went dead, leaving Téa staring at him with death and dismemberment in her eyes.

"Well?" Nonna prompted. "Luc is still with Téa?"

Madam nodded slowly. "Interesting, yes?"

"Very." Nonna's expression turned crafty and she tapped her finger against her lower lip while she considered the possibilities. "They could not have been discussing the job every minute of all this time, could they?"

"No." Madam drew out the word. "I didn't get that impression."

"So? What do you think they were doing?"

Madam peered carefully around to make certain Primo was out of earshot. She dropped her voice to a whisper. "I think they were having the sex."

Nonna fought back a grin, while struggling to appear appropriately shocked. "Well, we thought we saw signs of The Inferno all those years ago when they first met at the lake as children. Little baby fizzes that suggest at what is to come. The same thing happened between Lazzaro and Ariana and look how happy they are together. This simply confirms our suspicions and means we did the right thing when we set this up." A hint of satisfaction crept into her voice.

"You were right," Madam conceded. "But then, you always are."

"Once The Inferno strikes there is nothing they can do but give in to its demands. And maybe, if we are very fortunate, it will keep them too busy to ask uncomfortable questions."

"What questions?"

"You have to admit, that story about Téa needing a bodyguard will not hold up for long," Nonna said. "Luciano will soon discover that she is absentminded and when preoccupied prone to walk into walls, but is not in any real danger. We are lucky she had that little accident today or we might never have convinced him to help out."

"Lucky!"

"Now, now. It could not have worked better if we had planned it. No one was hurt and it added credibility to our story." Nonna patted Madam's arm in a reassuring manner. "Luciano is a good boy. Do not worry about your Téa."

"I have always worried about her." Madam's dark eyes glistened with tears. "No one else does. She takes so much on her shoulders. Ever since her parents died. She blames herself, you know."

"Luciano will ease her burden." Nonna's hazel eyes narrowed in thought. "So, step one is complete."

"Step two will be far more difficult," Madam warned.

Nonna lifted a shoulder in a shrug that spoke volumes. "There is always a way to get caught in the act, especially if nature is busy taking its course."

"And once caught?"

Nonna's smile grew cat-swallowing-canary smug. "Why, step three. A wedding, of course."

Luc winced at the expression on Téa's face. She stalked in his direction and snatched the cell phone from his hand. "I can't believe you did that."

"I'm sure she didn't catch the subtext."

Téa lifted an eyebrow. "And if she did?"

Luc felt dull color inch across his face. "Hell."

"You think?" She marched to her handbag and carefully began reorganizing it. "You were right earlier," she said as she arranged.

"Of course I was." He paused a beat. "What was I right about?"

"I also vote to end things right now. Two 'yes' votes… that makes it unanimous. The motion carries. As of this minute our relationship is strictly business."

He didn't bother commenting, since ending the relationship was what he wanted, as well. Though why he had a sudden urge to argue the point, he couldn't say. Instead he frowned as the cell phones vanished into her shoulder bag. "Just out of curiosity, why do you have three phones instead of just one?"

"I tried that. There were so many messages, my cell exploded."

His mouth twitched and he found himself relaxing. "Cell phones don't explode."

"Mine did." Her graceful fingers continued sorting and arranging, dancing over her possessions with all the skill of a concert pianist. "After just twenty-four hours the poor thing whimpered like a baby. Then this mushroom shaped cloud erupted out of my purse and the phone melted into a puddle of electronic goo all over everything. It made a terrible mess." She paused, a wistful expression creeping across her face. "A shame really. It was a pretty little thing. I quite liked it."

He folded his arms across his chest and propped his shoulder against the wall. "That's when you bought the individual phones?"

"Oh, no. Then I switched to one of those all-purpose PDA phones."

"And?"

"It's recovering nicely at the sanitarium. The doctors have high hopes it can be retrained as a dictionary or address book."

Luc grinned, unexpectedly charmed. "And then?"

At long last she appeared satisfied with how she'd packed her shoulder bag and flipped open her briefcase. It was one of those with endless little cubbyholes and slots and zip sections. "Organization is important to me," she said, stating the all-too obvious. "So, I assigned one phone for each need. My three sisters on one, my grandmother on the second and—"

"And?" he prompted again.

She shrugged, burying her head deeper in her briefcase. He suspected it was to avoid looking at him. "And a private line just for me."

"Ah." His focus narrowed, his hunting instincts going on full alert. "Who calls you on that one?"

For a moment, he didn't think she'd respond, wouldn't tell him whether there was someone special in her life. Then she admitted, "Sometimes work." For a split second she appeared intensely vulnerable and self-conscious. "I've been meaning to cancel it. There's really no point in keeping it since I rarely use it."

For some odd reason it took a moment to respond. "Don't," he insisted gruffly. "Don't cancel it."

Now she did look at him, all ruffled and defenseless and clinging gallantly to her dignity. "Why ever not?"

"That one will be our phone."

"*Our* phone?" She frowned. "We don't need a shared phone. We'll be together often enough that you can just tell me whatever you need to in person."

"There may be times over the next six weeks when we're not together and I'll have to get in touch with you." For some reason he found himself speaking gently. "If you'd rather not give me the number, I don't mind sharing with your sisters."

She dismissed the suggestion out of hand. "No, that won't do."

"What about my using Madam's line?"

"Not a chance." She sighed. "No. I guess it'll have to be my private cell."

He searched his pockets until he unearthed his phone. "Give me the number."

Reluctantly she relayed it and he punched it in. "Once I turn twenty-five I'm going to cancel the service," she warned. She couldn't have made herself any clearer if she'd announced, "In six weeks I'm deleting you from my phone, my work, my life…and my bed."

"Understood," he said, the word ripe with irony.

She stood, and he could tell she was intent on leaving. "Could you call me a cab?"

"Sure. Just as soon as we clarify one thing."

"Which is?"

"This."

He crossed to confront her, his arms closing around her. To his surprise, she didn't attempt to slip from his grasp. Instead her curves settled against his, fitting like a key to a lock. Only this key and this lock were filled with heat and demand. Even more important, this key and lock opened a treasure beyond compare, one he'd never believed existed. One that tempted and seduced.

One he wasn't quite certain he could walk away from in six weeks…though he'd find a way.

"We weren't going to do this again," she protested.

"We weren't going to do this again once we started working together," he corrected. He swung her into his arms. "Our working relationship doesn't begin until tomorrow."

"Your leg!"

"My leg will survive." His lips curved into a wry smile. "It's the rest of me that's questionable."

She teetered on a knife's edge between resistance and capitulation and he waited to see which way she tipped. Then her expression softened into exquisite surrender.

"Well, guess what?" Her arms crept upward and wrapped around his neck. Her lips nuzzled into the hollow at the base of his throat. "Some things may be questionable for you, but I believe I have the answers. Shall we see if I'm right?"

He eyed her with amused appreciation as he carried her to the bedroom. "If you insist."

"Oh, I do insist. In fact, I demand."

"A demand is it?" He deposited her on his bed. "I guess a man has to do what a man has to do," he said with a gusty sigh, and reached for his belt buckle.

Four

Luc wasn't the least surprised when he woke the next morning to find Téa long gone, no doubt with her briefcase, shoulder bag and cranky cell phones in tow. Some bodyguard he was, allowing his assignment to slip away with such ease.

The apartment felt strangely empty and silent, qualities that until a few hours ago he'd not only prized, but actively sought. He glanced toward the bedside table where he'd stashed his cell phone. He was tempted to try the number she'd given him, but since he'd see her soon at work, there wasn't much point.

He rolled over, planning to get up and shower and make tracks. But something stopped him, the faintest of scents. It sweetened the air next to him, coming from the indentation that was all that remained of Téa. He snagged the pillow and breathed her in.

Her light, crisp perfume saturated his lungs and made

him hungry for her. Hungry to repeat the excesses of the night before. But there was another reaction he hadn't anticipated, one that was far worse. His palm throbbed and itched and he found himself rubbing at the sensation just as he'd seen Dante men do their entire lives.

As much as he wanted to deny it, he could feel The Inferno stirring like some great dragon waking from a deep sleep. Flames sparked and crackled, surging through his veins and heating his blood. Not good, he realized in alarm. Not good at all. Somehow, someway, he'd have to return the dragon to its eternal rest. Because if there was one thing he intended to avoid experiencing, it was The Inferno.

He refused to consider that it might be far too late.

Luc arrived at Billings less than an hour later. It was an impressive place, he decided. Thick pearl-gray carpet sucked up all peripheral noise. Not that there was much. The few people he saw spoke in hushed undertones. The furniture was all heavy wood, stained a deep, somber shade of brown. A jungle of plants sprouted from every corner, dense enough to hide a tiger if one wandered in by mistake.

It was all a bit on the stuffy, pretentious side, especially when compared to Dantes. Still, if the purpose of the decor was to give the visitor the impression of wealth and prestige, it succeeded.

The attractive, impeccably tailored receptionist seated behind an intimidating fortress of wood and electronics assured him that not only was Ms. de Luca there, but expecting him. After making a discreet phone call, she examined his identification and presented him with credentials that would allow him to breach the upper echelon of the company's executive offices.

She then escorted him to a bank of elevators and actually pressed the call button for him. He couldn't quite decide if it was the limp that made her so solicitous, or if she just thought men with limps had trouble pushing buttons.

Before he could ask, a gleaming elevator accented in mahogany and chrome and playing a soft operatic aria in the background arrived and carried him directly to the executive level where another impeccably tailored receptionist—this one male—escorted him down a heavily forested hallway. He didn't see any tigers lurking in the brush, which disappointed him. But at least this receptionist didn't have to press any buttons for him.

Instead he knocked on a door and opened it before motioning Luc into a corner office. A small break in the march of skyscrapers outside Téa's window allowed for a sliver of sunshine to creep through, along with a splash of grayish-blue water. Luc stepped inside the office and closed the door in the receptionist's face, if only to prove himself capable of that much.

"How nice," he said to Téa, squinting at the sliver of water. "You have a view of the bay."

Téa looked up from her computer screen. For an instant, he saw their last waking moments together reflected in the turbulent blue-green of her eyes. Then she smiled at his jest, robbing him of breath and making his palm throb. Other parts throbbed, as well, but he did his best to ignore those.

"Good morning," was all she had to say to make the throbbing intensify.

"You left." He didn't mean to say that, let alone growl it. For some reason, he couldn't stop himself. "You left without saying goodbye."

"I did."

He didn't quite know what to respond to such a simple and ingenuous admission. He crossed to the window and snatched at his tie, tearing at the knot that threatened to choke him. "Maybe now would be a good time to decide how this bodyguarding stuff is going to work, don't you think?"

"We were supposed to do that last night."

He released a short laugh. "We seemed to spend a lot of last night doing what we weren't supposed to and not doing what we were. How is today going to be any different?"

"We'll start fresh," she said lightly. "See if we can't get it right this time."

He spun to face her. "It felt like we got it right last night."

"Don't."

Images ripped through his mind. Téa splayed across his bed, her glorious hair captured in the final rays of sunlight turning each strand to a blazing, vibrant russet. Téa, her pale skin soaking up the moonlight and glowing with a soft, pearl-white radiance. Those silken limbs twined around him, holding him in the cradle of her hips with surprising strength. The look in her eyes when he joined with her. The sound she made when she climaxed.

His mouth twisted. "Tell me how to stop and I will."

A wistfulness crept into her expression, a hint of the want she'd expressed with such generosity the night before. He could see her swing, light as a summer breeze, between desire and her precious logic.

"Luc." His name escaped on the swing toward desire. "I—"

Before she could complete the thought, a tinny

version of "Here Comes the Bride" filled the air. Every scrap of passion vanished as though it had never been. Without another word, she took the call. From what little he caught of the one-sided conversation, Juliana's fiancée was in the military and stationed overseas, which probably explained why Téa was involved in so many of the decisions. The conversation seemed to go on forever and it wasn't only passion that drained from her face, but energy. She'd just wrapped up that call when Davida rang with an update on her college woes, followed by Madam with a series of financial questions. At least Katrina held off, but maybe that was because someone had locked her in a classroom. Or better yet, detention. He could only hope.

Completing the call, Téa snapped the phone closed and regarded him with an appealing hint of bewilderment. "I'm sorry. What were we discussing?"

Best to let it go. After all, they'd elected to avoid that particular entanglement. "It wasn't important." He tilted his head to one side and decided to probe. He doubted it was germane to the job at hand, but he wouldn't know for certain until he had all the facts. "Is your family always so demanding?" he asked curiously.

She shrugged. "I'm sort of the mother figure."

He asked the next logical question. "What happened to yours?"

"She and my stepfather were killed in a car accident when I was a teenager."

He saw it then, the curtain that whisked across her emotions, hiding them from view and could tell there was a lot more to that simple statement than she was letting on. Way more. Took one to know one. He also had an incident that he kept carefully curtained. Knew how hard she must have practiced to perfect that calm, matter-of-fact tone. How carefully she worded the explanation so it contained the clear statement: *Don't go there. I don't want to discuss it.*

He let her off the hook. "I gather Madam took you in."

Téa nodded. "She raised us. But it was my responsibility to fill in for our mother."

Interesting. "Who told you that?"

"Who…?" The question knocked her off stride and she blinked at him, a hint of confusion causing her brow to wrinkle. "No one told me. No one had to."

"Uh-huh." He made some swift calculations in his head and came up with…way too young. "Just out of curiosity, how old are your sisters?"

"Juliann is twenty-two, Davida is twenty-one, and Katrina is eighteen. She graduates from high school in a couple months. Maybe."

That pretty much confirmed what he suspected. "Which makes you only two years older than Juliann."

"Almost three." This time her response came with a hint of defensiveness.

He throttled back, keeping his comments gentle and understanding. "Right. But even so, it's not quite enough of a gap to make you a mother figure in their eyes." He shot her an easy, confiding sort of grin, one meant to link them in some nebulous way. "I mean, we're both stuck in the same predicament. We're the oldest. We're supposed to set the example for the younger ones. But, my sister, Gia, is six years younger than me and I guarantee she doesn't see me as a father figure. Not even close."

Téa mulled that over, no doubt searching for a flaw in his logic. Eventually she came up with something, though it took her a minute. "Probably because your father's still alive," she said with a hint of triumph. "But when our parents married, they sort of looked at me as if I were—" She broke off with another shrug, her logic running out of steam since her stepfather and mother would have still been alive then, too.

"A mother figure? At nine?" he asked gently.

"Not exactly," she conceded. "But…more mature and distant. An aunt or something. I guess it evolved into a mother figure after my parents died."

He tried not to wince. In other words, they made her feel like the odd man out, despite the fact that their father eventually adopted her. He thought back to that long-ago summer at the Dante family cabin. How she'd kept herself apart from the rest of them. Now that he thought about it, she'd been different in every possible way from her sisters. In looks—like a flame dancing in the middle of a pile of coal. In attitude—a helpless fawn flitting among a pack of rambunctious panther cubs. In action—an oasis of calm amidst a storm of juvenile turbulence.

"I remember the first time I saw you," he confessed.

"You mean in the intersection?"

He shook his head. "No, I mean the very first time. At the lake when we were kids." He tilted his head to one side, watching the play of emotions that chased across her face, the unexpected vulnerability. "Don't you remember?" he asked softly.

She fiddled with a thick file folder on her desk, flipping it open and then closed again. "Yes," she said after a moment. She lifted eyes gone dark with memories.

"You made me itch even then." The words escaped of their own volition.

She stiffened. Her fingers played across the palm of her hand, though he doubted she even noticed. "Itch?"

He wouldn't admit it might have been the early signs of The Inferno. He wasn't willing to look at it that closely. But something about her had gotten under his skin, even then. "You irritated me."

She didn't press, made a face instead, then accused, "You were a bully. You all were."

It was his turn to shrug. "It wouldn't surprise me. We were probably operating under a pack mentality back then. And you didn't fit in."

She flinched. "No, I didn't."

He leaned across the desk toward her, sweeping a lock of hair off her brow and tucking it behind one ear. His fingers lingered, stroking. "You didn't want to fit in."

"Not then," she agreed, leaning into the caress. "I wasn't used to so much noise and confusion. Before we became de Lucas, it was just me and my mom. We lived a fairly quiet existence except when my Billings grandparents descended. Then it got a bit rocky."

That snagged his attention and his hand fell away. "Why is that?"

"I don't remember much, but according to Mom, Grandfather Billings was somewhat controlling." She gave a quick half smile, confiding, "Of course he'd have been excruciatingly polite about it—not like the de Lucas who handle any disagreement at top volume."

Luc grinned. "The Dantes have been known to go at it a time or two, though Nonna will bring us to a fast stop if it continues too long."

"As will Madam. She'll rap her knuckles on the table and if there isn't instant silence…" Téa shuddered.

"She can be intimidating."

"She terrified me during those early years," Téa confessed.

It was a telling comment. "So how did Grandfather Billings take the news that your mother was going to remarry?"

"Not well. He was dead-set against it. In fact, he cut us off when she married Dad." She leaned in closer still and dropped her voice, possibly because they were deep in Billings's territory. Perhaps on some level old man Billings still infused the walls with his essence and she didn't want to chance him overhearing. "It surprised the hell out of me when he named me his successor in the will. Until then I'd planned to get a law degree."

And probably surprised the hell out of her cousin, Conway Billings. Luc decided against saying as much. "You call your stepfather Dad. And you use his name. I assume he adopted you?"

"Yes, when I turned sixteen. Six months later—" She broke off, but he caught the glint of tears in her eyes.

He gathered up her hand. Heat licked across his skin where their palms joined. It was a pleasant sensation. Reassuring on some level. It was as though what had been parted was once again joined and he could relax. "I'm sorry. Losing both of your parents like that must have been rough."

"It would have been far worse if Madam hadn't taken all of us in."

"And now it's time to pay her back for her generosity."

For some reason that provoked a smile. "Is that so wrong?"

"You're the one who almost got taken out by a cab because you were so distracted. You tell me."

"It's temporary," she whispered. "As soon as I turn twenty-five—"

"You'll take over the reins of a huge company with limited experience. Your workload will increase dramatically and you'll still have three demanding sisters and a grandmother to worry about."

"You think I should just give it all up?"

"There are options."

"None that will allow me the financial freedom I need." She broke off at the knock on her door and snatched her hand from his. He watched her fight to compose herself before calling out, "Come in."

A man in his mid-forties stuck his head through the opening of the door and gave a patently fake start of surprise. "Oh, you have company. Am I interrupting?"

A smile bloomed on Téa's face and she waved the man in. "You're never interrupting, Connie. Come on in. I'd like to introduce you to Luc Dante. Luc, this is my cousin, Conway Billings."

A man hovering somewhere in those unfortunate inches between medium and short entered the office. Out of sheer habit, Luc made a swift assessment. Conway was dressed in an expensive navy suit with a snowy white shirt, the collar held in place by pretentious gold clips rather than buttons. Matching clips decorated the cuffs of his sleeves. He wore his thinning auburn hair as short as Luc's and was painfully clean-shaven. He also sported an old-fashioned pocket watch on a real gold chain—no doubt a subtle advertisement of Billings's wares, had gold-rimmed glasses perched on the ball of his stub nose and kept his shoes polished to a mirror shine. Unlike Téa's creamy complexion, his glowed an uncomfortable shade of red that clashed with his hair.

For some reason, Luc's hackles went up. Maybe it was Conway's pretense of surprise and ridiculous opening question. The door was closed. He had to have heard their voices. Of course he was interrupting. How could he not be? But then, this man ran Billings. At least, for the moment. No doubt his position meant that no matter who or what he interrupted, it wasn't an interruption.

Luc also suspected that someone had alerted him to the fact that a Dante was in the building talking to Téa. And since Dantes was Billings's biggest client, no doubt Cousin Connie wanted to find out what the hell was going on.

Luc stuck out his hand. "A pleasure," he lied.

"Yes, it is," Conway lied right back.

Luc's eyes narrowed. Okay, at least he knew where he stood. He edged his hip onto the corner of Téa's desk, staking his claim, only to ruin the possessive maneuver with a wince of pain. Damn hip. "Nice place you have here," he managed to say.

"Thanks." Pride rippled through the single word. "Billings has been the gold standard ever since my great-uncle established it, two and a half decades ago."

He placed enough emphasis on the words "gold standard" that Luc realized it was meant as a play on words. Supplier of gold. Gold standard. Ha-ha. Luc bared his teeth in a grin. "Don't sweat it. Dantes doesn't mind doing business with newcomers like Bling."

Conway stopped laughing. Either Cousin Connie didn't care for the company's nickname, or he didn't appreciate the reminder that Dantes had been around twice as long as Billings.

"Why are you here, Mr. Dante?" he asked bluntly.

"Make it Luc." He waited.

"Luc," Conway repeated through gritted teeth.

"I'm here on behalf of Dantes." He picked up on Téa's incipient protest and turned to her. Catching her hand in his, he gave it a light squeeze. "Just six more weeks, isn't it? We've almost left it too long."

"Left what too long?" Conway asked sharply.

He hadn't missed the touch Luc and Téa had exchanged, an intermingling of fingers that could be taken as a sign of intimacy—and in this case most assuredly was. He regarded the man with the sort of patience one did a child. Good ol' Connie caught the look, interpreted it as just that and bristled in offense.

"Téa takes over Billings then, doesn't she?" Luc didn't wait for confirmation. "As your largest and most important customer, Dantes wants to make certain all our needs will be met before, during and after the transition. So, I plan to work closely with Téa these next few weeks to ensure everything proceeds smoothly."

Téa's eyes narrowed on Luc in warning before she offered her cousin a reassuring smile. "You don't mind, do you, Connie?" she asked.

Conway seized the question with grim determination, using the opportunity to regain control of the situation. "As a matter of fact, I do, Téa," he informed her gravely. "If Dantes wants my assurance that Billings will continue to provide excellent goods and service—"

Luc cut him off without hesitation. "It's not *your* assurance I'm interested in. You're no longer the one in charge. Your cousin is."

Beside him, Téa stiffened. "Luc," she murmured in protest.

A sweep of heightened color darkened Conway's

cheekbones and a protest tumbled out before he could prevent it. "Not for another six weeks, she isn't."

Luc lifted an eyebrow. Interesting. Her cousin sounded a bit possessive for a man who—how had Téa described him? Oh, right. As a man who couldn't wait to get out from under his responsibilities. It might be interesting to find out just what sort of business Conway intended to start up…assuming there actually was one.

Luc shook his head with a mock frown. "Six weeks isn't very long. It might be just enough time for Dantes to satisfy ourselves that your gold standard will be upheld after the transition." He lifted an eyebrow. "You don't have any objection to my being here, do you?"

"As a matter of fact—"

"Hey, no problem," Luc interrupted and stood. "If you don't want me around, I'm gone."

"I think that would be best," Conway said with a decisive nod. He appeared more assured now that he'd regained the upper hand. Or at least, thought he had. He smoothed his suit jacket like a bird unruffling its feathers. "I'm sure you understand, Dante. But this is my company—"

"*Our* company," Téa interrupted with a spark of irritation.

Conway started. "Right, right. *Our* company." His tone turned aggrieved. "You must agree, Téa, that it wouldn't be appropriate to have someone looking over *our* shoulders, as it were."

"Got it." Luc retrieved his cell phone from his pocket and began pressing buttons. "Let me apprise Sev of these latest developments. It's an unfortunate setback, but my cousin is accustomed to those. Very decisive and proactive that cousin of mine."

"Is this really necessary?" Conway demanded.

Luc paused. "What? The phone call or my being here?" He shrugged. "Not that it matters. I assure you both are critical to our continued good relationship."

Téa sliced neatly through the testosterone thickening the air with icy shards of feminine disapproval. "If Conway objects to your being here, Luc, then that's that. Here's what I suggest in order to straighten this out and satisfy all parties involved." She clicked off her suggestions like a general commanding her troops. "Luc, please call Sev and ask if he'll take a meeting. The three of us will go over, sit down with him and see what can be arranged. But make it clear that we'll do everything in our power to ensure the transition goes off without a hitch. Connie, since our contract with Dantes is up soon, I suggest we pull together some numbers in order to begin preliminary negotiations on a new one."

Conway stiffened and Luc had the distinct impression he wasn't used to his cousin being quite so assertive. And he sure as hell wasn't accustomed to her issuing instructions to him. "That won't be necessary, Téa," he stated. "I have the contract details well in hand." Frustration ate at his expression before he finally capitulated. "Okay, fine. Mr. Dante, if you must oversee certain aspects of the transition—"

"Luc."

Silence reigned for an entire thirty seconds until Conway bit out, "*Luc*. If you insist it's necessary to be here—"

"I do."

Conway shot his cousin a smoldering glare. "Since you'll soon be running the show, Téa, you work out all the various details, though I must insist that any changes to established routine be run by me beforehand." He hesitated, sparing Luc a suspicious glance. "As for you, Mr.—*Luc*. I think it only fair you be as forthcoming as possible about your intentions."

"My intentions?"

The question caught Luc off guard and Conway picked up on that fact. He pounced with something akin to triumph. He rocked onto the balls of his feet with a quick bounce and jabbed his index finger toward Luc. "Exactly. Are you really here to ensure a smooth transition, or is this about the renewal of our contract? If you're looking for a better price…"

Huh. Luc cocked his head to one side. "Can you offer one?"

"No, I just meant…" He eyed the two, his suspicion deepening. "I hope you don't think Téa will offer you a better deal because she's a woman, and therefore susceptible to masculine influence."

"Masculine influence," Luc repeated. He didn't need to fake how much the comment offended him. "By that I assume you mean sexual influence." He slowly stood, allowing every intimidating inch of his six-feet-three to loom over Billings's five-feet-squat. "Just who the hell do you think I am? Who do you think *she* is?"

Conway retreated toward the door. "No! I didn't mean—" A heavy flush stained his cheeks and he made a production of checking his watch. "Since I have an urgent appointment in a few minutes, we'll have to finish this discussion some other time." He fumbled for the door handle behind him. "Téa, you and Luc carry on. I'll be in my office if you need me." With that, he exited the room with as much dignity as he could muster.

Luc waited until the door banged closed before glancing at Téa. To his relief, he saw amusement glittering in her eyes. He edged his hip on the corner of her desk again, managing not to wince this time. "I'm curious," he said. "Could I use sex to persuade you to give Dantes a better deal?"

"Not a chance."

He heaved a disappointed sigh. "Didn't think so, but I had to ask. Sev would have been annoyed if I hadn't at least tried."

"I understand."

"In that case, we better do what Conway ordered."

A delightful confusion spread across her face. "I'm sorry?"

Luc grinned. "Didn't you hear him? He told us to carry on. I suggest we get started." He leaned in, feeling the pull of The Inferno and allowing it to consume him. "He is, after all, the boss."

Her smile turned grim. "Only for six more weeks."

And then she, too, surrendered to the heat.

Five

The next week passed, at moments feeling as though it were on wings. Other times Téa was certain some sadistic creature had paused the minutes in order for her to fully experience the weight of desire building with each additional day she spent in Luc's company.

It was a desire she couldn't allow. One she didn't have time to explore, not when she faced so many more urgent demands. Mostly it was one she didn't deserve, not after the destruction she'd left in her wake all those years ago—a destruction she could never fully repair even though she'd do her best to mend the few rents within her capability.

Luc kept his word. Except for the single embrace they exchanged after the confrontation with Connie, he hadn't touched her. At least, he didn't touch her the way she longed to be touched. He kept their physical interaction as brief and distant as possible, though she sensed that it was as much a struggle for him as it was for her.

His struggle wasn't implicit in what he said, but she caught his reaction in small and significant ways. The deepening tenor of his voice. The slight hitch in his movement when he reached for her, as though he were deliberately switching gears from intimate to impersonal. A flash of awareness that turned his golden eyes molten with hunger before he deliberately banked the flames.

She didn't find the process any easier. She had an urgent job to accomplish right now—to learn everything she could about her grandfather's company before assuming the reins, while still carving out enough time each day to care for her family's needs and demands... not to mention the unending phone calls. The last thing she could handle was another disruption. Unfortunately Luc excelled at disrupting her on every conceivable level—including hiding her phones whenever their constant demands threatened to overwhelm her.

She couldn't say what clued her in the first time, other than the fact that she'd enjoyed several hours of blissful silence before noticing that her phones were no longer lined up along the edge of her desk. She stared at the empty space for an entire minute, on the verge of panic, before her gaze veered toward Luc and understanding dawned.

"Give them back."

He flipped the page on the journal he read, something that had to do with electronic security. "Relax, Téa. Nothing can be that urgent. If it were, they'd call Bling directly."

"That's not the point. You can't just take my cell phones." Her voice rose and she struggled to lower it, even out the shrillness. "They're lifelines to my family. Madam and my sisters depend on me."

He shot her a dangerous look, filled with a hard decisiveness she suspected was a natural part of his personality. Until now he'd never used it on her. "It's vital to trust your team, to rely on them. But it's just as vital to be self-sufficient enough to take care of business if one of those team members is lost."

"In English, please?"

"If you take self-sufficiency away from your sisters, they become less effective on all levels, personal, as well as professional."

"My family isn't some sort of military unit," she protested.

"They'll also never learn to fend for themselves if you wipe their noses every time they sneeze. Your sisters need to learn independent thought and action." His eyes narrowed, disapproval stirring in the deep gold depths. "Unless you want them dependent on you. Is that why you do everything for them? It makes you feel wanted? Needed?"

"No!"

"Are they incompetent? Handicapped in some way?"

"Of course not," she snapped.

"Then why the obsession to micromanage?"

Her mouth tightened and she shook her head, refusing to answer.

He shrugged. "Then, barring emergency, they're perfectly capable of handling their own affairs until after you've finished work for the day. Since I'm in charge of keeping you safe and distraction free, I've made the executive decision to confiscate your phones. I'll return them at five."

"And if there is an emergency?"

"There are enough brain cells between the four of them to call through to the Bling switchboard and alert you to that fact."

She didn't dare admit that not having the constant barrage of phone calls came as a tremendous relief. But it did. And Luc was as good as his word. The moment they stepped foot in her office he took possession of the phones, returning them at five on the dot.

Realizing that she'd been staring into space for the past fifteen minutes while he watched on, she forced her attention back to the spreadsheets piled in front of her. "You're not supposed to put your feet on my desk, remember?" she said absently as she scanned the numbers.

"I vaguely recall you saying something to that effect."

"And yet, I'm still seeing an impressive pair of size fourteens sitting here in front of me."

"Elevating my feet makes my knee and hip feel better."

She peered at him over the top of her reading glasses. "That's low, even for you."

"Are you calling me a liar?"

"I wouldn't dream of it. I would dream of telling you to move your feet elsewhere while I'm working."

She returned her attention to the numbers. Something didn't add up, but despite her affinity with all things accounting, she couldn't quite figure out what was bothering her. She blew out a sigh. Maybe she'd have better luck if part of her weren't constantly distracted by the golden-eyed panther lounging nearby, one that took great delight in ruffling her tidy little world.

"What's wrong?" he asked.

It didn't surprise her that he picked up on her frustration. The man was beyond observant. "I don't know. Nothing."

He dropped his feet to the floor and leaned forward in his chair. "If it were nothing you wouldn't be analyzing the same report for the fifth time this week."

"I'm having focus issues. I'm distracted." She didn't dare admit aloud that a huge part of that distraction was due to him. "That's one of the reasons you're here, remember? To save me from my own distraction."

His mouth twitched, but he answered seriously enough. "All too well. Part of your problem is that you don't get enough sleep."

"I get plenty." She couldn't say for certain, but it was possible the testy note in her voice gave lie to her claim.

"According to Madam you get maybe five hours a night."

She waved that aside. Maybe she'd have been in a better position to argue the point if the numbers weren't doing a bizarre rumba across the page. "It won't be for much longer."

"No, it won't." He caught her hand in his and tugged her to her feet. "Come on."

"What are you doing?" she protested. "I'm working here."

He shot a sardonic glance toward her spreadsheets, then checked his watch. "It's Friday and it's almost four. In my book, that's quitting time."

"Not in mine," she retorted.

"Yeah, well, I'm expected at my grandparents soon for a family celebration. It's Rafe's birthday."

"Oh."

She tugged fruitlessly at her hand before giving it up

and leaving it captured within his. Somehow the throb in her palm didn't bother her as much when their hands were interlaced. Instead it calmed her, steadied her, even as it stirred the banked fires of desire kindling between them. She couldn't decide which disturbed her the most, not having the connection created by their touch, or dealing with the urge to tug him into her arms and have her wicked way with him.

She cleared her throat, hoping it would also clear her thoughts. Not that it succeeded. "Well, you go ahead to the party. I have a few more hours to put in here and then, I promise, I'll go straight home." She offered a reassuring smile. "I'll even pay attention to what I'm doing and dive for cover anytime I see a cab."

For the past week he'd escorted her from door-to-door, unwilling to so much as debate the issue. No matter how early she attempted to leave for the office, or how late she stayed, he was always right there to shepherd her to and fro. She had a strong suspicion that Madam played a huge part in alerting him to any unexpected changes in Téa's schedule. After a few days of attempting to circumvent their efforts, she'd given up trying since it proved a ridiculous waste of both time and energy.

"I have a better suggestion," Luc countered. "Why don't you come with me to the party. Then I'll see you home, as usual."

She spared a brief glance toward the stack of accounting reports. They held all the appeal of a root canal. She'd much rather spend the next few hours with Luc. Maybe if he hadn't used the word "party" she'd have considered it. But that word carried negative associations, pushing every last one of her guilt buttons. Duty. Responsibility. Family obligation. They were brands she wore, ones burned into her heart and soul.

Something in her expression must have given her away. "What is it?" he asked sharply. "What's wrong?"

"Nothing." Not that the denial fooled him.

"Bull. You look like someone threatened with a firing squad. Why?"

She lifted her chin and forced herself to regard him with cool composure. "I don't do parties."

He studied her for an endless moment. "How about family dinners?" he asked neutrally. "You have a family, don't you?"

"You know I do," she retorted.

"And your family has dinners, right?"

"Yes, but—"

"And sometimes those dinners are to celebrate a birthday?"

She pushed out a sigh. She could see where this was going. What she couldn't see was a logical way out of it. "It's been known to happen," she admitted.

"That's what this is. A dinner to celebrate my brother's birthday. I'd like you to come with me." And then he turned downright mean and underhanded. "Please, Téa. Come with me," he said softly.

She caved. But then, how could she do anything else? Not only did she want to, but she flat-out couldn't resist the temptation, particularly when it was issued by such a bone-melting masculine package. "Fine. I'll come." She glanced down at her tailored slacks and jacket, the combination in a dignified, somber black. They screamed, "business." "I'm not sure I'm dressed appropriately for a party, though."

"You look gorgeous, as always. Just casual it up."

She blinked at him. "Excuse me?"

"You know how women do." He gestured with his hands. "Undo certain stuff. Fluff other parts."

"Undo and fluff." Maybe if her sisters were here to interpret it would help. Particularly Vida. Téa suspected that her flirty middle sister excelled at the art of undoing and fluffing. "That's man-speak for…?"

"Here. I'll show you."

Before she could stop him, he'd stripped off her jacket and tossed it aside. Then he released the first three buttons of her blouse. While she rebuttoned two of them, he ran his fingers through her hair, releasing the elegant little knot she'd fashioned that morning and sending her hair tumbling down her back in a cascade of exuberant auburn curls.

"Do you mind?" she demanded in exasperation.

"Not at all. All undone and fluffed." He tilted his head to one side. "But there's still something missing."

He took a step back and examined her while she did her best not to feel too self-conscious. "Well?" she asked, squirming just a bit. "What's wrong with me?"

"There's nothing wrong with you. It's just…" He snapped his fingers. "Got it." Reaching out, he plucked her reading glasses from the tip of her nose and set them carefully among the papers scattered on her desk. He studied her upturned face and offered a lazy smile filled with blatant male approval. "Much better."

"I need those to read." She wasn't quite sure why she uttered such an inane comment. He just had that effect on her.

"You won't need to read at the party," he answered gravely. "The cake will say Happy Birthday, Rafe."

Her lips quivered in the direction of a smile. "Thank you for letting me know."

"Glad to help."

Téa tidied up her desk and snagged her jacket on the way out of the office. "My phones," she reminded, holding out her hand. For some reason, she felt reluctant to take them when he handed them over. That was a first.

She paused by her assistant's desk on her way out and told him to take off early, before giving in to the pressure of Luc's hand urging her toward the elevators. Five minutes later they were in his car, battling the start of rush hour traffic as they headed toward the Golden Gate Bridge. She used the drive time to deal with the accumulated calls, fighting a headache from the pressure of dealing with her sisters' latest crises. The instant she finished, Luc stole the phones.

"For the next couple hours you're off duty," he said by way of explanation.

By the time they arrived in Sausalito and climbed the winding roads overlooking the bay, late afternoon was easing toward evening, resting a gentle hand on their surroundings and gilding it with a soft glow. Luc parked the car outside a wooden gate, squeezing in among the other cars piled up there. The gate led to a lush backyard, with rambling flowerbeds that rioted in color and fragrance. Carefully pruned black acacia and bay trees shaded portions of the large, fenced oasis while a mush oak spread its protective arms over a wrought iron table and chairs. The dining area offered the perfect place for an outdoor lunch or supper, with its glorious view of the bay, Angel Island and Belvedere. Currently it was the gathering place for nearly a dozen people, all of whom were talking and laughing at full volume, some in English and some in Italian.

Luc didn't approach immediately, but pulled Téa close and murmured in her ear. "Hang on a minute.

You met the original Dante clan when we were children, but I don't expect you can put names and faces together after all these years."

"Not a chance," she admitted.

"I'll give you a quick rundown. First up are the cousins." He indicated one of the men sitting near the table. He was a couple years older than Luc and bore a striking similarity in appearance. "Have you taken any meetings with Sev, yet?"

"Connie's covering that for now." She couldn't explain why she felt so reluctant to admit as much. Nor why she hastened to add, "I expect I'll have the chance to sit down with Sev when we finalize a new contract."

"Well, you can at least press the flesh tonight." He indicated two particularly gorgeous men with dark brown hair and Nonna's hazel eyes. "Those are the twins, Marco and Lazz. And their youngest brother, Nicolò, is sitting in the grass with his wife, Kiley."

Next Luc indicated a heavily pregnant blonde snuggled in Sev's arms. "That's his wife, Francesca. She and Kiley, are due…" He made a production of checking his watch.

"That soon?"

"Oh, yeah."

"Marco's wife, Caitlyn, is talking to Lazz's wife, Ariana. And my sister, Gia, is the one pouring the wine. Come on and I'll introduce you to everyone." He offered a swift grin. "Take a deep breath…"

"And dive right in?"

"The water's nice and warm."

Téa expected to feel like an outsider, but the Dantes soon proved her wrong. Perhaps it was because the family was so large and sprawling or because there were so many diverse personalities, but they instantly made her feel like one of them.

Gia, the most outgoing and vibrant of the bunch, gave her a quick hug and pressed a glass of wine into her hand. And while the men discussed all things sports related, the women talked at length about the additions that were soon to grace the family.

"So far Nonna is batting a thousand." Ariana dropped the comment into a lull in the conversation, speaking with the lightest of Italian accents.

"What do you mean?" Kiley asked.

"Well, she said you both would have boys and that's what the ultrasound shows, yes?"

"True," Francesca admitted, rubbing the taut mound of her belly. "But then, she also said you'd have the only girl out of all these Dantes sprawled around here."

"Also true," Ariana said.

It took a split second for comprehension to sweep through the family. The instant it did, a half dozen different voices exploded in everything from cheers of excitement to a rapid-fire peppering of questions.

"When are you due?"

"Is it really a girl?"

"Why didn't you tell us sooner?"

Lazz held up his hands with a laugh. "She's due in a bit under six months. We wanted to keep it to ourselves for a while without you lot driving us crazy. And yes, the ultrasound confirmed today that it's a girl. A bit early for them to know, or so I've been told, but apparently the baby was positioned just right for the doctor to make the determination."

Téa and Luc enjoyed the added celebratory mood of the family while they finished their drinks. Then he urged her to her feet. "Let's go inside and say hello to Primo and Nonna."

They found Primo supervising the kitchen, a bottle of homemade beer at his elbow. The room was enormous, with huge bluish-gray flagstones decorating the rustic kitchen floor. Overhead, rough-hewn redwood beams stretched across the twelve-foot plaster ceiling. A long, broad table, one designed for the largest of families, took up one end of the room, while appliances suitable for a gourmet kitchen filled the other. Several more Dantes were busy carrying out Primo's orders as they put the finishing touches on the various dishes they were preparing for dinner. To Téa's surprise all of them were male.

"I'm beginning to like your family," she told Luc in an undertone.

He grinned, quick on the uptake. "Because the men cook?"

"Darn right. Makes a nice change. Of course, there aren't any men in my family, only women, so we get stuck with all the chores."

"Cooking and gardening are my grandfather's two favorite pastimes. Wait until you try his *pollo al Marsala con peperoni rossi*." Luc closed his eyes in ecstasy. "There are chefs from all over the world who'd give their eyeteeth for the recipe."

"Chicken Marsala with red peppers?" she hazarded a guess. "My Italian isn't that great, much to Madam's displeasure." She slanted him a quick, teasing grin. "Except when it comes to food."

"We'll have to see what we can do to change that."

The expression in his eyes made her feel as though she were free-falling at fifteen thousand feet without a parachute. Heat exploded deep in her belly and spread outward in waves of lapping fire. All thought vanished, except for one indisputable fact. This was her man. She didn't know how it had happened or why, but he belonged to her every bit as much as she belonged to him. Even as the crazy thought took hold, she struggled to dismiss it. It was wrong to put her personal desires first. But some thoughts couldn't be so easily dismissed.

Primo paused in the middle of barking an order to greet them. "So," he said, the flavor of his Tuscany homeland filling his words with a lyrical warmth. "This is the one, yes?"

Téa wasn't certain who appeared more alarmed, her or Luc. She'd always considered herself in control of her emotions and able to keep them well hidden from curious eyes. She hoped she'd nailed the ability, considering she'd been practicing since the tender age of sixteen. But, with Primo… It was as though he looked into her heart and laid it bare. And she didn't like it one bit. Deciding to take control of the situation, she stuck out her hand.

"How do you do, Mr. Dante. I'm Téa de Luca. Luc and I are working together. Temporarily." Though who that final word was aimed at—Luc, his grandfather, or herself—she couldn't quite say.

"Mr. Dante?" he repeated with an offended click of his tongue. He wrapped her up in a powerful hug filled with the distinctive scent of a fragrant cigar and a variety of the spices he'd used in the preparation of their dinner. "I am Primo, you understand?"

"Primo," she said, accepting the enthusiastic kisses he planted on each of her cheeks. "It's a pleasure to meet you."

He drew back in mock offense. "We met when you

were a little girl. You do not remember me? With most people I make a big impression."

She fought to control her amusement, not wanting to offend. "I'm sorry. I remember the cabin and the lake, but not too much else."

Primo lifted a sooty eyebrow and fixed her with ancient gold eyes that were identical to Luc's. "Well, no matter. I remember you. You were a pale, shy thing, overwhelmed by so many people. All bright red hair and white, skinny arms and legs." He touched the tip of her nose. "Always had this stuck in a book, yes?"

"That was me," she admitted with a laugh.

Primo turned and slapped the shoulder of one of the men behind him with a hand heavy enough to knock him to the floor. Maybe it would have if he hadn't possessed a powerful Dante build. "This is Luc's *babbo*, Alessandro."

Luc's father, Téa realized. At least, the Tuscany version of the word. "It's a pleasure."

"I'm stirring or I'd come over and say hello." Alessandro tossed a friendly smile over his shoulder. "Hello, anyway."

"You stir, I say hello," Primo instructed. He pointed to the next one in line. "This is Rafe. He is one of the pretty Dantes. We only have two, thank the good Lord above for that small blessing. One is a girl, my precious Gianna, which is as it should be. We keep the other despite his being as pretty as the girl. If he did not have a brain, I would have drowned him as a child."

"I believe you tried that, Primo," Rafe offered, "and discovered I could swim like a fish."

"I should have tried harder." Primo whacked his next helper. "And this good-for-nothing is Draco. I am not certain what use he is."

"I'm the charming one."

"Marco is the charming one. You are *l'istigatore*. The troublemaker."

Draco shrugged, not bothered by the accusation. "That, too."

"That, alone," Primo corrected before addressing Luc once again. "*Cucciolo mio*, go find Nonna and Elia and introduce Téa. Maybe she will remember your *mammina* better than she remembers me." He leaned toward Téa, confiding, "I do not let them in the kitchen until it is time to eat."

"Sounds perfect to me," Téa said with sincere appreciation.

Primo grinned. "I like you. You come back when all is ready and sit next to me."

The offer touched her. "Thank you. I look forward to it."

The night seemed to fly by after that. As ordered, Téa took the seat of honor beside Primo and surprised herself by eating every morsel put in front of her. She also discovered that Luc was right. Primo's *Marsala* was sheer ambrosia. Dinner took hours, the process a raucous occasion filled with genuine family affection and laughter.

The cake did indeed say, Happy Birthday, Rafe, and after it was consumed, the presents opened and the dishes washed, the women swept Téa off to enjoy coffee and talk babies some more. She threw a panicked glance over her shoulder in Luc's direction, but he just chuckled at her dismay. The last view she had of him was his glorious grin before it dissolved into a sudden frown. It took her a moment to understand why. But then she saw it. He was staring down at his hands. Staring at the unconscious massage of left thumb against right palm. Staring as though his hands didn't quite belong to his own body.

Staring at the undeniable proof that The Inferno had claimed another victim.

"So, it has finally struck," Primo said the instant the women had left.

Luc glanced up in confusion while his brother, Rafe, looked on with an amused expression on his too-handsome face. "Excuse me?"

"The Inferno." His grandfather gestured toward his grandson's hands. "Do not bother denying it, Luciano. The signs are all there."

"What this?" He deliberately gave his palm a final scratch and forced a laugh. "Just an itch."

Primo snorted. "What you feel is a fifty year itch, boy. Longer if you are very lucky."

"Téa de Luca is an assignment, nothing more."

Primo rolled his eyes heavenward. "Why are they always so stubborn? So reluctant to believe the truth even when it strikes as hard and dazzling as a lightning bolt?"

He crossed to one of the cabinets and pulled out a canister that read, Dried Manroot. Popping the lid, he extracted a cigar while Luc struggled to suppress a snort of laughter, thoroughly enjoying his grandfather's sense of the absurd.

"Nonna will have a fit if she sees you with that," Rafe warned, his jade-green eyes gleaming in shared amusement.

"Then we will make certain she does not see." He took a moment to prep the cigar, then light it. "Luciano, you have witnessed The Inferno every day of your life. With my beloved Nonna. With your parents. One by one, with each of your cousins." He lifted a snowy eyebrow. "Did you believe yourself immune?"

Luc set his jaw at a stubborn angle. "Yes."

Primo blew a ring of smoke skyward and shrugged. "You were wrong."

"I'm not interested in settling down," Luc protested. "I'm sure as hell not interested in marriage and children."

"Because of what happened?" his grandfather asked shrewdly.

There was no point in denying the truth. "Yes."

Luc shied from the memories, knowing if he didn't build a strong enough bulwark they'd consume him. One key lesson had come from the incident, an undeniable fact he'd learned about himself. He never wanted to give so much of himself to another person that he couldn't live without her. To trust to that extent. To risk so much. Rafe had warned him when his own marriage had ended in disaster. But the accident that had ruined Luc's knee had brought the fact home in spades.

Primo stabbed his cigar in Luc's direction. "The Inferno is not something you can simply turn off. It has happened and you will have to deal with it. You can do as your uncle did—God rest my Dominic's soul." He crossed himself, grief still haunting his black eyes. "Like Dominic, you can turn from it and destroy your life. Or you can follow your parents' excellent example. You can embrace it and discover a happiness unlike anything you could imagine."

"And when it ends?" Luc demanded.

Primo regarded him in bewilderment. "Who says it must end? What is this ending?"

"All things end," he insisted in a hard voice. "Love is a gamble, the ultimate gamble. When it ends, you don't just lose. It can destroy you. I've seen it happen. That's why I'll never give into it, why I only bet when I know I can win."

Understanding dawned in his grandfather's face and an uncomfortable compassion settled into the deep lines bracketing his mouth. "You speak of the accident, yes? That unfortunate family?" He didn't wait for a response. "Death is part of life, Luciano, just as love is. No one can control it. You witnessed that during your military service. Everything in life is a risk. But you can't win unless you play. Take the love while you have the chance. Worrying about the other does you no good."

Nonna's voice drifted in from the backyard, warning of her approach. Without hesitation, Primo snatched his cigar from between his teeth and shoved it into Luc's hand. By the time his wife entered the kitchen, he was across the room with a virtuous expression pinned to his face.

Nonna's hazel eyes landed on Luc before arrowing toward Primo. "You know what the doctor said about smoking. No more cigars."

"Do you see a cigar in my hand, old woman?"

"Do you think me a fool, old man?" After nearly sixty years of marriage, her imitation of her husband was uncanny.

Primo held his hands out. "*Che cosa?* I have no idea what you are talking about."

"You look as innocent as a wolf with a lamb between its teeth, Primo Dante. My Luciano does not smoke." Nonna planted her hands on her hips. "You think I do not know the meaning of dried manroot? I know all about that canister in your spice cabinet."

"Dried cucumber," he protested. "Just a bit of seasoning."

"Hah! A joke at my expense, is what it is. Only the joke is on you when I tell all our friends that Primo Dante keeps his dried manroot in a jar in our kitchen cabinet!"

"You would not dare…!" He thumped his chest. "I am your husband and I am telling you—"

She lifted an eyebrow.

Primo cleared his throat. "And I am telling you that as of tonight there will be no dried manroot in my spice cabinet."

She nodded in satisfaction. "I thought that might be what you wanted to tell me."

Six

The evening didn't end as well as it began.

Téa expected Luc to join her after he'd finished his conversation with Primo. But instead, Sev Dante, the head of Dantes, the family's international jewelry empire, slipped into the seat next to hers. She offered him a smile, one he didn't return.

Her smile faded. "Is something wrong?"

He frowned, adding to her concern, and kept his voice low, so their conversation didn't carry to the other Dantes sprawled around them. "I know a birthday party isn't the appropriate venue for this discussion, but Francesca insisted I speak to you," he began on an ominous note. "She's usually right about these things."

"What things?" Téa asked warily.

"Business matters."

She stiffened. This couldn't be good, not when it involved so much frowning. "Business matters…

as in Billings's contract with Dantes?" At his nod of confirmation, she said, "I thought Connie was handling that."

He studied her with a golden gaze remarkably similar to Luc's, if perhaps a shade tawnier. "Let's just say that your cousin hasn't been very responsive to the concerns I've raised. So, if he's representing you in this matter, he's not doing a very good job of it." He hesitated, then asked, "You'll be in charge of Bling soon, won't you?"

"Five more weeks," she acknowledged.

"Then you should know there's a strong possibility that Dantes won't re-up our contract."

She fought to keep all emotion from her expression while she figured out how to deal with the unexpected— and alarming—information. All the while, a thread of panic wormed through her. If they lost the Dantes account, the company would be in serious jeopardy. Other accounts might follow suit and her inheritance would go from impressive to nonexistent.

And that meant she'd fail her family.

"Can you tell me why you've changed your mind about doing business with Billings?" she asked with impressive calm.

"It's a quality issue. Yours has gone down while your prices have skyrocketed. Conway says it's at your insistence. We've had another company approach us offering far better prices and top-notch quality."

Téa straightened in her chair. She carefully returned her cup and saucer to the wrought iron table and swiveled to confront Sev directly. "No one offers better quality than Billings."

"Once upon a time that would be true," he acknowledged. "But not any longer."

She searched desperately for a solution. "What if I can guarantee both? Would you re-evaluate your decision?"

"Your guarantee doesn't hold a lot of weight considering the quality of the merchandise we've been receiving." He hesitated, then nodded. "But since our two companies have always enjoyed such a stellar relationship, I'll give you a couple of weeks to get to the bottom of the problem."

"Thank you. I'll look into the matter and call you Monday, at the latest."

Sev inclined his head. "One last thing…"

He shot a look over her shoulder. Téa didn't need to follow his glance to know that Luc was approaching. She could feel him. Feel him as though he were a rising tide and she the waiting shoreline.

"Yes?" she prompted.

"Your…association…with Luc won't influence my decision," Sev warned quietly. And with that, he stood and returned to his wife.

Luc shot a glance in Téa's direction and grimaced. Ever since they'd left his grandparents' house she hadn't said more than a half dozen words, but had wrapped herself in silent gloom. Streetlights flickered over her, giving a harsh highlight to the tension scoring her face.

"Okay, what happened?" he demanded.

She was so lost in thought he couldn't be certain she'd heard him until her voice slipped out, soft as the night. "Nothing happened. It was a lovely evening." Then as an afterthought, she added politely, "Thank you for inviting me."

"You're welcome. Now what the *hell* is wrong? And don't tell me nothing. Something happened."

She swiveled slightly to face him. "Maybe I will tell you what happened. I realized where I've been going wrong all this time. I realized that my distraction is causing me endless problems and that it has to stop."

That was good, right? "That's good, right?" So why had his alarm bells kicked in?

"It's excellent." She managed a wobbly smile that didn't convince either of them. "In fact, it's so excellent I'm not going to need your services any longer."

His hands tightened on the steering wheel. "Good try, but… Not a chance in hell."

"Madam hired you because I was distracted," she reminded him. "I'm not distracted, anymore. I've never seen the situation so clearly."

He wished he could accuse her of having consumed too much of the wine that had flowed like water that evening. But he'd be surprised if she'd sampled more than the single glass she'd been handed when they first arrived. He didn't know who had said what this evening, but he wasn't about to let her off the hook just because a single night with his relatives had—hallelujah—given her 20/20 vision.

He used the only lever he possessed. "I'm your birthday present, remember?" Was it his fault if the words came out gravel-rough? "You can't unwrap or return me until you turn twenty-five."

She didn't so much as crack a smile. "You can insist on babysitting me for the next five weeks. It's not like I'm strong enough to turf you out, not with Madam and Nonna in your corner. But I don't need your assistance any longer. I'm more focused than I've ever been in my life."

He shot her a curious look before returning his

attention to the road. "Uh-huh. And what brought that on?"

"Tonight helped me figure out my priorities."

That was good, right? "That's good, right?" he repeated.

"That's excellent," she confirmed again. "From now on, I follow the Dantes' stellar example. I put family first. I have to if I'm going to protect them."

"Uh… Great?" Damn it.

"Yes, great." Her face settled into a grim, determined expression that set his alarm bells ringing to the max. "Because it means I put all my time and focus into taking over Billings."

That was *not* good. Not even a little. "*All* your time and attention?"

"Twenty-four/seven," she confirmed.

"That's what you learned from someone at Primo's tonight?"

"That's what I learned."

"Got it."

He didn't know which Dante was gonna die, but one of them was going down for whatever bug they'd stuck in Téa's ear. He'd been where she was, devoting his life to a cause. And it had just about killed him. Literally. It was bad enough when she was striving for some sort of balance between work and family and the teeny-tiny sliver of a piece he'd managed to coax out of her for play. Now it would only get worse. And someone would pay. Someone *always* paid the price for that sort of dedication.

He just didn't want it to be Téa.

First thing Monday, frustrated as a tiger with its tail in a knot, Luc watched Téa take the first step in her campaign. She marched into Conway Billings's office—a huge, palatial room with a prime view of the city—and slammed the door in Luc's face. The conversation between cousins went on at some length before she returned. She didn't even glance at him, though one look at her burning eyes and taut jaw warned that her conversation with "Cuz" didn't go well. She made a beeline for her own office and the spreadsheets she'd left there on Friday. She spent three straight hours poring over them, her expression more severe than he'd ever seen it.

At one point, she sent him from the room while she made a series of phone calls. Something was definitely up. He waited outside her office, glancing in the general direction of Conway's and flipped open his cell. He scrolled through the names until he hit on the one he wanted and placed the call.

"Juice? It's Luc. I need you to run a full background check on someone for me."

"What happened to hello?" his former associate complained in a rumbling bass voice. "You used to at least soften me up with a, 'how's it going?' before you started in. I feel so used when you insist we just get straight to it."

Luc felt his mouth relax into a grin. "Then you shouldn't let strangers pick you up in bars."

Juice sighed. "True enough. What can I get you?"

Luc gave him the details. "Rush it, will you?"

"That's not what they usually say."

"Yeah, but at least I'll still respect you in the morning. And I promise I'll call you soon. Honey."

Juice snorted. "Stuff it," he said before the line went dead.

Luc turned to find Téa standing there, arms folded across her chest, her vivid teal-blue eyes glaring through the sparkling lenses of her reading glasses. "If you're quite finished?"

"All done," he confirmed cheerfully.

"I'm going on a business trip which means you get the next couple of days off."

He waited a beat. "No, I believe it means I'm going on a business trip, too," he corrected.

She sliced a hand through the air. "Unnecessary and out of the question. It's a matter of confidentiality."

"I'm all about confidentiality."

"Not this time. I need to do this on my own. Connie insists and I'm forced to agree."

"Oh, well. If Connie insists…" He backed her into the office, slammed the door closed and shoved his nose against hers. Awareness shimmered through him, an awareness he did his level best to ignore. "Then I'm absolutely going."

Her eyes narrowed and he could practically see the gears spinning. Then she drew back and offered a wide, insincere smile. "Fine," she said with a careless shrug. "You can come, too."

He didn't need any alarm bells to know she'd given in way too easily. Plus, there was the small matter of her utter and total inability to lie. "When and where?"

"Wednesday morning, first thing."

"Got it." He lifted an eyebrow. "I'll pick you up at the usual time tomorrow?"

Her smile returned, sunny with insincerity. "Of course."

Of course.

Luc was right.

He'd suspected Téa planned to sneak out bright and early Tuesday morning and she didn't disappoint him.

He stood wrapped in early morning dew and shadows, and rested his hip against the brick wall that guarded the de Luca family row house. Somehow, the Italianate Victorian suited them, with its trademark gingerbread accents, top-heavy cornices and long, hooded windows. The garage door opened and Téa backed her car carefully out before the electronic mechanism engaged and slid the door closed again. He shifted until he stood directly in her path.

The instant she caught sight of him in her rearview mirror, her brakes squealed and the car bounced to a stop. After turning off the ignition, Téa erupted from the car. She made a beeline toward him, the decisive click of her heels bouncing off the concrete driveway. Somebody didn't look happy to see him. He was crushed.

"I. Should. Have. Known." She bit off each word as if they were chewed nails.

"Yeah, you should have." He held out his hand. "Keys."

"You're not coming."

He didn't bother arguing. He let his expression say it all.

She stewed for an entire sixty seconds before relenting. "If you must come, then I insist on driving."

He simply stood there, as immobile as a rock, hand outstretched.

"I'm sure there's a rule somewhere that says that bodyguards ride shotgun." When he still didn't budge, she slapped the keys in his hand. "Fine. I'll navigate."

"Excellent decision."

"It's not like I had a choice," she grumbled.

"Sure you did."

She lifted an eyebrow. "I could have canceled the trip?"

His mouth kicked up at the corners. "You got it."

He keyed the fob and popped the trunk. Picking up his duffel bag from where he'd stashed it on the sidewalk, he stowed it alongside Téa's case. By the time he finished Téa was already in the car, her nose buried in a map book.

Luc eased his tall frame behind the wheel and adjusted the seat to accommodate his long legs and cause his knee the least amount of strain. Twitched the mirrors. Did a quick check of the various controls. The engine turned over with a soft purr that spoke of a well-maintained vehicle. Knowing Téa he was willing to bet she rolled in for servicing at the exact same instant that the odometer rolled past each three thousand miles.

He didn't really need directions for getting out of the city, but if telling him where to go helped Téa come to terms with his crashing her business trip, he'd put up with it.

"How did you know?" she finally asked once they cleared the city.

"I know you." He shot her a speaking look. "Plus, you have to be the world's worst liar. Probably comes from lack of practice."

"You say that like it's a bad thing."

"It can be. I'm willing to bet every one of your sisters excels at the art."

She mulled that over before conceding the truth of it. "There are a lot of arts my sisters excel at that I don't."

No doubt it was part of the reason she'd never quite fit in. "Thank God for that." He gave her a moment to digest his comment, then asked, "Care to tell me where we're going and why?"

"Connie asked me to visit some of our smaller

accounts along the coast between San Francisco and L.A., so we can all get to know each other before I take over."

"Uh… I hate to tell you this, but Sacramento isn't between San Francisco and L.A. And that's the direction you have us headed."

"That's because I'm not going to visit those accounts."

"I'm shocked." And he was. "You're flouting Conway's authority?"

"Why, yes. I believe I am. I've always wanted to learn how to flout." Her chin took on a stubborn slant. "And today's the day."

He couldn't help himself. He chuckled. "Where are we going, instead?"

"To talk to the former manager of our manufacturing plant." She pulled out a piece of paper from her shoulder bag and checked the directions against the map book. "He retired to some small town called Polk about the time I started at Bling. It's located in the Sierra Nevada Mountains."

"Never heard of the place. Why do you want to talk to him?"

She hesitated for a telling moment. "To find out why he retired and what changes have been instituted since he left."

He considered how she'd obsessed over the accounting spreadsheets, obviously troubled by something she'd found there. It wasn't difficult to put two and two together and come up with Cousin Cunning. "I thought you trusted Connie implicitly."

Her expression threatened to rip out his heart. "So did I," she whispered.

"I'm sorry."

"Me, too."

Despite traffic, they made the drive to Sacramento in just under three hours. She spent most of the drive dividing her time between Madam's cell phone and her sisters' until he finally confiscated them. To his intense satisfaction, she turned them over without a single objection. It was a gorgeous late spring day, bright and sunny, the roads reasonably clear of traffic. Blue and violet lupine and camas lilies covered the foothills, interspersed with spindles of lemon aster. Their destination took them off the beaten path, on to twisty roads that clung to the sides of rock-strewn cliffs, but offering breathtaking vistas of the mountains.

Luc touched the brakes as he rounded one of the hairpin turns and frowned. "How much farther, Téa?" he asked.

The sharpness in his tone had her head coming around. "What's wrong?"

He gave it to her straight. "The brakes are soft. I'm not sure how much longer they're going to hold. Look for a safe place we can turn off."

"This isn't a good section of road to have the brakes go out." Other than a thread of anxiety that underscored the comment, she remained impressively calm.

"No, it isn't."

He touched the brakes again, alarmed by the way the pedal depressed straight to the floor. They needed a pull-off and fast. Unfortunately on Téa's side was sheer rock and on his side an endless drop off the mountain. The car swept around the next bend and the speedometer inched ever higher. He pumped the brakes, hoping to rebuild enough pressure to stop the car. It didn't help, but he kept trying. And hoping.

"Hold on," he warned. "I'm going to use the engine to slow us."

Punching in the clutch, he downshifted. The car bucked, shimmied. He wrestled with the wheel, fighting to keep the car on the road. The back tires slid sideways and the engine screamed in protest. Another sharp curve loomed ahead and he took it wide, dragging the car through the gravel along the shoulder, hoping the extra friction would slow the car.

"I'm going to downshift again."

"I'm okay. Do it."

Her soothing voice acted like a balm. It eased his concerns about her and allowed him to give his full focus to the task at hand. He downshifted once again, wincing at the sound of gears clashing and grinding. If he stripped them, they'd really be in trouble. The road flattened out briefly and he used the opportunity to play with the emergency brake on the console between the two front seats. He pushed in the button on the end of the stick and eased it backward. The car slowed but fishtailed so badly he was forced to let go of the lever in order to control the car.

"I need your help," he said.

"Tell me what to do."

He waited until he successfully steered them around the next bend. "I need you to push in the button on the emergency brake handle and pull it backward until you feel resistance. It'll engage the rear brakes. But if you yank too hard I'll lose control. So do it gently."

Early afternoon daylight flickered through the trees, dancing across the grim determination that lined her face. She reached for the brake handle, the slight tremor of her hand giving away her agitation. She played with the brake, first too gently, then too much pressure, before finding that sweet spot between the two. They rounded another curve, taking it far too fast.

The next instant he saw it. A straight stretch of road lined with heavy brush on Téa's side. There were trees, as well, but they were a solid twenty feet off the road. He wouldn't get a better opportunity than this.

"I'm going to crash the car into the brush. Cover your face."

She limited herself to a single word. "Damn."

Skidding onto the gravel-covered shoulder, he dragged the passenger side of the car against the thick brush. Téa instinctively flinched away. Branches slashed against the metal, tearing at it, clawing at the vehicle. The car slowed and he arced more fully into the bushes. The wheel jerked from his hand and the car spun in a sharp 180, flinging itself into the embrace of the roadside shrubs before careening into a ditch and plowing sideways against a towering fir.

The scream of metal was followed by simultaneous explosions. The first, the ringing impact of tree against car, followed instantaneously by the bang of the airbags inflating. Fine powder filled the air and he felt a sharp sting. The coating from the airbags, no doubt. Or maybe the sting came from the impact of the bags, themselves. It had happened too fast for him to be certain. He could recall the sensation from his last car wreck, though, and shied from the memory. The powder made him cough and irritated his eyes. Then silence descended, broken by the wheeze of the engine and the whirr of one of the tires that continued to spin.

"Téa?" Luc cut the engine. The car was tilted, driver side down and her weight sagged against him. "Are you hurt?"

To his relief she shifted. "I…I'm okay. I think. Dizzy."

"Did you hit your head?"

"I don't know." She felt for it. "Small bump on the side."

"The back windows blew out. Are you cut? Can you tell?"

Her sigh sounded amazingly normal. "To be honest, I can't see a damn thing. My eyes are watering from all this dust."

"Hang on." He shoved the deflated airbags out of the way until he uncovered Téa. "Hello, gorgeous."

She managed a smile. "That bad?"

"That good."

He eased a wealth of curls away from her face. He'd never seen a more beautiful sight. Unable to help himself, he leaned in and kissed her. Inhaled her. Allowed himself a full minute to lose himself in celebration that they'd survived such a close call. She wound her arms around his neck and kissed him back with gratifying enthusiasm. Finally he pulled away and cupped her face, his fingers skating gingerly over her face and into her hair. He found the bump she'd indicated, saw her wince and skimmed past it as he checked the rest of her.

"If we manage to get out of this with only a small bump and a batch of scrapes and bruises, we can consider it a miracle."

"No, the miracle is that you were behind that wheel instead of me," she replied. "If I'd been on my own—" She broke off with a shudder.

Luc's eyes narrowed and he filed the comment away for future consideration. "Any chance you can open your door? Mine's wrapped around the tree."

"I'll try." She squirmed around, wedging her shapely

backside against him while she fumbled with the door. "It's too heavy. I can't lift it."

"Okay. How about you dig out one of your cell phones so we can call for help?"

"I'm not sure where my purse ended up."

He shifted, fighting back a curse when his knee issued a sharp complaint. Great. Just what he needed. He poked around the floor of the car until he found her bag and passed it over.

"Everything's jumbled," she murmured. "Okay, here's one. Oh. It's our phone."

For some reason the comment gave him a warm, possessive feeling. "Perfect."

She placed the call and within twenty minutes the car swarmed with emergency personnel who extracted them in no time. While the EMTs examined Téa, Luc had a private conversation with one of the county deputies, whose nametag read Sandford. Together they walked the path the car had taken and the deputy shook his head in disbelief.

"That's one hell of a piece of driving. I think you picked the only stretch on this road where you could have gotten away with ditching the car the way you did." Sandford gestured farther down the road. "If you'd kept going you'd have ended up driving right off the mountainside. Sorry to say, I've seen the results of that once before. Just as soon never see it again."

"Not much choice but to ditch. The brakes went out on me."

"Bad place to have that happen."

It would have been just as bad if they'd taken the coast road Conway had requested, Luc realized. Long sections were a steep drop into the Pacific on one side and a wall of rock on the other. "I want the car checked from top to bottom." Luc spared a glance over his shoulder and grimaced. "At least, what's left of it."

Sandford's eyebrows shot upward. "You think someone messed with the brakes?"

"Let's just say I want to cover all the bases."

"I'll have it impounded, Mr. Dante."

"And the less said to Ms. de Luca, the better."

Sandford shrugged. "Nothing to tell her. Yet." He jerked his head in the direction of the ambulance. "I suggest you get that leg checked out. We're not big enough to warrant an actual hospital, but we have a decent medical center down the road a piece. They're going to want to transport you there to get checked out and I advise you to let them."

Luc didn't have the energy to argue, though the next few hours weren't the most pleasant he'd ever experienced. After a battery of tests, they were finally released. They discovered that Sandford had rescued their belongings from the mangled remains of the car and dropped them off at the medical center. Téa took the time to send text messages to her sisters letting them know she'd arrived safely—"safely" being a relative term. She was careful not to mention the accident. On their way out the door, one of the nurses recommended a nearby bed-and-breakfast over the local mom-and-pop motel where they could spend the night while they arranged for transportation home.

The proprietress welcomed them with open arms and tutted over their accident. Then she insisted on giving them her best accommodations, a honeymoon cabin tucked under a stand of pines and overlooking a small, private lake.

"Nothing better to ease your aches and pains than a view from the back deck. And if that's not enough, there's a hot tub out there that will do the trick. Just had it put in. You two will be the first to give it a whirl."

"Sounds like heaven," Téa admitted with a weary smile.

The two of them limped down the path toward the lake. Luc unlocked the door and shoved himself and their bags over the threshold. Téa made a beeline toward the bedroom, and of more interest, the king-size bed. Kicking off her shoes, she dropped face-first onto the mattress.

"Come on," she mumbled around the feather pillow. "There's enough room here for a small army."

He didn't need a second invitation. He invaded the bed, an army of one, scooped Téa into his arms and was asleep before she'd finished spooning that glorious backside up against his thighs.

Seven

Téa surfaced slowly, aware of a delicious warmth surrounding her and an intense feeling of peace and security, both of which made her reluctant to open her eyes in case it caused the sensation to vanish. She might have drifted back to sleep if Luc hadn't stirred.

"Damn knee," he muttered.

Instantly she sat up and twisted to face him. "What can I do?"

He massaged the joint. "Just need to take an anti-inflammatory."

"Would soaking in the hot tub help?"

Early evening sunshine slipped through the shaded window and highlighted the grin that creased his face. He regarded her speculatively, the color of his eyes a sleep-laden tawny gold, filled with the sort of hunger that caused her heart rate to kick up a tad.

"It would help, but only if you join me."

Her concern eased and an answering smile flirted with her mouth. "How would my being there help your knee?"

"It would take my mind off the pain," he offered hopefully.

"No doubt." She escaped the bed and winced. Bruises she hadn't even known she possessed made themselves known. "Maybe it'll take both of our minds off the pain."

His amusement vanished. "Where do you hurt? Do we need to go back to the medical center?"

"No, no," she reassured. "A few scrapes and bruises. They warned me that it would get worse before it got better. I think a soak in a hot tub is just what the doctor ordered."

"First food. We skipped lunch, if you recall."

"Sounds good. But no alcohol for twenty-four hours."

"Spoilsport." He yawned. "I wonder if there's anywhere around here that delivers."

"I'll call the front desk and ask."

There was a nearby pizza place and, after calling in an order, Téa closeted herself in the bathroom for a quick shower. She wasn't surprised when Luc joined her. He wrapped his arms around her and drew her against his chest. She tilted her head back and relaxed against him.

"You shouldn't be here."

Somehow he'd found the soap and he traced her curves with slick, sudsy hands. "Or doing this?"

She moaned. "Probably not. The pizza is due to arrive any minute."

He nuzzled the sensitive skin in the curve of her neck. "Do you want to eat it in the hot tub?"

She sank against him in clear surrender. "Probably be better than eating it in the shower."

They never made it to the hot tub. The minute Luc paid off the delivery boy, they carried the pizza to the bedroom. Téa climbed into his lap and fed him a slice while helping herself to one, as well. Somehow the box ended up on the floor, along with the terry cloth robes they'd found hanging on the back of the bathroom door.

She feathered a string of kisses from shoulder to mouth. "We weren't supposed to do this again, not while we were working together," she reminded him.

He settled her more firmly on his lap. "I won't tell, if you don't."

"Works for me."

He rolled her under him and gave her his close and undivided attention. She was soft and sweet from her shower, though the bruises she'd sustained from the car crash were already purpling her ivory skin. He kissed each and every one, wishing he could kiss away the hurt as easily. It horrified him, how close they'd come.

"If you hadn't been there…" Her words echoed his thoughts.

"But I was."

"Have I thanked you, yet, for saving my life?"

"That's not nec—"

He never finished his sentence. She inhaled the last word, drinking him in, and he sank into the mattress with her. Sank into her mouth, over her body, and into the warmth and passion she so openly offered. The Inferno hummed between them, a livewire that quietly pulsated no matter how far apart they were. But here, in her arms, in this bed together, it crackled with a deep and abiding need that drove him to possess the woman he considered his and his alone.

It was temporary, he reminded himself. He wasn't made for love or marriage or commitment. The accident five years ago had brought that fact home. But somehow, in this moment out of time, it seemed less imperative.

He sculpted her shape with his hands, lingering over the sleek, toned curves. "So perfect," he murmured.

"Funny. I was going to say the same about you."

She pushed at his shoulders and obliging, he rolled onto his back. She drifted over him, delicately. Tenderly. Massaged the tension from his arms and shoulders, then ran her fingertips across his chest. Just the lightest of touches. Sheer torture. He reached for her, but she pushed him away.

"No. Not yet. I'm not through," she protested.

"I am." Heaven help him. "Or I will be if you don't stop."

"And here I thought you were such a tough guy," she teased.

"Hell," he muttered. "So did I."

Her laugh whispered in the gathering dark. "Then, control yourself, tough guy."

She continued along her path of destruction, wreaking havoc with each new caress. He sucked in air, his hands fisting in the sheets so they wouldn't fist in her hair and yank her back into his arms. And still she continued, drifting ever lower until she found the rigid length of him.

There she paused. There she lingered. There she took him, as he'd once taken her. It was beyond intimate. Beyond glorious. Beyond thought and description. He'd never fully surrendered to a woman before, never lost control of what happened in bed. Never felt safe enough to let go of that final shred of containment. But something about Téa…

Something about this woman loosened all he'd kept wrapped up tight. Something about her slipped beneath his guard and allowed her to breach every last one of his defenses. He could feel her within him. He drew her in with every breath. Felt her sweep through his veins with every beat of his heart. Felt her feminine strength and power to the very marrow of his bones. Held her in a soul-deep grip that he'd never willingly let go.

He called to her, his voice hoarse and desperate. And she answered him, giving of herself in the most generous way possible. He didn't hold back. Couldn't. Afterward, they curled together, locked tight within each other's embrace.

He regained consciousness hours later while dark lay full around them. He eased into her, waking her in the sweetest way possible. She sighed in pleasure, wrapping him up as he gave all he had to her. Driving the storm that swirled within them before riding with her on the wild wind that swept them away.

Then once again they slept, two parts made whole.

"No!"

Téa jerked upright at the visceral shout, her heart pounding. "Luc?"

Beside her, he twisted in the bedcovers, clearly in the throes of a nightmare. "I won't do it!"

She caught her bottom lip between her teeth, not quite certain whether or not she should touch him, in case he hit out in panic. She'd read somewhere of that possibility. Instead she scooted to the far side of the bed and called to him. "Luc. Wake up. You're dreaming."

"Got to stop the bleeding."

She flinched. "Luc." This time she raised her voice, speaking firmly. "Wake up. Now."

To her relief, he came to. Unlike her, he didn't jump up, but froze, swiftly assessing the situation before his tension slackened. He scrubbed a hand across his face. "Aw, hell."

"Bad dream?" she asked in as neutral a voice as possible.

"Yeah." He levered up on one elbow, squinting at the bedside table. "Can you see what time is it?"

"A little before eight." She hesitated. "Do you want to talk about it?"

He spared her a brief glance. "Do you suppose that hot tub is still up and running?"

He hadn't answered her question. Then again, maybe he had. "Should be."

He caught her hand in his and tugged. "Can't hurt to find out."

They snatched up their bathrobes on the way to the back porch where the sun peeked over the mountaintops and skipped across the stillness of the lake. In the distance, a loon gave a startled cry, the eerie sound echoing over the water. Other than the birds and deer, the place was deserted, protected from curious eyes by a tall privacy fence. They removed the cover from the hot tub and draped their robes across a nearby bench. Shivering from the morning mountain chill, they climbed into the gently steaming water.

To Téa's amusement they both sighed in unison as they sank into the warmth. Luc pushed a button on the inset panel next to him and the water began to gently churn. Satisfied, he scooped her close, settling her in the vee of his legs. She relaxed against his chest. It was as though she'd been gifted with a taste of heaven and she savored the unexpected moment. They sat for a while in peaceful silence, simply enjoying the view and each other.

Then Téa gathered up her courage and said, "I have nightmares, too." She waited a second before continuing. "Not…not just bad dreams. But waking up screaming, in a total sweat type nightmares."

"Sounds familiar. Your parents?" It didn't surprise her that he was so quick to pinpoint the cause.

"Yes." The word was barely audible over the sound of the jets. "It was my fault, you know."

"What happened?" For some reason, the simple question sliced neatly through the scars, straight down to the source of the infection.

"I went to a party I'd been forbidden to attend. They found out and tracked me down. They were on the sidewalk outside, approaching the house when one of the girls started screaming that we were about to get busted. The boy I was with jumped in his car. He was drunk, of course." She shrugged. "It was over in an instant. He didn't see them, they couldn't get out of the way in time."

"I'm sorry."

"Aren't you going to tell me it wasn't my fault?"

"You already know that," he startled her by saying. "But I understand now why you've taken on the role of mother to your stepsisters. Why you feel obligated to put your family ahead of your own needs and wants. I can't see you doing anything else. Not until you're ready to forgive yourself."

Tears flooded her eyes and she blinked hard to hold them at bay. "What about you? What are you blaming yourself for?"

Luc sighed. "Takes one to know one?"

"Something like that." She made an educated guess. "I gather this is in some way related to your injured knee?"

"Yeah. Same incident."

She turned, curled into him, rested her cheek against his chest while the water frothed around them. It felt right to be with him, held like this. "Must have been bad if you still have nightmares about it."

He held on to her as though she anchored him against the pull and drag of a turbulent sea. "Five years bad."

She winced. "If you'd rather not—"

"You did. Seems only fair that I should, too." He took another minute to gather himself. "I owned my own security firm after I left the military. We specialized in personal protection."

"Dangerous."

"Boring," he corrected, "with the occasional splash of terrifying."

"Got it. This must have been one of the terrifying episodes."

"This was *the* terrifying episode."

"What went wrong?" Because, clearly, something had.

"There was a married couple. Sonya and Kurt Jorgen." She felt him swallow. "They had a young child, maybe five. Kurt asked me to help them disappear for a while. I knew something wasn't quite right. Hell, my internal alarm system went haywire even during that first meeting. I questioned him, but he kept insisting they wanted to reconsider the direction they were taking in life and just needed to get away from it all for a while."

She had to agree with Luc. Something didn't add up. "How did Kurt explain the need for a bodyguard?"

"He claimed to have a lot of money. That taking off would leave him vulnerable. He just wanted some protection until they settled in somewhere. Mainly, he wanted me to show him how to get lost for a couple months."

"But that wasn't the real problem." She didn't phrase it as a question.

"Hell, no. It turns out the husband witnessed an incident at work he shouldn't have, but neglected to mention that detail when he hired me. On the way to disappearing, goons of Kurt's employer caught up with us and ran us off the road. I failed to do then what I succeeded in doing yesterday."

"A controlled crash," she murmured numbly.

"A controlled crash. The husband was killed instantly." She felt the harsh swallow again. Heard the choke in the rumble of words. "The kid, too. Sonya was badly hurt. The goons managed to take themselves out at the same time they took us out. Since they weren't a problem, I worked on saving Sonya."

"She died, too?"

"No. I saved her." He waited a beat before dropping the other shoe. "Unfortunately she didn't want to be saved. She begged me to let her die so she could be with her husband and son."

Téa tightened her grip, wrapped him up in as much warmth as she could muster, hanging on tight. "Oh, Luc."

He relaxed into her embrace, though she could feel the emotional walls he erected pushing at her, trying to hold her at a distance. "When I visited the wife in the hospital she became so hysterical they had to sedate her. She just kept screaming at me that she hated me. That I should have let her die."

"I'm so sorry. She was out of her mind with grief."
Téa tilted her head back to look up at him. "You must
realize that?"

"Of course I realize it. Just as I realize it wasn't my
fault when she attempted to take her own life three
months later." His voice grew even more grim, if that
were possible. "Didn't succeed."

"What ultimately happened to her?"

"I have no idea." He closed his eyes and shook his
head. "I'm afraid to find out."

"You think she's gone, don't you?"

He shrugged. When he opened his eyes again
they were the darkest she'd ever seen. Hard. Remote.
Dispassionate. "If you're that determined to die, chances
are excellent you'll eventually succeed."

"You did the right thing. You do understand that,
don't you?" she asked urgently. "It wasn't your fault."

He didn't bother to point out the irony of her
statement. "Trust me, I've looked at this from every
possible direction. If the husband had warned me when
he first hired me. If I'd hit the brakes sooner. Later.
Turned left instead of right. The bottom line is…" He
shrugged dismissively. "I took the job. People died. End
of story. Afterward, I dissolved the business and went
to work for Dantes Courier Service."

But it wasn't. She could see it wasn't. The incident
had struck hard and deep, and left wounds that still
hadn't healed, just as hers hadn't. "What aren't you
telling me?"

He looked at her with tarnished eyes, the expression
so distant. So emotionless. "I don't know what you're
talking about."

She shivered despite the warmth of the water. "Yes,
you do." She'd never been more certain of anything

in her life. "Something else happened that day. What was it?"

He hesitated, then offered a cool smile. "Okay, fair enough. It wasn't part of the accident, merely a decision I made as a result of it. Just like you made the decision to fill in for your parents."

Every feminine instinct she possessed warned her to let it go. To change the direction of the conversation. To offer some lighthearted quip that would cut through the thickening tension. But she couldn't. Wouldn't. Not while that look of pain and grief darkened Luc's eyes. Not while the poison still swept through his veins, infecting every aspect of his life. Not while her palm itched and throbbed, warning that whatever existed between them would always be tainted by the hideous events of that day.

"Go on," she whispered. "Tell me what you decided."

"I decided that I'd never marry."

With that, he shifted her to one side and erupted from the hot tub. He padded across the deck like some great, sleek jungle cat to where they'd discarded their robes. He shrugged into his and held the other out to her.

"I gather we're done soaking?" she asked in a neutral voice.

"Since this is a bed-and-breakfast, I thought we'd go and find the breakfast portion of our stay. According to my stomach, that pizza is a fond but distant memory."

Téa didn't bother arguing. One look at Luc's face convinced her of that. She switched off the jets and hurried from the steaming warmth of the tub into the protective covering of her robe, doing her best to limit her exposure to the crisp mountain air. Luc opened the French doors that led into the living area of the cabin and picked up the phone. Téa waited while he spoke to the owner.

"It would seem that one of the benefits of the honeymoon cabin is private dining," he explained once he'd hung up. "They'll bring breakfast to us."

"I guess we should dress."

"Then I need to arrange for a rental car. We should also decide if we're staying another night or returning to the city."

He spoke calmly, as though his earlier announcement was of little concern. Maybe it wasn't to him. But she'd always been hampered by a logical nature and she didn't understand the connection between the two incidents. Deciding to bide her time, she returned to the bedroom to dress. Luc was on the phone arranging for a car to be brought in from Lake Tahoe when a staff member arrived with a loaded tray.

"There's a coffee machine in the kitchenette," he informed Téa. "I'll start a fresh pot for you. Or would you prefer tea?"

"Coffee is fine," Téa confirmed.

As soon as the coffee finished brewing, she and Luc took their breakfast onto the deck. The temperature had crept upward, warmed by the sunshine splashing down from a cloudless sky. They fell on their meal as though they hadn't eaten in a week, polishing off every bite before relaxing in their chairs to enjoy a steaming cup of coffee.

"Go on," Luc surprised her by saying. "Ask."

She didn't bother pretending. There wasn't any point. Plus, there was that small matter of being, quote, the world's worst liar, end quote. "Fine. I'll ask." She tried for an indifferent attitude, as though she couldn't care less. She suspected she failed miserably at the attempt.

"What has the accident got to do with your decision to never marry?"

He hesitated. "You have to understand my world. The Dante world," he offered on a roundabout way. "Primo and Nonna. My parents. My uncle and his disaster of a marriage."

Téa lifted a shoulder. "I'm sorry. I'm not following." Her brows drew together. "Wait. Is this about The Inferno?"

"Yes." He refilled his coffee cup and topped off hers. "All my life I've heard about The Inferno. Lived with The Inferno. Had it stuffed down my throat."

Téa attempted a light laugh. "Luc, it's just a story. A charming family legend."

He shook his head. "It's more than legend for the Dantes. You've seen my grandparents. They'll turn eighty soon and they still can't keep their hands off each other. My parents aren't any better. Nor are my cousins. And every last one of them claims it's because of this damn Inferno."

"What about your uncle?" Téa strove for normalcy. "You said his marriage was a disaster. Doesn't that prove The Inferno doesn't always work?"

He laughed without humor. "Uncle Dominic proves just the opposite. You see, he didn't marry for love, even though he was madly in love with one of his jewelry designers and had a torrid affair with her. Instead he married Aunt Laura for her money. Primo warned it would end in disaster. And it did. Uncle Dom and my aunt were killed years ago in a boating accident while in the throes of a divorce discussion. I gather he'd decided to marry this jewelry designer, after all. When my aunt and uncle died, my grandparents took in Sev and my cousins and raised them."

So much tragedy! "Oh, Luc. I'm so sorry."

"Of course, that only solidified the legend in everyone's eyes. Turned your charming fairy tale into truth."

"But it's not," she insisted.

He reached across the table and took her hand in his, intertwined their fingers so their palms met and mated. "Isn't it?"

She shuddered. "I—" She snatched an uneven breath. "What we're experiencing is just a bad case of physical attraction. Anything else would be illogical."

"I'm glad to hear you say that. Because that's what it's going to stay," he warned, even as a spark of desire caught hold and roared to life. "I won't be forced into a marriage I don't want because of a make-believe fairy tale."

"No one is forcing you to do anything," she protested.

"Aren't they?" He released her and sat back. A hint of cynicism played about his mouth and burnished his eyes. "Maybe it would have occurred to me sooner if *I* hadn't been so distracted. But there's a lot that doesn't add up. For instance, why have I been hired as your bodyguard?"

She offered a self-deprecating smile. "Apparently because I can't put one foot in front of the other without tripping over it."

"Funny." He cocked his head to one side. "In the couple of weeks we've spent together I haven't noticed that about you."

"The first time we met—" she began.

"Had me worried," he agreed with a nod. "But how many incidents have there been since?"

"Well, none," she admitted. "But I assumed that was

because you were there." She broke off with a frown. "Now that I say that out loud it doesn't make the least bit of sense, does it?"

"No, it doesn't. I've just recently concluded there's only one reason we were brought together."

She gave a disbelieving laugh. "You can't think it's because of The Inferno. How could anyone possibly know that we'd be a match?"

Luc lifted his cup and stared at her over the rim, his gaze enigmatic through the steam. "That stopped me, too, until it occurred to me that we met once before, remember?"

"That was ages ago," she said with a dismissive shrug. "We were children."

"Really? Lazz and Ariana first met as children. Primo claims that Uncle Dominic saw early signs of The Inferno even then. As a result, he and Ariana's father contracted a marriage between them right then and there."

Téa's mouth opened, then shut again, before she managed to say, "You must be joking."

"Not even a little."

"And you suspect your parents or grandparents caught something similar between us? How is that possible?" she scoffed. "We hardly said two words to each other. We despised each other at first sight."

"Don't you remember why?"

"I…" She thought back, struggled to recall that miserable, uncomfortable summer. "You kept pestering me. Teasing me."

"Zapping you," he said softly.

"That's right. I remember now. It was like you were filled with static electricity. And you loved jumping out at me when I least expected it to give me a shock." Her eyes narrowed. "Brat."

"Think about it," he urged. "Wouldn't that be a gentler, more childish version of what we experienced when we first touched as adults?"

She drew back in her chair, closing in on herself. "I thought you didn't believe in The Inferno," she accused.

"I don't."

"Then—"

"But my parents and grandparents believe implicitly."

Her eyes widened in outrage. "And because of that zapping…"

He nodded. "I'm now guessing they decided we were experiencing The Inferno. Primo made me stop and told me not to go near you for the rest of your visit. And when Primo lays down the law…" Luc lifted a shoulder. "So, the years passed. I'm willing to bet Nonna and Madam decided it was time to put us together again and see if anything happened between us. I'm also guessing they drummed up your distraction as the perfect excuse."

Téa returned her cup to the saucer with a sharp click. "Fine. Let's say for the sake of argument that the reason we're in our current predicament is because of what happened at the lake all those years ago. That certainly doesn't mean we have to act on it. And I still don't understand what The Inferno has to do with the car crash and your decision not to marry."

Darkness settled over him and she could tell he wasn't seeing her. That she'd lost him to those long-ago events. "The Dantes believe that once mated through

The Inferno, it's a lifetime love affair. One man. One woman. One love."

"Isn't that the idea with all marriages, at least going in?" she asked gently.

He nodded. "That's how it was between the Jorgens. Even I could see that much, despite the limited amount of time we spent together. One second they were a loving family. The next she was alone. Her life ended when theirs did, but she was still alive. Empty. Broken. And forced to live that way for the rest of her life—a life she appeared determined to end."

Téa struggled to put the pieces he was showing her into a logical whole. "And you're afraid that will happen to you?"

Luc focused on her. "Sonya gave every part of herself to Kurt and their son. When they were gone there was nothing left. As far as she was concerned, without them her life had ended. Someone had just forgotten to turn out the lights for her."

"Sonya isn't you," Téa argued.

"No, she isn't. Because I won't surrender that much of myself to another person. I watched Rafe do it with his wife, Leigh, and watched her gut him on her way out the door. I won't be another Sonya. I won't be Rafe after the death of his marriage." He turned his haunted gaze on her. "So, I won't marry."

Téa shook her head. "You're wrong, Luc. It's not that you won't marry. What you've decided is that you won't love. Funny thing about love." She shoved her empty coffee cup aside. "You're assuming you have some control over it."

"I do."

"That's where you're wrong." She pushed back her

chair and stood. "Unfortunately for you, love chooses. And it chooses whether you're willing or not."

With that Téa turned and forced herself to walk away from what she'd just discovered she wanted most in the world.

Eight

A couple hours later, the rental car was delivered and Luc signed the necessary papers to take possession. The owner of the bed-and-breakfast asked if they wanted the cabin for a second night and Luc glanced at Téa.

"It's your call," he said without expression.

Téa hesitated. "I don't know how long it'll take to locate the former manager of our plant and convince him to talk. Plus, Connie expects me to be gone at least two days, if not three. I'd rather he not find out I didn't go where he requested."

"There's weather moving in late this afternoon," the owner offered tentatively. "Don't want to be on these mountain roads when it hits. Should be clear again by tomorrow morning."

Téa gave a decisive nod. "We'll stay another night, if that's all right."

The owner beamed. "Our next reservation doesn't

arrive until Friday. We'd be happy to have you until then."

Téa shook her head apologetically. "One more night should do it." She spared Luc a wistful glance, one that clearly told of her preference to remain for the entire week. That look—one that said that a single word from him would be enough to have her prolong their stay— would have slayed a weaker man. He forced himself to remain impassive beneath it. She sighed. "There's a lot of work sitting on my desk. Plus I have to replace my car."

No doubt an added expense and distraction she didn't need right now. "I'll help with that."

"That's not necessary," she replied with cool politeness.

"It's the least I can do considering I'm the one who crashed it," he replied just as politely.

She let it go and turned to address the owner who'd been watching their byplay with an indulgent expression. "Could you give me directions to the town of Polk?"

Luc waited patiently while the two women inched their way over Téa's map book. A short time later they were on the road again. He shot her a fleeting glance. She appeared a shade paler than usual, her slight dusting of freckles standing out more sharply than usual, and she had a grim set to her mouth. More telling, her hands were laced together in a death grip, her knuckles bleached white.

"You okay?" he asked after the first series of hairpin turns. He'd deliberately kept their speed a full five miles beneath the posted limit.

"I'll survive."

They arrived in Polk shortly before noon and Luc suggested they have lunch before tackling the manager.

Téa settled on a local café with boxes of colorful flowers outside and a homey setup inside. The menu was varied and their lunch choices were attractively plated when they arrived.

"What's this guy's name you plan to visit?" Luc asked while they ate.

"Krendal. Douglas Krendal."

"Does he know you're coming?"

She hesitated. "I thought I'd surprise him. I called to make certain he was in. Pretended I was a telemarketer." She winced and rubbed her ear. "Mr. Krendal doesn't mince words."

"You may find that helpful when you talk to him."

"That's what I'm hoping." She hesitated, playing with her fork and pushing her lunch around her plate. "Listen, I want to speak privately with him. I suspect he'll be more open if it's just the two of us."

Luc cocked an eyebrow. "In other words, the conversation is none of my business?"

"Okay, yes."

"No problem."

"Really?" she asked skeptically. "You're not going to argue the way you have about Connie?"

He shrugged. "The situation with your cousin is different. I don't trust the guy. So, I've made a point of sticking close whenever he starts yanking on the puppet strings."

She stiffened. "I gather I'm the puppet?"

"Time will tell." He gestured toward her plate. "You done?"

"Yes." She shoved her half-eaten lunch to one side. "Let's get this over with."

They found the Krendal place without too much trouble, the cottage perched on top of one of the endless hillsides that surrounded the town of Polk. It was a small rambler on a large piece of property, tucked beneath a towering stand of pine trees. Luc pulled into the driveway and parked along one edge of the small circle of gravel on the side of the house. Téa exited the car and followed the cement walkway to the front door. He watched while she knocked and the door opened. Saw her introduce herself and Krendal's grim resistance. Caught the instant it began to fade beneath Téa's warmth. At long last, the door swung wide and she disappeared inside.

His cell phone vibrated about five minutes into the wait and he checked the caller ID. "Yeah, Juice," he said by way of greeting. "What did you find out about Billings?"

"The man or the business?"

"Okay, now you've got my attention." Luc frowned as he listened, his frown deepening with each new revelation. "Well, hell," he said when Juice completed his report.

"That was my reaction. What are you going to tell the de Luca woman?"

"Everything."

"She's not going to be happy."

"Furious would be my guess."

"Glad you're the one handing her the news and not me."

"Chicken."

"Cluck-cluck." And with that, the line went dead.

Twenty minutes later Téa emerged from the house. She shook hands with Krendal and then returned to the car, her heels rapping out a hard, staccato beat on the walkway leading to the gravel driveway. She climbed into the car and slammed the door closed.

"That bastard!"

Luc folded his arms along the top of the steering wheel and assessed the level of her anger. If he were to guess, he'd say steaming, bordering on, "thar she blows." "I hope that comment's aimed at Cousin Connie and not Mr. Krendal," he said.

"Oh, it's definitely aimed at Cousin Connie…or maybe I should say Cousin Con Artist." She gave an imperious wave of her hand. "Let's go. I need to drive off some of this mad."

Little did she know. "Okay."

He headed back toward their rental cabin in silence, giving her the opportunity to stew. Maybe once she'd come to terms with the information Krendal had dumped on her, she'd be in a better position to deal with his news. In the distance, the first evidence of the storm they'd been warned about boiled up over the tops of the nearby mountains, the clouds filled with threat and turmoil. They were a perfect punctuation mark to Téa's mood. He checked his watch, judged the distance and decided they'd get to the cabin with time to spare.

By the time they parked in front of the cabin, the sky had turned nighttime dark. Luc hustled Téa inside and flicked on lights to dispel the gathering gloom. While he went in search of a flashlight or candles in case the storm knocked out the power, Téa checked her various cell phones and frowned.

"What's wrong?"

"No signal. I hope Madam and the girls aren't worried." She brightened. "Maybe they haven't tried to call."

He set out a sleeve of candles he found in one of the drawers in the kitchenette, along with a box of matches. "What do you suppose the odds are of that happening?"

Her hopeful mood vanished. "Zero to less than zero." She released a sigh. "I need a drink."

He opened the door to the small refrigerator. "You're in luck. It would seem the honeymoon cabin also comes with a complimentary bottle of champagne. Are we cleared to drink, do you suppose?"

Téa checked her watch and nodded. "We're just past the twenty-four-hour time frame we were given by the doctor."

"Good enough."

Luc pulled out the bottle and removed the foil and wire, before cautiously uncorking it. Digging through the cupboards, he unearthed a pair of Lucite flutes and poured them each a glass. Téa took a tentative swallow and wrinkled her nose at the explosion of bubbles.

"Surprisingly good," she said with a hint of surprise. "Is it a California wine?"

"Yes. Carneros region."

"That explains it." She drank another couple sips, stalling. Then finally, said, "There's something I need to tell you."

"About Krendal?"

She waved that aside. "No. It's about the night we were at Primo's for Rafe's birthday party."

He wondered when they'd get back to that. "I gather you're about to tell me the real reason you were so upset when we left. Why you suddenly decided to put all your focus on work and protecting your family."

"Yes." She spared him a speculative glance. "Sev never said anything to you?"

"No." And Sev would pay for that small oversight. "What happened?"

"Your cousin warned me that there was a quality issue with our product."

He took a moment to absorb that, to put it together with the information Juice had provided. "I gather that explains your confrontation on Monday with Conway." Luc sampled the champagne, also approved it and topped off their glasses. "I can't wait to hear his explanation."

"He claimed it was all a huge error and he'd look into it."

"And you bought that?"

She waved her glass at him. "Don't be ridiculous. Of course I didn't buy it. The man is as bad a liar as I am."

Luc choked on a laugh. "Must run in the genes."

"No doubt. Anyway, he insisted I stay out of it and even when I pointed out that I'd be right in the middle of the fiasco in five short weeks—about a month now—he told me that was fine. In five short weeks I could handle it. In the meantime, he was in charge and he'd get in touch with Sev. That I wasn't to contact your cousin under any circumstances."

"That's when you came storming out and buried your nose in the spreadsheets."

"There was something about them…" Her eyes glittered darkly in the deepening gloom. "Once I understood the underlying problem, I knew what to look for."

"Your cousin has been cutting corners."

She nodded. "And charging more for an inferior product. That's what I didn't catch in the accounting records. You see, the price we charge our customers has gone up, but when I looked more carefully, our manufacturing costs have actually dropped, despite the fact that our overall profit remains the same."

Even without an accounting background, Luc could add that together to equal something was definitely fishy.

"If your manufacturing costs have gone down, your cost to customers increased, the profit margin should have skyrocketed."

"You would think," she agreed. "And the bottom line would have skyrocketed if that profit hadn't vanished into the cost of purchasing new equipment. On paper it appears legit."

"Huh."

She tilted her head to one side. "You look like a puzzle piece just fell into place."

"It did. First tell me what Krendal said, and then I'll explain."

"Okay." She helped herself to more champagne. "Douglas Krendal was the production manager of our manufacturing plant. He claims that Connie forced him out."

"Because Krendal caught on to what Billings was doing," Luc guessed.

"Yes. And he was rather vocal in his disapproval. He'd worked for my grandfather for years and was outraged that Connie wanted to cut corners by producing an inferior product."

"So, Conway fired him."

"Retired him," she corrected with a shrug. "But, essentially, you're right. He got rid of Douglas at the earliest opportunity."

Luc hesitated, knowing the time had come to give her the rest of the bad news. He blew out a breath. "You're not going to like this next part."

She stilled, a look of intense vulnerability sweeping across her face. "Please tell me you're not a secret operative for my cousin."

The sheer unexpectedness of her comment provoked a laugh. "No, I'm not a spy," he said tenderly. To his relief, his reassurance restored her confidence. "But I did ask a former associate to dig into your cousin's background." He grimaced. "It's not good, Téa."

She sank into a nearby chair. "Let me have it."

"Essentially, he's broke."

Her mouth dropped open. "How is that possible? I happen to know what he makes running Bling and it's a pretty penny."

"Right, except he doesn't receive a percentage of the profits from the company the way he would if he were the owner. He's on salary with modest bonuses approved by the board. And he's been funneling all available funds into this new start-up business he's about to launch." He allowed that to sink in before adding, "There's more."

"Of course there is," she murmured.

"I think I know what he's up to."

"Is he embezzling?"

"Not funds." He waited a beat. "Equipment."

"The purchases he made with the profits." She frowned. "I don't understand. What does he want with the equipment?"

"This is sheer conjecture, but I'm pretty sure I'm right. I think he's going to start up a competing business."

Téa inhaled sharply. "The poor quality merchandise—"

"—gets your customers angry. Makes them easier to steal away from Bling." Luc downed the last of his champagne and set the glass aside. "Oh, he's going to turn the family business over to you. He's just going to make sure it's nothing more than a shell when he does it. Then, when you're on the verge of bankruptcy because you've lost all your customers to him—"

"—he comes sweeping in and offers to buy me out for pennies on the dollar," she finished his sentence for him. "Connie's new start-up company then takes over the Billings name and he has everything my grandfather didn't leave him. The business, the name and all the money."

"That's what I suspect."

"And I suspect you're right." She closed her eyes and thought about it. "The question is, what can I do to stop him? He's had ages to set all this up. I still don't take over for another four and a half weeks. He must know I'm close to figuring it out. Which means he has a full month to bring his plans to fruition while I watch helpless from the sidelines."

"He doesn't know you're on to him, yet," Luc attempted to reassure. "There's still time to do something."

Téa shook her head. "Not while he controls Bling. If I could just take over now..." She froze. Slowly her gaze shifted to fix on Luc. He didn't care for the speculative gleam in her eyes. "There *is* a way I can do that."

"Well, okay." He snatched up his glass, annoyed to find it empty. "Then do it."

"I need your help to put my plan into action."

A plan. Action. He was all over that. "You know I'm willing to do whatever I can."

She smiled. "I was hoping you'd say that."

For some reason, her expression worried him. It had turned calculating, filled with the same drive and determination he'd noticed the night of Rafe's birthday party.

"I'm almost afraid to ask, but... What do you want me to do?"

"It's quite simple, really. I want you to marry me."

Luc stared at Téa in disbelief. "Excuse me?"

To her credit, she was smart enough to show a trace of

nervousness. "You heard me." She gulped champagne. "I want you to marry me. Temporarily, of course."

"Oh, of course."

She flinched at his sarcasm. "Luc—"

He cut her off without hesitation. "I believe we had this discussion already." Anger ripped through him, accompanied by the first rumbling of the storm. "What part of 'I'm never going to get married' didn't you understand? The 'never' part or the 'married'?"

"Let me explain." She approached, showing either an impressive amount of bravery or proving just how badly she'd misjudged his current mood. "There's a clause in the will that says that if I marry I inherit Billings outright, so long as I'm over the age of twenty-one."

"Outstanding. I wish you every success in finding someone to marry you."

"I don't think you understand."

"I understand perfectly," he snapped. "You're the one who doesn't understand. The answer, Ms. de Luca, is not just no, but *hell* no."

"I'll try not to be offended by that." A matching anger flared to life in her eyes, while outside lightning flashed, causing the electricity to sputter. "Don't you see that it's the perfect solution? For both of us, Luc."

He folded his arms across his chest. "Okay, this I have to hear. How is marrying you the perfect solution for me?"

"Your entire family believes we've been struck by The Inferno, right?"

"Unfortunately."

"So, we give them what they want." Thunder crashed overhead and she had to wait for it to die down before continuing. "We give them a wedding between Inferno soul mates. A couple months down the road…say six or seven…we inform everyone that it didn't work out. We divorce."

"Dantes don't divorce."

"Rafe did," she retorted, stung.

"Technically he's a widower."

That stopped her. "Oh. I didn't realize. I'm sorry."

"You don't need to apologize to me."

She waved that aside. "We're getting off track here."

"I understand where you're going with this, Téa. I recommend you let it go."

Luc turned his back on her and crossed to stare out into the stormy darkness. A bolt of lightning streaked overhead, the reflection forking across the surface of the lake, while thunder boomed, the echo from it bouncing off the surrounding mountains. He could see the logic of her suggestion, just as he could see all the dangerous pitfalls along the way.

Pitfalls like the itch of The Inferno that would only grow stronger and burrow deeper with each additional day in her company. Pitfalls like having her in his bed and discovering he couldn't bring himself to let her go. Pitfalls like pregnancy.

Or love.

He could see her reflection mirrored in the glass of the French door, picked up on her tension from the set of her shoulders and the way she fiddled with her empty flute. Despite his anger, he still wanted her, could feel the unwelcome connection pulsating between them.

With a sigh, he turned to face her. "You think that if we marry, wait a reasonable amount of time and then claim it didn't work out, my family will leave me alone. Stop forcing this nonsense about The Inferno down my throat. Is that your plan?"

She nodded eagerly. "Exactly. Since they believe I'm your Inferno bride, they won't keep nagging you about marrying again."

"No." He folded his arms across his chest. "They'll just keep nagging me about getting back together with you."

"Oh." She sighed. "I hadn't thought of that."

He smiled dryly at the bitter disappointment in her voice. "That's because you don't know my family."

She was quick to regroup. "Well, when I marry for real that will put an end to it, won't it? They'll leave both of us alone."

He stilled. "Marry for real?"

"It's possible." She lifted her chin. "More than possible. Because unlike you I'm not afraid of love. Seeing your family, seeing how happy the various couples are, it's made me think. Maybe once my family is safe and financially secure I can fall in love and get married, too. Start a family like Kiley and Francesca."

For an endless moment he couldn't think straight. Couldn't breathe. Images filled his head of Téa, heavy with a baby. *His* baby. And then the image shifted. Twisted. And suddenly it wasn't his baby any longer, but another man's. Her husband's. A man who had the right to put his hands on her. To take her to his bed. To share every intimacy with her.

To give her a baby.

He heard a low snarl fill the room, barely aware it had been ripped from his throat. One minute he stood silhouetted by the pounding storm and the next he was across the room. He reached for her, swept her into his arms.

"Luc," she gasped. "What are you doing."

"You're the one with all the answers. You figure it out."

Luc reached the bed in fewer than a dozen limping steps and dropped Téa to the mattress. He followed her down, his mouth closing over the questions trembling on her lips. He had no memory of stripping off her clothes, of stripping away his own. Thunder crashed around them while lightning bleached the ebony from the night. He had a quick flash of Téa, a stunning palate of ivory splayed across a canvas of black. Only her hair and eyes offered any color, a spill of vibrant, fiery red, and a blue-green as deep and mysterious as the ocean.

The elements tore across the night, setting flame to the explosive passions trapped within the room. They came together, a clash of masculine and feminine that somehow found a melding point, a place where they joined with undeniable perfection and became one. Their bodies mated, moving to the rhythm of the storm, echoing its power and ferocity, giving no quarter and expecting none. They followed each other into the very heart of the tempest, riding it, driven by it to an exquisite climax.

Luc felt Téa peak, heard her cry of pleasure. That was all it took. He followed her up and over. He heard his name on her lips. Answered the cry with one of his own, with her name, the sound of it a stamp of possession. It grounded him as nothing else could have. Slowly the tumult calmed. And when it was finished, he gathered her close. Gently. Tenderly. Safe within the harbor of his arms.

She pressed close, twining herself around him until

he couldn't tell where she began and he ended. He simply held her, felt the steady beat of her heart filling his palm.

And he slept.

Téa woke the next morning feeling better than she had in her entire life. She had no idea what had gotten into Luc. He hadn't given her much opportunity to ask. But she could only hope it happened again. And soon. She stretched, feeling the pull of well-worked muscles, along with the twinge of lingering bruises.

Luc stirred and groaned. "Is the hot tub still out there?"

She snuggled, finding his warmth, pleased when he dropped a powerful arm over her and tucked her in close. "It's there unless it washed away in the storm."

"Is it still raining?"

"I don't hear anything. And I think that yellow stuff coming in through the drapes is sunshine."

"Okay. Just this once I'll let you carry me out to the hot tub. But only this once."

"I'll get right on that." She paused. "Are we there, yet?"

He pulled back slightly and frowned down at her. "You're not very good at this. Considering the number of times I've hauled you around, the least you could do is return the favor."

"Very inconsiderate of me," she said apologetically.

"I'll say." He escaped the bed and dragged her out, protesting all the way. "Come on. Let's go soak before we pack up."

"What about our robes?"

"Let them find their own hot tub."

Moving quickly, they stripped off the cover and climbed into the tub, allowing the heat and swirling jets of water to ease sore muscles. Téa stirred, picking up on an odd noise coming from the interior of the cabin. "I think I hear something." She sat up and craned her neck, thought better of it and ducked lower in the water. "What if it's one of the staff members with our breakfast?" she whispered frantically.

Luc grinned. "Then someone's going to be really embarrassed. And I'm willing to bet it won't be me."

She heard it then. Heard the voices coming closer. Voices that shouldn't be here. She had a whole two seconds to stare wild-eyed at Luc before Madam stepped onto the deck, followed closely by Téa's three stepsisters. Her grandmother's distinctive voice cut across the peaceful serenity of the morning.

"Madre del Dio! Girls, don't look!"

But of course, they did.

Nine

Luc opened the door of the rental car and waited until Téa slid in before closing it. Then he limped around to the driver's side and climbed behind the wheel. He didn't start the engine.

"How did Madam find us?" he asked abruptly.

Téa answered readily enough. "Apparently the claims adjuster at my insurance agency called the house with a few more questions about the wrecked car. Madam took the call and then tried to get hold of me. When she couldn't—remember the service went out?—she assumed the worst. That we'd been injured in the accident." She rolled her eyes. "Though how I was well enough to call the insurance company but too badly injured to speak to her, I have no idea. Madam's not always the most logical person in the world." She paused. Flinched. "Oh, dear. I'll bet she was remembering the night my parents died."

"That still doesn't explain how she found us."

Téa shrugged, preoccupied with settling her shoulder bag and fastening her seatbelt. "I guess from the insurance company. If you recall I had to provide the claims adjuster with the location of the car. He must have passed that information on to Madam. She probably called the nearest medical facility. I know I would have. From there it would be a short hop to this place." She paused, studying him with a growing frown. "What's with the third degree?"

"Let's just say that her showing up and catching us naked in a hot tub is a bit too convenient for my taste," he said in a detached voice.

"Convenient? Convenient!" Téa leaned in, enunciating carefully. "For your information, Luciano Dante, there was absolutely *nothing* convenient about what just went down in that cabin this morning."

Time would tell. "How bad was it?" he asked.

She sat back, but he could see she was still simmering. "I'm guessing about as bad as your conversation with Primo."

"Damn."

"Oh, yeah." She released a long sigh. "What did your grandfather have to say?"

He watched her closely, interested in her reaction. "He said we're now officially engaged."

Téa's eyes widened in shock. "Tell me you're joking."

"I'd love to. Unfortunately I'm not. I'm open to any suggestions you might have for getting us out of this mess."

"Okay, here's one. Tell your grandfather no."

"That'll work." He turned the key in the ignition and

the engine started with an extra roar, echoing his own irritation. "Not."

"So, that's it?" she asked. "Now we just get married?"

"Isn't that what you wanted?"

"Well, yes, but not like this." She folded her arms across her chest. "Be reasonable, Luc. It's not like anyone can force you to marry me."

"Oh, really? And what did Madam have to say after catching us naked in a hot tub after a night of raw passion?" He cupped a hand to his ear. "What's that? I can't hear you."

Téa cleared her throat. "I said... She's disappointed."

"Me, too. I had plans for that hot tub."

"She also said it was so unlike me. Selfish. Impulsive. And worst of all, I was setting a bad example for the girls."

"I'd have said it was exactly like you. Generous. Inventive. And those three witches you call sisters don't need any help riding their broomsticks to Badville. I'd say they invented the place. Especially Goth Girl."

"That's Katrina. It's just a phase."

"Scary."

"She's not scary. She's wonderful. All my sisters are wonderful."

"Particularly the one who would have stuck her tongue down my throat if you'd left us alone for a minute longer than you did." He shot Téa a quelling look when she opened her mouth to argue. "Don't tell me. I shouldn't take it personally. She's like that with all the men."

"Davida's naturally exuberant," she retorted, stung.

"Exuberant. That's a catchy name for it. Well, Vida's *exuberance* came across loud and clear."

Téa closed her mouth again and released a long, tired sigh. Luc winced. He felt like the worst kind of bully. It wasn't her fault that her stepsisters were hellions. Or that they hadn't received the right sort of discipline, though Téa had chosen to shoulder the blame for that, as well as the death of her parents.

"You know… There's an easy way out of this mess," he suggested.

"Which is?"

"We drop your sisters off at Primo and Nonna's. My grandparents will have them straightened out within a week. Then we gag and tie Cousin Connie and hide him in a dusty closet somewhere so you can start running Bling the minute we return."

She offered a reluctant smile. "And what about our impending nuptials? How do you propose we handle that small detail?"

"Huh." He frowned. "Okay, you got me there. I don't have a clue how to handle it."

"I do."

"Great. Why didn't you say so."

"I'll speak to Primo when we get back to San Francisco. Explain how everyone leaped to the wrong conclusions."

"Wrong conclusion," he repeated. "Naked plus hot tub equals not much of a leap."

Téa grimaced. "It also didn't help that the owner told Madam we were in the honeymoon cottage. At first, she assumed we'd eloped. When she found out we hadn't…"

"I gather the conversation went downhill from there."

"Oh, yeah."

Luc's cell phone rang and he dug it out of his pocket and tossed it to Téa. "See who that is, will you?"

She flipped open the phone and checked the caller ID. "It's Primo."

"Perfect. Go ahead and answer it. You can explain to him why we're not getting married."

"Okay," she agreed, though she didn't sound quite as sure of herself as she had earlier. "Hi, Primo, it's Téa. Yes, Luc is still with me. But he's driving, so—" She listened at length, tossing in several, uh-huhs and oh, dears.

"Tell him!" Luc encouraged.

She waved him silent. "Uh-huh. Oh, dear." She cleared her throat. "The thing is, Primo, Luc and I... Well, we don't want to get married. Right. I understand. Okay. No, you're right. Lake Tahoe isn't all that far."

"What the hell are you saying?" Luc bit out. "Just tell him no and hang up!"

"Excuse me a moment, Primo." She covered up the phone. "Would you please try not to wreck another car? If you can't drive straight, pull over. You're making me very nervous."

"*I'm* making *you* nervous? Give me that phone!"

"He doesn't want to talk to you. He wants to talk to me. Yes, Primo, I'm still here." Her eyes widened and she inhaled sharply. "Um. You're sure they're planning to print that? You do understand we don't want to get married, right? I made that clear? No, no. That's fine. I guess we'll see you tomorrow. Yes, I'll be sure to tell Luc. Bye."

Jamming on the brakes, Luc swung onto a pull-off on the side of the road and cut the engine. "So?" he demanded. "Did you tell him?"

Téa's head bobbed up and down. "Oh, I told him.

Didn't you hear me tell him? I told him flat-out that we didn't want to get married."

"And he accepted that?"

She squirmed. "Sort of."

"Are we still engaged?"

"Not for long."

"Well, okay, then." He started the engine again and continued down the road. It took two miles for him to fully process her words. "Just out of curiosity, what do you mean by 'sort of' and 'not for long'?"

"It means we have to take a short detour on the way home."

"Where?"

She swallowed. "Reno, Vegas or Lake Tahoe. Our choice."

Swearing more virulently, Luc swerved into a dirt lane and killed the engine. "What. Did. You. Do?"

"You don't understand." The words escaped in a rush.

"Explain it to me so I will."

"You remember that gossip magazine that caused so much trouble for your cousins? *The Snitch*?"

"Unfortunately. What's that got to do with us?"

"Well, they somehow got hold of the story that we eloped. I have no idea how it happened," she hastened to add.

"Let me take a wild guess here. Which of your sisters is the most broke?"

"Vida, but—"

"Then that's my guess."

"My sister wouldn't…" She hesitated, her brows pulled together and she altered course. "That's not really the point. *The Snitch* is going to print the story in the morning. Primo said that if we don't marry immediately, it will have a serious effect on my future at Bling. That I'll lose the respect of both employees and customers."

Luc grimaced. He wished he could refute his grandfather's claim, but he couldn't. He had a feeling his grandfather had it exactly right, and if their suspicions about Conway Billings were correct, Cousin Connie would be all over this news and use it to Téa's disadvantage. With each new revelation, Luc could feel the trap tightening around him, edging him deeper and deeper into an inescapable corner.

"Plus," she added in a rush. "There's one other small problem."

"What's the other small problem? I think I can take it. Maybe."

"Primo said that if you wish to remain a Dante, you'll marry me. But I don't think he was serious." She turned to him. "Do you?"

"You did meet my grandfather, didn't you?"

"You know I did."

"I think that answers your question." He started the car again and pulled onto the road.

"So what now?" Tea asked tentatively.

"Now, we drive to Lake Tahoe and get married."

They arrived in Nevada by midday and made short work of obtaining the necessary license. Despite the rush and reluctance, Luc insisted they stop at a boutique for more appropriate clothing—a formal suit for Luc, while Téa chose an ivory calf-length skirt and tailored jacket accented with seed pearls. The shop owner suggested a simple Mantilla style veil with embroidered edges that suited her outfit perfectly. A short time later, Téa emerged from the boutique to discover Luc waiting for her, holding a bridal bouquet of multicolored roses in one hand, and a jeweler's box with two plain wedding bands in the other.

They made the short trip to the venue they'd selected and were given the choice of having the ceremony performed in the chapel, itself, or in a glorious flower-filled garden just behind the small stucco building. To Téa's surprise, Luc didn't hesitate, but selected the garden. She couldn't help but wonder if it was because it reminded him of Primo's backyard.

Both had large, sprawling shade trees and well-tended flower beds, bursting with a riot of colors. They took their vows beneath an arching arbor draped with deep red roses that filled the air with their lush scent. Twenty short minutes later they were pronounced husband and wife.

Téa didn't recall much of the drive back to San Francisco. She knew they kept the conversation light and casual. But she had no idea what either of them said. Awareness returned when Luc bypassed the turn for Madam's row house and continued on toward his apartment.

"Aren't you going to drop me off at home?"

He glanced in her direction. "Why would I do that? We're married, remember?" he asked with devastating logic. "I think your grandmother and stepsisters would find it extremely odd if you spent your wedding night under their roof instead of mine."

She blushed, feeling like an utter fool. "Oh. Of course. I didn't think."

Luc parked the rental car, said something about returning it in the morning and grabbed their bags while she gathered up the rest of their paraphernalia. The elevator ride to his apartment was accomplished in strained silence. The minute the doors parted, he carried his duffel through to his bedroom and then put her case just inside the doorway of the spare room.

Message received, loud and clear.

"Would you like a drink?" he offered politely.

She debated, then nodded. "I wouldn't say no to a glass of wine."

"Red?"

"Please." He poured her a glass and then fixed himself a whiskey. "It's almost identical to the last time I was here," she observed. "Except for the marriage part."

He eyed her broodingly. "That's a big exception."

She gently placed her bouquet on the table beside the couch. The flowers were already beginning to wilt, she realized with a sad pang. It seemed fitting, all things considered. Soon they'd have to return to reality, which meant putting her focus on work and family, while Luc went back to avoiding commitment at all costs. "I know you have something eating at you. Why don't you just say what you need to so we can go to bed?"

"All this worked out to your advantage, didn't it?"

She closed her eyes. She suspected that was what he thought. It hurt to have it confirmed. "You think I set it up, don't you?"

He took a moment to swallow his drink. "The thought crossed my mind."

"Let it uncross your mind," she said sharply. "You said no to marriage. I accepted that. End of story."

"And yet, within hours my ring ended up on your finger."

"Because of your family, Luc. Yours. Not mine. Madam was merely disappointed in me. I could have lived with her disappointment. It was Primo who forced the issue."

"You're forgetting that Primo pushed because someone leaked the news to *The Snitch*. There are only a limited number of people who could have done that."

She lifted an eyebrow. "All of whom are de Lucas?"

"Pretty much."

She took a step in his direction. "You always claimed I was a lousy liar. Look at me, Luc. Hear me." She spoke quietly. Forcefully. "I didn't trick you into marrying me. I didn't ask anyone in my family to get in touch with *The Snitch*. I would never do such a thing to you."

He inclined his head. "Fair enough."

"Do you believe me?" she pressed.

"I believe you."

"But you still want someone to blame."

"Yes. No." He released his breath in a sigh. "I'm as much to blame as anyone."

"Thank you for that much," she said dryly.

"I want you to understand something, Téa." His eyes glittered darkly, with just a hint of gold. "This doesn't change anything."

"What do you mean?"

"You know what I mean. This is temporary. In a few months I plan to walk away."

"I know." And she did. She'd just hoped… She set her glass down, exercising extreme care. "I don't think I want a drink after all. I'm exhausted. If you don't mind, I'll turn in."

He stopped her as she started from the room. Just a brush of his fingers along her arm. "Téa…"

The Inferno stirred, flared to life, sizzling and crackling with unmistakable urgency. She longed to turn and step into his arms. To beg him to allow her in.

To give her a chance. "Don't. I can't..." She shook her head, struggling for control. "Please, don't."

Without another word, he let her go.

She got ready for bed, moving mindlessly through her nighttime regimen. At long last, she slid between the sheets and curled into a ball. Just a few short hours ago she'd been married. This was her wedding night. Never in her wildest dreams had she imagined she'd spend it alone. Or that the man she married would have given almost anything to rip the ring from his finger, and her from his life.

Tears burned against her eyelids, slipped out and left scalding streaks down her cheeks. She buried her face in the pillow, fighting not to make any sound as she cried. She never heard the door to her room open. Never heard Luc limp across the floor. One minute, she was huddled in her bed, the next she was curled against his chest as he lifted her and carried her to his room.

"What are you doing?" she choked out the question.

"It's my wedding night," he said, echoing her earlier thoughts. "And I'll be damned if I'm going to spend it alone."

He deposited her in his bed, then joined her there. In the silence of the night, he gathered her up. Her nightgown whispered away, melting into the darkness. Then his hands found her. Stroked her. Spoke the words he refused to. With every touch, every caress, he gave of himself, allowing what he guarded so carefully free rein.

Where before they came together in clashing power, now they gently slid, one into the other. Sweetly. Tenderly. The climax, when it came, was every bit as powerful, but it contained a different quality. A need answered. Two hearts united. A consummation of not just bodies, but of souls.

Just before sleep consumed her, he wrapped her up in his arms, hands intertwined, palms meshed. From a great distance she heard his whisper. "Good night, my Inferno bride."

"Good night, my Inferno husband," someone answered. Not her. It couldn't have been her. "Oh, Luc. I do love you."

When Tea awoke, she was alone in the bed.

A quick search of Luc's apartment confirmed that he'd gone, though the scent of freshly brewed coffee drew her to the kitchen. Beside the pot, she found a note that read: *Don't go in to Bling until I get back.* The word "don't" was underlined several times. It took two cups of coffee to figure out why. If she planned to oust her cousin and assume the reins of Billings, she'd better do it with a plan. Because, guaranteed, Connie had one.

After a quick shower, she ate breakfast and drafted a press release announcing the change in management, fussing over each and every word, striving to get it just right. It took several hours to perfect. She'd just finished when Luc returned. He was accompanied by a tank-size black man whom he introduced as Juice.

She offered her hand, amused when it got swallowed up in his. "Pleased to finally meet you," he said. "Luc's had a lot to say about you."

"Some of it good, I hope."

"Good enough to make me wonder why you'd waste your time on him when I'm available."

She grinned. "Maybe if I'd met you first…?"

He waggled his eyebrows at her. "You'd be counting your lucky stars and singing praises on high."

"If you're done hitting on my wife," Luc interrupted, "I'd like to give her an update."

Téa buried a smile. "I just brewed a fresh pot of coffee. I drank the last one while drafting a press release."

"You read my mind."

Once everyone had fresh coffee, they gathered at the dining room table. Luc took the lead. "First, let's deal with the issue of the new equipment Conway has been purchasing. FYI, Juice was my top researcher when I owned my own security business. He was able to locate where Connie had the equipment stashed."

"How did you do that?" Téa asked in amazement.

"Uh…" Juice darted Luc a panicked look. "Best if I don't tell you. It's not exactly leg— That is to say…"

"It's none of your business," Luc cut in. "We also have temporarily relocated said equipment. My men should be finished moving it by noon."

"Wait a minute. You *stole* Connie's machinery?"

The two men exchanged glances. "Well, technically, it belongs to Billings since he used company money to purchase it," Luc explained. "Which means it's yours to move if you want. I merely decided that's what you wanted and acted on it."

"Of course." She didn't know why that didn't occur to her. "Will that be sufficient to keep him from starting up a competing business?"

"That's the hope."

Téa nodded in satisfaction. "Then the next step is to get Connie out with as little fuss as possible while keeping our current customers." She put the press release she'd drafted on the table. "See what you think about this."

Luc and Juice scanned it. "Oh, Connie's not going to be happy," Luc said, with a merciless grin. "Particularly when he reads the part about being a distant relative of your grandfather who, quote, has been forcibly removed as CEO for failing to maintain Billings's high standard of producing top quality merchandise, which is the number one priority for Daniel Billings's granddaughter, the company's new CEO. End quote." He shoved the release back across the table toward her. "One major error."

Téa snatched up the paper. "What? Where?"

"Your name. It says Téa de Luca. It should say Téa Dante."

The correction brought tears to her eyes. Considering how he felt about their marriage, it meant the world to her that he'd insist she use the Dante name. "Silly of me," she murmured. "I'll change it right away."

Luc nodded in satisfaction. His cell rang just then. "Yes, Sandford," he said as he left the table to take the call. "What did you find out?"

It took Téa a moment to place the name, but then she remembered the deputy who'd been so helpful after their car crash. She only caught snatches of Luc's conversation, but when he returned a grim fury clung to him. He gave Juice a nod before turning to Téa.

"Let's go," he announced. "Time for you to kick Cousin Connie to the curb."

Ten

Conway Billings didn't take kindly to being kicked to the curb.

Téa swept into his office without bothering to knock, followed closely by Luc and Juice. Conway looked up, his face darkening in outrage. "What the hell do you mean by waltzing in here without permission? You may take over in another month, Téa, but until then this is still my office."

"You're mistaken, Connie. It's now *my* office." She took a stance in front of his desk, her hands planted on her hips. "And don't call me Téa. The name is Mrs. Dante."

Her cousin's mouth opened and closed several times. "When…?"

She lifted an eyebrow. "Did I get married? Luc and I were married yesterday."

"Yesterday? I… You…" He resorted to bluster. "You

were supposed to be getting to know our clients. How are you ever going to learn what you need to—"

"That's no longer your concern," she interrupted. "As of this minute, you're no longer in charge."

"There's still another month until it's official, Téa." Luc and Juice both took a single step forward and Conway's eyes bulged. "Mrs. Dante," he hastened to correct. "You don't take possession of Billings until next month."

"I suggest you go back and reread the will, Connie." She circled the desk, putting herself on his side of it. Then she edged her hip onto the corner in a decidedly possessive maneuver. "In case you overlooked it, I also take possession of the company the day I marry. Since that happy event took place yesterday, I'm now the new owner of Billings."

"Don't be ridiculous, Te—" a quick look at Luc "—Mrs. Dante. You're not ready to assume control."

"That's quite possible. Time will tell. What I can say with absolute certainty is that you're through. I have security waiting outside the door. They'll escort you off the premises."

His breath hissed in surprise. "What's brought this on?" His gaze shot to Luc and narrowed. "He's responsible for this, isn't he?"

"No, Connie," she corrected very gently. "You are. Did you think I wouldn't figure it out?"

He stiffened. "Figure what out?"

"The equipment. Billings Prime. I did get the name right, didn't I? That's what you plan to call your new company?"

"I have no idea what you're talking about."

"Stop. I uncovered it all. The way you cut corners to save money and churn out inferior merchandise. The business you planned to start up. The new manufacturing equipment you bought with the extra profits you gained from overcharging *my* customers. How you planned to use the drop in quality to convince those same customers to switch to Billings Prime. The sale you're currently drafting so that your company can buy the new manufacturing equipment from Billings for only pennies on the dollar. That was particularly slick, Connie."

"And if I did all that, so what?" He shoved back his chair, fury reddening his face. "This should have been my company! I worked here my entire life." He didn't bother to conceal his disgust. "You're not even a Billings. You gave up your rights to this company when you let de Luca adopt you."

She straightened, faced him down. "That decision was my grandfather's to make. Obviously he didn't agree with you since he left Billings to me, not you." She tilted her head to one side. "I wonder why that is? He must have figured you out long ago."

Conway smoothed the front of his suit jacket and drew himself up to his full height, as little as that was. "It's too late for you to do anything about it. That equipment now belongs to me. I wasn't planning to bring Billings Prime online for another month, but I won't have any difficulty moving up my agenda."

"I think you'll not only find that difficult, but impossible," Téa replied. "I rescinded the sale of the manufacturing equipment between Billings and Billings Prime first thing this morning and I've confiscated that equipment. All you have left is a name. No equipment, no merchandise to sell and when my press release hits, not much of a reputation, either."

"That's impossible! I'll…I'll sue."

"I wish you would." She smiled coldly. "But I doubt

you will, considering that when all the facts are brought to light you'll most likely find yourself sitting in a jail cell."

Luc stepped forward. "And if by some chance the judge is inclined toward leniency, it won't last long. Not when he discovers that you tampered with Téa's brakes before sending her on a dangerous drive. I'm guessing you arranged that sometime Monday when her car was parked in Billings's garage. I suspect it was shortly after you ordered her to take that trip to L.A. No doubt you were hoping it would end up being a one-way trip."

Téa swung around to face her husband. She didn't even attempt to conceal her shock. "What?"

"Deputy Sandford called. Someone mixed transmission fluid in with your brake fluid. It's slower than simply cutting the lines. No doubt he wanted to give you plenty of time to get on some of the more treacherous stretches of road before your brakes went out. Might have worked, too."

Téa fought to breathe. "It would have worked if you hadn't been driving."

She turned to face her cousin. She saw his mouth moving, could hear the denials that spilled out. But her brain couldn't seem to process them. Instead all she saw was the guilt burning like acid in his unrepentant blue eyes.

"I want him out of here," she said, her voice cutting through whatever her cousin was saying. It took every ounce of self-control to keep from physically attacking him. He must have sensed it because he fell back as she approached. "Just so you know, Connie? Just so it's crystal clear. My sisters will inherit the business if anything happens to me. And every last scrap of information that my husband has uncovered about your activities is going to be turned over to the appropriate authorities. I suggest you find yourself a good lawyer."

"Screw finding a lawyer," Luc said. "Find yourself a nice, deep hole, *Cuz*. Somewhere I won't find you. Because if I ever see you again, I swear I'll take you apart."

Billings's security stepped in then and with Juice's assistance, escorted Conway out of the office, out of the building—and she sincerely hoped—out of her life. The instant the door closed behind them, Téa sank into the chair behind Connie's—*her*—desk.

"That's that," she murmured.

Luc inclined his head. "You're now the boss. Congratulations."

A tiny frown tugged at her brow. "Thanks to you."

"Happy to help." He shoved his hands into his trouser pockets and strolled across the spacious room to stand in front of the windows. "I guess my job is done now."

Maybe if he hadn't said it with such finality, she'd have known how to respond. She hesitated, before conceding, "I guess it is."

He threw her a look over his shoulder. "You okay?"

"Sure. Fine." Only she wasn't. Not even a little.

"Anything else I can do for you?"

Love me. Stay with me. Make our marriage real. She silently shook her head.

"If you're sure, then I'll push off."

"Thanks again for all your help," she managed to say.

For ten minutes after Luc left, Téa continued to sit behind the huge desk, numb. So this was it. In the blink of an eye, he'd given her everything she thought she wanted, and she owed him more than she could ever repay.

Because he suspected her cousin might be attempting something underhanded, he used his time, skill and associates to look into Connie's background. More, he and Juice uncovered her cousin's plan and moved to circumvent it. And thanks to Luc agreeing to marry her, she'd gained control of her inheritance in time to stop Connie from gutting it. With a lot of hard work and dedication, she'd turn Billings around and salvage her family's finances. But she'd lose something far more important.

Luc.

Her mouth trembled. Of course, that was assuming she'd ever had him. She leaned back and closed her eyes, fighting exhaustion. She loved her husband. Loved him with all her heart and soul. Loved him with every fiber of her being. And because she loved him, she'd let him go. Knowing Luc, that wouldn't be easy, despite his aversion toward marriage. She'd need to prove she could stand on her own two feet. And she'd have to find a way to get him out of their marriage without his looking like the bad guy.

Unfortunately she knew precisely how to do it, too. Even more unfortunate, she'd give him up, regardless of the personal cost. She just wished she could offer him something in return to show him how much she appreciated everything he'd done for her.

A light tapping sounded at the door and Juice peeked in. "What happened to Luc?" he asked.

"He's gone." A sudden idea struck her. One final way she could even the scales. She straightened in her chair, energized. "Juice, I wonder if you'd do one more favor for me."

"Sure." He stepped into her office. "Name it."

"There's someone I need you to find…"

Luc checked his watch and grimaced. He was late for his dinner date with Téa. Not badly, but more than he liked. Maybe it had been his subconscious way of putting off the inevitable. Because he suspected he knew what she wanted. She wanted to end their marriage so she could return to her default setting—taking care of her family. Of course, he wanted to end their marriage, too. No long-term commitments for him. He'd made that abundantly clear.

So, why the reluctance?

It couldn't have anything to do with those words she'd whispered on their wedding night. Words that burned a path straight to his heart. Words he wasn't even sure she remembered speaking. Words that confessed how much she loved him. For some reason they resonated, wrapped around him, through him, binding them as surely as the itch in his palm bound them.

"Luc Dante," he practically growled at the maître d'. "I'm meeting someone."

"Yes, Mr. Dante. She's already arrived. I'll show you to your table." He gestured toward the interior of the restaurant. "This way."

Luc followed the winding pathway through the various tables to a small alcove where a woman waited. It took an instant to realize that she wasn't Téa. The maître d' made a flourishing gesture, then retreated before Luc could explain that he'd been shown to the wrong table. He offered the woman an exasperated smile.

"Sorry about the mistake. I was supposed to meet my wife and—"

"There's no mistake," the woman said. She tilted her

head to one side. "You don't recognize me, do you? Would it help if I told you that you saved my life five years ago?"

Luc hesitated and looked more carefully. There was something familiar about her… Then it hit him. The car wreck. Kurt and the Jorgen boy, dead. The wife, pleading, begging him to let her die. *"Sonya?"*

Téa checked her watch and bit down on her lip. Right about now Luc and Sonya Jorgen would be getting reacquainted, assuming Luc stayed to talk after learning that his wife had set him up. A big if. Since she hadn't received an outraged phone call, she could only hope the impromptu meeting yielded positive results instead of all going hideously wrong. A distinct possibility, she was forced to concede. But if it worked… She closed her eyes and fought a rush of tears. If it worked, it would be the first of her parting gifts, gifts she could only pray would pay him back for all he'd done for her. Now for gift number two.

She let herself into the home that until recently she'd shared with Madam and her three sisters. She'd deliberately chosen a time when she was certain they'd all be together—the dinner hour. It was all part of her plan to try to put Luc's life back on track before their divorce. If he no longer had to worry about her, he'd feel free to move on.

She found the de Luca clan in the kitchen, squabbling over dinner preparations. She couldn't help smiling. Some things never changed. It took them a moment to realize she was there. The instant they did, they turned to greet her, the volume going up by several hundred decibels.

"What's for dinner?" she asked with a wide smile. "I'm starving."

"What are you doing here?" Madam demanded. "Where's Luc?"

"He has an appointment this evening, so I thought I'd have dinner with you." She eyed each in turn. "We need to talk."

"Actually," Sonya said, "it's not Jorgen, anymore. It's Thompson."

"You remarried?"

His shock must have shown because she smiled and waved him toward the chair across from her. Once he was seated she studied him with frank curiosity. "It's been five years and you haven't changed a bit, Luc," she murmured. "You still have the saddest eyes I've ever seen. You know, it was the first thing I noticed about you."

He took his time replying. "I may not have changed, but you have," he surprised himself by saying. "Your eyes aren't sad at all."

She lit up. "No, I guess they wouldn't be."

She shook out her napkin and spread it across her lap. Luc's gaze followed her movements, dropping downward. He froze. "You're—"

"Pregnant?" she asked with a lilting laugh. "Why, yes, I am."

"What's this about, Téa?" Madam asked apprehensively. "Has something happened between you and Luc?"

"Yes. We're going to be divorcing soon." She held up her hand when everyone began talking at once. "That's enough."

For some reason the quietly spoken words worked, cutting through the cacophony of feminine voices. Odd. It had never worked before. But then, she'd never been this serious or determined before.

"I'm not going to discuss it or answer any questions. I'm just going to say that the relationship didn't work out. As a result, I've decided to make some changes. A lot of changes." She eyed each in turn before settling on Juliann. "I've been a lousy wedding planner, Jules. I'm sorry about that."

"It hasn't been so bad," Juliann instantly denied.

"Yes, it has." Téa reached into her shoulder bag and pulled out the shiny black cell phone with its neon-pink kisses. She placed it on the table. "I appreciate you including me in the preparations, but I think what I'd enjoy most is just being there for you on your special day."

Juliann's eyes misted. "That's all I ever wanted, too. But you've always tried to fill in for Mom, and I figured…"

Téa closed her eyes. Of course. "You were trying to let me play the traditional mother role, weren't you?" She blinked back tears and offered her sister a wobbly smile. "Thank you. To be honest, I don't want to be your mother, anymore. But I'd love to be your sister."

For some reason, her confession caused all her sisters to tear up. Then there were hugs all around before Davida said, "I gather I'm next?"

"Yes," Téa confirmed. She nudged the phone farther away. "Stay in college or don't. It's your decision. But I'm not bailing you out anymore."

Davida nodded. "You're not going to have to. The professor whose exam I missed? He sat me down and we had a long talk. I realized that what I really want to do is design jewelry. Luc put me in touch with Sev's wife, Francesca. She's going to mentor me while I take the classes I need."

Téa blinked. "*Luc* put you in touch…?"

Davida made a face. "I'm sorry you two are getting divorced. I like him. He's nice."

Katrina held out her hand, gloved palm up. "Finish it, Téa. I know it's my turn to get cut off."

Téa slid the phone the rest of the way across the table. "Not cut off, just cut down to reasonable, although I am canceling this line."

"That's okay. And FYI? You don't have to worry about me, either. I've decided I'm going into the military. That or I'm gonna be a cop."

Téa could only stare. "You must be joking," she finally said.

"Nope. I've gotten to know a lot of cops over the past year." She shot Madam a nervous glance. "You know. Community service projects."

Madam simply narrowed her eyes at her granddaughter and let it pass.

"Anyway, it got me interested in law enforcement." Katrina lounged back in her chair and lifted a pierced eyebrow. "So, we done?"

Madam cleared her throat. "You…you haven't mentioned me," she said with heart-wrenching dignity. "You may give me my phone, too, if you wish."

Téa hastened to her grandmother's side and enfolded her in a tight hug. "Never. I'll always be there for you." She looked at her sisters and in that moment finally forgave herself for her parents' death. "I'll always be there for all of you. But as a sister. As a granddaughter."

Madam dabbed at her eyes. "I think that can be arranged."

* * *

Luc was surprised to discover he enjoyed the hour he spent with Sonya. "I assume Téa arranged this?" he said, taking a not-so-wild guess.

"Your wife? Yes. Such a lovely woman. She tracked me down and explained that you were still dealing with the aftermath of what happened all those years ago." Remorse swept across Sonya's face. "I'm so sorry, Luc. I'd give anything to take back those hideous things I said to you. I was out of my mind with grief."

"I understood." He tossed some money into the billfold the waiter had left and set it to one side. "I never blamed you."

Sonya's mouth twisted. "I'm not so sure. That's why I jumped at the opportunity to meet with you, so I could thank you."

"*Thank* me?" Of all the things he'd imagined her ever saying to him, this was bottom of the list. Hell, it didn't even make the list.

She pushed aside her decaf coffee, picking her words with care. "I was so angry with you, Luc. I wanted to die and you forced me to live. I hated you for that. I even attempted to commit suicide. Did you know?" At his silent nod, she shrugged. "Somehow I'm not surprised. Afterward, much to my amazement, I realized I no longer wanted to die. It took time and a lot of counseling, but I discovered I had a very simple choice. I could open myself up to love again, or continue to live a barren life. When I chose to open up, I found love." A radiant smile played at the corners of her mouth. "Actually I found my soul mate."

"I thought that was Kurt," Luc said, startled.

"So did I. I was wrong," she replied simply. "What I loved about my life with Kurt was being married. What

I loved was—" Her voice broke. "My son. I still miss him, Luc. I'll always miss him. But I can and will honor his memory by moving on and giving him brothers and sisters. He may never know them, but they'll always know him. I'll see to that."

Luc's jaw clenched and it took him a minute before he could speak. "I'm glad you made it through. That you found love again."

"You can, too." She leaned forward, speaking with a hushed intensity. "I'm reading between the lines here, but… Don't make the mistake I almost did. Don't turn away from life. Take the gamble, Luc, before it passes you by. Everyone experiences heartache. But that's going to happen whether you're alone or with someone you love. It's love that gets you through. Téa strikes me as a woman who can both fill your life with love, and be strong enough to ride out the heartache with you."

A short time later, Luc climbed into his car. He didn't bother to start the engine, but simply sat, mulling over the events of that evening. It occurred to him that when he saved Sonya, he'd given her back her life, but had shut down his own. She was right about a lot of things. He did have a choice. He could continue on as he had before Téa tumbled into his life or he could take a chance. He could open his heart and take the risk.

He thought about his grandparents and nearly sixty years of profound love and devotion, laughter and tears. It was the same with his parents. With his cousins. Would they avoid love if it meant avoiding the tears? He didn't even have to think about that one. They'd choose love every time.

He considered what his life would be like if he moved forward without Téa. Losing her warmth and generosity.

Her humor and passion. God help him, her love. And he remembered her murmured declaration on their wedding night and felt something hard and cold begin to loosen and break.

It was the ultimate gamble. Either he loved Téa and wanted to spend the rest of his life with her, was willing to open himself to her in every possible way. Or he let her go. Watched from afar as she moved on and found someone else to love. Someone else to give all that she'd given him.

He shook his head. No. No way in hell. As though in reaction, his palm itched and he stared at it. He was an idiot. He'd turned away from the best, most important parts of his life. And why? Because he'd been too much of a coward to take a risk. Well, screw that! It was past time that he took back his life. That he went after what he wanted most.

And what he wanted most was Téa—the woman he loved with all his heart and soul. His Inferno soul mate.

Before he could start the engine, his cell phone rang. He checked the caller ID and flipped it open. "What's up, Nonna?"

She spoke in rapid-fire Italian. "Your wife is here," she said without preamble. "You must come. Now."

He shot up in his seat. "What's wrong?"

"Téa is explaining to Primo why your marriage is a mistake. That he must not interfere in the divorce. What is this talk of a divorce, *cucciolo mio?*" she demanded. "You have only just married."

Hell. "Has Primo taken her apart, yet?"

"No, no. He is being very patient. Very understanding." His grandmother sighed. "She is a determined one, though, that wife of yours. Determined to get her head handed to her."

"Nonna, I need you to do me a favor."

"Anything."

"Break out Primo's homemade beer and *stall*." He cut the connection and immediately dialed Sev. "I need you to meet me at the Dante vault. Yes, now. She's *what*? Hell. Well, can you meet me on the way to the hospital? You're damn right it's an emergency. It's a matter of life and... And love."

Téa blinked owlishly at Primo and waved her bottle of beer at him. So far, her third gift to Luc wasn't going so well. At this rate, she'd never even up those scales. "So, you understand, right?" she asked hopefully.

Primo slanted a look in Nonna's direction, gritted his teeth and said, "Maybe if you explain one more time?"

"Oh." She suppressed a burp and lifted a hand to her aching head. "To be honest, I'm not sure I can."

"Good. We talk of other things now, yes? How do you like babies?" he asked expansively. "You and Luc will make many good babies. Inferno babies with red Inferno hair, okay?"

Téa sniffed. For some reason his question had tears welling up in her eyes. "Haven't you been listening? There aren't going to be any babies."

He leaned back in his chair and grinned. "There are always babies when your husband is a Dante." He fixed his attention on a spot over her shoulder. "Is this not true, Luciano?"

"Absolutely, Primo."

Téa swung around and almost fell off her chair.

"Oh, dear," she murmured as the room did a slow 360 around her.

"How many?" Luc asked Nonna with a sigh.

His grandmother shrugged. "Three or four."

"Maybe five," Primo offered helpfully.

"Damn. I was hoping she'd remember tonight."

"I'll remember tonight," Téa protested. "Why won't I remember?"

Luc tipped her face up to his. "Because, darling wife," he said, enunciating clearly. "You're drunk."

"Am not."

He gave his grandfather a stern look. "Coffee and lots of it. In the meantime…" He swept his wife into his arms. "Let's hope some fresh air will do the trick. By the way, you might want to give Sev a call. Francesca's in labor and they're on their way to the hospital."

Téa tipped her head back as Luc carried her into the garden. A dazzling canopy of stars glittered and burned like Dantes legendary fire diamonds. Cool spring air swirled around and over her in soft revitalizing currents. It helped clear her head and she stirred, suddenly aware that she'd somehow ended up where she most longed to be—in Luc's arms.

"Where did you come from?" she asked dreamily. "Or am I just imagining you?"

"Oh, I'm real enough," he claimed.

Not that she believed him. Having him here like this was just too good to be true. "This is so nice." Since he was a dream, she could indulge herself and she scattered her kisses across his bronzed skin, like the stars scattered their dust across the heavens. "We can pretend to still be married and have another glorious wedding night."

He smiled with breathtaking tenderness. "We don't need to pretend. We are still married."

"Not for long."

"True. Only a half dozen decades or so."

She laughed. "Now I know I'm dreaming."

He lowered her to a wrought iron bench situated beneath one of Primo's shade trees. The cold metal brought her surroundings into sharp focus. Luc really was here. And he really was holding her in his arms.

"Seriously," she said, her brain slowly coming online. "What are you doing here?"

"I wanted to thank you for arranging the meeting with Sonya tonight."

Sonya? Her brow crinkled. Oh! Sonya. "I was afraid you might be angry with me," she confessed.

"Not even a little."

"I'm so glad. I asked Juice to help me find her." She nestled against him, resting her head in the crook of his shoulder, allowing herself this one final indulgence. "How did it go?"

"She's remarried, but I guess you knew that." At Téa's nod, he added, "And she's pregnant."

Téa looked up at Luc, startled. "Is she really? That's good, right?"

"It's very good. She was...ecstatic."

"Pregnant." Téa frowned. "Wait a minute. Did I hear you tell your grandparents that Francesca was in labor, or was that part of my dream?"

"It wasn't a dream. She's in labor and Sev isn't very happy with me."

"Why ever not?"

"Because I made him stop off at the Dantes vault on the way to the hospital."

"I'm confused," Téa confessed with a sigh. "And it's all Primo's fault."

"Nonna's actually. I told her to feed you beer until I got here."

It took all her courage to ask. "Why?"

"So I could give you this…"

He held out a small jewelry box and flipped open the lid. Inside was nestled the most beautiful ring she'd ever seen. The band was platinum gold, Billings gold, Téa realized, a type her grandfather had dubbed, Platinum Ice. The band took the shape of two hearts linked together with a magnificent fire diamond set where the hearts joined.

It took several tries before she could speak. "I don't understand."

"I love you, Téa. And I want a real marriage. A permanent one."

"No," she whispered, shaking her head. "That's not what you want. You want to be apart. Alone."

"I was wrong. I can't live like that. Not anymore. Not since meeting you." She watched as he struggled to find the right words, to open himself in a way he never had before. "I can't promise I'll be perfect at it. I've spent a lot of years holding people at an emotional distance. But for you… I'm willing to give you everything I have. And with luck, we'll spend the rest of our lives getting it right."

"Oh, Luc. I came here to let you go." She gazed in the direction of the house and fought an onslaught of tears. "But I couldn't get your grandparents to listen to me. To understand and let you off the hook."

"Because they knew you were the one. My Inferno bride."

His admission melted her. "Oh, Luc. I love you so much."

"And I love you, Téa, more than I ever thought possible. My life would be empty without you and I think I've had all the emptiness I can bear." He slid the ring on her finger. It fit perfectly. But then, he knew it would. It was destiny. "It's from our new line of eternity rings. It has a name, if you're interested. It's actually the reason I chose it."

It took her two tries to get the question out. "What's the name?"

He lowered his mouth to hers. "Why, Dante's Inferno, of course."

Epilogue

Nonna touched her wineglass to Madam's. "*Salute.*"

Madam smiled tremulously. "We did it, didn't we?"

Nonna eyed Luc and Téa with smug satisfaction. "That we did. Of course, it was your managing to accomplish Step Two that allowed Primo to insist on Step Three." She released a contented sigh. "And that just leaves Step Four."

"Step Four?" Madam's eyes widened in concern. "What step is this?"

"Babies. More precious Dante babies. Boys for these two." Nonna lifted her glass in the direction of her grandson. "But that step I will leave to Luc. I believe he has the matter well in hand."

From his position at the kitchen window, Rafe Dante regarded Luc and his bride, Téa, with a cynical smile. They were in Primo's garden, enjoying the party thrown to celebrate their elopement, and accepting the congratulations of all the well-wishers. Babies abounded: one from Francesca, as well as Kiley's contribution. Both sons, of course. The two mothers were comparing everything from birthing experiences to feeding schedules. Hell, they were even comparing toes.

To Rafe's amusement, Luc looked on, taking an actual interest. Unheard of! But then, his poor brother was the latest victim of The Inferno. Of all the Dantes, Rafe had always figured that he and Luc were the two least likely to ever succumb to the family plague. For some reason, it made him feel fiercely alone. Which was the way he wanted it, right? God knows, Leigh had caused him enough heartache that he never wanted to give another woman that much power over him. But watching his family...

He deliberately turned away.

Luc joined him midway through the festivities, taking the tumbler of whiskey Rafe offered. "I hear we've been cleared to return to work."

"As of today," Rafe confirmed. "Dantes Courier Service reopens first thing Monday morning. You coming back?"

"You can't keep me away."

Rafe nodded in satisfaction. "Congratulations, by the way. Téa's a beautiful woman." He paid the compliment with complete sincerity. "You're a lucky man." Okay, maybe that wasn't quite as sincere.

"Yes, I am," Luc agreed. He fixed Rafe with a speculative eye. "I know you're one of the unbelievers."

"Check mark firmly in that column," Rafe confirmed.

"I guess we have Leigh to thank for that." Luc rested his hip against the kitchen counter. "Tell me something. Did you believe in The Inferno when you first fell in love with her? When the two of you first married?"

Rafe took a long swallow of his drink. "What makes you think that?'"

Luc froze. "Wait a sec. You didn't feel…?" He rubbed his palm.

"Don't be ridiculous. Of course not."

Luc straightened. "Are you telling me you never felt The Inferno for Leigh?"

Rafe released an incredulous laugh. "You're as crazy as the rest of them. Don't you get it? *There is no Inferno.*"

Luc simply smiled.

A hint of anger ripped through Rafe. "Don't. Don't give me that smug, knowing look. You and the rest of our deluded relatives fell in love. That's all there is to it. But because of our family's ridiculous myth, you're calling this emotion that has you drooling all over your bride The Inferno. Well, I've got news for you, brother. It's illogical. Not to mention messy." He leaned forward, speaking distinctly. "In my book that means The Inferno doesn't exist."

"I'm sure that explains the itch," Luc said, straight-faced.

"That itch is called lust. Now, you want to talk lust?" Rafe downed the rest of his drink. "Happy to oblige. Been there, sated that. Moved on."

This time Luc didn't bother to conceal his grin. "Keep talking, Rafe. And keep telling yourself you're immune. But I'm giving you fair warning. Clearly Leigh wasn't the right woman."

Rafe lifted an eyebrow. "You think?"

"You're missing the point. If Leigh wasn't the one, that means your Inferno bride's still out there. And when you find her, you'll know." Luc jabbed his index finger against his brother's chest. "Then we'll see who has the last itch, pretty boy."

* * * * *

**"Is *that* why you brought me here?"
she asked, watching closely, giving
him the chance to deny it.**

"Depends," he said, cocking his head. "On what
you mean by *that.*"

"Because you thought I'd sleep with you?"

"It had crossed my mind," he admitted.

"You are the most egotistical, opportunistic—"

"Hey, you were the one who was dressed to kill
and insisted on 'taking a ride in my jet plane.'"

"That *wasn't* a euphemism for sex."

"Really?" He looked genuinely surprised. "It
usually is."

Amber compressed her lips. How had she been
so naive? How could she have been so incredibly
foolish? Royce wasn't some knight in shining
armor. He was a charming, wealthy, well-groomed
playboy.

IN BED WITH
THE WRANGLER

BY
BARBARA DUNLOP

All the characters in this book have no existence outside the imagination of
the author, and have no relation whatsoever to anyone bearing the same name
or names. They are not even distantly inspired by any individual known or
unknown to the author, and all the incidents are pure invention.

Published in Great Britain 2011
by Mills & Boon, an imprint of Harlequin (UK) Limited,
Eton House, 18-24 Paradise Road, Richmond, Surrey TW9 1SR

© Barbara Dunlop 2010

ISBN: 978 0 263 88221 6

51-0611

Harlequin (UK) policy is to use papers that are natural, renewable and
recyclable products and made from wood grown in sustainable forests. The
logging and manufacturing processes conform to the legal environmental
regulations of the country of origin.

Printed and bound in Spain
by Blackprint CPI, Barcelona

For my husband.

Barbara Dunlop writes romantic stories while curled up in a log cabin in Canada's far north, where bears outnumber people and it snows six months of the year. Fortunately, she has a brawny husband and two teenage children to haul firewood and clear the driveway while she sips cocoa and muses about her upcoming chapters. Barbara loves to hear from readers. You can contact her through her website at www.barbaradunlop.com.

Dear Reader,

Welcome to book number two in the *Montana Millionaires: The Ryders* series from the Desire line. I love writing about siblings, and I hope you enjoy reading Royce's story in *In Bed with the Wrangler* along with his brother Jared and his sister Stephanie's stories in the companion books.

The idea for this series goes back a long time. When I was ten years old, my parents took me to visit my aunt and uncle's ranch during the summer. Even at that young age, I spun fanciful stories about the people living and working on the cattle ranch. I thought the cowboys were exotic and exciting, and I loved the space and isolation that gave such a sense of community.

Montana is one of my favorite states, and since my husband is a pilot, a cowboy and a business owner all rolled into one, the stories came together quite naturally.

Happy reading!

Barbara

One

Strains from the jazz band followed Royce Ryder as he strode across the carpeted promenade between the ballroom and the lobby lounge of the Chicago Ritz-Carlton Hotel. He tugged his bow tie loose, popping the top button on his white tuxedo shirt while inhaling a breath of relief. His brother, Jared, and his new sister-in-law, Melissa, were still dancing up a storm in the ballroom, goofy smiles beaming on their faces as they savored every single moment of their wedding reception.

But it had been a long night for Royce. He'd stood up for his brother, joked his way through an endless receiving line, then toasted the bride and the bridesmaids. He'd socialized, danced, eaten cake and even caught the garter—a reflexive action that had everything to do with his years as a first baseman in high school and college, and nothing whatsoever to do with his future matrimony prospects.

Now his duty was done, and it was time for a final night in the civilized surroundings of downtown Chicago before his sentence began in Montana. Okay, so managing the family ranch wasn't exactly hard labor in Alcatraz, but for a man who'd been piloting a jet plane around the world for the past three years, it was going to be a very long month.

It wasn't that he begrudged Jared his honeymoon. Quite the contrary, he was thrilled that his brother had fallen in love and married. And the better he got to know Melissa, the more he liked her. She was smart and sassy, and clearly devoted to both Jared and their younger sister, Stephanie. Royce wished the couple a fantastic, well-deserved trip to the South Pacific.

It was just bad luck that McQuestin, the family's Montana cattle ranch manager, had broken his leg in three places last week. McQuestin was down for the count. Stephanie was busy training her students for an important horse jumping competition. So Royce was it.

He slipped onto a padded bar stool, the majority of his focus on the selection of single malts on the mirrored, backlit shelf as he gave the woman next to him a passing glance. But he quickly did a double take, disregarding the liquor bottles and focusing on her. She was stunningly gorgeous: blond hair, dark-fringed blue eyes, flushed cheeks, wearing a shimmering, skintight, red-trimmed, gold dress that clung to every delectable curve. Her lips were bold red, and her perfectly manicured fingers were wrapped around a sculpted martini glass.

"What can I get for you?" asked the bartender,

dropping a coaster on the polished mahogany bar in front of Royce.

"Whatever she's having," said Royce without taking his gaze from the woman.

She turned to paste him with a back-off stare, her look of disdain making him wish he'd at least kept his tie done up. But a split second later, her expression mellowed.

"Vodka martini?" the waiter confirmed.

"Sure," said Royce.

"You were the best man," the woman stated, her voice husky-sexy in the quiet of the lounge.

"That I was," Royce agreed easily, more than willing to use tonight's official position to his advantage. "Royce Ryder. Brother of the groom. And you are?"

"Amber Hutton." She held out a feminine hand.

He took it in his. It was small, smooth, with delicate fingers and soft skin. His mind immediately turned to the things she could do to him with a hand like that.

"Tired of dancing?" he asked as the waiter set the martini in front of him. He assumed she would have had plenty of partners in the crowded ballroom.

"Not in the mood." Her fingers moved to the small plastic spear that held a trio of olives in her glass. She shot a brief glance behind her toward the promenade that led to the sparkling ballroom. Then she leaned closer to Royce. He met her halfway.

"Hiding out," she confided.

"From?" he prompted.

She hesitated. Then she shook her head. "Nothing important."

Royce didn't press. "Any way I can be of assistance?"

She arched a perfectly sculpted brow. "Don't hit on me."

"Ouch," he said, feigning a wounded ego.

That prompted a smile. "You did ask."

"I was expecting a different answer."

"I'll understand if you want to take off."

Royce gazed into her eyes for a long moment. Past her smile, he could see trouble lurking. Though women with trouble usually sent him running for the hills, he gave a mental shrug, breaking one of his own rules. "I don't want to take off."

"You one of those nice guys, Royce Ryder?"

"I am," he lied. "Good friend. Confidant. A regular boy next door."

"Funny, I wouldn't have guessed that about you."

"Ouch, again," he said softly, even though she was dead right. He'd never been any woman's good friend or confidant.

"You strike me as more of a playboy."

"Shows you how wrong you can be." He glanced away, taking a sip of the martini. Not a lot of taste to it.

"And you left the party because…"

"I wasn't in the mood for dancing, either," he admitted.

"Oh…" She let her tone turn the word into a question.

He swiveled on the stool so he was facing her. "I'm a jet pilot," he told her instead of explaining his mood. Time had proven it one of his more successful pickup lines. Sure, she'd asked him not to hit on her, but if, in the course of their conversation, she decided she was interested, well, he had no control over that, did he?

"For an airline?" she asked.

"For Ryder International. A corporate jet."

Her glass was empty, so he drained his own and signaled the bartender for another round.

"Getting me drunk won't work," she told him.

"Who says I'm getting you drunk? I'm drowning my own sorrows. I'm only including you to be polite."

She smiled again and seemed to relax. "You don't strike me as a man with sorrows, Mr. 'I'm a Jet Pilot' Best Man."

"Shows you how wrong you can be," he repeated. "I'm here celebrating my last night of freedom." He raised his skewer of olives to his mouth, sliding one off the end.

"Are you getting married, too?"

He nearly choked on the olive. "No."

"Going to jail?" she tried.

He resisted the temptation to nod. "Going to Montana."

She smiled at his answer. "There's something wrong with Montana?"

"There is when you were planning to be in Dubai and Monaco."

Her voice turned melodic, and she shook her head in mock sympathy. "You poor, poor man."

He grunted his agreement. "I'll be babysitting the family ranch. Our manager broke his leg, and Jared's off on his honeymoon."

Her smile stayed in place, but something in her eyes softened. "So, you really are a nice guy?"

"A regular knight in shining armor."

"I like that," she said. Then she was silent for a moment, tracing a swirl in the condensation on the full glass in front of her. "There are definitely times when a girl could use a knight in shining armor."

Royce heard the catch in her voice and saw the tightness in her profile. The trouble was back in her expression.

"This one of those times?" he found himself asking, even though he knew better.

She propped an elbow on the polished bar and leaned her head against her hand, facing him. "Have you ever been in love, Royce Ryder?"

"I have not," he stated without hesitation. And he didn't ever intend to go there. Love guaranteed nothing and complicated everything.

"Don't you think Melissa looked happy today?"

"I'm guessing most brides are happy."

"They are," Amber agreed. Then she lifted her head and moved her left hand, and he realized he'd missed the three carats sparkling on the third finger.

Rookie mistake. What the hell was the matter with him tonight?

Amber should have had more sense than to attend a wedding in her current mood. She should have made up an obligation or faked a headache. Her mother was in New York for the weekend, but it wasn't as if her father needed moral support at a social function.

"You're engaged." Royce Ryder's voice pierced her thoughts, his gaze focused on her ring.

"I am," she admitted, reflexively twisting the diamond in a circle around her finger.

"Don't I feel stupid," Royce muttered.

She cocked her head, and their gazes met and held.

"Why?" she asked.

He gave a dry chuckle and raised his martini glass to

his lips. "Because I may be subtle, but I *am* hitting on you."

She fought a grin at his bald honesty. "Sorry to disappoint you."

"Not your fault."

True. She had been up-front with him. Still, she couldn't help wondering if there was something in her expression, her tone of voice, or maybe her body language that had transmitted more than a passing interest. Not that she'd cheat on Hargrove. Even if…

She shut those thoughts down.

She'd never cheat on Hargrove. But there was no denying that Royce was an incredibly attractive man. He seemed smart. He had a good sense of humor. If she was the type to get picked up, and if he was the one doing the picking, and if she wasn't engaged, she might just be interested.

"What?" he prompted, scanning her expression.

"Nothing." She turned back to her drink. "I'll understand if you leave."

He shifted, and his tone went low. "I'll understand if you ask me to go."

Her brain told her mouth to form the words, but somehow they didn't come out. A few beats went by while the bartender served another couple at the end of the bar, a smoky tune vibrated from the ballroom and a group of young women laughed and chatted as they pulled two tables together in the center of the lounge.

"He here?" asked Royce, cutting a glance to the ballroom. "Did you have a fight?"

Amber shook her head. "He's in Switzerland."

Royce straightened. "Ahh."

"What ahh?"

His deep, blue-eyed gaze turned cocky and speculative. "You're lonely."

Amber's mouth worked in silence for an outraged second. "I am *not* lonely. At least not that way. I'm here with my father."

"What way, then?"

"What way what?" She stabbed the row of olives up and down in her drink.

"In what way are you lonely?"

Why on earth had she put it that way? What was wrong with her? "I am not lonely at all."

"Okay."

"I'm…" She struggled to sort out her feelings.

In a very real way, she *was* lonely. She couldn't talk to her parents. She sure as heck couldn't talk to Hargrove. She couldn't even talk to her best friend, Katie.

Katie was going to be the maid of honor at Amber's wedding next month. They'd bought the bridesmaid dress in Paris. Oriental silk. Flaming orange, which sounded ridiculous, but was interspersed with gold and midnight plum, and looked fabulous on Katie's delicate frame.

Hargrove Alston was the catch of the city. And it wasn't as if there was anything wrong with him. At thirty-three, he was already a partner in one of Chicago's most prestigious law firms. He had a venerated family, impeccable community and political connections. If everything went according to plan, he'd be running for the U.S. Senate next year.

She really had no cause for complaint.

It wasn't as if the sex was bad. It was perfectly, well, pleasant. So was Hargrove. He was a decent and pleasant man. Not every woman could say that about her future husband.

She downed the rest of her martini, hoping it would ease the knot of tension that had stubbornly cramped her stomach for the past month.

Royce signaled the bartender for another round, and she let him.

He polished off his own drink while the bartender shook a mixture of ice and Gray Goose that clattered against the frosted silver shaker. Then the man produced two fresh glasses and strained the martinis.

"His name is Hargrove Alston," she found herself telling Royce.

Royce gave a nod of thanks to the man and lifted both glasses. "Shall we find a table?"

The suggestion startled Amber. She gave a guilty glance around the lounge, feeling like an unfaithful barfly. But nobody was paying the slightest bit of attention to them.

She'd started dating Hargrove when she was eighteen, so she'd never taken up with a stranger in a bar. Not that Royce was a stranger. He was the best man, brother of her father's business associate. It was a completely different thing than encouraging a stranger.

She slipped off the bar stool. "Sure."

At a quiet, corner table, Royce set their drinks down. He pulled one of the padded armchairs out for her, and she eased into the smooth, burgundy leather, crossing her legs and tugging her gold dress to midthigh.

"Hargrove Alston?" he asked as he took the seat opposite, moving the tiny table lamp to one side so their view of each other was unobstructed.

"He's going to run for the U.S. Senate."

"You're marrying a politician?"

"Not necessarily—" She cut herself short. Wow. How

had *that* turned into real words? "I mean, he hasn't been elected yet," she quickly qualified.

"And what do you do?" asked Royce.

Amber pursed her lips and lifted the fresh drink. "Nothing."

"Nothing?"

She shook her head. It was, sadly, the truth. "I graduated University of Chicago," she offered.

"Fine Arts?" he asked.

"Public Administration. An honors degree." It had seemed like a good idea, given Hargrove's political aspirations. At least she'd be in a position to understand the complexities of his work.

"You've got my attention," said Royce, with a look of admiration.

"Only just now?" she joked. But the moment the words were out, she realized what she'd done. She was flirting with Royce.

His blue eyes twinkled with awareness. Then they darkened and simmered. He eased forward. "Amber, you had my attention the second I laid eyes on you."

She stilled, savoring the sound of her name, wrapping her mind around his words as a dangerous warmth sizzled up inside her. The rest of the room disappeared as seconds ticked by, while he waited for her response.

Then his smiled softened, and the predatory gleam went out of his eyes. "I take it that was an accident?"

"I'm not sure," she admitted.

"Well, let me know when you decide."

If flirting with him wasn't an accident, it was definitely a mistake. She needed to get herself back under control. "Tell me about Montana," she tried. "I've never been there."

He drew back, tilting his head to one side for a second, then obviously deciding to let her off the hook. "What do you want to know?"

"Your ranch," she rushed on. "Tell me about your ranch."

"We have cattle."

A cocktail waitress set a small bowl of mixed nuts on the table and took note of their drink levels as Royce thanked her.

"How many?" asked Amber as the woman strode away.

"Around fifty thousand head."

"That's a lot of cows to babysit."

"Tell me about it."

"Horses?" she prompted, determined to keep the conversation innocuous.

"Hundreds."

She plucked an almond from the clear bowl. "I took dressage lessons when I was eleven."

His wide smile revealed straight, white teeth. "In Chicago?"

"Birmingham Stables." She nibbled on the end of the nut. "I didn't last long. I wasn't crazy about sweat and manure."

"You'd hate Montana."

"Maybe not. Tell me something else about it."

"My sister has a horse ranch up in the hills. It has huge meadows with millions of wildflowers."

"Wildflowers are nice." Amber was pretty sure she'd like fields of wildflowers. "What else?"

"She jumps Hanoverians."

"Really? Is she good?"

"We expect her to make the next Olympic team."

"I bet she loves it." Amber tried to imagine what it would be like to be so passionate about something that you were one of the best in the world.

Royce nodded. "Ever since she was five." The glow in his eyes showed his pride in his sister.

Amber sighed and took a second almond. "I wish I loved something."

He considered her words for a few seconds. "Everybody loves something."

She dared to meet his eyes and rest there. "What do you love?"

He didn't hesitate. "Going Mach 1 in a Gulfstream. On a clear night. Over the Nevada desert."

"Get to do it often?"

"Not often enough."

Amber couldn't help but smile. "Are you good?"

His gaze flicked to the low neckline of her dress as his voice turned to a rumble. "I am very, very good."

"You are very, very bad," she countered, with a waggle of her finger.

He grinned unrepentantly, and the warmth sizzled up inside her all over again.

"Your turn," he told her.

She didn't understand.

"What do you love?"

Now, there was a question.

She bought herself some time by taking a sip of her drink.

"Designer shoes," she decided, setting the long-stemmed glass back down on the table.

He leaned sideways to peer under the table. "Liar."

"What do you mean?" She stretched out a leg to show off her black, stiletto sandals.

"I've dated women with a shoe fetish."

"I never said I had a fetish."

"Yours are unpretentious." Before she knew it, he'd scooped her foot onto his knee. "And there's a frayed spot on the strap." His thumb brushed her ankle as he gestured. "You've worn them more than twice."

"I didn't say I was extravagant about it." She desperately tried to ignore the warmth of his hand, but her pulse had jumped, and she could feel moisture forming at her hairline.

"Try again," he told her.

"Birthday cake." She was more honest this time. "Three layers with sickly, sugary buttercream icing and bright pink rosebuds."

He laughed and set her foot back on the floor.

Thank goodness.

"How old are you?" he asked, scooping a handful of nuts.

"Twenty-two. You?"

"Thirty-three."

"Seriously?"

"Yeah. Why?"

She shrugged, hesitated, then plunged in. "Hargrove is thirty-three, and he seems a lot older than you."

"That's because I'm a pilot—daring and carefree. He's a politician—staid and uptight. No comparison, really."

"You've never even met him." Yet the analysis was frighteningly accurate.

Royce's expression turned serious. "Why are you hiding out?"

"What?"

"When I first saw you over at the bar, you said you were hiding out. From what?"

What, indeed.

Amber took a deep breath, smoothing both palms in parallel over her hair. She scrunched her eyes shut for a long moment.

She was hiding out from the glowing bride, the happy guests and the pervasive joy of happily-ever-after.

But even as she rolled the explanation around, she knew it wasn't right. She didn't begrudge Melissa her happiness.

Truth was, she was hiding out from herself, from the notion that she was living a lie, from the realization that she'd wrapped her life around a man she didn't love.

The truth was both frightening and exhausting, and she needed time to figure it all out. More than an evening. More than a day. Even more than a weekend.

She needed to come to terms with the colossal mess she'd made of her life and decide where to go next. Ironic, really. Where Royce dreaded his ranch in Montana, she'd give anything—

Her eyes popped open, and she blinked him into focus. "Take me with you."

His brow furrowed. "What?"

"Take me with you to Montana." Nobody would look for her in Montana. She'd be free of dress fittings and florists and calligraphers. No more gift registries or parties or travel agents.

No more Hargrove.

The thought took a weight off her shoulders, and the knot in her stomach broke free. Not good.

"Are you joking?" asked Royce.

"No."

"Are you crazy?"

"Maybe." Was she crazy? This certainly felt insane. Unfortunately, it also felt frighteningly right.

"I'm not taking an engaged woman with me to Montana."

"Why not?"

He held out his palms, gesturing in the general vicinity of her neckline and the rest of her dress. "Because… Because… Well, because your fiancé would kill me, for one."

"I won't tell him."

"Right. That plan always ends well."

"I'm serious. He'll never know."

"Forget it."

No. She wouldn't forget it. This was the first idea in weeks that had felt right to her.

She pulled off her diamond ring, setting it on the table between them. "There. No more fiancé. No more problem."

"It doesn't have to be on your finger to count."

"Yeah?" she challenged.

"Yeah," he confirmed.

"What if I wasn't engaged?" Her words cut to absolute silence between them. The other sounds in the room muted, and time slowed down.

His gaze took a methodical trip from her cleavage to her waist, then backtracked to her eyes. "Sweetheart, if you weren't engaged, I'd say fasten your seat belt."

She snapped open her handbag. "Then how about this?" Retrieving her slim, silver cell phone, she typed a quick message and handed it over to Royce.

He squinted in the dim light, brows going up as he read the typed words.

I'm so sorry. I can't marry you. I need some time to think.

"Press Send," she told him. "Press Send, and take me to Montana."

"*There you are,* pumpkin." Amber's father stepped up behind her, and his broad hand came down on her shoulder.

Shock rushed straight from her brain all the way to her toes. She whipped her head around to look up. "Daddy?"

"The limo's at the curb." Her father's glance went to Royce.

Royce placed the cell phone facedown on the table and stood up to hold out his hand. "Royce Ryder. Jared's brother."

Her father shook. "David Hutton. We met briefly in the receiving line."

"Good to see you again, sir."

"You've been entertaining my daughter?"

"The other way around," said Royce, his gaze going to Amber. "She's an interesting woman. You must be proud."

Her father gave her shoulder a squeeze. "We certainly are. But it's getting late, honey. We need to get home."

No, Amber wanted to yell. She didn't want to go home. She wanted to stay here with Royce and completely change her life. She wanted to break it off with Hargrove and escape to Montana. She truly did.

Royce picked up the phone and slipped it back into her purse, clicking the purse shut with finality then handing it to her. "It was fun meeting you."

Amber opened her mouth, but no words came out.

Her father scooped a hand under her elbow and gently urged her to her feet.

She stared at Royce, trying to convey her desperation, hoping he'd understand the look in her eyes and do something to help her. But he didn't. And her father took a step, and she took a step. And another, and another.

"Amber?" Royce called, and relief shot though her. He knew. He understood. He was coming to her rescue.

But when she turned, he was holding out her engagement ring.

"Amber," her father admonished, shock clear in his tone.

"My hands were swelling," she answered lamely.

Royce didn't bother making eye contact as he dropped the diamond into the palm of her hand.

Two

"Who was that?" Stephanie's voice startled Royce as he watched Amber exit the lounge on her father's arm.

Tearing his eyes from the supple figure beneath the gold-and-red dress, he turned to face his sister. Stephanie looked young and unusually feminine in her ice-pink, strapless, satin bridesmaid dress. It had a full, flowing, knee-length skirt and a wide, white sash that matched her dangling, satin-bead earrings.

"Are all women crazy?" he asked, trying to recall the last time he'd seen Stephanie in anything other than riding clothes.

"Yes, we are," she answered without hesitation, linking her arm with his. "So you probably don't want to upset us. Like, for example, turning down our perfectly reasonable requests."

Royce sighed, steering her back to the table as he

pushed the bizarre conversation with Amber out of his mind. "What do you want, Steph?"

"A million dollars."

"No."

"Hey," she said, sliding into Amber's vacated seat as the cocktail waitress removed the empty martini glass. She kicked off one sandal and tucked her ankle under the opposite thigh on the roomy chair. "I'm a woman on the edge here."

"On the edge of what?" He pushed his half-full drink away. Had Amber's text message been an elaborate joke? If so, how warped was her sense of humor?

"Sanity," said Stephanie. "There's this stallion in London."

"Talk to Jared." Royce wasn't getting caught up in his sister's insatiable demands for her jumping stable.

"It's Jared's wedding night. He already went upstairs. You're in charge now."

Royce glanced at his watch. "And you think I'm a soft touch?"

"You always have been in the past."

"Forget it."

"His name's Blanchard's Run."

"I said forget it." He had time for maybe four hours of sleep before he had to get to the airport and preflight the jet.

"But—" Stephanie suddenly stopped, blinking in surprise as she glanced above his head.

"I sent it," came a breathless voice that Royce already easily recognized.

He jerked his head around to confirm it was Amber.

"Sent what?" asked Stephanie.

Amber's jewel-blue eyes were shining with a mixture of trepidation and excitement.

She hadn't.

She wouldn't.

"Where's your father?" asked Royce. Was this another warped joke?

"He left. I told him to send the limo back for me later."

Royce shook his head, refusing to believe any woman would do something that impulsive. "You did not send it."

But Amber nodded, then she glanced furtively around the lounge. "I figure I have about ten minutes to get out of here."

"What did you send?" Stephanie demanded. "To *who?*"

Amber slipped into the vacant third seat between them and leaned forward, lowering her voice. "I broke off my engagement."

Stephanie looked both shocked and excited. She reached for Amber's hand and squeezed it. "With *who?*"

"Hargrove Alston."

"The guy who's going to run for the Senate?"

Royce stared at his sister in astonishment.

"I read it in *People,*" she told him with a dismissive wave of her hand. Then she turned her attention back to Amber. "Is he mad? Is he after you now?"

"He's in Switzerland."

"Then you're safe."

"Not for long. As soon as Hargrove reads my text, he'll call my dad, and my dad will turn the limo around."

Stephanie's lips pursed into an O of concern, and her breath whooshed out.

Amber nodded her agreement, and both women turned expectantly to Royce.

"What?"

"We have to go," said Stephanie, her expression hinting that he was a little slow on the uptake.

"To Montana," Amber elaborated.

"Now," said Stephanie with a nod of urgency.

"They'll never think to look for me in Montana," Amber elaborated.

"I'm not taking you to—"

But Stephanie jumped up from her chair. "To the airport," she declared in a ridiculously dramatic tone.

"Right." Amber nodded, rising, as well, smoothing her sexy dress over her hips as she stood on her high heels.

"Stop," Royce demanded, and even the laughing women at the table next to them stopped talking and glanced over.

"Shh," Stephanie hissed.

Royce lowered his voice. "We are *not* rushing off to the airport like a bunch of criminals."

Stephanie planted both hands on the tabletop. "And why not?"

"Six minutes," Amber helpfully informed them.

He shot her a look of frustration. "Don't be such a wimp. If he yells at you, he yells at you."

Amber's brows rose. "I'm not afraid he'll yell at me."

"Then, what's the problem?"

"I'm afraid he'll talk me out of it."

"That's ridiculous. You're a grown woman. It's your life."

"It is," Amber agreed. "And I want to come to Montana."

The look she gave him was frank and very adult. Perhaps his first instinct had been right. Maybe there was something between them. Maybe he was the reason she'd made the decision to finally dump the loser fiancé and move on.

He felt a rush of pride, a hit of testosterone and, quite frankly, the throb of arousal. Having Amber around would definitely make Montana more palatable. Only a fool would put barriers in her way.

He stood and tossed a couple of twenties on the table. "The airport, then."

Since he'd had the martinis, it would be a few hours before he could fly. But there was plenty to do in preparation.

By the time they arrived at the Ryder Ranch, Amber had had second, third, even fourth thoughts. Both her father and Hargrove were powerful men. Neither of them took kindly to opposition, and she'd never done anything remotely rebellious in her life.

Hargrove was probably on a plane right now, heading back to Chicago, intending to find her and demand to know what she was *thinking.* And her father was likely out interrogating her friends this morning, determined to find out what had happened and where she'd gone.

Katie would be flabbergasted.

Amber had been questioning her feelings for Hargrove for a couple of months now, but she hadn't shared those fears with Katie. Because, although Katie was a logical and grounded lawyer, she was saddled with an emotional case of hero worship when it came to Hargrove. She thought the sun rose and set on the man. She'd never understand.

Amber had sent her father a final text last night from the airport, assuring him that he didn't need to worry, that she needed some time alone and that she'd be in contact soon. Then she'd turned off her cell phone. She'd seen enough crime dramas to know there were ways to trace the signal. And Hargrove had friends in both high and low places. Where the police couldn't accommodate him, private investigators on the South Side would be happy to wade in.

The sun was emerging from behind the eastern mountains as Amber, Royce and Stephanie crossed the wide porch of the Ryder ranch house. She was dead tired but determined to keep anyone from seeing her mounting worry.

In the rising light of day, she admitted to herself that this had been a colossally stupid plan. Her father and Hargrove weren't going to sit quietly and wait while she worked through her emotions. Plus, she had nothing with her but a pair of high heels, her cocktail dress and a ruby-and-diamond, drop necklace with a set of matching earrings.

And of all the nights to go with a tiny pair of high-cut, sheer panties—sure, they smoothed the line of her dress, but that was their only virtue.

"You heading home?" Royce asked his sister as he tossed a small duffel bag onto the polished hardwood floor, against the wall of a spacious foyer.

"Home," Stephanie echoed, clicking the wide double

doors shut behind her. "I can grab a couple hours' sleep before class starts."

Amber turned to glance quizzically at Stephanie. "Home?" She'd assumed they were already there. The sign on the gate two miles back had clearly stated Ryder Ranch.

"Up to my place." Stephanie pointed. "I've got students arriving this afternoon."

"You don't live here?" Amber kept her voice even, but the thought was unsettling. Sure, Royce was the brother of her father's business associate, but he was still a stranger, and there was safety in numbers.

Stephanie was shaking her head. "They kicked me out years ago."

"When your horses took over the entire yard." Royce loosened his tie and moved out of the foyer. He'd changed out of his tux at the airport in favor of a short-sleeved, white uniform shirt and a pair of navy slacks.

Stephanie made to follow him into a massive, rectangular living room with a two-story, open, timber-beamed ceiling and a bank of glass doors at the far end, flanking a stone fireplace. Amber moved with her, taking in a large, patterned red rug, cream and gold, overstuffed furniture groupings and a huge, round, Western-style chandelier suspended in the center of the room.

"You want me to show Amber a bedroom?" asked Stephanie. She was still wearing her bridesmaid dress.

"She's probably hungry," Royce pointed out, and both looked expectantly at Amber.

"I'm...uh..." The magnitude of her actions suddenly hit Amber. She was standing in a stranger's house, completely dependent on him for food, shelter, even clothes. She was many miles from the nearest town, and every normal support system—her cell phone, credit card and chauffeur—were unavailable to her, since they could be traced.

"Exhausted," Stephanie finished for her, linking an arm with Amber's. "Let's get you upstairs." She gently propelled Amber toward a wide, wooden staircase.

"Good night, then," Royce called from behind them.

"You look shell-shocked," Stephanie whispered in her ear as they mounted the staircase.

"I'm questioning my sanity," Amber admitted as the stairs turned right and walls closed in around them.

Stephanie hit a light switch, revealing a half-octagonal landing, with four doors leading off in separate directions.

"You're not insane," said Stephanie, opening one of the middle doors.

"I just abandoned my fiancé and flew off in the middle of the night with strangers."

"We're not that strange." Stephanie led the way into an airy room that fanned out to a slightly triangular shape.

It had a queen-size, four-poster brass bed, with a blue-and-white-checked comforter that looked decadently soft. Two royal blue armchairs were arranged next to a paned-glass balcony door. White doors led to a walk-in closet and an ensuite bath, while a ceiling fan spun lazily overhead and a cream-colored carpet cushioned Amber's feet.

Stephanie clicked on one of two ceramic bedside lamps. "Or do you think you're insane to leave the fiancé?"

"He's not going to be happy," Amber admitted.

"Does he, like, turn all purple and yell and stuff?" Stephanie looked intrigued and rather excited by the prospect.

Amber couldn't help but smile. "No. He gets all stuffy and logical and superior."

Hargrove would never yell. He'd make Amber feel as though she was a fool, as though her opinions and emotions weren't valid, as though she was behaving like a spoiled child. And maybe she was. But at least she was out of his reach for a little while.

"I hear you." Stephanie opened the double doors of a tall, cherrywood armoire, revealing a set of shelves. "My brothers are like that."

"Royce?" Amber found herself asking. In their admittedly short conversation Royce hadn't seemed at all like Hargrove.

"And Jared," said Stephanie. "They think I'm still ten years old. I'm a full partner in Ryder International, but I have to come to them for every little decision."

"That must be frustrating." Amber sympathized. She had some autonomy with her own credit cards and signing authority on her trust fund. She'd never really thought about independence beyond that.

Well, until now.

"There's this stallion," said Stephanie, selecting something in white cotton from the shelves. "Blanchard's Run, out of Westmont Stables in London. He's perfect for my breeding program. His dam was Ogilvie and his sire Danny Day." She shook her head. "All I need is a million dollars." She handed Amber what turned out to be a cotton nightgown.

"For one horse?" The price sounded pretty high.

"That's mine," said Stephanie, nodding to the gown.

"You should help yourself to anything else in the dresser. There's jeans, shirts, a bunch of stuff that should fit you."

"If it's any consolation," said Amber, putting her hand on Stephanie's arm, "I can't see Hargrove ever letting me spend a million dollars, either."

"And *that's* why you should leave him."

"I'm leaving him—" Amber paused a beat, debating saying the words out loud for the first time "—because I don't love him."

Stephanie's lips formed another silent O. She nodded slowly for a long moment. "Good reason."

Amber agreed.

But she knew her parents would never accept it. And it wasn't because they had some old-fashioned idea about the value of arranged marriages or about love being less important than a person's pedigree. It was because they didn't trust Amber to recognize love one way or the other.

And that was why Amber couldn't go home yet. Nobody would listen to her. They'd all gang up, and she'd find herself railroaded down the aisle.

As usual, it was frighteningly easy for Royce to slip back into the cowboy life. He'd stretched out on his bed for a couple of hours, then dressed in blue jeans, a cotton shirt and his favorite worn cowboy boots. Sasha had quick-fried him a steak, and produced a big stack of hotcakes with maple syrup. After drinking about a gallon of coffee, he'd hunted down the three foremen who reported directly to McQuestin.

He'd learned the vet had recommended moving the Bowler Valley herd because seasonal flies were impacting the calves. A well had broken down at the north camp and the ponds were drying up. And a lumber shipment was stuck at the railhead in Idaho because of a snafu with the letter of credit. But before he'd had a chance to wade in on any of the issues, an SOS had come over his cell phone from Barry Brewster, Ryder International's Vice President of Finance, for a letter from China's Ministry of Trade Development. The original had gone missing in the Chicago office, but they thought Jared might have left a copy at the ranch.

So Royce was wading through the jumble of papers on the messy desk in the front office of the ranch house, looking for a letter from Foreign Investment Director Cheng Li. Without Cheng Li's approval, a deal between Ryder International and Shanxi Electrical would be canceled, costing a fortune, and putting several Ryder construction projects at risk.

Giving up on the desk, and cursing out his older brother for falling in love and getting married at such an inconvenient time, Royce moved to the file cabinet, pulling open the top drawer. His blunt fingers were awkward against the flimsy paper, and the complex numbering system made no sense to him. What the hell was wrong with using the alphabet?

"The outfit seems at odds with the job duties," a female voice ventured from the office doorway.

He turned to see Amber in a pair of snug jeans and a maroon, sleeveless blouse. Her feet were bare, and her blond hair was damp, framing her face in lush waves. There was an amused smile on her fresh, pretty face.

"You think this is funny?" he asked in exasperation.

"Unexpected," she clarified.

"Well, don't just stand there."

"Should I be doing something?"

He directed her to the desktop. "We're looking for a letter from the Chinese Ministry of Trade and Development."

She immediately moved forward.

"Do you know what it looks like?" she asked, picking up the closest pile of papers.

He grunted. "It's on paper."

"Long letter? Short letter? In an envelope? Attached to a report?"

"I don't know. It's from Cheng Li, Foreign Investment Director. I need his phone number."

She moved on to the next pile, while Royce went back to the filing cabinet.

"Have you tried Google?" she asked.

"This isn't the kind of number you find on the Internet."

She continued sorting. "I take it this is important?"

"If I don't get hold of him today, we're going to blow a deal."

"What time is it in China?"

"Sometime Monday morning. Barry says if the approval's not filed in Beijing by the end of business today, we're toast."

"Their time?" Amber asked.

"Their time," Royce confirmed. "What the hell happened to the alphabet?"

She moved closer, brushing against him. "You want me to—"

"*No,*" he snapped, and she quickly halted.

He clamped his jaw and forced himself to take a breath. It wasn't her fault the letter was lost. And it wasn't her fault that his body had a hair-trigger reaction to her touch. "Sorry. Can you keep looking over there? On the desk?"

"Sure." Her features were schooled, and he couldn't tell if she was upset.

"I didn't mean to shout."

"Not a problem." She turned back.

He opened his mouth again, but then decided the conversation could wait. If she was upset, he'd deal with it later. For now, he had three more drawers to search.

"Something to do with Shanxi Electrical?" she asked.

Royce's head jerked up. "You found it?"

She handed him a single sheet of paper.

He scanned his way down to the signature line and found the number for Cheng Li's office. "This is it." He heaved a sigh, resisting the urge to hug her in gratitude.

Then he took in her rosy cheeks, her jewel-blue eyes, her soft hair and smooth skin. The deep colored blouse molded to her feminine curves, while the skintight blue jeans highlighted a killer figure. There was something completely sexy about her bare feet, and he had to fight hard against the urge to hug her.

"Thanks," he offered gruffly, reaching for the phone.

He punched in the international and area codes, then made his way through the rest of the numbers.

After several rings, a voice answered in Chinese at the other end.

"May I speak with Mr. Cheng Li?" he tried.

The voice spoke Chinese again.

"Cheng Li? Is there someone there who speaks English?"

The next words were incomprehensible. He might have heard the name Cheng Li, but he wasn't sure.

"English?" he asked again.

Amber held out her hand and motioned for him to give her the phone.

He gave her a look of incomprehension while the woman on the other end tried once more to communicate with him.

"I'm sorry," he said into the phone, but then it was summarily whisked from his hand.

"Hey!" But before he could protest further, Amber spoke. The words were distinctly non-English.

Royce drew back in astonishment. "No way."

She spoke again. Then she waited. Then she covered the receiver. "Your phone number?" she whispered.

He quickly flipped open his cell to the display, and she rattled something into the phone. Then she finished the call and hung up. "Cheng Li will call you in an hour with an interpreter."

"You speak *Chinese?*" was all Royce could manage.

She gave a self-deprecating eye roll. "I can make myself understood. But for them, it's kind of like talking to a two-year-old."

"You speak Chinese?" he repeated.

"Mandarin, actually." She paused. "I have a knack." When he didn't say anything, she bridged the silence. "My mother taught me Swedish. And I learned Spanish in school." She shrugged. "So, well, considering the potential political impact of the rising Asian economies, I decided Mandarin and Punjabi were the two I should study at college. I'm really not that good at either of them."

He peered at her. "You're like a politician's dream wife, aren't you?"

Her lips pursed for a moment, and discomfort flickered in her eyes. "Are you saying I have no life?"

"I'm saying he's going to come after you." Royce put a warning in his tone. "I sure as hell wouldn't let you get away."

She blinked, and humor came back into her blue eyes. "I doubt I'd make it very far from here. After all, there is only one road out of the ranch."

Royce wasn't in the mood to joke. "He *is* going to come after you, isn't he?"

She sobered. "I don't think he'll find me."

"And if he does?"

She didn't answer.

"What's the guy got on you?"

From what Royce could see, Amber was an intelligent, capable woman. There was no reason in the world for her to let herself get saddled with a man she didn't want.

"Same thing Jared has on you," she answered softly. "Duty, obligation, guilt."

"Jared needs me for a month," said Royce, not buying into the parallel. "What's-his-name—"

"Hargrove."

"Hargrove wants you forever." Royce felt a sudden spurt of anger. "And where the hell are your parents in all this? Have you told them?"

"They think he's perfect for me."

"He's not."

Amber smiled. "You've never even met him."

"I don't have to. You're here. He's there." Royce ran

his brain through the circumstances one more time. "Your cell's turned off, right?"

She nodded.

"Don't use your credit cards."

"I didn't bring them."

"Good."

"Not really." She hesitated. "Royce, I have no money whatsoever."

"You don't need money."

"And I have no clothes, not even underwear."

Okay, that gave him an unwanted visual. "We have everything you need right here."

"I can't live off your charity."

"You're our guest."

"I forced you to bring me here."

Royce set the letter back down on the desktop and tucked his phone back into his shirt pocket. "Ask anybody, Amber. I don't do anything I don't want to do." He let his gaze shade the meaning of the words. He'd brought her home with him because she was a beautiful and interesting woman. It was absolutely no hardship having her around.

"I need to earn my keep."

Royce resisted the temptation to make a joke about paying her way by sleeping with him. It was in poor taste, and the last thing he wanted to do was insult her. Besides, the two were completely unrelated.

He hoped she was attracted to him. What red-blooded man wouldn't? And last night he had been fairly certain she was attracted to him. But whatever was between them would take its own course.

Her gaze strayed to the messy desk. "I could…"

He followed the look.

"…maybe straighten things up a little? I've taken business management courses, some accounting—"

"No argument from me." Royce held up his palms in surrender. "McQuestin's niece, Maddy, usually helps out in the office, but she's gone back to Texas with him while he recovers." He spread his arms in welcome. "Make yourself at home."

Three

Several hours later, eyes grainy from reading ranch paperwork, Amber wandered out of the office. The office door opened into a short hallway that connected to the front foyer and then to the rest of the ranch house. It had grown dark while she worked, and soft lamplight greeted her in the empty living room. The August night was cool, with pale curtains billowing in the side windows, while screen doors separated the room from the veranda beyond.

Muted noise came from the direction of the kitchen, and she caught a movement on the veranda. Moving closer, she realized it was a plump puff ball of a black-and-white puppy. Amber smiled in reaction as another pup appeared, and then a third and a fourth.

They hadn't seen her yet, and the screen door kept them locked outside. Just as well. They were cute, but

Amber was a little intimidated by animals. She'd never had a pet before. Her mother didn't like the noise, the mess or the smell.

Truth was, she dropped out of dressage riding lessons because one of the horses had bit her on the shoulder. She hadn't told the grooms, or her parents, or anybody else about the incident. She was embarrassed, convinced that she'd done something to annoy the horse but not sure of what it might have been. When a creature couldn't talk or communicate, how did you know what they wanted or needed?

The pups disappeared from view, and she moved closer to the door, peeking at an angle to see them milling in a small herd around Royce's feet while he sat in a deep, wooden Adirondack chair, reading some kind of report under the half-dozen outdoor lamps that shone around the veranda.

Then the pups spotted her and made a roly-poly beeline for the door, sixteen paws thumping awkwardly on the wooden slats of the deck. She took an automatic step back as they piled up against the screen.

Royce glanced up from the papers. "Hey, Amber." Then his attention went to the puppies. He gave a low whistle, and they scampered back to him.

"It's safe to come out now," he said with a warm smile.

"I'm not…" She eased the door open. "I'm not scared to come out."

Royce laughed. "Didn't think you were. Shut the screen behind you, though, or these guys will be in the kitchen in a heartbeat."

She closed the screen door behind her. "Your puppies?"

He reached down to scratch between the ears of the full-grown border collie sprawled between the chair and the railing. "They belong to Molly. Care to take one home when you leave?"

"My mother won't have pets in the house." The puppies rushed back to Amber again.

Royce gestured for her to take the chair across from his. "Is she allergic?"

"Not exactly." Warm, fuzzy bodies pressed against her leg; cool, wet noses investigated her bare feet and she felt a mushy tongue across the top of her toes. She struggled not to cringe at the slimy sensation. "She doesn't want any accidents on the Persian rug."

"The price you pay," said Royce.

Amber settled into the chair. One of the pups put its paws on her knee, lifting up to sniff along her jeans.

"Most people pet them." Royce's tone was wry.

"I'm a little…" She gingerly scratched the puppy between its floppy, little ears. Its fur was soft, skin warm, and its dark eyes were adorable.

"It's okay," he said. "Not everybody likes animals."

"I don't dislike them."

"I can tell."

"They make me a little nervous, okay?"

"They're puppies, not mountain lions."

"They—" Another warm tongue swiped across her bare toes, and she jerked her feet under the chair. "Tickle," she finished.

"Princess," he mocked her.

"I was once bitten by a horse," she defended. Her interactions with animals hadn't been particularly positive so far.

"I was once gored by a bull," he countered with a challenging look.

"Is this going to be a contest?"

"Kicked in the head." He leaned forward and parted his short, dark hair.

She couldn't see a scar, but she trusted it was there.

"By a bronc," he finished. "In a local rodeo at fourteen."

Amber lifted her elbow to show a small scar. "Fell off a top bunk. At camp. I was *thirteen*."

"Did you break it?"

"Sprained."

"What kind of camp?"

"Violin."

His grin went wide. "Oh, my. Such a dangerous life. Did you ever break a nail? Get a bad wax job?"

"Hey, buddy." She jabbed her finger in the direction of his chest. "*After* your first wax job, we can talk."

Devilment glowed in his deep blue eyes. "You can wax anything I've got," he drawled. "Any ol' time you want."

Her stomach contracted, and a wave of unexpected heat prickled her skin. How had the conversation taken that particular turn? She sat up straight and folded her hands primly in her lap. "That's not what I meant."

He paused, gaze going soft. "That's too bad."

The puppies had grown bored with her feet, and one by one, they'd wandered back to Royce. They were now curled in a sleeping heap around his chair. The dog, Molly, yawned while insects made dancing shadows in the veranda lights.

"You hungry?" asked Royce.

Amber nodded. She was starving, and she was more than happy to let their discussion die.

He flipped the report closed, and she was reminded of their earlier office work.

"Did you talk to Cheng Li?"

"I did," said Royce. "He promised to fax the paperwork to the Ryder financial office."

"In Chicago."

"Yes." He rose cautiously to his feet, stepping around the sleeping puppies. "Disaster averted. Sasha'll have soup on the stove."

"Soup sounds great." It was nearly nine, and Amber hadn't eaten anything since their light snack on the plane around 5:00 a.m. Any kind of food sounded terrific to her right now.

They left the border collies asleep on the deck and filed through the living room, down a hallway to the kitchen on the south side of the house.

"Have you talked to your parents?" asked Royce as he set a pair of blue-glazed, stoneware bowls out on the breakfast bar.

The counters were granite, the cabinets dark cherry. There were stainless steel appliances with cheery, yellow walls and ceiling reflecting off the polished beams and natural wood floor. A trio of spotlights was suspended above the bar, complementing the glow of the pot lights around the perimeter of the ceiling.

"I texted them both before I got on the plane."

"Nothing since then?" He set a basket of grainy buns on the breakfast bar, and she slipped onto one of the high, padded, hunter-green leather chairs.

She shook her head. "I don't know how this GPS and triangulating-the-cell-towers thing works."

Royce's brows went up, and he paused in his work.

"Crime dramas," she explained. "I don't know how much of all that is fiction. My dad, and Hargrove for sure, will pull out all the stops."

Royce held out his hand. "Let me see your phone."

She pulled back on the stool and dug the little phone out of the pocket of her blue jeans.

He slid it open and pressed the on button.

"Are you sure—"

"I won't leave it on long." He peered at the tiny screen. "Nope. No GPS function." He shut it off and tossed it back to her. "Though they could, theoretically, triangulate while you're talking, but you're probably safe to text."

"Really?" That was good news. She'd like to send another message to her mother. And Katie deserved an explanation.

He set out two small plates and spoons while she tucked the phone back into her pocket. She'd have to think about how to phrase her explanation.

Royce ladled the steaming soup into the bowls and set them back on the bar, taking the stool at the end.

"Thanks," she breathed, inhaling the delectable aroma.

Royce lifted his spoon. "So, how long have you known?"

She followed suit, dipping into the rich broth. "Known what?"

"That you didn't love him?"

Royce knew his question was blunt to the point of rudeness, but if he was going to make a play for Amber, he needed to know the lay of the land. He knew he'd be a temporary, rebound fling, which was not even remotely a problem for him. In fact, he'd gone into the situation *planning* to be her temporary, rebound fling. She wasn't going to stay the whole month. She probably wouldn't even last a week. But he was up for it, however long it lasted.

Last night, he'd known Amber was beautiful. Today, he'd learned she was positively fascinating. She was intelligent, poised and personable, and she could actually speak Chinese. Her reaction to the puppies was cute and endearing. While her fiancé's and family's ability to intimidate her made him curious.

Why would such an accomplished woman give a rat's hind end what anybody thought of her decisions?

She stirred her spoon thoughtfully through the bowl of soup. "It's not so much…" she began.

He waited.

She looked up. "It's not that I knew I didn't love him. It's more that I didn't know that I did. You know?"

Royce hadn't the slightest idea what she meant, and he shook his head.

"It seems to me," she said, cocking her head sideways, teeth raking momentarily over her full bottom lip, "if you're going to say 'till death do us part' you'd better be damn sure."

Royce couldn't disagree with that. His parents obviously hadn't been damn sure. At least his mother wasn't. His father, on the other hand, had to have been devastated by her betrayal.

Amber was right to break it off. She had absolutely no business marrying a man she didn't love unreservedly.

"You'd better be damn sure," Royce echoed, fighting a feeling of annoyance with her for even considering marrying a man she didn't love. This Hargrove person might be a jerk. So far, he sounded like a jerk. But no man deserved a disloyal wife.

Amber nodded as she swallowed a spoonful of the soup. "Melissa looked sure."

"Melissa *was* sure."

Amber blinked at the edge to Royce's tone. "What?"

"Nothing." He tore a bun in half.

"You annoyed?"

He shook his head.

"Melissa and Jared seem really good together."

"You do know it's kinder to break it off up front with a guy." Royce set down his spoon.

"I—"

"Because, if you don't, the next thing you know, you'll have two or three kids, the PTA and carpool duty. You'll get bored. You'll start looking around. And you'll end up at the No-Tell Motel on Route 55, in bed with some young drifter. And Hargrove, whoever-he-is, will be going for his gun."

"Whoa." Amber's eyes were wide in the stark kitchen light. "You just did my whole life in thirty seconds."

"I didn't necessarily mean you."

"What? Are we talking about Melissa?"

"No." Royce gave himself a mental shake. "We are absolutely not talking about Melissa."

"Then who—"

"Nobody. Forget it." He drew a breath. So much for making a play for her. It wouldn't be tonight. That was for sure. "I just don't understand why you're feeling guilty," he continued. "You are absolutely doing the right thing."

"I believe that," she agreed.

He held her gaze with a frank stare. "And anybody who tries to talk you out of it is shortsighted and just plain stupid."

"You know you're talking about my father."

"I know."

"He's Chairman of the City Accountants Association, and he owns a multimillion-dollar financial consortium."

"Pure blind luck, obviously."

A small smile crept out, though she clearly fought against it. "The No-Tell Motel?"

"Metaphorically speaking. I'm sure you'd pick the Ritz."

"I've never been unfaithful."

Royce knew he should apologize.

"I've dated Hargrove since I was eighteen, and even though he's not the greatest—" She snapped her mouth shut, and a flush rose in her cheeks as she reached for one of the homemade buns.

Okay, this was interesting. "Not the greatest what?"

"Nothing."

"You're blushing."

"No, I'm not." She tore into the bun.

Royce grinned. "Were you going to say *lover?*"

"No." But everything in her body language told him she was lying.

He gazed at her profile for a long minute.

Eighteen. She was eighteen when she took up with Hargrove. Royce could be wrong, but he didn't think he was. Amber hadn't had any other lovers. She was dissatisfied with Hargrove, but she had no comparison.

Interesting. He chewed a hunk of his own bun.

A woman deserved at least one comparison.

"What did you find?" Royce's voice from the office doorway interrupted Amber's long day of office work.

The sun was descending toward the rugged mountains, while neat piles of bills and correspondence had slowly grown out of the chaos on the desktop in front of her.

Now she stretched her arm out to place a letter on the farthest pile. It was another advertisement for horse tack. She was fairly sure the junk mail could be tossed out, but she wasn't about to make that decision on her own.

"You've got some overdue bills," she answered Royce, twisting her head to see him lounging in the doorway, one broad shoulder propped against the doorjamb, his hair mussed and sweaty across his forehead and a streak of dirt marring his roughened chin. She met his deep blue gaze, and a surge of longing clenched her chest.

"Pay them," he suggested in a sexy rumble, crossing his arms over his chest.

"You going to hand over your platinum card?"

His lips parted in a grin. "Sure."

"Then you better have a high limit. Some of them are six figures." Feed, lumber, vet bills. The list went on and on.

He eased away from the door frame and ambled toward her. "There must be a checkbook around here somewhere."

"I didn't see one." Not that she'd combed through the desk drawers. There was plenty to do sorting through what was piled on top. "How long did you say McQuestin had been off?"

"Three weeks. Why?"

"Some of these bills are two months old. That's hell on your credit rating, you know."

He moved closer, and she forced herself to drag her gaze from his rangy body.

To distract herself, she lifted the closest unopened envelope and sliced through the seam with the ivory-handled opener, extracting another folded invoice. The distraction didn't help. Her nostrils picked up his fresh, outdoorsy scent, and his arm brushed her shoulder, sending an electric current over her skin as he slid open a top desk drawer.

Lifting several items out of the way, he quickly produced a narrow, leather-bound booklet and tossed it on the desk. "Here you go. Start protecting my credit rating."

"Like the bank would honor my signature." She knew she should shift away, but something magnetic kept her sitting right where she was, next to his narrow hip and strong thigh. She didn't even care that his jeans were dusty.

Not that it would matter if anything rubbed off. She was dressed in a plain, khaki T-shirt and a pair of faded jeans she'd borrowed from Stephanie's cache in the upstairs bedroom. She could press herself against Royce from head to toe, and simply clean up later with soap and water.

The idea was far too appealing. She felt heat flare in the pit of her stomach as an image bloomed in her mind.

"I'll sign a bunch for you." His voice interrupted her burgeoning fantasy as he flipped open the checkbook.

She blinked herself back to reality. "I assume you're joking."

"Why would I be joking?" He leaned over, hunting through the drawer again, bringing himself into even closer contact with her.

She shifted imperceptibly in his direction, and his cotton-clad arm brushed her bare one. She sucked in a tight breath.

He retrieved a pen.

She suddenly realized he was serious, and placed her hand over the top check. "You can't do that."

He turned, pen poised, bringing their faces into close proximity. "Why not?"

"Because I could write myself a check, a *very big* check, and then cash it."

He rolled his eyes

"Don't give me that 'shucks ma'am' expression—"

"'Shucks, ma'am'?"

"You didn't just wander in off the back forty. You know I could drain your account."

"Would you?"

"I *could*," she stressed. Theoretically, of course.

He twirled the pen over two fingers until it settled into his palm. "And then what?"

"And then I disappear. Tahiti, Grand Cayman."

"I'd find you."

"So what?" She shrugged. "What could you do? The money would already be in a Swiss bank account."

He braced one hand against the desk and moved the other to the back of her chair, bending slightly over. "Then I'd ask you, politely, for the number."

She was blocked by the V of his arms. It was

unnerving, but also exciting. He emanated strength, power and raw virility.

"And if I refuse to tell you?" she challenged, voice growing breathy.

"I'd stop being polite."

"What? You'd threaten to break my legs?"

He smiled and leaned closer. Self-preservation told her to shrink away, but the chair back kept her in place. His sweet breath puffed against her skin. "Violence? I don't think so. But there are other ways to be persuasive."

She struggled for a tone of disbelief. "What? You kiss me and I swoon?"

His grin widened. "Maybe. Let's try it."

And before she could react, he'd swooped in toward her. She gasped as his smooth lips settled on hers. They were warm and firm, and incredibly hot, as the contact instantly escalated to a serious kiss.

It took her only seconds to realize how much she'd longed for his taste. His scent filled her, and his hands settled on her sides, surrounding her rib cage as he deepened the kiss. Her head tipped back, and her mouth responded to his pressure by opening, allowing him access, drinking in the sensation of his intimate touch.

She clutched his upper arms, steadying herself against his hard, taut muscles. He flexed under her touch, and she imagined she could feel the blood coursing through his body. She could definitely feel the blood coursing through her own. It heated her core, flushed her skin and made her tingle from the roots of her hair to the tips of her toes.

His hands convulsed against her body, thumbs tightening beneath her breasts. Her nipples hardened almost painfully as arousal thumped its way to the apex of her thighs. She gave him her tongue, answering his own erotic invitation. A river of sound roared in her ears as he drew her to her feet, engulfing her, pressing her against his hard body.

His touch was unique, yet achingly familiar, as if she'd been waiting for this moment her entire life. Her palms slid across his shoulders, around his neck, stroking the slick sweat of his hairline as their kiss pulsed endlessly between them.

His hands slipped to her buttocks, pulling her against the cradle of his thighs, demonstrating the depth of his arousal and shocking her back to her senses.

She jerked away, hands pressing against his chest, putting a barrier between them. He leaned in, trying to capture her mouth.

"I can't," she gasped.

He froze.

"I'm…uh…" She wasn't exactly sorry. That had definitely been the best kiss of her life. But she couldn't take things any further. They barely knew each other. She'd only just left Hargrove. And she hadn't come to Montana for casual sex.

"Something wrong?" he asked.

She tried to take a step back, but the damn chair still blocked her way. "This is too fast," she explained, struggling to bring both her breathing and her pulse rate back under control.

He heaved an exasperated sigh. "It was a kiss, Amber."

But they both knew it was more than a kiss. Then, to her mortification, her gaze reflexively flicked below his waistline.

He gave a knowing chuckle, and she wished the floor would swallow her whole.

"Are you blushing?" he asked.

"No." But she couldn't look him in the eyes.

"You seemed a whole lot more sophisticated when we met in the lounge," he ventured.

She couldn't interpret his flat tone, so she braved a glance at his expression. Was he annoyed?

He looked annoyed.

She hadn't intended to lead him on. Nor had she meant for the kiss to spiral out of control.

Surely he could understand that.

Or was he always so quick to leap to expectations?

Then, an unsettling thought hit her. What if Royce hadn't leaped to expectations in the past two minutes? What if his expectations had been there since their meeting in the lounge?

Had she been hopelessly naive? Did he consider her a one- or two-night stand?

"Is *that* why you brought me here?" she asked, watching closely, giving him the chance to deny it.

"Depends," he said, cocking his head and giving her a considering look. "On what you mean by *that*."

"Because you thought I'd sleep with you?"

"It had crossed my mind," he admitted.

Her embarrassment turned to anger. "Seriously?"

He sighed. "Amber—"

"You are the most egotistical, opportunistic—"

"Hey, you were the one who was dressed to kill and insisted on 'taking a ride in my jet plane.'"

"That *wasn't* a euphemism for sex."

"Really?" He looked genuinely surprised. "It usually is."

Amber compressed her lips. How had she been so naive? How could she have been so incredibly foolish? Royce wasn't some knight in shining armor. He was a charming, wealthy, well-groomed pickup artist.

Her distaste was replaced again by embarrassment. She'd proposed paying her way here by doing office work. He'd had a completely different line of work in mind.

She pushed the wheeled chair aside and moved to go around him. "I think I'd better leave."

She'd have to call her parents to rescue her, head back to Chicago with her tail between her legs, maybe even reconsider her relationship with Hargrove, since, as the three of them so often told her, she was naive in the ways of the real world.

At least with Hargrove, she knew where she stood.

"Why?" Royce asked, putting a hand on her arm to stop her.

She glanced at his hand, and he immediately let go.

"There's obviously been a misunderstanding." She'd hang out in the upstairs bedroom until a car could come for her. Then she'd head back to the airport, home to her parents' mansion and back to her real life.

This had been a crazy idea from beginning to end.

"Clearly," said Royce, his jaw tight.

She moved toward the door.

Royce's voice followed her. "Running back to Mommy and Daddy?"

Her spine straightened. "None of your business."

"What's changed?" he challenged.

She reached for the doorknob.

"What's changed, Amber?" he repeated.

She paused. Then she turned to confront him. No

point in beating around the bush. "I thought I was a houseguest. You thought I was a call girl."

A grin quirked one corner of his mouth, and her anger flared anew.

"Are you always this melodramatic?" he asked.

"Shut up."

He shook his head and took a couple of steps toward her. "I meant what's changed on your home front?"

"Nothing," she admitted, except it had occurred to her that her parents might be right. She had been protected from the real world for most of her life. Maybe she wasn't in a position to judge human nature. They'd always insisted Hargrove was the perfect man for her, and they could very well be right.

"So, why go back?" Royce pressed.

"Where else would I go?" She could sneak off to some other part of the country, but her father would track her down as soon as she accessed her bank account. Besides, the longer she stayed away, the more awkward the reunion.

Royce took another step forward. "You don't have to leave."

She scoffed out a dry laugh.

"I never thought you were a call girl."

"You thought I was a barroom pickup."

"True enough," he agreed. "But only because it's happened so many times before."

"You're *bragging?*"

"Just stating the facts."

She scoffed at his colossal ego.

"You're welcome to stay as a houseguest." He sounded sincere.

"Are you kidding?" She couldn't imagine anything

more uncomfortable. He'd been planning to sleep with her. And for a few seconds there, well, sleeping with Royce hadn't seemed like such a bad idea. And he must have known it. She was sure he'd known it.

Their gazes held.

"I can control myself if you can," he told her.

"There's nothing for me to control," she insisted.

He let her lie slide. "Good. Then it's settled."

"Nothing is—"

He nodded toward the desk. "You organize my office and pay my bills, and I'll keep my hands to myself." He paused. "Unless, of course, you change your mind about my hands."

"I'm not going to—"

He held up a hand to silence her. "Let's not make any promises we're going to regret."

She let her glare do the talking, but a little voice inside her acknowledged he was right. She didn't plan to change her mind. But for a few minutes there, it had been easy enough to imagine his hands all over her body.

Four

Royce felt the burn in his shoulder muscles as he hefted another stack of two-by-fours from the flatbed to a waiting pickup truck. The two ranch hands assigned to the task had greeted him with obvious curiosity when he joined the work crew. Hauling lumber in the dark, with the smell of rain in the air, was hardly a choice assignment.

But Royce needed to work the frustration out of his system somehow. How had he so completely misjudged Amber's signals? He could have sworn she was as into him as he was her.

He slid the heavy stack across the dropped tailgate and shifted it to the front of the box, admitting that he'd deluded himself the past few months in the hotel fitness rooms. High-tech exercise equipment was no match for the sweat of real work.

"Something wrong?" came Stephanie's voice as she appeared beside him in the pool of the yard light. She tugged a pair of leather work gloves from the back pocket of her jeans. "You looked ticked off."

"Nothing's wrong," Royce denied, turning on the dirt track to retrace his steps to the flatbed, passing the two hands who were on the opposite cycle. "Where'd you come from?"

Stephanie slipped her hands into the gloves, lifting two boards to Royce's five, balancing them on her right shoulder. "I drove down to join you for dinner. I wanted to see how Amber was doing."

"She's fine.

"She inside?"

He shrugged. "I assume so."

"You have a fight?"

"No. We didn't have a fight." An argument, maybe. In fact, it was more of a misunderstanding. And it was none of his sister's damn business.

"Something wrong with Bar—"

"No!" Royce practically shouted. Wait a minute. His sister might have changed topics. He forced himself to calm down. "What?"

"With Barry Brewster," she enunciated. "Our VP of finance? I talked to him earlier, and he sounded weird."

Royce slid his load into the pickup then lifted the boards from Stephanie's shoulder and placed them in the box. "Weird how?"

It was Stephanie's turn to shrug. "He yelled at me."

Royce's brow went up. "He *what?*"

They stepped out of the way of the two hands each carrying a load of lumber.

Stephanie lowered her voice. "With Jared gone. Well, Blanchard's Sun, an offspring of Blanchard's Run, took silver at Dannyville Downs, and—"

"*S-o-n* son?" Royce asked.

"*S-u-n.* It's a mare."

"You don't think that will get confusing?"

Stephanie frowned at him. "I didn't name her."

"Still—"

"Try to stay on topic."

"Right."

The temperature dropped a few degrees. The wind picked up, and ozone snapped in the air. Royce went back to work, knowing the rain wasn't far off.

Stephanie followed. "Blanchard's Run is proving to be an incredible sire. With every week that passes, his price will go up. So I called Barry to talk about moving some funds to the stable account."

"Did you really expect him to hand over a million?"

"Sure." She paused, sucking in a breath as she hefted some more lumber. "Maybe. Okay, it was a long shot. But that's not my point."

"What is your point?"

The first, fat raindrops clanked on the truck's roof, and one of the hands retrieved an orange tarp from the shed. Royce increased his pace to settle the last of the lumber on the pickup, then accepted the large square of plastic.

"You two get the flatbed," he instructed, motioning for Stephanie to move to the other side of the pickup box.

"My point," Stephanie called over the clatter from

the tarp under the increasing rain, "is Barry's reaction. He went off on me about cash flow and interest rates."

"Over a million dollars?" Royce threaded a nylon rope through the corner grommet of the tarp and looped it around the tie-down on the running board. It was a lot to pay for a horse, sure. But there weren't enough zeros in the equation to raise Barry's blood pressure.

"I felt like a ten-year-old asking for her allowance."

"That's because you behave like a ten-year-old." Royce tossed the rope over the load to his sister.

"It's a great deal," she insisted as lightning cracked the sky above them. "If we don't move now, it'll be gone forever."

"Isn't that what you said about Nare-Do-Elle?"

"That was three years ago."

"He cost us a bundle."

"This is a completely different circumstance. I'm right this time." She tossed the rope back. "You don't think I've learned anything in three years?"

Royce cinched down the tarp. He wasn't touching that question with a ten-foot cattle prod. "What exactly do you want me to do?" he asked instead.

"Talk to Barry."

"And say what?"

"Tell him to give me the money."

Royce grinned.

"I'm serious." The rain had soaked into her curly auburn hair, dampening her cheeks, streaking down her freckled nose.

"You're always serious. You always need money. And half the time you're wrong."

She waggled her leather gloved finger at him. "And half the time I'm *right*."

"So I'll get you half a million."

"And you'll lose out on generations of champion jumpers."

Royce walked the rope around the back of the pickup, tying it off on the fourth corner. "Sorry, Steph."

Her hands went to her hips. "I own a third of this company."

"And I have Jared's power of attorney."

"You two have *always* ganged up on me."

"Now you're sounding like a child."

"I'm—"

"I'm not giving a million dollars to a child."

Her chin tipped up. "You weren't giving it to me anyway."

"True," Royce admitted. He couldn't resist chucking her under that defiant chin. "You've got a perfectly adequate operating budget. Live within your means."

"This is an extraordinary opportunity. I can't begin to tell you—"

"There'll be another one tomorrow. Or next week. Or next month." He'd known his sister far too long to fall for her impassioned plea.

"That's not fair."

"Life never is."

Thunder clapped above them, and the heavens opened up, the deluge soaking everything in sight. The ranch hands ran for the cook shed, and Royce grabbed Stephanie's hand, tugging her over the muddy ground toward the lights of the house.

Amber stood in the vast Ryder living room, rain pounding on the ceiling and clattering against the windows in the waning daylight as she stared at the cell phone in her hand. Royce had been a gentleman about it, but that didn't change the fact that she'd put herself in a predicament and behaved less responsibly than she'd admitted to herself.

She really needed to let someone know where she was staying. She also needed to make sure her parents weren't worrying about her. Her father tended to blow things out of proportion, and there was a real chance he was freeing up cash, waiting for a ransom note.

She pressed the on button with her thumb, deciding she'd keep it short and simple.

"Calling in the cavalry?" came Royce's dry voice.

Amber glanced up to see him and Stephanie in the archway leading from the front foyer.

"Did you hear the thunder?" Stephanie grinned as she stepped forward, stripping off a pair of leather gloves and running spread fingers through her unruly, wet hair.

Amber nodded. The storm had heightened her sense of isolation and disquiet.

"I love storms," Stephanie continued, dropping the gloves on an end table. "As long as I'm inside." She frowned, glancing down at her wet clothes. "I'm going upstairs to find something dry. Is that lasagna I smell?" Her pert nose wrinkled.

Amber inhaled the aromas wafting from the kitchen. "I think so."

"My fav." Stephanie smiled. "See you in a few." She skipped up the stairs.

As he stood there in the doorway, the planes and angles of Royce's face were emphasized by the yellow lamplight reflecting off the wood grain walls.

An hour ago, she'd come to the conclusion that she couldn't really blame him for thinking she was attracted to him. She imagined most women who requested a ride in his plane were coming on to him. Not that she blamed them. His shoulders were broad in his work clothes. His dark, wet hair glimmered, and those deep blue eyes seemed to stare right down into a woman's soul.

"Did you decide to leave after all?" he asked, his deep voice reverberating through her body, igniting a fresh wave of desire.

She shook her head. "I'm just reassuring my parents."

Royce moved into the room with an easy, rolling gait. He struck her as different than the man in the hotel lobby lounge. In just a couple of days, the wilds of Montana had somehow seeped into him.

"Not worried they'll track you down?" His steps slowed as he stopped in front of her, slightly closer than socially acceptable, just a few inches into her personal space, and she felt her heartbeat deepen.

"I'm worried they might be raising the ransom."

Royce quirked a brow. "Seriously?"

"I've never done anything like this before."

"No kidding."

"Royce." She wasn't sure what she was going to say to him, or how she should say it.

But before she could formulate the words, his voice and expression went soft. "I'm sorry."

She shook her head. "No. I'm the one who's sorry. I gave you the wrong impression. It wasn't on purpose, but I realize now that—"

"It was wishful thinking on my part."

"You flat out told me you were hitting on me."

"I was."

She fought a reflexive smile. "And I'm honored." She found herself joking.

"I don't want you to be honored." His expression said the rest.

"I know exactly what you want."

He eased almost imperceptibly closer. "Yes, you do."

They both went silent, sobering. Thunder rumbled overhead, and the moisture-laden air hung heavily in the room.

Stephanie's light footsteps sounded on the landing above.

"You should make that call," said Royce, stepping back.

Amber nodded, struggling to get her hormones under control. She'd never been pursued by such a rawly masculine man. Come to think of it, she'd never been pursued by any man.

Oh, she received her fair share of flirtatious overtures on a girls' night at the clubs, but a flash of her engagement ring easily shut the guys down. Plus, usually she was out with Hargrove. And they generally attended functions where he was known. Nobody was about to hit on Hargrove Alston's fiancée.

While Stephanie skipped down the stairs, Amber pressed the speed-dial button for her mother. It rang only once.

"Sweetheart!" came her mother's voice. "What happened? Are you okay? Are you having a break-down?"

Amber turned away from Royce, crossing the few steps to an alcove where she'd have a little privacy.

"I'm fine," she answered, ignoring the part about a breakdown.

"Your father is beside himself."

Royce's and Stephanie's footfalls faded toward the kitchen.

"And Hargrove," her mother continued. "He came home a day early. Then he nearly missed the Chamber dinner tonight worrying about you. He was the keynote, you know."

"He *nearly* missed it?" asked Amber, finding a hard tone in her voice. Hargrove hadn't, in fact, missed his big speech while his beloved fiancée was missing, perhaps kidnapped, maybe dead.

As soon as the thoughts formed in her mind, she realized she was being unfair. She'd sent a text saying she was fine, and she had expected them to believe her. She wanted Hargrove to carry on with his life.

"The Governor was there," her mother defended.

"I'm glad he went to the dinner," said Amber.

"Where are you? I'll send a car."

"I'm not coming back yet."

"Why not?"

"Didn't Dad tell you?"

"That nonsense about not marrying Hargrove? That's crazy talk, darling. He wowed them last night."

"He didn't wow me." As soon as the words slipped out, Amber clamped her lips shut.

"You weren't there." Her mother either missed or ignored the double entendre.

"I wanted to let you know I'm fine." Amber got back on point.

"Where are you?"

"It doesn't matter."

"Of *course* it matters. We need to get you—"

"Not yet."

"Amber—"

"I'll call again soon." Amber didn't know how long it took to trace a cell phone call, but she suspected she should hurry and hang up.

"What do you expect me to tell your father?"

"Tell him not to worry. I love you both, and I'll call again. Bye, Mom." She quickly disconnected.

A slightly plump, fiftyish woman, who Amber had earlier learned was Sasha, was pulling a large pan of lasagna from the stainless steel oven when Amber entered the kitchen. Stephanie was tossing a salad in a carved wooden bowl on the breakfast bar, while Royce transferred warm rolls into a linen-napkin-lined basket.

For the second time, she was struck by his domesticity. The men she knew didn't help out in the kitchen. Come to think of it, the women she knew didn't, either. And though Amber herself had taken French cooking lessons at her private school, the lessons had centered more on choosing a caterer than hands-on cooking.

"There's a wine cooler around the corner." Stephanie was looking to Amber as she indicated the direction with a toss of her auburn head. "Italian wines are on the third tier, left-hand side."

Royce didn't turn as Amber made her way to a small alcove between the kitchen and the back entryway. The cooler was set in a stone wall, reds in one glass-fronted compartment, whites in the other.

"See if there's a Redigaffi." Royce's voice was so close behind her that it gave her a start.

She took a bracing breath and opened the glass door, turning a couple of bottles on the third shelf so that she could see their labels.

"How'd the call go?" he asked.

"Fine."

There was a silence.

"That's it?" he asked. "Fine?"

"I talked to my mother. She wants me to come home." Amber found the right bottle of wine and slid it out of the holder, straightening and turning to discover Royce was closer than she'd expected. She pushed the glass door closed behind her.

"And?" he asked.

"And what?" She reflexively clutched the bottle.

"Are you going home?"

Though they'd agreed she'd merely be a houseguest, the question seemed loaded with meaning as his eyes thoroughly searched her expression.

"Not yet," she answered.

"Good."

She felt the need to clarify. "It doesn't mean—"

"I meant it's good because you don't love Hargrove, so it would be stupid to go back."

She gave him a short nod.

"Not that the other's gone away," he clarified.

Amber didn't know how to respond to that.

His gaze moved to the bottle. "Did you find one?"

She raised it, and he lifted it from her hands.

"Perfect," he said.

"Move your butts," called Stephanie from the kitchen, and Amber suddenly realized that her world had contracted to the tiny alcove, Royce and her wayward longings.

She gave herself a mental shake, while he took a step back and gestured for her to lead the way into the kitchen.

Stephanie was setting wineglasses at three places at the breakfast bar, while Sasha had disappeared. The Ryder family was a curious mix of informality and luxury. The glasses were fine, blown crystal. The wine was from an exquisite vineyard that Amber recognized. But they were hopping up on high chairs at the breakfast bar to a plain, white casserole pan of simple, beef lasagna.

"Did you talk to your mom?" asked Stephanie as she took the end seat.

Amber took the one around the corner, and Royce settled next to her. He was both too close and too far away. She could almost detect the heat of his body, felt the change in air currents while he moved, and she was overcome with a potent desire to touch him. Of course, touching him was out of the question.

"I talked to her," she told Stephanie.

"What did she say?"

"She wants me to come home and, well, reconcile with Hargrove, of course."

"And?" Stephanie pressed. "What did you tell her?"

"That I wasn't ready." Amber found herself deliberately not looking in Royce's direction as she spoke.

"Good for you," said Stephanie with a vigorous nod. "We girls, we have to stick to our guns. There are too many people in our lives trying to interfere with our decisions." She cast a pointed gaze at her brother.

"Give it a rest," Royce growled at his sister, twisting the corkscrew into the top of the wine. "You're not getting a million dollars."

"You're such a hard-ass."

"And you're a spoiled brat."

"You *are* spending an awful lot for vet supplies and lumber," Amber put in. "Those are the bills I found stacked up on the office desk."

Stephanie blinked at her. "Oh."

Royce popped the cork and reached for Amber's wineglass. "Amber has some questions about the accounts. Who does McQuestin deal with at head office?"

"I think he talks to Norma Braddock sometimes."

Royce handed the wine bottle to his sister then whisked his cell phone from his pocket. "I'll go straight to Barry."

"I'd watch out for him," Stephanie advised, forehead wrinkling.

Royce rolled his eyes at the warning.

Amber decided to stay quiet.

"Barry?" said Royce, while Stephanie handed the salad bowl to Amber.

Amber served herself some of the freshest-looking lettuce and tomatoes she'd ever seen.

"Royce, here."

Then she leaned toward Stephanie and whispered, "From your garden?"

Stephanie nodded, whispering in return. "You'll want to get out of here before canning season."

Amber grinned at the dire intonation.

"Sorry to bother you this late," Royce continued. "We've hired someone on to take care of the office while Jared and McQuestin are away." He gave Amber a wink, and something fluttered in her chest. She quickly picked up her wineglass to cover.

"She has some questions about the bank account. There have been a number of unpaid bills lately." He paused for a moment. "Why don't I let you talk to her directly?"

Amber hadn't expected that. She quickly swallowed and set down the glass. Good thing her questions were straightforward. She tucked her hair out of the way behind her ears, accepting the phone from Royce, ignoring the tingle when his fingers brushed hers.

"Hello?" she opened.

"Who am I speaking to?" asked Barry from the other end of the line.

"This is Amber, I'm—"

"And you're an employee at Ryder Ranch?" he asked directly.

She paused. "Uh, yes. That's right."

"Administrator? Bookkeeper?" There was an unexpected edge to the man's tone.

"Something like that." She gave Royce a confused look, and his eyes narrowed, crinkling slightly at the corners.

"Do you have a pen?" Barry asked, voice going even sharper.

"I—"

"Because you'd better write this down."

Amber glanced around at the countertops. "Just—"

"Sally Nettleton."

"Excuse me?"

"Sally Nettleton is the accounts supervisor. You can speak to her in the morning."

"Sure. Do you happen to have her—"

"And a warning, young lady. Don't you *ever* go above my head to Royce Ryder again."

Amber froze, voice going hollow. "What?"

"Share this conversation with him at your own peril. I don't tolerate insubordination, and he won't always be there to protect you."

Amber's mouth worked but sounds weren't coming out. Nobody had dared speak to her that way in her life.

"You're not the first, and you won't be the last. Don't fool yourself into thinking anything different." He stopped speaking, and the line fairly vibrated with tension.

She didn't know what to say. She had absolutely no idea what to tell this obnoxious man. Imagine if she really was an employee, dependent on her job. It would be horrible.

She heard a click and knew he'd signed off.

"Goodbye," she said weakly for the benefit of Royce and Stephanie.

"Told you he was feeling snarky today," said Stephanie.

"What did he say?" asked Royce. "You okay?"

"She looks a little pale," Stephanie put in.

"I'm fine," said Amber, debating with herself about what to tell Royce as she shut down the phone and handed it back.

"You didn't ask many questions," Royce ventured.

"He gave me a name. Sally Nettleton." She took a breath, framing her words carefully. "He was, well, annoyed that you'd put me in direct touch with him."

Royce frowned.

"He seems to think I broke the chain of command."

"So what?"

"I tell you, something's wrong with that man,"

Stephanie put in, dishing some of the crisp salad onto her plate.

Amber made up her mind, seeing little point in protecting Barry. In fact, she probably owed it to the rest of his staff to tell Royce the truth. "He seems to think I'm your lover."

It was Royce's turn to freeze. "He *said* that?"

"He said he didn't tolerate insubordination, and you won't always be around to protect me. That you'd lose interest."

A ruddy flush crept up Royce's neck, and he reached for his phone.

Amber put her hand over his. "Don't," she advised.

"Why the hell not?"

"Because he'll think you *are* protecting your lover."

"I don't give a rat's ass what—"

"Did I miss something?" asked Stephanie, glancing from one to the other, her tone laced with obvious anticipation and excitement. "Lovers?"

"No," they both shouted simultaneously.

"Too bad." She went back to her salad. "That would be cool."

Amber turned to Stephanie. "That would be tacky. You can't sleep with a man you've barely met." She silently commanded herself to pay close attention to those words.

"Sure you can," Stephanie chirped with a grin.

"No," Royce boomed at her. "You can't."

Stephanie giggled. "Good grief, you're an easy mark. There's nobody around here for me to sleep with anyway."

Some of the fight went out of Royce's posture, but his hand still gripped his phone.

Amber rubbed the tense hand. "Let it go."

"It's a firing offence."

"No, it's not."

"Yes, it is."

"At least give it some thought first." Barry had been a jerk, but she didn't want anyone getting fired on her account. "Maybe ask around. See if this was an isolated incident."

"He was rude to me this morning," said Stephanie.

"You're not helping," Amber warned.

Royce folded his arms across his chest. "It was *my* decision to call him directly. He doesn't get to second-guess me."

"Did you explain the circumstances?"

"I don't have to."

"So, he made an assumption. You can't fire a man for making an assumption."

He pasted her with a sharp look. "You like being spoken to that way."

"Of course not." But she'd like being Royce's lover. Heaven help her, she was pretty sure she'd like being Royce's lover.

Their gazes locked and held for a long moment, and she could have sworn he was reading her mind.

"The lasagna's getting cold," Stephanie pointed out conversationally.

Royce ended the moment with a sharp nod. "We'll talk about it later."

"Sure," Amber agreed, wondering if they were going to talk about Barry or about the energy that crackled between them like lightning.

Five

In Royce's mind, the issue was far from settled.

The storm had passed, leaving a bright moon behind. He closed the office door behind him for privacy, leaving Amber and Stephanie chatting out on the veranda, puppies scampering around them. He, on the other hand, flipped on the bright overhead light and crossed to the leather desk chair, snagging the desk phone and punching in Barry's home number.

It was nearly midnight in Chicago, but he didn't give a damn. Let the man wake up.

"Hello?" came a groggy, masculine voice.

"Barry?"

"Yes."

"It's Royce Ryder."

"Yes?" A shot of energy snapped into Barry's voice. "Anything wrong, Royce?"

There was plenty wrong. "Were you able to give Amber the information she needed?"

A pause. "I believe I did. Sally can cover anything else in the morning."

Royce waited a beat. "When I called you earlier, it wasn't because I wanted her to talk to Sally in the morning." Full stop. More silence.

"Oh. Well... I assumed—"

"Did you or did you not answer Amber's questions?" Royce repeated. And he could almost hear the wheels spinning inside Barry's head.

"I don't think you did," Royce said into the silence. "And the reason I don't think you did is because I was sitting right next to her during the call, and she didn't get a chance to ask you any questions." Once again, he stopped, giving Barry an opportunity to either contribute or sweat.

Hesitation was evident in the man's voice. "Did she... Mmm. Is she there?"

"No. She's not *here*. It's eleven o'clock. The woman's not working at eleven o'clock."

Silence.

"Here's my suggestion," said Royce. "To solve the problem. You hop on a plane in the morning. The corporate jet is unavailable, so you'll have to fly commercial. I'm thinking coach." He picked up an unopened envelope from the desktop and tapped it against the polished oak surface, dropping all pretense of geniality. "You get your ass to the ranch, and you apologize to Ms. Hutton. Then you answer any and all of her questions."

"I... But... Did you say Hutton?"

"David Hutton's daughter. But that couldn't matter less."

"Royce. I'm sorry. I didn't realize—"

"Apologize to *her*."

"Of course."

"You'll be here tomorrow?"

"As soon as I can get there."

Satisfied, Royce disconnected. Amber only needed to be sure funds would be available in the account. But that wasn't the point anymore.

He gazed at the envelope in his hand. It was windowed. From North Pass Feed. Typical bill.

Curious after Amber's concern about his credit rating, he slit it open. Then he glanced through the other piles she'd made, arming himself with some basic information on the ranch expenses.

Half an hour later, he thought he had a picture of the accounts payable situation, so he headed back down the hallway to find Amber and Stephanie in the front foyer.

Stephanie was on her way out the door, and she gave him a quick kiss and a wave before piling into a pickup truck to head for home. As he closed the door behind her, the empty house seemed to hold its breath with anticipation.

Amber looked about as twitchy as he felt.

"You want to talk about Barry?" she asked, moving from the foyer into the great room.

"Taken care of," he answered, following a few paces behind her, letting his gaze trickle from her shoulders to her narrow waist, to her sexy rear end and the shapely thighs that were emphasized by her snug-fitting blue jeans.

She twisted her head. "What do you mean?"

"He'll be here in the morning."

She turned fully then. "I don't understand."

"He's coming by to apologize. And to answer your questions in person."

Her eyes widened in shock, red lips coming open in a way that was past sexy. "You didn't."

"He insisted."

"He did not."

Royce moved closer. "I suspect he understood the stakes."

She tipped her chin. "I don't need somebody to travel a thousand miles to offer me an insincere apology."

"But I do."

She didn't appear to have a comeback for that, and it was all he could do not to lean in for a kiss. She looked as if she wanted one. Her lips were full, eyes wide, body tipped slightly forward. If this was any other woman, at any other time…

But she'd made her position clear.

And he'd respect that.

Unless and until she told him otherwise.

Midday sun streaming through the ranch office window, Amber clicked through the headlines of a national news station on the office computer, reflecting with curiosity that she didn't feel out of touch with the rest of the world. She'd become a bit of a news junkie while finishing her degree, always on the lookout for emerging issues that might impact on her research. Having gone cold turkey in Montana, she should have missed watching world events unfold.

Of course, she had been a little distracted—okay, a

lot distracted by a sexy cowboy who was quickly making her forget there was a world outside the Ryder Ranch.

She'd half expected him to kiss her last night.

He'd stared down at her with those intense blue eyes, nostrils slightly flared, hands bunched into fists, and the muscles in his neck bulging in relief against his skin. She'd imagined him leaning down, planting his lips against hers, wrapping his arms around her and pulling her into paradise all over again.

But then he'd backed off, and she hadn't been brave enough to protest.

Now she sighed with regret as she clicked the mouse, bringing up a live news broadcast from a Chicago network. The buffer loaded, and the announcer carried on with a story about a local bridge repair.

She turned back to the desk, lifting the stack that was the day's mail. Barry Brewster hadn't arrived to confirm the bank balance yet, so she couldn't make any progress paying the backlog of bills.

Truth was, she was dreading the man's arrival. No matter what he said or did, it was going to be embarrassing all around. Royce might think she needed an apology, but Amber had spent most of her life with people being polite to her because they either admired or were afraid of her father or Hargrove. She didn't need the same thing from Barry today.

"The Governor's Office can no longer get away with dodging the issue of Chicago's competitiveness." The familiar voice startled Amber. She whirled to stare at the computer screen, where a news clip showed Hargrove posed in front of the Greenwood Financial Tower with several microphones picking up his words.

"His performance at the conference was shameful,"

Hargrove continued. "If our own governor won't stand up for the citizens of Chicago, I'd like to know who will."

Guilt percolated through Amber, and she quickly shut off the sound. She watched his face a few seconds longer, telling herself her actions had been defensible. If she'd stayed, she'd probably be standing right next him, holding his hand, the stalwart little fiancée struggling to come to terms with her role in his life.

He looked good on camera. Then, he'd always had a way with reporters, dodging their pointed questions without appearing rude, making a little information sound like a detailed dissertation. It was the reason the party was grooming him for the election.

A child shouted from outside the window, and Amber concentrated on the sound, forcing her mind from the worry about Hargrove to the seclusion of the ranch. Then another child shouted, and a chorus of cheers went up. Curious, she wandered to the window to look out.

Off to the left, on a flat expanse of lawn, a baseball game was underway. It was mostly kids of the ranch staff, but there were a few adults in the field. And there in the center, pitching the baseball, was Royce. She smiled when he took a few paces forward, lobbing a soft one to a girl who couldn't have been more than eight.

The girl swung and missed, but then she screwed her face up in defiance and positioned herself at the plate, tapping the bat on the white square in front of her. Royce took another step forward.

Amber smiled, then she glanced one more time at Hargrove on the computer screen—her old life.

As the days and hours had slipped by, she'd become more convinced that her decision was right. She had no intention of going back to her old life. And she owed it to Hargrove to make that clear.

She searched for her cell phone on the desktop, powered it up and dialed his number.

"Hargrove Alston," he answered.

"Hargrove? It's Amber."

Silence.

"I wanted to make sure you weren't worried about me," she began.

"I wasn't worried." His tone was crisp.

"Oh. Well, that's good. I'm glad."

"Your parents told me you were fine, and that you'd taken the trouble to contact them."

Amber clearly heard the "while you didn't bother to contact me" message underlying his words.

"Are you over your tantrum, then?" he asked.

She couldn't help but bristle. "Is that what you think I'm doing?"

"I think you're behaving like a child."

She gritted her teeth.

"You missed the Chamber of Commerce speech," he accused.

"I hear you didn't," she snarked in return.

Another silence. "And what is that supposed to mean?"

"Nothing."

"Honestly, Amber."

"Forget it. Of course you gave the speech. It was an important speech."

Her words seemed to mollify him. "Will you be ready in time for dinner, then? Flannigan's at eight with the Myers."

Amber blinked in amazement at the question.

She'd been gone for three days. She'd broken off their engagement.

"I'm not coming to dinner," she told him carefully.

He gave a heavy sigh on the other end of the phone. "Is this about the Switzerland trip?"

"Of course not."

"I explained why I had to go alone."

"This is about a fundamental concern with our compatibility as a couple."

"You sound like a self-help book."

Amber closed her eyes and counted to three. "I'm breaking our engagement, Hargrove. I'm truly sorry if I hurt you."

A flare of anger crept into his tone. "I wish you'd get over this mood."

"This isn't something I'm going to get over."

"Do you have any idea how embarrassing this could get?"

"I'm sorry about that, too. But we can't get married to keep from being embarrassed." She flicked a gaze to the baseball game, watching two colorful young figures dash around the bases.

"Are you trying to punish me?" asked Hargrove, frustration mounting in his tone. "Do you want me to apologize for…" He paused. "I don't know. Tell me what you think I've done?"

"You haven't done anything."

"Then get ready for dinner," he practically shouted.

"I'm not in Chicago."

He paused. "Where are you?"

"It doesn't—"

"Seriously, Amber. This is getting out of hand. I don't have time to play—"

"Goodbye, Hargrove."

"Don't you dare—"

She quickly tapped the end button then shut down the power on her phone. Talking around in circles wasn't going to get them anywhere.

She defiantly stuffed the phone into her pocket and drew a deep breath. After the tense conversation, the carefree baseball game was like a siren's call. Besides, it was nearly lunchtime, and she was tired of looking at numbers.

Determinedly shaking off her emotional reaction to the fight with Hargrove, she headed outside to watch.

Stephanie was standing at the sidelines.

"Looks like fun," said Amber, drawing alongside and opening the conversation. She inhaled the fresh air and let the cheerfulness of the crowd seep into her psyche.

"Usually it's just the kids," Stephanie told her. "But a lot of the hands are down from the range today, and Royce can't resist a game. And once he joined in, well…" She shrugged at the mixed-age crowd playing and watching.

A little girl made it to first, and a cocky, teenage boy swaggered up to the plate, reversing his baseball cap and pointing far out to right field with the tip of his bat.

Royce gave the kid an amused shake of his head, walked back to the mound and smacked the ball into the pocket of his worn glove. Then he shook his head in response to the catcher's hand signals. Royce waited, then smiled, and nodded his agreement to the next signal.

He drew back, bent his leg and delivered a sizzling fastball waist high and over the plate. The batter swung hard but missed. Royce chuckled, and the kid stepped out of the batter's box, adjusting his cap then scuffing his runners over the dirt at home plate.

"That's Robbie Nome," Stephanie informed her. "He's at that age, constantly challenging the hands."

"How old?" asked Amber, guessing sixteen or seventeen.

"Seventeen," Stephanie confirmed. "They usually settle down around eighteen. But there's a hellish year there in between while their brain catches up to their size and their testosterone level." She shook her head as Robbie swung and missed a second time.

"Royce seems pretty good," Amber observed, watching him line up for another pitch. She knew she was staring way too intently at him, but she couldn't help herself.

He was dressed in faded jeans, a steel-gray T-shirt and worn running shoes. His bare arms were deeply tanned, and his straight, white teeth shone with an infectious grin.

"He played in the College World Series."

"Pitcher?" asked Amber, impressed.

"First base."

Royce rocketed in a third pitch, and the batter struck out.

The outfielders let out a whoop and ran for the sidelines. The shoulders of the girl on first base slumped in dejection. Royce obviously noticed. He cut to her path, whispered something in her ear and ruffled her short, brown hair. She smiled, and he gave her a playful high five.

Then he spotted Amber and Stephanie, and made a beeline for them. Amber's chest contracted, and her heart lifted at the thought that his long strides were meant to bring him closer to her.

His gaze flicked to Stephanie but then settled back on Amber.

"Impressive," she complimented as he drew near.

He shrugged. "They're kids."

Stephanie held out her hand, and Royce smacked the glove into her palm. "You want to play?" she asked Amber.

Amber shook her head. "I need to get back to work." Then, as Stephanie trotted toward the outfield, she confided in Royce. "I've never been much of an athlete."

His gaze traveled her body. "Could've fooled me."

"Pilates and a StairMaster."

"I bet you'd be a natural at sports."

"We're not about to find out." She'd never swung a bat in her life. There were eight-year-olds out there who would probably show her up.

"I'd lob you a soft one," Royce offered, beneath the cheers and calls from the teams.

"Think I'll stick to bookkeeping."

He sobered. "You worked all morning?"

She nodded.

"Anything interesting?"

She shook her head. Actually, she'd found a couple of strange-looking payments in the computerized accounting system. But they were probably nothing, so she didn't want to bother Royce with that. And she sure wasn't about to tell him about her conversation with Hargrove.

"You surprise me," he said in an intimate tone.

"How so?"

"I had you pegged for a party girl."

"No kidding," she scoffed, rolling her eyes at his understatement.

"I didn't mean it that way."

She looked him straight on. "Yeah, you did."

He raked a hand through his sweat-damp hair, giving a sheepish smile. "Okay, I did for a while. But I got over it."

She paused, debating for a few silent seconds, but then deciding she was going to quit censoring herself. "So," she dared, with a toss of her hair. "What do you think of me now?"

His eyes danced, reflecting the color of the endless summer sky. "It could go one of two ways."

"Which are?"

"Royce!" someone called. "You're on deck."

He twisted his head to shout over his shoulder. "Be right there." Then he turned back, slowly contemplating her.

"Well?" she prompted, ridiculously apprehensive.

His hand came up to cup her chin, his thumb and forefinger warm against her skin. "You're either shockingly ingenuous or frighteningly cunning." But his tone took the sting out of the labels.

"Neither of those are complimentary," she pointed out, absorbing the sparks from his touch.

His tone went low. "But both are very sexy."

Then his hand dropped away, and he turned to the game, trotting toward the batter's box as a player took a base hit.

Amber skipped down the staircase, recalling Royce smacking a three-base hit, bringing ten-year-old Colby

Jones home to win the game by one run. She and Stephanie had decided to dress up for dinner, and she wore a white, spaghetti-strap cocktail dress and high-heeled sandals. She rounded the corner at the bottom of the stairs and caught sight of him in a pressed business suit. He was even sexier now than he'd been this afternoon in his T-shirt and jeans.

And he didn't look out of place in the rustic setting. She was glad she'd gone with the dress.

His gaze caught hers, dark and brooding, and she faltered on her high heels. This afternoon, he'd been almost playful. Had she done something to annoy him?

And then she caught sight of the second man, nearly as tall as Royce, somewhat thinner, his suit slightly wrinkled at the elbows and knees. The man turned at the sound of her footsteps, and she knew it had to be Barry Brewster. His jaw was tight, and beads of sweat had formed on his brow.

"Ms. Hutton," Royce intoned. "This is Barry Brewster. You spoke to him on the phone last night."

Amber fought an urge to laugh. The whole charade suddenly struck her as ridiculous. "Mr. Brewster," she said instead, keeping her face straight as she came to a stop and held out her hand.

"Barry, please."

"You can call me Amber."

"No, he can't."

"Royce, please."

But Royce didn't waver, shoulders square, expression stern.

"Ms. Hutton," Barry began, obviously not about to run afoul of his boss. "Please accept my apology. I was rude and insulting last night. I am, of course, available for anything you might need."

The irritation in his eyes belied the geniality of his tone. But then she hadn't expected him to be sincere about this.

"Thank you," she said simply. "I do have a couple of questions." She looked to Royce. "Should we sit down?"

"Unnecessary. Barry won't be staying."

"This is ridicul—"

Royce's hard expression shut her up, and she silently warned herself not to get on his bad side.

"I was hoping you could tell me the balance in the ranch bank account," she said to Barry. "There are a number of unpaid bills, so I wondered—"

"You don't need a reason to ask for the bank balance," Royce cut in.

"I'd need to look it up," said Barry, shifting from one black loafer to the other. He flexed his neck to one side and straightened the sleeves of his suit.

"So, look it up," said Royce.

"I don't have access to the server."

"Call someone who does."

Barry hesitated. "It's pretty late."

"Your point?"

"I guess I could try to catch Sally." With a final pause, Barry reached into his pocket for his phone.

While he dialed, Amber moved closer to Royce, turning her back on Barry.

"Is this completely necessary?" she hissed.

"I thought you wanted the bank balance."

"I do."

"Then it's completely necessary."

"You know that's not what I'm talking about."

"Let me handle this."

She took in the determined slant to Royce's chin while Barry's voice droned on in the background.

"Do I have a choice?" she asked.

"No."

"You can be a real hard-ass, you know that?"

"He insulted you."

"I'm a big girl. I'm over it."

"That's not the point."

She fought against a sudden grin at his need to get in the last word. "Do you ever give up?"

"No."

Barry cleared his throat, and Amber smoothly turned back to face him.

"Sally is looking into the overdraft and the line of credit to see where—"

"The balance," said Royce.

Barry's neck took on a ruddy hue, and he tugged at the white collar of his shirt. "It's, uh, complicated."

"I'm an intelligent man, and Amber has an honors degree."

Barry's gaze flicked to Amber, and she could have sworn she saw panic in its depths.

"I'd really rather discuss—"

"The balance," said Royce.

Barry drew a terse breath. "At the moment, the account is overdrawn."

There were ten full seconds of frozen silence.

Stephanie entered the room from the kitchen, stopping short as she took in the trio.

"Say again?" Royce widened his stance.

"There's been… That is…" This time when Barry

glanced at Amber, he seemed to be pleading for help. There was no help she could give him. She didn't have a clue what was going on.

Royce's voice went dangerously low. "Why didn't you transfer something from corporate?"

Barry tugged at his collar again. "The China deal."

"What about the China deal?" Royce asked carefully. "Was the transfer held up?"

Barry swallowed, his Adam's apple bobbing, voice turning to a raspy squeak. "The paperwork. From Cheng Li. It didn't make the deadline."

Stephanie's eyes went wide, while Royce cocked his head, brows creasing. "They assured me the fax would go through."

"It did. But…well…"

Royce crossed his arms over his chest.

"Our acknowledgment," said Barry. "The time zone difference."

"You didn't send the acknowledgment?"

"End of day. Chicago time."

"You missed the deadline?" Royce's voice was harsh with disbelief.

"I've been trying to fix it for thirty-six hours."

Royce took a step forward. "You *missed* a fifty-million-dollar deadline?"

Barry's mouth opened, but nothing came out.

"And you didn't call me?" Royce's voice was incredulous now.

"I was trying to fix—"

"Yesterday," Royce all but shouted, index finger jabbing in Barry's direction. "*Yesterday,* I could have called Jared at his hotel. Today, he's on a sailboat somewhere in the South Pacific. You have…" Royce raked a hand through his hair. "I don't even know how much money you've lost."

"I—"

"What in the *hell* happened?"

"It was the time zones. Technology. The language barrier."

"You are *so* fired."

Amber's gaze caught Stephanie's. She felt desperate for an exit. She didn't want to witness Royce's anger, Barry's humiliation. She wanted to be far, far away from this disturbing situation.

"You're done, Barry," Royce confirmed to the silent man.

Barry hesitated a beat longer. Then his shoulders dropped. The fight went out of him, and he turned for the door.

The room seemed to boom with silence as Barry's footsteps receded and the car pulled away outside.

Stephanie took a few hesitant steps toward her brother. "Royce?"

"Cancel his credit cards," Royce commanded. "Wake up someone from IT and change the computer passwords. And have security reset the codes on the building."

"What are we going to do?" Stephanie asked in a whisper.

Royce's hands curled into fists at his sides. He looked to Amber. "I have to call Beijing. If we don't fix this, the domino effect could be catastrophic."

Amber nodded. "Just tell me what you need."

"Can we talk to Jared?" asked Stephanie.

Royce shook his head. "Not a chance. Not for a week at least."

Six

Amber hung up the phone after their fifth call to China, her expression somber as Royce's mood.

"That's it." He voiced his defeat out loud.

"Are you sure?"

"Can you think of anything else?"

She shook her head.

He slipped the phone from her hands, setting it on the end table next to the sofa in the living room. The deadline was the deadline, and they hadn't been able to penetrate the Chinese bureaucracy to make their case to Cheng Li. The deal was canceled.

It was nearly 3:00 a.m. Only a few lights burned in the house, and Stephanie had headed to her own ranch an hour ago. Amber tipped her head back on the gold sofa cushion, closing her eyes. She'd struggled through translations for hours on end, and the strain was showing in her pale complexion.

Royce gave in to the temptation to smooth a lock of hair from her cheek. "You okay?"

"Just sorry I couldn't help."

He dropped his hand back down. "You did help."

She opened her eyes. "How so?"

"I understand now what is and isn't possible."

"Nothing's possible."

"Apparently not."

She blinked her dark lashes, and her hand covered his. "How bad is it?"

He rested his own head against the sofa back. "It'll play havoc with our cash flow. We may have to sell off some of our companies. But, to start off, I'm going to have to call the division heads to keep them from panicking. Firing Barry was a significant move."

"Will they be angry?"

He shrugged. "That's the least of my worries."

Amber didn't answer, and Royce was content to sit in silence. He turned his hand, palm up, wrapping it around her smaller one. For some reason, it gave him comfort. Simply sitting here quietly, with her by his side, made the problems seem less daunting.

Her hand went limp in his, and he turned to gaze at her closed eyes and even breathing. She was astonishingly beautiful—smooth skin, delicate nose, high cheekbones and lustrous, golden hair that made a man want to bury his face against it.

He felt a shot of pity for the hapless Hargrove. Imagine having Amber in your grasp then having her disappear? Not that the man wasn't better off. Royce glanced at the portrait of his parents on their wedding day. He usually put it away while he was at the ranch, unable to bear the look of unbridled adoration on his father's face.

And that's the way it would have been with Amber, too. Her husband would have gone completely stupid and helpless with longing, only to have her change her mind and move on. Poor, pathetic Hargrove. He wouldn't have known what hit him.

Royce extricated his hand from hers, shifting to the edge of the couch, positioning himself to lift her into his arms.

"Amber?" he whispered softly, sliding one arm around her back and the other beneath her knees.

She mumbled something unintelligible, but her head tipped to rest against his shoulder. He lifted her up, and she stayed sleeping, even as he adjusted her slight body in his arms.

She weighed less than nothing. She was also soft and her scent appealing. There was something completely right about the scent of a beautiful woman, particularly this beautiful woman, fresh, like wildflowers, he supposed, but sweeter, more compelling.

He moved his nose toward her hair, guessing it was her shampoo. Hard to tell, really. He mounted the staircase, taking his time, reluctant to arrive at her room where he'd have to put her down.

His imagination wandered to that moment. Should he help her undress? Slip her between the sheets in her underwear? Would a gentleman wake her up or leave her in her clothes? Never having been a gentleman, Royce wasn't sure.

This had to be the first time he'd put a woman to bed without immediate plans to join her. He couldn't help a self-deprecating smile. It figured. He also couldn't remember a moment in his life when he'd been more eager to join a woman in bed.

He pushed open her door, carefully easing her through the opening. Then he crossed to the queen-size, brass bed and leaned down, laying her gently on top of the comforter.

She moaned her contentment, and his longing ratcheted up a notch. Their faces were only inches apart, his arm around her back, the other cradling her bare legs. He knew he had to leave her, but try as he might, he couldn't get his body to cooperate.

"Amber," he whispered again, knowing that if she woke he'd have no choice but to walk away.

"Mmm," she moaned. Then she sighed and wriggled in his arms.

His muscles tensed to iron. His gaze took in her pouty lips and, before he knew it, his head was dipping toward hers. Then he was kissing her sweet lips.

Just to say good-night, he promised himself. Just a chaste—

But then she was kissing back.

Her arms twined around his neck, and her head tipped sideways, lips parting, accommodating his ravenous kiss. Her back arched, and her fingertips curled into his short hair, even as her delicate tongue flicked into his mouth.

He leaned into her soft breasts, stroking the length of her bare legs, teasing the delicate skin behind her knees, tracing the outline of her shapely calves and daring the heat of her smooth thighs.

He wanted her, more than he'd ever wanted a woman in his life. Passion was quickly clouding reason, and his hormones warred with intelligence. Another minute, another second, and his logic would switch completely off.

He dragged his mouth from hers. "Amber?" he forced himself to ask. "Are you sure you're ready for this?"

Her eyes popped open, and she took a sudden jerk back against the pillow. She blinked in confusion at Royce's face, and in a split and horrible second, he realized what had happened.

The woman had been dreaming.

And Royce wasn't the man she'd been dreaming about.

In the morning, Amber was grateful to find Stephanie in the kitchen at breakfast. She needed a buffer between her and Royce while she got over her embarrassment.

She'd hesitated a moment too long last night. When she'd realized it wasn't a dream, she should have kept right on kissing him. She should have pressed her body tightly against his and sent the signal that she was completely attracted to him, nearly breathless with passion for him, and that making love was exactly what she wanted.

Instead, all he'd seen was her shock and hesitation. He'd been offended and abruptly left the room. She didn't blame him. And she wasn't brave enough to try to explain.

"Morning, Amber." Stephanie was her usual bright self as she bit into a strip of bacon, legs swinging from the high chair at the breakfast bar.

"Morning," Amber replied, daring a fleeting glance at Royce.

He gave her a cool nod then turned his attention

back to Stephanie. "Two days at the most," he told Stephanie.

"I'll definitely get you something," she responded and blew out a sigh. "This is the worst possible time."

"I can't imagine there being a best possible time." Royce stood from the breakfast bar and carried his plate and coffee mug over to the sink. He downed the last of the coffee before setting everything on the counter.

Amber helped herself to a clean plate from the cupboard and took a slice of toast from the platter.

"Royce has to call a division heads meeting," Stephanie told her. "We need to ask for financial reports from everybody. But he's worried about panic."

"Who would panic?" Amber addressed her question first to Royce, but when he didn't meet her eyes, she turned back to Stephanie.

"I need a pretext for the meeting," said Royce. "Barry Brewster's firing is bad enough. Add to that a sudden meeting and financial reports, and the gossip will swirl.

"We have over two thousand employees," he continued. "Some very big contracts, and some very twitchy clients." His gaze finally went to Amber, but his face remained impassive, his tone flat. "If you don't mind, we'll start a rumor you were the cause."

"You mean the cause of Barry Brewster being fired, not the money problems?"

Royce didn't react to her joke. "Yes."

"Are you leaving today?" asked Stephanie.

At first Amber thought Stephanie meant her, and the idea made her clench her stomach in regret. But then she realized Stephanie was talking to her brother.

Royce nodded.

"Where—" Amber clamped her jaw to slow herself down. It was jarring to think of him leaving with this tension between them. "Where are you going?" she finished, feigning only a mild interest.

"Chicago."

"You don't think that will bring on the gossip?"

She assured herself her caution was sincere. It wasn't merely an attempt to keep Royce here at the ranch.

His eyes narrowed.

"If you come rolling into the office, people are sure to think something's up."

"She's right," Stephanie put in.

"I don't see an alternative. I have to talk to the division VPs."

"Bring them here," suggested Amber.

Both Royce and Stephanie stared at her.

"There's your pretext. Come up with a reason to bring them here. Something fun, something frivolous, then take them aside and have whatever discreet conversation you need to have." She paused, but neither of them jumped in.

"A barbecue." She offered the first thing that popped into her mind.

Royce's voice turned incredulous, but at least there was an emotion in it. "You want me to fly the Ryder senior managers to Montana for a barbecue?"

"They'd never suspect," she told him.

"A barn dance," Stephanie cried, coming erect on the seat. "We'll throw a dance to christen the new barn."

"You're both insane," Royce grumbled.

"Like a fox," said Stephanie. "Invite the spouses. Hire a band. Nobody throws a dance and barbecue when the company's in financial trouble."

Amber waited. So did Stephanie.

Royce's brows went up, and his mouth thinned out. "I find I can't disagree with that statement."

Finished with her own breakfast, Stephanie hopped up and transferred her dishes to the sink. She gave Royce a quick peck on the cheek. "See you guys in a while. I have to get the students started."

As she left the room, Amber screwed up her courage. She definitely needed to clear the air. "Royce—"

"If you have time today," he interrupted, "could you give me as much information as possible on the cattle ranch finances?" His voice was detached, professional, and his gaze seemed to focus on her hairline.

Amber hated the cold wall between them. "I..."

"Stephanie's going to pull something together for the horse operation, and I'll be busy—"

"Of course," Amber quickly put in, swallowing, telling herself she had no right to feel hurt. "Whatever you need."

He gave a sharp nod. "Thanks. Appreciate you helping out." Then he turned and strode out of the kitchen, boot heels echoing on the tile floor.

Amber was curled up on the webbed cushions of an outdoor love seat on the ranch house deck, clouds slipping over the distant mountains, making mottled shade on the nearby aspen groves. She flipped her way through a hundred-page printout from the ranch's financial system, highlighting entries along the way.

Gopher, one of Molly's young pups, had curled up against her bare feet. At first, she'd been wary of his wet nose and slurpy tongue. But then he'd fallen asleep, and she found his rhythmic breathing and steady heartbeat rather comforting.

She hadn't seen Royce since breakfast, and Stephanie was obviously busy getting her own financial records together. Amber's thoughts had vacillated from heading straight for home, to confronting Royce about last night, to seducing Royce, to helping him sort out his business problems and earning his gratitude.

She sighed and let her vision blur against the page. For the hundredth time, she contemplated her mistake. Why had she panicked last night? Why hadn't she kissed him harder, hugged him tighter and waited to see where it would all lead?

She was wildly attracted to him. She was truly free from Hargrove now, and there was no reason in the world she couldn't follow her desires. So what if she'd only known him a few days? They were both adults, and this was hardly the 1950s.

Gopher shifted his warm little body, reminding her of where she was and that, 1950s or not, she'd blown her chance with Royce. The choices left were to leave him, seduce him or impress him. Since she was completely intimidated by the thought of seducing a man she'd already rebuffed, she decided to go with impressing him.

She forced herself to focus on the column of numbers in her lap.

There it was again.

She stroked the highlighter across the page.

Yet another payment to Sagittarius Eclipse Incorporated. It was for one hundred thousand dollars, just like the last one, and the one before that.

She skipped back on the pages, counting the payments

and pinpointing the dates of the transactions. They fell on the first day of every month. Where other payments in the financial report were for obvious things like feed, lumber, tools or veterinary services, the Sagittarius Eclipse payments were notated only as "services."

Amber's curiosity was piqued. She flipped to the back page. Scanning through the total columns, she discovered one-point-two million dollars had been paid out to Sagittarius Eclipse in the current year, the same amount the year before.

She pulled her feet from the love seat cushion. Gopher whimpered and quickly scooted up next to her thigh, flopping against her.

She smiled at the little puff ball, set the financial report aside and scooped him into her arms. He wiggled for a moment, but then settled in next to her like a fuzzy baby.

"I suppose if I hold on to you, you can't do any harm," she whispered to him, checking Molly and the other pups as she rose to her feet. They were curled together at the far end of the deck. Nobody seemed to notice as she carried Gopher through the doorway.

There was a computer close by in the living room, and she sat down in front of it, moving the mouse to bring the screen back to life. She hadn't graduated in Public Administration without knowing how to search a company. Using her free hand, she called up a favorite corporate registry search program.

An hour later, she knew nothing, absolutely nothing about Sagittarius Eclipse Incorporated. They had to be an offshore company, and a hard-to-trace one at that. She could hear her father's voice inside her head, warning her that when something didn't seem right, something definitely wasn't right. But since she wasn't nearly as suspicious as her father, she refused to jump to any conclusions.

Shifting the sleeping puppy, she dug into her pocket to retrieve her cell phone, dialing Stephanie's number.

"Yo!" came the young woman's voice.

"It's Amber."

"I know. What's going on?"

"You ever heard of a company called Sagittarius Eclipse?"

"Who?"

Amber repeated the name.

"What are they, astrologers or something?"

"I hope not." Amber nearly chuckled. If Ryder Ranch was paying for a hundred grand a month of astrology services, they'd better be accurately predicting the stock market.

"Never heard of them," said Stephanie. "How are things looking at your end?"

"Best I can come up with is to stop work on the new barn," said Amber. And maybe quit paying for unidentified "services." But something stopped her from mentioning the strange payments to Stephanie.

"I hate to say it," Stephanie returned, "but I'd better not buy Blanchard's Run."

"I thought that was a foregone conclusion."

"A girl can hope."

This time, Amber did laugh at the forlorn little sigh in Stephanie's voice. "Suck it up, princess."

"Easy for you to say. It's not your business being compromised."

Amber couldn't deny it. What's more, she couldn't ignore the fact that she didn't have a business to compromise. Nor did she have a career to compromise. The only thing she'd ever been able to call a vocation was her role as Hargrove's loyal fiancée and future wife. And she'd completely blown that job yesterday.

"What else have you got?" she asked, shoving the disagreeable thoughts to the back of her mind.

"Let me see." Stephanie shuffled some papers in the background. "I can delay a tack order, struggle through with our existing jumps. Man, I hate to do that. But the horses have to eat, the employees need paychecks, and we don't dare cut back on the competition schedule."

Royce's deep voice broke in from behind Amber. "I see you've changed your mind."

She jerked around to face him in his Western shirt and faded jeans. A flush heated her face. Yes, she'd changed her mind. She'd changed her mind the second he left her bedroom last night.

But he was staring at the puppy in her lap, and she realized he was referring to a completely different subject.

"Royce is here," she said into the mouthpiece.

"Tell him I'll be down there before dinner."

"Sure." She signed off and hung up the phone, adjusting Gopher's little body when she realized her arm was beginning to tingle from lack of circulation. "He's very friendly," she told Royce.

"Are you taking him home?"

"Have you ever heard of a company called Sagittarius Eclipse?" she countered, not wanting to open the subject of her going home. She'd pretend she didn't notice he was anxious for her to leave.

"Never," he answered, watching her closely, the

distance and detachment still there in his expression and stance.

She debated her next move, unable to shake the instinct that told her the payments were suspicious.

"Why do you ask?" he prompted.

"The ranch is making payments to them."

"For what?"

"That's just it. I can't tell."

"Tools? Supplies? Insurance?"

"Insurance, maybe." She hadn't thought of that. "The entries only say 'services.'" She reached behind her for the report, and Gopher wriggled in her lap.

"Better put him back outside," Royce suggested.

Amber moved to the screen door, deposited the puppy on the deck and returned to point out the entries to Royce.

"I searched for the company on the Internet," she offered while he glanced through the pages she'd noted. "I can't find anything on them, not domestically, not offshore."

He raised a questioning brow.

"I learned corporate research at U of C."

Royce's jaw tightened, and she could feel the wheels turning inside his head.

She dared voice the suspicion that was planted inside her brain. "Do you think McQuestin could be—"

"No."

"His niece?"

"Not a chance. Not for these amounts."

"McQuestin had to know, right?" The man worked with the business accounts on a daily basis. Whatever was going on with Sagittarius Eclipse, McQuestin had to be aware.

"It's legit," Royce said out loud, but his spine was stiff, and he was frowning.

"What do you want to do?" she asked. Maybe this was the tip of the iceberg. Maybe Sagittarius Eclipse would help them solve some kind of embezzlement scheme. Maybe she could even help alleviate the company's cash flow problems.

He reached into the breast pocket of his blue-and-gray plaid shirt, retrieving his cell phone and searching for a number. His hair was damp with sweat, face streaked with dust, sleeves rolled up to reveal his tanned, muscular forearms. Amber's gaze went on a wayward tour down his body, her hormones reaching with predictability to his sex appeal.

He pressed a button on the phone, and the ringing tone became audible through the small speaker.

Amber pointed to the screen door. "Do you want me to—"

Royce shook his head. "You're the one that found it. Let's hear what McQuestin has to say."

A woman's voice bid them hello.

"Maddy? It's Royce."

"Oh, hey, Royce. He's doing okay today. They think they got the last of the bone fragments, and the infection's calming down."

"Good to hear," said Royce. "Can I talk to him for a minute?"

Maddy hesitated. "He's pretty doped up. Can I help with something?"

"It's important," said Royce, an apology in his voice.

"Well. Okay." The sounds went muffled for a few moments.

"Yeah?" came a gravelly voice.

"It's Royce, Mac. How're you feeling?"

"Like the bronc won," McQuestin grumbled.

Amber couldn't help but smile.

"You married yet?" McQuestin's voice was slightly slurred.

"That was Jared," Royce corrected.

"Mighty pretty girl," McQuestin mused. "Should have married her yourself."

"Jared might have had an objection to that."

"He's too busy… Hey! Did you wash the ears?"

Royce and Amber glanced at each other in amusement.

"Mac," Royce tried.

"What now?" MacQuestin grumbled.

"You know anything about Sagittarius Eclipse?"

There was a silence, during which their amusement turned to concern.

"I paid 'em," said McQuestin, obviously angry. "What else would a man do?"

"What exactly did you pay them for?"

McQuestin snorted. "You tell Benteen…" Then his voice turned to a growl. "Somebody should have shot the damn dog yesterday."

Maddy's voice came back. "Can this wait, Royce? You're really upsetting him."

"I'm sorry, Maddy. Of course it can wait. Keep me posted, okay?"

"Will do." McQuestin's voice still ebbed and flowed in the background. "Better go."

Royce signed off.

"Who's Benteen?" asked Amber.

Royce's voice was thoughtful, and he placed the phone

back in his pocket. "My grandfather. He died earlier this year. You think you could dig a little deeper into this?"

Amber nodded. Her curiosity was piqued. She'd like nothing better than to sleuth around Sagittarius Eclipse and figure out its relationship to the Ryder Ranch.

Seven

"Royce?"

Royce's body reacted to the sound of Amber's voice. He hefted a hay bale onto the stack, positioning it correctly before acknowledging her presence.

"Yeah?" He didn't turn to look at her. It was easier for him to cope if only one of his senses was engaged with her at a time. He only hoped she'd keep her sweet scent on the far side of the barn.

Her footsteps echoed. So much for that plan.

"I didn't find any more information," she said. "I'm going to have to try again tomorrow."

He nodded, moving to the truckload of hay bales, keeping his gaze fixed on his objective.

"It's getting late," she ventured, and there was a vulnerability in her voice that made his predicament even worse. Though he didn't look at her now, an image of her this afternoon, in that short denim skirt, a peach tank top, her blond hair cascading softly around her bare shoulders, was stuck deep in the base of his brain. It was going to take dynamite to blast it out.

"I know." He gave the short answer.

"What are you doing?"

He grabbed the next bale, binder twine pressing against the reinforced palms of his leather work gloves. "Moving hay bales."

He retraced his steps. Extreme physical work was his only hope of getting any sleep tonight. If he wasn't dead-dog exhausted, he'd do nothing but lie awake and think about Amber sleeping across the hall.

"Is it that important?" she pressed.

"Horses have to eat."

"But do you—"

"Is there something you need?" he asked brusquely.

Her silence echoed between them, and he felt like a heel.

"No," she finally answered in a soft voice. "It's just…"

He didn't prompt her, hoping she'd take the hint and leave. He'd never found himself so intensely attracted to a woman, and it was physically painful to fight it.

"I'm surprised is all," she continued.

He mentally rolled his eyes. Couldn't the woman take a hint? Did she like that she was making him crazy? Was she one of those teases that got her jollies out of tempting a man then turning up her prissy little nose at his advances?

"When you said you had to babysit the ranch—"

How the hell long was she going to keep this up?

"—I thought you meant in a more managerial sense. I mean, can't somebody else move the hay?"

He turned to look at her then. Damn it, she was still wearing that sexy outfit. Only it was worse now, because the cool evening air had hardened her nipples, and they were highlighted against the soft cotton where she stood in the pool of overhead light.

The air whooshed right out of his lungs, and he almost dropped the bale.

"I'd rather do it myself," he finally ground out.

"I see." She held his gaze. There was something soft in the depths of her eyes, something warm and welcoming.

At this very second, he could swear she was attracted to him. But he'd been down that road before. Down that road was a long night in a very lonely bed.

He went back to work.

"Royce?" Her footsteps echoed again as she moved closer.

He heaved the bale into place, gritted his teeth and turned. "What?" he barked.

"I'm…" She glanced at the scuffed floor. "Uh… sorry."

He swiped his forearm across his sweaty brow. "Not as sorry as I am."

She glanced up in confusion. "For what? What did you do?"

"I didn't *do* anything."

"Then, what do you have to be sorry about?"

"You want to know why I'm sorry?" He'd reached the breaking point, and he was ready to give it to her with both barrels. "You really want to know why I'm sorry?"

She gave a tentative nod.

"I'm sorry I walked into the Ritz-Carlton lounge."

Her eyes widened as he stripped off his gloves.

"And I'm sorry I brought you home with me." He tossed the gloves on the nearest hay bale. "And I'm sorry you're so beautiful and desirable and sexy. But mostly, *mostly* I'm sorry my family's future is falling down around my ears, and all I can think of is how much I want you."

Their eyes locked.

For a split second, it looked as though she smiled.

"You think this is *funny?*"

She shook her head. Then she took a step forward. "I think it's ironic."

"You might not want to get too close," he warned, drinking in the sight, sound and scent of her all in one shot, wondering how many seconds he could hold out before he dragged her into his arms.

"Yeah?" She stepped closer still.

"Did you not hear me?"

She placed her flat palm against his chest. "I heard you just fine." Her defiant blue eyes held one of the most blatant invitations he'd ever seen.

He hoped she knew what she was doing.

Hell, who was he kidding? He couldn't care less if she knew or not. Just so long as she didn't back off this time.

His arms went around her and jerked her flush against him, all but daring her to protest.

Then he bent his head; his desire and frustration transmitted themselves into a powerful kiss. He all but devoured her mouth, reveling in the feel of her thighs, belly and breasts, all plastered against his aching flesh.

He encircled her waist, pulling in at the small of her back, bending her backward, kissing deeper as his free hand strummed from hip to waist over her rib cage to capture the soft mound of her breast.

She groaned against his mouth, lips parting farther, her tongue answering the impassioned thrusts of his own. Her nipple swelled under his caress, fueling his desire and obliterating everything else from his brain. He bent his knee, shifting his thigh between hers, pushing up on her short skirt, settling against the silk of her panties.

Her hands gripped his upper arms, nails scraping erotically against his thin shirt, transmitting her passion to the nerves of his skin. He lifted her, spreading her legs, hands cupping her bottom, shoving the skirt out of the way and pressing her heat against him.

Her arms went around his neck, legs tightening, her lips hot on his, her silky hair flowing out in all directions around her shoulders. She braced her arms on his shoulders, fingers delving into his short hair. Her kisses moved from his mouth to his cheek, his chin and his neck. She tugged at the buttons of his shirt, loosening them, before dipping her head and trailing her kisses across his chest.

He tipped back his head, drinking in the heat and moisture of her amazing lips. Then he took a few steps sideways, behind the bale stack, screening them from the rest of the cavernous room. He shrugged out of his loose shirt, dropping it on a bale before settling her on top. He braced his arms on either side of her and pulled back to look.

Her eyes were closed, lips swollen red. Her chest

heaved with labored breaths, and his gaze settled on the outline of her breasts against the peach top.

"Royce?"

His name on her lips tightened his chest and sent a fresh wave of desire cascading through his veins. He swiftly stripped her top off over her head, revealing two perfect breasts peeking from a lacy, white bra that dipped low in the center and barely camouflaged her dusky nipples.

"Gorgeous," he breathed, popping the clasp and letting the wisp of fabric fall away. "Perfection."

Her lash-fringed lids came up, revealing blue eyes clouded with passion.

They stared at each other for a long suspended breath. Then he reached out, his tanned hand dark against her creamy breast. He stroked the pad of his thumb across her nipple.

She gasped, and he smiled in pure satisfaction.

He repeated the motion, and she grabbed for his waist, tugging him toward her. But he stood his ground, his gaze flicking to the shadow of her sheer, high-cut panties, the skirt pulled high to reveal her hips.

He traced the line of elastic, knuckle grazing the moist silk. She moaned, head tipping back against the golden hay, her arms falling to her sides, clenching her fists tightly.

He could feel his anticipation, his own blood singing insistently through his system, hormones revving up, his passion making demands on his brain. But he wasn't ready. He wasn't ready to let the roar toward completion hijack his senses.

While his fingertips roamed, he leaned forward,

taking one plump nipple into his mouth, curling his tongue around the exquisite texture.

A deep sound burbled in Amber's throat, and her hands went for his belt buckle, the snap of his jeans, his zipper, his boxers, and then he was in her hand, and he knew time was running out.

He hooked his thumbs over the sides of her panties, stripping them down, letting them drop to the floor. Then his body moved unerringly to hers.

Her legs wrapped around his waist, and he raised his head, gazing into her eyes as he flexed his hips, easing slowly as he could to her center and into her core. Her eyes widened with every inch, she clenched her hands on his hips, and her sweet mouth fell open in a pout of awe.

Unable to resist, he bent his head, her features blurred as he grew close. Then her mouth opened against his, and his tongue thrust in, mimicking the motions of his hips as nature took over and he let the primal rhythm throb free between them.

He cupped her face, caressed her hair, kissed her neck, her temple, her eyelids. His hands roamed free, stroking her thighs, her bottom, her belly and breasts. Her panting breaths were music to his ears, her nails crescenting into his back transmitted her fervor.

Then she cried his name, urging him on, playing havoc with his self-control. But she was with him, and the small tremors contracting her body catapulted him over the edge into oblivion.

Amber blinked open her eyes.

She was vaguely aware of hay strands tickling her bare back. But she was much more aware of Royce's hard, hot body engulfing her own. Her lungs were struggling to get enough oxygen, and every fiber of her muscles danced with the aftershocks of lovemaking.

Royce's palm stroked over her hair, and he kissed her eyelids. Despite her exhaustion, her lips curled into a smile. But she was a long way from being able to speak.

Her skirt was in a bunch around her waist, her other clothes scattered. Her hair was wild and disheveled, tangled with hay, while her lips tingled with the heat of his kisses.

"I don't know what to say," Royce whispered in her ear.

She struggled through a few more breaths. "Well, I'm definitely not sorry," she managed, and she heard him chuckle.

"Definitely not sorry," he echoed.

He eased back, taking in her appearance.

"Bad?" she asked.

He pulled some straw from her hair. "Telltale."

She raked spread fingers through her hair in an attempt to tame it while he refastened his jeans.

He bent and picked up her bra from the floor, frowned at the dirt streaks on it and tucked it into his back pocket. He located her tank top, gave her breasts one last, lingering look, then pulled her top back over her head. The peach color was blotted with dust. And Royce's attempts to brush it off made things worse.

"We'll probably want to sneak you in the back way," he joked as she tugged down her skirt. He watched her movements closely.

She slipped his wrinkled shirt from beneath her butt

and held it out to him. "You're not looking so sharp yourself, cowboy."

"I've been working hard." As he shrugged into his shirt, his gaze strayed from the top of her head to the tips of her toes, and his tone went soft and intimate. "What's your excuse?"

"Someone stole my underwear."

He reached for the wisp of silk caught on the side of a bale and tucked it into his pocket with her bra.

"That's my only pair."

"Yeah?" He gave her body another long look. "Lucky me."

He fastened his buttons then helped her down, tucking her hand in his as they headed across the barn. "I hope you know you're sleeping in my bed tonight."

"Only if you give my underwear back."

"Maybe."

"Maybe?"

He turned to gaze at her. "Talk me into it."

Her footsteps slowed, and so did his. With their joined hands, he reeled her in, then he smoothed her hair back once more, moving closer still, voice intimate. "You know, you are stunningly gorgeous."

A smile tickled the corners of her mouth. "Is that why you're sneaking me in the back way?"

"I'm keeping you all to myself," he whispered, lips coming down on hers.

The kiss nearly exploded between them. For all that they'd just made love, Amber's arousal was strong as ever. She wrapped her arms around his neck, came up on her toes, welcomed his tongue and reveled in the feel of his warm hands as they stroked over her back, across her buttocks, down her thighs, then back up beneath her skirt.

She pressed her body against his as the kiss went on and on. A groan slipped from her lips.

"Again?" he asked, voice husky.

She nodded.

"Here or in bed."

"I don't care." She truly didn't. Royce could make her body sing, and propriety didn't appear to have a lot to do with it.

He backed off slightly on the kiss and smoothed her skirt back down. "In bed."

"Really?"

He grinned at the disappointment in her tone. "I want to make love to you for a very, very long time."

She cocked her head sideways. "And you need a bed for that?"

"I don't plan to be able to move afterward."

She breathed a mock, drawn-out sigh. "If you think I'll wear you out…"

"Is that a challenge?"

She gave a teasing half smile and rapidly blinked her lashes.

In return, he planted a playful swat on her buttocks. "You're on, sweetheart."

Amber stifled a yawn in the bright, midday sunshine, stretching her taut thigh muscles as she leaned on the railing of the ranch house deck. The puppies were below, chasing each other and rolling around on the meadow that sloped toward the river. Off the end of the deck, Amber could see the ranch hands putting up five giant tents in preparation for Saturday's barbecue and barn dance.

She was dividing her time between the Sagittarius Eclipse mystery and the barbecue. She'd never planned an event quite like this before. They'd hired a local band. Hamburgers and hot dogs were making up the main course, while salads, potato chips and condiments seemed to round out the rest. They had plans for a giant cake for dessert, with papers plates, soft drinks and canned beer all around.

Amber wasn't sure how the Ryder International executives would react to the dinner, though she was sure their kids would love the wagon rides, horseshoes and baseball game Stephanie had planned. When she'd broached the possibility of steaks, wine and real china with Sasha, the woman looked at her as though she'd lost her mind.

Okay, so they did corporate entertaining a little differently here in Montana. Amber could conform. And at least the event wasn't likely to damage the Ryder International bottom line.

Tucking her windblown hair behind one ear, she pressed the on button of her cell phone, and dialed Katie's work number.

"Katie Merrick," came the familiar voice.

"It's Amber."

"What? Finally! Have you gone stark raving mad?"

"You've been talking to my mom, haven't you?"

"Of course I've been talking to your mom. And your dad. And Hargrove. You've got him completely confused."

"I thought I cleared up the confusion yesterday."

"By breaking it off over the phone?" The accusation was clear in Katie's tone.

"I'm a little ways away, Katie."

"Where?"

Amber scratched her fingernail over a dried flower petal the rain had stuck to the painted railing, deciding she couldn't keep it a secret forever. "Montana."

Silence.

"Katie?"

"Did you say Montana?"

"Yes. I'm staying with a…well, friend. I need your help with something."

"I'd say you need a whole lot more than *my* help. The dress arrived yesterday."

"What dress?"

"Your *wedding* dress." Katie's voice was incredulous. "The one from Paris. The one with antique alençon lace and a thousand hand-sewn pearls."

"Oh." Right. That dress. Amber supposed they'd have to put it on consignment somewhere. "The thing I wanted to talk to you about at the moment, though, was business."

"What do you mean?"

"I have a problem."

"What problem?" Katie's voice immediately turned professional.

"It's a company called Sagittarius Eclipse. I haven't been able to trace it, but I think it's got to be offshore somewhere, maybe hiding behind a numbered company. It could be connected to embezzlement."

There was another moment's silence. "Where did you say you were?" asked Katie.

Amber drew a sigh. "You remember that thirty dollars I gave you last week?"

"To pay for the dry cleaning on my dress?"

"You're on retainer, Katie. I'm a client."

"*What* is going on?"

"Lawyer-client confidentiality. Say it."

"Lawyer-client confidentiality," Katie parroted with exasperation.

"I think Sagittarius Eclipse is involved in an embezzlement scheme against Ryder International."

"*Montana.*" Katie drew out the word in a triumphant voice, obviously making the connection with Amber's father's business.

Fine by Amber, she'd rather have Katie connecting her to Jared Ryder than to Royce. Even thinking his name brought up an image of last night, and Amber was forced to shake it away in order to concentrate.

"You going into my line of work?" asked Katie.

Creighton Waverley Security was famous in Chicago for specializing in corporate espionage, and they'd investigated plenty of other corporate crimes along the way.

"Just for the week." Though Amber could already see the appeal of the profession. The harder she looked for information, the more involved she became in the hunt.

"You looking for anything specific?"

"A bank account. A name. A guy named McQuestin might be involved."

Although Royce was sure McQuestin was honest, Amber wasn't prepared to rule anything out. She'd looked back as far as she could in the financial records this morning, and Sagittarius Eclipse had received millions over the years. Maybe McQuestin hadn't even broken his leg. Maybe he was on his way to some offshore haven even now.

"I'll see what I can find. And, Amber?"

"Yes?"

"You serious about this breakup?"

Amber didn't hesitate. "Yes."

"Why?"

Good question. Hard to put into words. "He's just not the right guy for me."

Katie's accusing tone was back. "When did he become not the right guy for you?"

"Katie."

"When he made his first million? When he bought you a three-carat diamond? When he received the party nod for the nomination? Or when he planned the honeymoon to Tahiti?"

"Hargrove planned a honeymoon to Tahiti?" It was the first Amber had heard about it.

"Yes! Just last night he was showing me some—"

"You saw Hargrove last night?"

There was a small pause. "He was desperate, Amber. He needed a date for that hospital thing with the Myers."

"You went on a date with Hargrove?"

"Of *course* not." But there was something in Katie's tone. "He couldn't show up stag, and I've met Belinda Myers before, so…"

Amber rolled the image of Katie and Hargrove around in her head. No problem for her. She really didn't care. "Did you have a good time?" she asked.

"That's not the point."

Royce appeared in Amber's peripheral vision, on

horseback, moving along the river trail between the staff cabins and the barbecue setup. Even at this distance, the sight of him took her breath away.

"Gotta go," she said to Katie. "Call me as soon as you find something."

"Uh… Okay, sure."

"Thanks, Katie. I miss you." Amber quickly signed off.

Royce spotted her, and the sizzle of his gaze shot right to her toes. He turned his horse toward the house, and she headed for the deck's staircase.

Glances and brief, public conversations were all Royce had managed to share with Amber throughout the day. So he was disappointed when he finally found her up at the jumping-horse outfit, and she was sitting on the front porch laughing with his sister and another man.

As he exited the pickup truck, Royce's first thought was that Hargrove had found her. The idea tightened his gut and sped up his stride. She certainly seemed happy to see this guy. She was listening to him with rapt attention, smiling, even laughing.

"Royce," Stephanie sang out as his boot hit the bottom stair. Amber glanced up, and the stranger twisted his head.

Royce immediately realized the man was too young to be Hargrove. Plus, he was wearing jumping clothes, not a business suit.

"Wesley, this is my brother, Royce. Wesley is our newest student. He was nationally ranked as a junior."

The young man stood up as Royce trotted up the remaining stairs.

"Good to meet you," Royce said with a hearty

handshake, ignoring how relieved he felt that the guy wasn't Hargrove. Wesley looked to be about twenty-one. Not much younger than Stephanie and Amber, but no immediate competition.

"You, too." Wesley nodded. "I'm honored to be working with Stephanie."

Royce smirked at his sister. "Well, we'll see how honored you feel a month from now."

"Hey," she protested, reaching out to swat his arm.

"Can I grab you a beer?" Wesley offered, nodding to a cooler against the wall. "I picked up a dozen at a microbrewery in San Diego."

"Thanks," Royce agreed, and the younger man headed for the far side of the porch.

"I've got something for you," Amber stage-whispered, and Royce's attention shot immediately to her dancing eyes.

His chest tightened, and he wondered if she was going to proposition him right here in front of Stephanie. Not that it would be a bad thing. They'd seemed to come to a tacit agreement to keep their relationship secret. But there was no real reason to do that. They were both adults. She'd officially broken off her engagement. They were entitled to date each other if they wanted.

"Sagittarius Eclipse," she said, and he realized his brain had gone completely off on the wrong track. "I have a name."

"Yeah?" He pushed an empty deck chair into the circle.

"Norman Stanton."

Royce froze, brain scrambling while Amber kept talking.

"He's an American, originally from the Pacific North—"

"Later," Royce barked.

Amber drew back, squinting at his expression.

He moderated his voice, forcing a smile when he realized Stephanie was staring at him in confusion. "I want to hear how things are coming with the barbecue."

Then he nodded to Wesley as he returned with the beer. "Thanks," he told him. "So, are you training for any competition in particular?"

Out of the corner of his eye, he could see that Amber was confused, probably hurt, but there was nothing he could do about that at the moment. He pretended to listen to Wesley's answer, while his mind reeled.

Stanton. Damn it. A name out of his worst nightmare. After all these years, they were being blackmailed by a Stanton?

How much did the bastard know? How long had he known it? And why the hell hadn't his grandfather or McQuestin told him before now?

Eight

Amber waited until they'd passed the lights of Stephanie's yard and were headed down the dark, ranch driveway before turning to Royce in the pickup truck. "What did I do?"

"Nothing." But his answer was terse, and she could tell he was upset. Their speed was increasing on the bumpy road, and she gripped the armrest to stabilize herself.

"I don't understand. It's good information. I don't know if you realize how hard I had to dig—"

"Where did you get it? Where did you come up with the name Stanton?"

"Katie found a bank account in the Cayman Islands."

Royce hit her with a hard glance, staring a bit too long for safety. "Who's Katie?"

"Watch the road," she admonished as a curve rushed up at them in the headlights.

He glanced back, but only long enough to crank the wheel. "Who is Katie?"

"She's my best friend, my maid of honor."

"I thought you weren't getting married."

"I'm *not* getting married." Amber took a breath. "She would have been my maid of honor. She's a lawyer. Her firm specializes in corporate espionage, but they investigate all kinds of criminal activity."

Royce's voice went dark. "McQuestin is not a criminal."

"I never said he was."

"You had no right to disparage a man's name—"

"I didn't disparage anything. Katie's my friend. She works for Creighton Waverley Security, and she's our lawyer now. Everything she finds out is confidential."

Royce didn't answer, but she could almost hear his teeth gritting above the roar of the engine and the creak of the steel frame as the truck took pothole after pothole.

"Who is Stanton?" she dared.

His hands tightened on the steering wheel, face stony in the dim dashboard lights. "Nobody you need to worry about."

Something inside Amber shriveled tight. She'd felt so close to Royce last night. Between lovemaking, they'd shared whispered stories, opinions, worldviews. She'd thought they were becoming friends.

"I have more," she told him, not above bribery.

"What else?"

She crossed her arms over her chest. "Who's Stanton?"

Royce glared at her. It was the first time she'd had his true anger directed at her. But she stiffened her spine. "Who is Stanton?"

"Forget it."

"*Why?* Why won't you let me help you?"

He geared down for a hill. "There are things you don't understand."

"No kidding."

"No offence, Amber. But I barely know you."

"No offence, Royce. But you've seen me naked."

"And that's relevant how?"

"I'm just saying—"

"That it's not about to happen again unless I talk?"

"You think I'd use sex to bribe you?"

He let go of the steering wheel long enough for a jerking hand gesture of frustration. "Why do you jump to the absolute *worst* interpretation?"

"I'm trying to understand you."

"Well, I'm not having the slightest success understanding you." He sucked in a deep breath.

She let a few beats go by in silence, forcing herself to calm down. In her mind, this argument was completely separate from any future sexual relationship. She moderated her voice. "Maybe if you told me what was going on."

"Maybe if you let me keep my private business private."

Okay, now that crack would probably impact on their future sexual relationship.

"Fine," she huffed. "There's this numbered holding company." She pulled a note from her pocket and checked it in the dim light. "One-four-nine-five-eight, twelve-zero-ninety-three is registered in Liechtenstein with bank accounts in Liechtenstein, Switzerland and Grand Cayman. Its only asset is a company called Eastern Exploration Holdings. Eastern Exploration owns several parcels of property, mostly in the Bahamas. It also owns one company, Sagittarius Eclipse. One-four-nine-five-eight, twelve-zero-ninety-three is solely owned by Norman Stanton."

The truck rocked to a halt in front of the ranch house.

"His last known address was in Boston, Massachusetts," Amber finished.

Royce killed the lights and turned the key, shutting down the engine. "You don't know where he is now?"

"Not yet." She yanked up on the door handle, and the door creaked wide.

"But you're looking?" Royce followed suit.

"We're looking," said Amber, sliding off the high bench seat and onto the dirt driveway. She'd taken to wearing a pair of tattered, flat, canvas runners she'd found in a closet by the back door. They weren't as sturdy as the cowboy boots favored by everyone else, but they beat the heck out of the high heels she'd arrived in.

"How long will it take?" he asked as they headed for the porch.

"I don't know." Her voice was still testy.

Royce frowned at her.

"It'll take as long as it takes. He could be hiding. He might have left the country." She headed up the stairs. "Maybe someone warned him McQuestin was hurt, and he's worried he'll get caught."

"Who would warn him McQuestin was hurt?"

Amber paused at the front door. "Maybe McQuestin."

Royce turned the knob and shoved open the door. "McQuestin wouldn't do that."

She walked inside. "You're putting a lot of faith in a man who's been authorizing secret payments."

"He has his reasons." The door slammed shut, and Royce moved up close.

Amber turned, then drew back from the intensity in his eyes.

He moved closer.

She stepped back again, coming up against the wall in the foyer.

He braced a hand on either side of her, dipping his head.

"Royce?"

"Yeah?" He kissed her, and her protest was muffled against his mouth.

He kissed her again, softer, deeper, and a flame of desire curled to life in the pit of her belly.

His hands cupped her chin, deepening the kiss, pressing his strong body flush against hers, evoking near-blinding memories of the night before.

"What are you doing?" she finally gasped.

"It's not obvious?" There was a thread of laughter deep in his throat, his warm breath puffing against her skin.

"No."

"Makeup sex."

"But I'm still mad at you."

"You are?" He feigned surprise as he kissed her neck, her collarbone, her shoulder. He found the strip of bare skin at the top of her jeans, skimming his knuckles across her navel. "Then let's see what we can do to change that."

* * *

Royce feathered his fingertips across Amber's stomach, the narrowing at her waist, the indentation of her navel and the small curve of her belly. Her skin was pale and supple, a light tan line at bikini level, barely above where the sheet covered her legs.

She was by far the most beautiful woman he'd ever seen. Her blond hair, mussed at the moment, was thick and lustrous, reflecting the pink rays of the rising sun. Her eyes were deep blue, a midsummer sky right now, but they'd been jewel bright last night while they made love. Her lips were full, deep red and tempting.

Even her ears were gorgeous, delicate and small, while her neck was graceful, her shoulders smooth, and her breasts were something out of his deepest fantasy. Add to that her quick wit, her intelligence and her sense of fun, and she was somebody he could keep in his bed for days on end.

He'd had sex with plenty of women over the years, slept with only some of them, ate breakfast with fewer still. And in all that time, he'd never had an urge to bare his soul to a single one.

Now, he did.

Now, he wanted to tell her anything and everything.

He let his fingers trace the curve of her hip bone, made up his mind and took the plunge. "My father killed a man named Stanton."

Amber's head turned sharply on the stark white pillow. "He what?"

"Killed him," Royce repeated, hand stilling, cupping her hip.

"Was it an accident?"

"Nope."

"I don't understand."

"It was on purpose. Frank Stanton was having an affair with my mother."

Amber's eyes widened and she rolled sideways, propping her head on one elbow. "Did they get into a fight?"

"I guess you could say that. My father shot him."

Amber stilled. The sun broke free from the horizon, and the pink rays morphed to white.

"Did your father go to jail?" Her voice was hoarse.

Royce shook his head. "He died that same day."

Amber swallowed. "And your mother?"

"Died with my father. Their truck went off the ranch road in the rain. They both drowned in the river."

"After he shot Stanton."

"I always assumed he panicked." Though Royce had never delved too deeply into his father's possible motivations for speeding down the ranch road with his unfaithful mother. "There was no trial, of course. Everybody chalked the shooting up to a failed robbery, and the accident was ruled just that, an accident. For years, I thought I was the only one who knew the truth."

"How did you know?"

"I found my mother's confession letter."

Amber sighed, eyes going shiny with sympathy. "Oh, Royce."

"I burned the letter, and the secret was safe. But then, on his deathbed, my grandfather Benteen told Jared he'd heard the shot. When my father drove away, Benteen dumped the gun in the river because he didn't want his son tried for murder."

Royce had wished that Jared never found out. But

now it was better that he had. "So, I know, and Gramps knew, and Jared knows." Royce blew out a breath.

"Plus McQuestin," Amber said softly, obviously putting the pieces together. "And somehow Norman Stanton."

"Allowing him to blackmail my family."

She lay back down. "To keep the secret?"

"Our reputation was important to Benteen."

"But, millions of dollars' worth of important?"

Royce had asked himself that same question, and he didn't have a good answer. What the hell were Benteen and McQuestin thinking? His father couldn't be tried. There wasn't a man in the state who'd fault Royce's father for retaliating against Stanton.

That left their mother's reputation. And, as far as Royce was concerned, she'd made her own bed. He couldn't imagine paying millions of dollars protecting a woman who'd betrayed her own family.

Well, from this point on, he and Jared were in charge, and not a single dime of Ryder money was getting into the hands of a Stanton.

"The payments stop now," he vowed to Amber. "And I want to know everything there is to know about Norman Stanton."

She put her hand on Royce's shoulder. "You're not going after revenge, are you?"

He turned his head to look her in the eyes. "I *am* going after my money."

"Royce."

He raised his eyebrows, all but daring her to argue.

She searched his expression. "I don't want you to get yourself in trouble."

His anger switched to resolve, and he couldn't help

but smile. Her sentiment was admirable, but completely unnecessary.

"Darlin'," he told her. "If I was you, I'd be worried about Norman Stanton, not about me."

Six worried Ryder International division heads stared back at Royce around the ranch house dining room table. The doors were closed to the rest of the house, but the windows were open, the happy sounds of an ongoing barbecue and baseball game a jarring counterpoint to the uncomfortable conversation.

If the four men and two women were unsettled by Barry Brewster's firing, they were positively rattled by the potential fallout from the loss of the China deal. Ryder International was a strong company, but it wasn't invincible. They were going to have to take quick and decisive action if they wanted to recover.

Jared was still out of touch, but it didn't take a rocket scientist to figure out the answer. Some of the Ryder companies would need to be sold, perhaps entire divisions, which explained the ashen faces around the table. Nobody wanted to be the sacrificial lamb.

"Construction is the bread and butter of the company," Konrad Klaus opened the conversation. He was out-front and aggressive as always. As the head of the largest and longest-standing division of the corporation, he wielded considerable influence with his counterparts.

"It's pretty shortsighted to mess with high tech," Carmen Volle put in.

Mel Casper threw down his pen. "Oh, sure. Everybody look at sports and culture. It's not always the bottom line, you know. We're carrying the marketing load for everybody else."

Royce cut them all off. "This isn't divide and conquer," he warned. "Jared's not coming back to a war. I've got your reports—"

"We wrote those before we had the facts," said Konrad.

Konrad's respect factor for Royce had never been high. But it was rare that it mattered. It mattered today.

Royce gave him a level look. "Precisely why I asked for them up front. I wanted the facts, not half a dozen individual lobbying efforts."

"So you can pick us off like fattened ducks?" asked Mel.

"*That's* the attitude you want to project?" Royce needed loyalty and teamwork right now. He wasn't looking to get rid of anybody else, but he wasn't looking to babysit any prima donnas, either.

"I say we wait for Jared to get back," said Konrad.

Royce turned to stare the man down. "What part of fifty million dollars didn't you understand?

Konrad glowered but didn't answer.

"We start today," said Royce. He might not be as involved in the operations of Ryder International as Jared, but he was still an owner, and he'd had about enough of people assuming he could be marginalized.

Barry Brewster would never have treated Melissa the way he'd treated Amber. Just because Royce flew a jet didn't mean he was incapable of anything else. Starting here and now, he was taking a stand—both with Norman Stanton, and with the brass at Ryder International.

"I don't see how we do that." Konrad tossed out a direct challenge to Royce's leadership.

"Did this company turn into a democracy when I wasn't looking?" Royce asked softly.

"Our loyalty is to Jared."

"Your loyalty should be to Ryder International."

Konrad compressed his lips. The rest of the division heads looked down at the table. Royce realized it was now or never. He had to firmly pick up the corporate reins.

"I'm hiring an expert to do a review," he announced, having made a split-second decision.

The group exchanged dubious glances, but nobody said anything.

"Creighton Waverley Security."

"You think we're criminals?" Konrad thundered across the table.

"I think they're one hell of a research firm," Royce countered calmly. "We're going to review every company we own, take stock and make our decisions. Anybody who's not on board with it is free to leave."

He looked to each of the people in turn around the table. Nobody was happy, but nobody was walking away, either.

Now that he'd taken the first step on the fly, he supposed the second step had better be to have Amber put him in touch with her best friend's firm.

Amber helped a waiting group of children into the back of the wooden wagon, while a Ryder cowboy double-checked the harnesses on the matched Clydesdale team out front. Sasha was handing out giant chocolate chip cookies while, off to one side, Wesley was teasing Stephanie with his lariat. Amber did a double take of the two. If she wasn't mistaken, Wesley had developed a crush on his riding instructor.

She smiled to herself. Wesley was a very attractive,

fun-loving man. It wouldn't surprise her in the least if the crush was reciprocated.

"I have to talk to you." The mere sound of Royce's voice behind her caused a little thrill to zip through Amber's body. But in contrast to Wesley, Royce sounded tense and serious.

"Something wrong?" She helped the last little boy into the wagon, dusting her hands off on the sides of her jeans.

Royce moved to the corner of the wagon and pushed up the tailgate, sliding the latch to keep everyone safely inside.

Stephanie planted a foot on the wagon wheel and jumped in with the kids. Wesley quickly followed suit, taking a seat next to her on one of the padded benches, and Amber was sure she'd guessed right.

Royce backed out of the way, towing Amber with him as a cowboy unhitched the lead horse and turned the team toward the road.

"I've been meeting with the division heads," said Royce.

"What did you find out?" Amber had realized Royce and the senior managers were missing, and she'd easily guessed they were talking business. She raised her hand to wave to the cheering children as the wagon creaked down the road.

Royce pulled her toward the shadow of the barn, speaking low into her ear, his voice bringing flash memories of their night together. "I was wondering if you could do something for me."

"I don't know, Royce." She glanced around at the crowds. "There's an awful lot of people in the barn right now."

"You have a one-track mind," he admonished.

She grinned at him. She did seem particularly obsessed with making love.

"Not that I'd say no to a more interesting offer," he clarified. "But I was hoping to get in touch with your friend Katie. I need to know the who's who of Creighton Waverley."

The request brought Amber back to reality. "I thought you were going to let *me* investigate Norman Stanton."

"What?"

"I'm doing a good job," she informed him, pursing her lips.

Royce suddenly grinned.

"What?"

"You. Jumping to conclusions."

"Quit laughing at me."

"Then stop being so entertaining."

"Stop being condescending."

"Stop pouting."

"I like investigating. I want to see this through."

Royce's smile turned sly, and he cocked his head meaningfully toward the barn. "Yeah?" he drawled.

"Now who's got a one-track mind?"

"Guilty," he agreed with an easy smile, but at the same time, he backed off.

A cheer went up at the baseball game, while a freshening breeze brought the aroma of hamburgers from the cook tent.

Amber brushed at a lazy fly.

"I'm commissioning a review of all the Ryder companies," said Royce. "We're going to have to make some tough decisions, and I thought Creighton Waverley might be able to help."

"So, I'm keeping my job?"

He brushed the back of his hand along her upper arm and leaned closer again. "Now *that* remains to be seen."

"I'm not bribing you with sex."

He exaggerated an offended tone. "I'd bribe you with sex."

She extracted her cell phone from her jeans pocket. "I'm bribing you with Katie's phone number."

"Fair enough. I'll bribe you for something else later."

Amber couldn't help but smile as she punched in Katie's cell number.

"Amber," came the breathless answer. "I was just about to call you. Are you at a hoedown or something?"

Amber glanced around for the source of a noise that might have made it through the phone. "What makes you ask that?"

"Checked tablecloths, cowboy hats, horses."

Amber glanced down at her phone, then put it back to her ear. "Do you have some kind of monitor on me?"

"No, I have a white Lexus, over in front of the house. At least I think it's the house. The building with the porch and, yep, it's a hitching rail."

Amber whirled around.

Sure enough, Katie was emerging from a low-slung sports car, wearing a short, blue, clingy dress, high-heeled pumps, with her honey-blond hair in a jaunty updo. Her small bag was beaded, and she reminded Amber of how long it had been since she'd had a manicure or a facial.

Amber took a reflexive step away from Royce. "What are you *doing* here?"

"I have to talk to you."

"That's what telephones are for." A sudden fear

gripped Amber. "There's nobody with you, is there?" Like Hargrove or her parents.

"Relax," said Katie as she picked her way along the edge of the baseball field. "Your secret is safe." She grinned and gave Amber a wave.

Several dozen cowboys followed her progress.

"That's Katie," Amber told Royce.

"She does know how to make an entrance," he muttered, watching as raptly as anyone else on the ranch.

Amber felt an unwelcome pinch of jealousy.

"Who's that with you?" asked Katie as she drew ever closer.

"Royce Ryder."

"Nice."

Okay, jealousy was silly. Katie was an attractive woman, and Royce was an attractive man. They'd noticed. So what?

"Do you have any idea how far away this place is?" Katie called across the grass, folding her phone closed now that she was in shouting range.

"It's Chicago that's far away," Royce countered. "Montana is right here."

Katie grinned as she stepped up, holding out her perfect, magenta-tipped hand. "Katie Merrick. Creighton Waverley Security." She shook, then opened her purse, dropped the phone inside and extracted a business card, handing it to Royce.

"I was about to call you," said Royce.

"Well, isn't that perfect," Katie returned, glancing around the ranch yard. "Any chance they're serving margaritas at this shindig?"

It was a slow walk back to the ranch house, where

Sasha whipped up a blender of margaritas while Amber, Royce and Katie settled in on the deck. Gopher immediately jumped into Amber's lap.

"You'll want Alec Creighton's help," said Katie. She'd been all business while Royce had explained his plans for Ryder International.

"Your boss?" asked Royce as he poured the frozen green concoction into tall glasses.

"My boss's son. He's not with Creighton Waverley. He's sort of a lone-wolf troubleshooter. We subcontract to him on occasion. I can give you a list of a hundred satisfied clients if you like." Katie accepted the drink with a nod of thanks.

"How do I get hold of him?" Royce handed Amber a drink. She still couldn't believe Katie had come all the way to Montana. And since they'd done nothing but discuss Ryder International business since she'd arrived, Amber couldn't begin to guess *why* she'd come all the way to Montana.

"I'll get him to call you." Katie took a sip of her drink. "He won't take on a client without a referral."

"Appreciate that," said Royce with a salute of his drink.

Amber couldn't keep quiet any longer, and her voice came out more demanding than she'd intended. "What are you doing here, Katie?"

Katie shrugged. "I missed you."

It didn't ring true. There was something in Katie's eyes—guilt, maybe fear.

Amber was suspicious. "Did you tell my parents I was here?"

"I can't believe you'd even ask me that. Can't a girl visit her best friend?" Katie took another swig, smiling far too brightly. "Okay if I stay over tonight?"

Nine

Wrapped in a fluffy robe, Katie sat cross-legged on the end of Amber's bed while Amber washed her face at the sink inside the en-suite bathroom door.

"Just how long are you planning to stay here?" Katie asked, her voice muffled by the gush of the running water.

"I haven't decided," Amber answered, dipping her face forward to rinse it, then blindly grabbing for a towel.

As the days went by, she thought less and less about going home. Oh, she knew she'd have to, and probably soon. But there simply wasn't anything tugging her in that direction.

"You know the wedding shower's coming up, right?"

Amber peeked out from behind the towel. "Nobody canceled it?"

"Nobody believed you were serious. There are people flying in from all over the country."

Amber tossed the towel over the rack and paced back into the room. "They're still putting on my wedding shower?"

Katie nodded, while Amber dropped down onto the bed.

"The shower cake's gorgeous," Katie offered.

"This is a disaster."

Katie reached out to rub Amber's arm. "You breaking it off with Hargrove was the disaster. The shower, the dress…" Her hand gripped on Amber's shoulder. Then she abruptly stood up and crossed the room.

"I tried on your dress," she blurted out, turning to brace her back against the bureau.

Amber blinked in surprise. "You did? How'd it look?"

"Gorgeous. Absolutely, stunningly gorgeous."

"It's too bad we'll have to sell it," said Amber. "I can't see ever wearing it."

Katie nodded, her eyes staring blankly into space. "Gorgeous. Really gorgeous."

Amber pictured her friend twirling in front of the mirror. Katie always did have a romantic streak.

Suddenly, Katie clenched her fists, and her eyes scrunched shut. "Oooh, you have to promise me you won't get mad."

"Why would I get mad?" Truth was, Amber wondered if Katie had taken pictures while she modeled the dress. It might be interesting to see how it had turned out.

"I…did something," Katie confessed in a harsh whisper.

"To the dress?"

Katie didn't answer, but the color drained from her face.

"Did you spill something on it? Tear it?" Amber waited for an emotional reaction to her wedding dress being ruined, but it didn't come.

Katie emphatically shook her head. "No. The dress is fine."

"Then what are you so worried about?"

Katie picked up a china horse figurine from the top of the bureau, stroking her fingertip across its glossy surface. She looked at Amber then drew a breath.

"Katie?"

"He saw me in it."

"Who saw you in what?"

"Hargrove. He saw me in the wedding dress."

Amber didn't exactly understand why that was a problem.

Katie set down the figurine, her words speeding up, hands clasping together. "After it was delivered, and I had it on and was prancing around my apartment, he knocked on the door. I didn't know it was him. And, well, when I opened it…" She stopped talking.

"That's when Hargrove saw you in the wedding dress?"

Katie nodded miserably.

Amber fought an urge to smile. "I don't think that's bad luck or anything."

"I'm not so sure."

"Seriously, Katie. I can imagine he was annoyed." Hargrove was nothing if not mired in propriety. "But we're selling the damn thing anyway."

Katie drew a deep breath and squared her shoulders. "Thing is, he really, uh, liked the dress."

"Well, at that price, he'd better have liked it."

"I mean, well…" Katie gazed down at her front, picking a dark speck from the terry-cloth pile of the robe. "He really liked *me* in it."

Amber blinked. "So?" It was probably a good fit. She and Katie were pretty close to the same size.

"And—" Katie buried her face in her hands "—turns out, he liked me out of it, too."

Amber was silent for a full ten seconds. "You're going to have to repeat that."

Katie spread her fingers, peeking out as if she was looking at a horror movie. "I am the *worst* friend *ever*."

Amber gave her head a little shake. "What are you saying?"

Katie just stared at her.

"Are you saying you *slept* with Hargrove?" It wasn't possible. Nothing made less sense than that.

But Katie nodded. "It happened so fast. One minute he was staring at me. Then he was kissing me. Then the dress came off, and well, yeah, there might have been a bit of a tear around the buttonholes—"

Amber shook her head. "You're not making any sense."

"I am *so* sorry," Katie wailed, pressing a fist against her mouth. "You must hate me."

"No. No, it's not that."

"I had to come and tell you in person."

"I'm confused, not mad." Amber tried to make her point. "Hargrove doesn't get overcome with passion and tear off dresses." Not the Hargrove she knew.

Katie blinked like an owl.

"He's staid, proper, *controlled*."

Katie blinked once more. A flush rose up from the base of her throat, coloring her face. "Actually..."

Amber rose from the bed. "Actually, what?"

"Sexually speaking, I wouldn't call him staid, and I definitely wouldn't call him proper."

"Are you telling me...?"

Katie gave a meaningful nod.

"You had wild, impulsive sex with Hargrove?"

Something deep and warm flared in Katie's eyes, and she nodded.

"And...it was...*good?*" Amber asked in disbelief.

"It was fantastic."

Amber tried to wrap her head around that. "But... What..." She gripped the bedpost to steady herself. "Sorry. We can't get technical about this." She paused. "Can we?"

Katie cocked her head. "I take it it wasn't always good for you?"

"It was, um..." How did she say this? "Kind of boring."

"No way. You mean he didn't—" Katie's blush deepened.

Amber was forced to stifle a laugh. "Whatever it is you're not saying, I'm pretty sure he didn't do it with me."

Katie fought a grin and lost. "So, you're not mad?"

Amber shook her head, sitting back down on the bed. "I broke up with him."

Katie crossed the room to sit beside her, relieved amusement coloring her tone. "You're probably not going to want the wedding dress back."

"Keep it. Maybe you should keep Hargrove, too. Think of them as a set."

"Maybe I will," Katie said softly.

Amber turned to gaze at her friend and saw the glow in Katie's eyes. She raised her brows in a question, and Katie nodded, wiping a single tear with the back of her hand.

Surprised, but not the least bit unhappy, Amber wrapped her arm around Katie's shoulders. "You do realize what this means, don't you?"

"What?"

"I get to wear the maid of honor's dress." Amber paused. "You know, I always liked that one better anyway."

"Take it," said Katie. "It's yours."

Amber drew a deep sigh. "Wow. Does Hargrove know?"

"That I slept with him?" There was a strengthening thread of laughter in Katie's voice.

"That you came here to confess."

Katie shook her head. "He thinks... Wait. I almost forgot." She bounced off the bed to her small suitcase. "I found something for you."

Hunting through her things, she extracted a manila envelope. "Pictures of Norman Stanton. And his brother, Frank. Also a sister and parents—the three of them died quite a few years back."

Amber accepted the envelope, her thoughts going to Royce. Now it was her turn to feel guilty.

"What?" Katie asked, gauging Amber's expression.

"There's something you don't know."

"About the investigation?"

Amber shook her head. "About me." She shut her eyes for a second. "Oh, hell. I'm sleeping with Royce."

Katie drew back. "Whoa. You cheated on Hargrove?"

"No." Amber swatted Katie with the envelope. "I did not cheat on Hargrove. I broke up with Hargrove. Lucky for you."

"True," Katie agreed. Then she sobered. "This cowboy dude? He rocks your world?"

"And how."

"So." Katie cocked her head toward the bedroom door. "What are you waiting for?"

"I didn't want to be rude."

"Unlike me who slept with your fiancé."

"Ex."

"Whatever. Go see your cowboy. I'll catch you at breakfast."

"You sure?"

"Of course I'm sure. *I* don't want to sleep with you."

Amber grinned, came to her feet and headed out the door.

On the way across the hall, she slit the envelope open, sliding out some eight-by-ten photos.

First one was labeled Norman. He had receding hair, dark, beady eyes and a little goatee. Yeah, she could see him as a blackmailer.

The next was Frank, an older picture. This was the guy who'd broken up Royce's family. He wasn't bad-looking, but not fantastic, either. He seemed a little on the thin side. But maybe that was a generational thing.

She flipped to the next picture, raising her hand to rap on Royce's door. But she froze, hand in midair, the picture of Frank and Norman's sister stopping her cold.

The young girl had a trophy in her hand and a broad smile on her face. Amber stared for a long minute, then slowly turned to the next picture. It was the parents, and the next one was a thirty-year-old family portrait. The final picture was another headshot of Norman.

Amber paged back to the picture of the sister for a final look. Then, stomach twisting around nothing, she rapped on Royce's bedroom door.

His voice was muffled and incomprehensible, but she opened the door anyway. He was lying in bed, a hardcover book in his hands, the bedside lamp glowing yellow against his natural wood walls.

"Hey." He smiled, letting the book fall to his lap.

"Hi." She clicked the door shut behind her.

"Something wrong?"

She nodded.

His smile immediately faded. "Katie?"

"Kind of." Amber moved across the room.

His eyes cooled. "News from…home?"

Amber sat down on the bed. "We have a problem."

He tossed the book aside. "You're reconciling with Hargrove."

"What? *No*. How could you say that?"

Royce didn't answer.

"This has nothing to do with Hargrove." She wanted to be annoyed with Royce for even thinking that it might have been Hargrove, but there wasn't time for that. Instead, she covered his hand, trying to prepare him. "I have pictures of the Stantons. And it's not what we think."

"What do we think?"

She slipped the pictures out of the envelope and spread them on the bed. "Look."

Royce clenched his jaw as he leafed through them. "I've seen Frank Stanton before. He lived on the ranch for a while. Worked with the horses. That's how they met."

"Look at the sister," Amber whispered.

Royce shifted his gaze. "She was into horses, too," he surmised. The trophy was obviously equestrian.

"Look at her chin," said Amber. "Her eyes, the hairline."

Royce glanced from the picture to Amber, brows furrowing.

"Stephanie, Royce."

"What about Stephanie?"

"Stephanie is the spitting image of…" Amber flipped the picture over to read the handwriting on the back. "Clara Stanton, Frank and Norman's sister."

"No." He glanced back down. "She doesn't look anything like…" Royce's breathing went deep.

"He's not blackmailing you over murder."

"Son of a bitch."

She didn't want to say it out loud.

"Son of a bitch!"

"Shh."

Royce turned to her with haunted eyes. "This can't be right."

There was nothing she could say to cushion the blow.

"It can't be real."

It was real all right. Stephanie was Frank Stanton's daughter.

"Who else knows?" he demanded.

"No one."

"Katie?"

Amber shook her head. "Not even Katie. I only figured it out in the hallway thirty seconds ago."

He glanced back down at the picture. "We can't tell Stephanie. It'll kill her. She was two years old when they died. She doesn't even know about the affair."

"I won't tell Stephanie." But Amber realized that meant paying off Norman again.

Royce rolled out of bed, pacing across the floor, photo still gripped in his hand. He was stark naked, but the fact didn't seem to register.

He strode past the bay window, raking a hand through his hair. "We…"

Then he turned at the wall, glanced at the picture and threw it down on a dresser. "I…"

He stopped dead, fisted both hands and glared at Amber. "There's got to be a way out."

"I'm sure there is," she agreed in the most soothing voice she could muster.

He crossed back over to the bed, sat down and uttered a crude cuss. "That bastard's got us by the balls."

Amber didn't know how to answer. It was true, but agreeing seemed counterproductive.

"We can't tell Stephanie," he reaffirmed.

Amber nodded.

Royce snagged his phone from the table. He punched a couple of numbers and put it to his ear.

"Who—" Amber stopped herself.

"Jared."

She knew Jared had been out of touch for several days now.

It appeared he still was.

Royce's voice was terse as he left the voice-mail message. "Jared. Royce. Call me now. Right now." He punched the off button then leaned back against the headboard.

She dared to reach out and touch his bare shoulder. It was hot, hard as a rock. "Anything I can do?"

"Short of fixing a deal with the Chinese, finding a sailboat in the middle of the South Pacific or giving Norman Stanton a fatal disease? Not really."

"Right." She slipped across the bed to sit close beside him, curling her arm around his tense back. "Moral support doesn't really cut it at the moment, does it?"

He wrapped one of his arms around her and then the other. Then he bent to kiss the top of her head. "Moral support is better than nothing."

She struggled to find a smile. "That's always been a dream of mine. To be better than nothing."

He gave her a gentle squeeze and whispered above her head. "Will you stay?"

She nodded against his neck, knowing she was falling fast and hard. His troubles were her troubles, and she'd be by his side just as long as he needed her.

In the morning, when Katie asked for a tour of Stephanie's jumping ranch, Royce resisted the temptation to tag along. Much as he'd love to spend the time with Amber, he was afraid he'd end up studying his sister's expressions, movements and mannerisms for traces of the man he'd hated for twenty long years.

She was still his baby sister. He loved her, and he'd move heaven and earth to protect her. But he needed some time to come to terms with the knowledge she was also Frank Stanton's daughter.

What the hell had his mother been thinking?

Had she known which man fathered Stephanie? What

was her plan? Was she going to take Stephanie with her and Stanton? Would she have destroyed that many lives for her own selfish happiness?

The knowledge crept like a cold snake into his belly.

He smacked open the front door, marching onto the porch to take a deep breath of fresh air. He didn't wish anybody dead, not even Frank Stanton. But he wasn't sorry his mother's plan had failed. He couldn't imagine his life without Stephanie.

An engine roared in the distance, dust wafting up at the crest of the drive. Royce squinted against the midmorning sunshine. He knew it was too early for Amber and Katie to return, but he couldn't help hoping.

Amber had been amazing last night. First she'd let him rail in anger. Then she'd offered practical advice. She seemed to have an uncanny knack for knowing when to stay quiet and when to talk. Finally, against all odds, she helped him find a touch of humor in the face of catastrophe.

Afterward, he'd stayed awake for hours, simply holding her in his arms, letting the feel of her body make his troubles seem less daunting.

It was a car that appeared over the rise. A dark sedan, dusty from the long road in, but unmistakably new, and undeniably expensive. The windows were tinted, and the driver moved tentatively around the potholes dotting dirt and sparse gravel.

Not a local, that was for sure.

Royce made his way down the front stairs, wondering if this could be the mysterious Alec Creighton, or perhaps someone from the Ryder Chicago office.

The car eased to a halt. The engine went silent. And the driver's door swung open wide.

Royce didn't recognize the tall man who emerged. He looked to be in his late thirties. He was clean shaven, his hair nearly black. He wore a Savile Row suit and an expensive pair of loafers. His white shirt was pressed, the patterned silk tie classic and understated.

To his credit, he didn't flinch at the dust, simply slammed the car door shut and gave Royce a genuine smile, stepping forward to offer his hand. "Hargrove Alston."

Royce faltered midreach but quickly recovered. "Royce Ryder."

He resisted the urge to grip too hard, though he squared his shoulders and straightened his spine, watching Hargrove's expression closely for signs that there was going to be a fight.

"Good to meet you," Hargrove offered. There wasn't a trace of anger or resentment in the man's eyes. Either he didn't know about Royce and Amber, or the man had one hell of a poker face.

"What brings you to Montana?" Royce opened.

A split second of annoyance narrowed the man's eyes. "For starters, I understand you're harboring my fiancée."

Royce resented the accusation. "It was at her request."

Hargrove's smile flattened. "I'm sure it was. I'd like to speak with her if you don't mind."

"She's not here." The statement was true enough. Amber might be close by, she wasn't specifically on the ranch this very moment.

Hargrove glanced to the house then back to Royce. "You have a reason to lie to me?"

"I have no reason to lie."

Hargrove regarded him with obvious impatience.

"I can try to pass along a message," Royce offered, folding his arms over his chest and planting his feet apart on the dusty drive.

"You do know who I am, right?"

"You said you were Hargrove Alston."

"I'm not accustomed to being stonewalled, Mr. Ryder."

"And I'm not accustomed to uninvited guests on my land, Mr. Alston."

Hargrove's expression went hard. "I know she's here."

"I told you she wasn't."

There was a pause while the entire ranch seemed to hold its breath.

"But you do know where she is."

Royce did. Since he preferred not to lie, he didn't answer.

Hargrove gave a cool, knowing smile. "She does bring out the protective instincts."

The assessment rang true. And it reminded Royce how well Hargrove knew Amber. She had been bringing out Royce's protective instincts from the moment they'd met.

He decided it was time to stop the pretense. "I assume you're here to drag her back to Chicago."

The shot of pain that flitted through Hargrove's eyes was quickly masked by anger. "I'm here to tell her she can't solve her problems by running away from them."

Guilt hit Royce square in the solar plexus. Amber

had, in fact, run away from Hargrove. And Royce had helped her.

His thoughts went to his father, and an unwelcome chill rippled up his spine. His mother had written a letter. Amber had settled for a text.

Not that Royce was anything like Frank Stanton. Looking back to his teenage memories, Frank had deliberately and methodically lured a woman away from her husband and children.

"Do you have any idea why she left?" he found himself asking.

"Only Amber knows the answer to that." Hargrove shook his head in disgust. "Forget that the wedding dress arrived from Paris this week, that the caterer's put the Kobe beef on hold, that the florist has a Holland order in limbo and that the press has been commenting on Amber's absence. We have fifty people arriving for the wedding shower on Saturday. Her mother's frantic with worry."

Royce swallowed, considering for the first time the destruction Amber had left in her wake.

Hargrove's dark eyes glittered. "I can't wait to sit her down and ask a few questions."

"Did you think about canceling everything?" Royce ventured. If it was him, and the bride went AWOL, as Amber had, Royce couldn't see himself waiting around.

"Are you married, Mr. Ryder?"

Royce shook his head.

"Ever been in love?"

"Nope."

"Well, once you get there, you'll find yourself making allowances for the most inappropriate behavior."

"So, you'd take her back?"

"You don't throw this away over some prewedding jitters. Our plans have been in the works for four years. Our relationship is built on mutual goals and respect. And the foundation of my entire campaign has been built around the fresh faces of Mr. and Mrs. Hargrove Alston. If we're lucky, she'll be pregnant by the primaries."

It sounded a little cold-blooded to Royce. But it also sounded as though Amber was fundamentally entwined in Hargrove's life. And he hadn't considered the situation from Hargrove's perspective.

Amber herself had admitted he was a decent guy. He wasn't malicious or abusive. He simply wasn't as exciting as she'd hoped.

Well, hell, honey, it had been four years. When you were in it for the long haul, the thrill of romance eventually turned into the routine of everyday life.

"There's no way you end something like this on a whim," Hargrove finished, and Royce couldn't deny the man's point.

Relationships took work. They took patience and commitment. They didn't need third party interference. An honorable man would have walked away the minute he saw her diamond ring.

And what the hell had Royce expected? Amber wouldn't stick with him any more than she'd stuck with Hargrove. In the end, he would have been left with nothing but a broken heart and the knowledge he'd destroyed another man's life.

Another engine sounded on the driveway. Before the blue pickup even crested the hill, Royce knew exactly who had arrived.

Ten

"You *didn't*," Amber rasped to Katie as the truck rocked to a stop behind Hargrove's car, and the dust cleared around them.

"I really didn't," Katie responded, her face pale.

"Did you talk to him last night?"

"Just about business."

"Did you tell him we were together?" Amber squinted at Hargrove, then at Royce, trying to interpret their posture.

Katie clutched the dashboard. "I hinted we were in Chicago."

"He knew I wasn't in Chicago. He must have tracked you here."

"Damn it," Katie cursed.

"You go talk to him," said Amber.

"No way."

"You're the one who slept with him. Maybe he's here for you."

Katie frantically shook her head. "Neither of us have even mentioned it. He's here for you."

"He doesn't want me."

But Hargrove's accusatory gaze was focused directly on Amber.

"I don't think he knows that," Katie offered.

This time Amber swore between clenched teeth. She grabbed the gearshift, setting up to pull it into Reverse. "I say we run for it."

"I don't think that's an option," Katie ventured, her gaze tracking Royce as he paced toward the truck.

He looked angry.

Had Hargrove been rude?

Royce reached for the handle and swung open her door. "There's somebody here to see you."

"I'm sorry, Royce. I didn't expect—"

"You knew he'd come," said Royce, hand gripping the top of the door frame. "*I* knew he'd come."

Amber had fervently hoped he wouldn't. She glanced at Katie, who sat completely still, eyes front. No help there. Finally, she took a breath and pulled the key from the ignition.

Royce stepped back out of the way, as Hargrove marched up.

"*Montana?*" Hargrove accused. "Honestly, Amber, could you make things any more difficult?"

Royce backed off farther, and she knew he was leaving.

"Royce, don't—"

But he shook his head, sliding his eyes meaningfully toward Hargrove.

And he was right. They might as well get this conversation over with.

"We need to talk," rasped Hargrove, moving in too close and pushing the truck door closed.

"There's not a lot left to say," she responded, pushing her windblown hair behind her ears and gathering her courage as Royce left.

It was hard for her to imagine what came after *you slept with the bridesmaid, and I fell for someone else.*

"Do you have any idea how much trouble you've caused?" Hargrove growled. "We've got a thousand people working on the wedding. Nobody knows whether to stop, go, or hold."

"I already told you. They can stop."

"You can't just shut this down on a dime, Amber. We had plans. There's the campaign, the press."

"I'm not marrying you to get good press, Hargrove."

He held up his hands in frustration. "This isn't a one-shot article, Amber. We're talking about my entire political career."

"Yours won't be the first high-profile wedding that was canceled."

"And do you *know* what happened to the others?"

"I don't care what happened to the others. I don't love you, Hargrove. And you don't love me."

"That's ridiculous."

"Then why did you sleep with Katie?"

His jaw went taut. "*That* was a mistake."

"Excuse me?" Katie squeaked from beyond the open window, reminding them both of her presence.

Hargrove's nostrils flared.

"A mistake?" Amber scoffed. "What? Did you trip and accidentally tear off the wedding dress?"

"I don't know what she told you."

"I'm right *here*," Katie pointed out, exiting the truck and slamming the passenger door for emphasis.

"She said you were wild with passion."

"That's ridiculous." But a flush rose up his neck.

"You never tore off *my* dress," said Amber.

"That was out of respect."

Amber shook her head at Hargrove. "It was out of disinterest. Admit it."

"I'm not here to fight with you."

"That's good," said Amber as she dared a glance to where Katie was glaring daggers at him. "Because I think I'd have to take a number."

Hargrove glanced at Katie. "Can you give us some privacy."

"No." She stood her ground.

"This isn't about you."

"The hell it isn't."

"*I'm* going to give *you two* some privacy," said Amber.

Hargrove quickly reached for her arm. "Amber—"

"It's over, Hargrove." She backed out of his reach. "I'm truly sorry about the press and the campaign, but I can't marry you."

"Amber!" He looked genuinely fearful. "You don't know what you're doing to me."

She shook her head. "You don't know what you're doing to yourself. Talk to Katie."

"This isn't about Katie."

"It should be." Amber backed up a few more steps. "Don't screw this up, Hargrove," she warned.

Then she turned away, scanning the yard and finding Royce in a round pen, doing groundwork with a black horse.

Heart still pounding, stomach still cramped, she made her way to the rail and leaned over to watch.

Royce shifted his arms, and the horse sped up. Then he slowed it down, turned it and had it trotting in the opposite direction. It was near poetry, and the tension leached out of her body.

Several minutes later, he approached the animal. He stroked its neck, clipping a lead rope to its bridle then tying it to a rail. He walked through the soft dirt toward Amber.

He braced his hands on the opposite side of the fence. "You here to say goodbye?"

She drew back in surprise. "No."

He nodded toward Hargrove. "He came a long way."

"I told you, I'm not marrying him."

"Why not?"

Amber peered at Royce in confusion. "What do you mean why not?" She leaned forward. "I've just spent the last week with you."

He shrugged. "That doesn't mean anything."

She opened her mouth, struggling to form words.

"I'm new, Amber." He stripped off a pair of leather gloves. "I seem interesting and exciting. You're on vacation, having a fling."

Amber's fingertips went to her temple. "A fling?"

He calmly tucked the gloves under his arm and adjusted his Stetson. "Hargrove is willing to take you back. You should seriously consider his offer."

Her frustration was turning to anger. "You said

anybody who told me that was short-sighted and stupid."

"Guess I was wrong."

She shook her head, but he stayed stubbornly silent.

She clenched her jaw, then enunciated her words slowly and carefully. "I do not love Hargrove."

"You don't know that for sure."

"I absolutely know that for sure. Because I love *you*, Royce."

The words went unanswered. But she wasn't sorry. This was no fling. He was falling for her, too. She'd bet her life on it.

No one had ever treated her the way Royce did. He was compassionate, attentive and so very sexy. And she was positive he didn't open up with many other people the way he'd opened up with her. He'd flat out told her nobody else knew about his father. And their lovemaking was off the charts.

He scoffed out a laugh. "You don't love me."

She smacked her hand on the rail in frustration. "What is the matter with you? Are you afraid of Hargrove?"

Royce's eyes glittered. "I'm not afraid of anybody."

"Well, I *know* you feel it, too."

He whipped off his hat, banging it on his thigh to release the dust. "If by *it,* you mean lust, then you're right."

"I don't mean lust."

"People don't fall in love in a week."

"People can fall in love in an hour."

"Not so it lasts." It was his turn to lean in. "It's lust, Amber. It's a fling. What you have with Hargrove is real, and you need to go back to him."

"Hargrove loves Katie."

Royce smacked his hat back on his head. "Then why's he here looking for you?"

"He doesn't know it yet." She realized that sounded lame, but it was completely true. Amber had very high hopes that Hargrove would wake up to the truth about Katie.

"Now you're grasping at straws. Go back to reality, Amber. Get married in that big cathedral and have beautiful babies for the campaign trail."

"Are you *listening* to yourself?" She gripped the rail. "You're willing to throw away everything that's between us?"

A part of her couldn't believe it. A part of her expected to wake up any second. But another brusque, insidious part of her realized she'd made a horrible mistake.

She might have fallen for Royce. But Royce hadn't fallen for her.

"You've spun a nice fantasy, here," he said. Then he nodded toward Hargrove's car. "But your reality is over there."

Her throat closed over, and she swallowed hard. "You're asking me to leave?"

His expression was unreadable. "I'm asking you to leave."

She gave a stiff nod, unable to speak. Royce didn't love her. He didn't want her. And she'd made a complete and total fool of herself.

Two days later, Amber alternated between misery and mortification. Royce might not have loved her, but her heart had fallen hard and fast for him.

It was easy to see what made him such a great pick-up artist. He must make every woman feel loved and cherished—at least temporarily. She wondered about the string of broken hearts he'd left behind.

Then she wondered who he'd be with next. But that thought hurt so much she banished it, blinking back the familiar sting in her eyes as she focused on her mother far across her family's great room.

The replacement-for-the-shower party was in full swing. But Amber didn't feel remotely like celebrating.

Maybe if Royce had simply sweet-talked her into bed, if they'd had fantastic sex, if he'd put her in a cab in the morning, maybe then she could have handled it. But he hadn't simply made love to her. He'd joked and laughed with her, shared his secrets with her, made her feel valuable, important, a part of his world.

"Amber?" Her mother, Reena, approached, concern in her expression.

Amber tried to smile at her mother. Her family had been told that she was the one to break it off with Hargrove. But nobody but Katie knew anything about Royce. Amber planned to keep it that way.

Reena's floor-length chiffon dress rustled to a halt. "Why aren't you visiting, sweetheart?"

"I'm a little tired."

"Are you sure that's all it is?"

"I'm sure." She mustered up a smile.

"That's the best you can do? You look like you're headed for the gallows."

Amber signed. "I'm really not in the mood for a party, Mom."

Reena moved in closer. "But I thought this was what you wanted."

"I didn't want a party."

"Well, you didn't want a shower, either. And the guests were already on their way."

Amber drew a shuddering breath, fighting the tears that were never far from the surface. Emotions alone shouldn't hurt this much. Still, a single teardrop escaped, trailing coolly down her cheek.

"Sweetheart," her mother entreated, drawing Amber close to her side. "Do you miss him so much?"

Amber startled in surprise. How had her mother guessed?

Reena cupped Amber's chin with gentle fingertips, peering deeply into her eyes. "Shall I give Hargrove a call for you? We might be able to talk him into—"

"She's not missing Hargrove," came Katie's voice as she swooped in to join them.

"Of course she is," said Reena. "Just look at her."

"I'm not missing Hargrove," Amber confirmed.

Katie gave Amber a level, challenging look. "She's missing Royce Ryder."

Amber sucked in a gasp.

"Who?" asked her mother, glancing from Amber to Katie and back again.

Katie gave Amber a helpless shrug. "What's the point in hiding it? It's obvious to anyone that you've had your heart broken."

"Who is Royce Ryder?"

"The man she met in Montana."

"I met him at Jared Ryder's wedding," Amber corrected. Where he'd picked her up in the bar for a quick fling. At least that's the way *he* remembered it.

Reena's jaw dropped a notch, and her hand went to her chest. "You were unfaithful to Hargrove?"

"I *wasn't* unfaithful to Hargrove." Frustration finally

gave Amber an emotion to replace despair. "In fact, Hargrove was unfaithful to me." She returned Katie's look. "With *Katie*."

Katie's face went pale, and Reena's jaw dropped another notch.

"They'd already split up," Katie hastened to assure Reena.

"That's true," Amber admitted. "Nobody was unfaithful to anybody."

Katie's voice went soft. "And she did fall in love with Royce."

Amber was too exhausted to deny it.

"Oh, sweetheart." Reena took Amber's hand. Her mother was a romantic to the core. "That terrible man broke your heart?"

"I broke my own heart." As she said the words out loud, Amber admitted to herself they were true. "We barely knew each other. And my expectations were… Well, he's just such an incredible man. You'd love him, Mom. You really would."

Reena's narrow arm curled around her shoulders. "I wouldn't like him at all. He broke my baby's heart."

Jared's familiar voice barked at Royce over the phone. "What the hell did you do?"

"Jared? Finally. Where are—"

"I need an explanation," Jared demanded.

Royce swiveled on the ranch house office chair, assuming Jared had been in contact with the Ryder office in Chicago. "I don't even know where to start."

"Start with how you broke Amber Hutton's heart and infuriated one of our most important clients."

Royce nearly dropped the phone. "Huh?"

"I've only been gone a week, and you screw up this badly."

"She *called* you?" Royce could hardly believe it. What was Amber doing running to Jared?

"David Hutton called me. He's threatening to cancel his lease. You are aware that he's our second-biggest client, right?"

"Don't patronize me."

"Then don't sleep with our clients' daughters."

What could Royce say to that? "It just…happened."

"Right. Well, un-happen it."

"I don't think that's physically possible."

"You know what I mean. Fix it."

"I can't fix it. She's engaged to someone else."

"What?" Jared's voice rose to a roar.

"Hargrove Alston."

"Then why did you sleep with her?"

Royce didn't have an answer for that. There wasn't an excuse in the world for what he'd done.

Jared was silent for a moment. "David thinks she's in love with *you?*"

"I'm not breaking up her engagement."

"Admirable," said Jared.

"Thank you."

"Could've thought of it *before* you slept with her."

Royce grunted.

"So, how're you going to fix it?"

"I'll talk to her."

"What are you going to say?"

"None of your business." Royce didn't have the first clue.

He'd been thinking about it for days, and had come to the conclusion that by bringing Amber to Montana, he'd turned a momentary hesitation into a life-altering event.

Whatever crazy fantasy Amber had spun around Royce wasn't real. She barely knew him. And he barely knew her. If relationships built on years didn't last, there was no hope at all for one that was built on a mere week.

"Make it my business."

"No."

Jared went silent on the other end of the line for a few beats. "You ever think…"

Royce drummed his fingers on the desktop.

"That maybe she's not…"

"Not what?" Did Jared have something intelligent to add here or not?

Jared drew a breath. "I mean, she might really be in love—"

"No!" Royce barked.

"Could happen."

"No, it could not."

"I'm a married man, Royce. And I'm telling you it could happen."

"You've been married a week. Talk to me in twenty years."

"You're going to make a woman wait twenty years?"

Royce felt his frustration level rise. "I'm going to make a woman wait until she's sure."

"How're you going to know that?"

"I'll just know."

"Like you do now?"

"What I know now is that she's taken, and she's

confused, and she has obligations that have nothing to do with me."

"She's not Mom," Jared said softly.

"Don't even go there."

"And you're not Frank Stanton."

"I'm hanging up now."

"Mom and Dad's relationship was demanding and complex. He worked too hard and she had stars in her eyes."

"And you don't think all marriages are demanding and complex?" That was what the long haul was all about. It meant sticking together through the rough times, knowing better times would come again. It didn't mean bailing the second life got a little humdrum.

"Did it ever occur to you that Dad might have shared the blame?"

"He didn't screw around on her," Royce practically shouted.

"Yeah, but he wasn't perfect. He had a temper. Hell, he shot a guy."

"The son of a bitch deserved it. I'd have shot him, too."

"You mean, if he slept with Amber?"

"Hell, yes."

"Gotcha."

Royce went silent, his jaw clamping down.

What had just happened? He was the illicit lover in this triangle, not the betrayed husband.

Jared's voice turned jovial. "Okay, fixing this is going to be way easier than I thought."

"Shut up."

Jared chuckled, and Royce bit down harder on his outrage. His brother could be positively infuriating.

"Let's move on to other problems," he ground out. He wasn't wrong, and Jared wasn't right. And it was definitely time to end this discussion.

His brother's tone changed. "What problems?"

"The China deal fell apart."

"Yeah," Jared sighed. "I was afraid of that."

"We're in a cash crunch because of it. I've got a guy taking a thorough look at our operations. I think we're going to have to streamline."

"He any good?"

"He came highly recommended." Royce drew a breath. "And, Jared. I fired Barry Brewster over China."

"Seriously?"

"He missed the deadline, blew the deal." He'd also insulted Amber, but Royce wasn't going anywhere near that conversation.

"There are a thousand ways to blow a deal with China."

"Yeah, well, he's gone."

"Okay. Your call. You need me to come back early?"

"Let's give it a few more days. There's one more thing…." Royce stopped himself. "You know what? It can wait."

If Jared learned about Norman Stanton and Stephanie, he'd be on the next plane back to the States.

But Royce had already made this month's blackmail payment. Norman Stanton had no idea they were on to him, and there was nothing Jared could do in the short term but worry.

"You sure?" asked Jared.

"I'm sure."

"And fix it with Amber, bro. She's not Mom. You're not Stanton. And everything's a leap of faith."

Amber and Katie stood side by side, gazing into the three-way mirror in Amber's bedroom.

"You don't think it would be too weird?" asked Katie as they admired their reflections in the sleek, sleeveless, pearl-adorned wedding gown and the dramatic oriental silk bridesmaid dress.

"Like I said before," Amber replied. "Think of them as a set. You know I like this one better." She turned and watched the orange, gold and midnight plum shimmer in the sunlight that streamed through her big windows.

"Did I miss something?" came a masculine voice from the doorway.

Amber and Katie whirled simultaneously to see all six foot two of Royce standing in the bedroom doorway. He was wearing a steel-gray business suit, a blue silk tie and a crisp white shirt. His face was freshly shaven, and his blue gaze hungry as he stared at her.

She swallowed the tears that were never far from the surface. His appearance was her dream come true. But she couldn't let herself hope.

"Where did you come from?" asked Katie.

Instead of answering, he strolled into the bedroom, gaze fixed on Amber as he grew closer. "Someone named Rosa said you were trying on your wedding gown."

Amber glanced down at the silk bridesmaid dress. "Something got lost in the translation."

"I was going to rip it from your body." The hunger in his eyes grew more intense.

Amber tipped her head, not sure what to think.

"I flew here at Mach 1," he told her. "All the way

over South Dakota, Iowa and Illinois, I told myself you belonged to Hargrove."

"I don't belong—"

"I told myself I'd reason with you, I'd make you understand you had an obligation to your fiancé, I'd explain again that nobody falls in love in a week, and what you thought you felt for me was an illusion."

He took her hands.

Katie took a few steps toward the door. "Uh, I'm… just going to…" She slipped outside and shut the door behind her.

"At least that's what I told myself," said Royce. "And then Rosa told me you were trying on your wedding dress. And I knew I had to stop you. I knew there was no way I could let you marry someone else."

"I'm not marrying—"

"I still find it impossible to believe a week is any kind of a foundation for a lifelong commitment. I looked up the mathematical odds on marital success. They're not good.

"But I do know I want you. And I know I'll shoot any guy who touches you. And I'm thinking maybe that's a sign that there's something to this."

Amber fought the smile that tightened her lips.

As declarations of love went, this left a whole lot to be desired. But this was Royce, and she knew his demons, and she knew just how difficult it was for him to even contemplate the possibility of happily ever after.

"I love you, Royce."

"You can't know—"

She put her fingertips over his lips. "I do know. And, guess what? I know you love me, too. And I know you're going to figure it out eventually. And if I have to wait a year, or ten or twenty, for you to decide we should stay together, that's fine with me."

His arm snaked around her waist, and he jerked her up tight against him. "I want to start staying together now."

"No problem." She smiled at him, trailing her palms over his chest, wrapping them loosely around his neck. "We'll hang out together while you give this love thing some serious thought."

He settled his other arm around her. "And by hanging out, I hope you mean living together, working together and sleeping together."

"I do," she told him.

"Good." He gave a decisive nod. "Then I'm thinking we'd better be married while we're hanging out. I don't want anyone else to try to steal you. Your father's already a little ticked off at my brother. And there's the whole propriety thing."

"You think it's logical for us to be married while we figure out if we're in love?"

"Completely logical," he said. "Especially if we want a few kids. You're not getting any younger—"

"Hey!" She smacked him on the shoulder.

"And who knows how long it'll take for us to be sure."

"Maybe twenty years?" she asked.

"Maybe even fifty." His expression sobered. His gaze caressed her as he slowly dipped his head. Then his warm, soft lips came down ever so gently onto hers, sealing their bargain.

"What do you say, Amber?" he whispered against her mouth. "Will you spend the next fifty or so years married to me, just in case I love you?"

She nodded, coming up on her bare toes to kiss him again, longer this time, more soundly.

"Yes, I will," she whispered. "Just in case."

His arms engulfed her, and he lifted her completely off the floor. His mouth slanted and his kiss deepened, and she clung to him, heart bursting with joy.

When he finally set her down, slowly sliding her along his body, his grin widened. "Well, what do you know."

"What?"

"I think it might be happening already."

She couldn't help but smile in return. "Imagine that."

He nodded. "And it's really easy. You know, I think I'm going to be very good at this."

"There's not a doubt in my mind."

His blue eyes stared down into hers. "I love you, Amber."

"I know you do, Royce."

"Forever."

"Absolutely."

"Who knew."

"I did."

"You did at that." And he bent to kiss her one more time.

Eleven

Royce couldn't think of a single thing he liked better than the sight of Amber at Hargrove's wedding—wearing the bridesmaid's dress. Katie had been radiant on her walk down the aisle. She'd beamed at Hargrove during the first dance, then laughed with him when they cut the cake. Royce caught the garter again, and this time he knew it was fate.

"She looked spectacular," said Amber as they walked, hand in hand, beneath the lighted tress of the waterfront patio. The reception was in full swing inside the restaurant, notables from both the business and political worlds dancing it up at the black-tie event.

"Your life's not going to be anything like hers," Royce observed, thinking about the reporters hovering in the parking lot.

"No, it's not." Amber grinned, turning to the rail to

stare out across the sparkling water. She took a sip of the bubbly liquid in her champagne flute.

Royce moved up behind her, tracing a fingertip along her bare shoulder. "Any regrets?"

"Yes," she sighed, and he felt a moment's pause.

But she covered his hand with her own, holding his touch against her skin. "I regret saying no to you in the hotel room earlier."

A surge of masculine pride swelled within him, and he leaned down to kiss her shoulder. "I told you so."

"You did."

"Weddings have a way of making women feel all romantic and mushy."

"It's true." She nodded, taking another drink.

"And all those romantic and mushy feelings have a way of turning to—"

"Lust?"

"Which could have been pre-empted," he whispered in her ear. "If you'd only let—"

"There you are, pumpkin," came David Hutton's hearty voice.

Royce immediately stepped back from Amber.

"Seems like I'm always finding you off in a corner with this Ryder fellow at wedding receptions."

"He does have a way of finding me," Amber joked, turning to face her father.

Royce was still a bit jumpy around the man. The two-carat solitaire on Amber's finger had mitigated some of the antagonism, but Royce wasn't sure David had forgiven him for breaking things off with Amber. He also wasn't sure that a jet pilot was an acceptable substitute for a senator as a son-in-law.

"You look amazing," David told his daughter, kissing her gently on the forehead.

"And you look handsome as always," Amber returned.

Royce held out his hand to shake, refusing to let David see anything but confidence. "Good to see you again, sir."

"I trust you'll be making your own wedding plans soon?" David asked him.

"Daddy," Amber admonished.

"Don't want to give the man time to change his mind again."

Royce held the handshake a little longer. "I'm not going to change my mind."

David harrumphed.

"I love your daughter, Mr. Hutton." Royce wrapped an arm around Amber's shoulder and drew her close. "I'm going to marry her and make her happy for the rest of her life."

"I would hope so. What with all the turmoil you caused."

"Daddy, I stopped loving Hargrove before Royce got anywhere near me."

Royce nearly choked on her choice of words. "The wedding will be soon," he assured David.

Amber glanced up at him in surprise. "Royce, we haven't—"

"Very soon." He gave Amber a meaningful squeeze.

David cracked a smile. "You keep my baby girl happy, son. And we'll get along just fine."

"I will," Royce assured the man.

"Call me David."

"Okay."

David winked at Amber and started away. "Don't stay out too late."

"I'm not coming home tonight," she warned him.

David turned his attention to Royce again. "Soon." He waggled a warning finger before he turned away.

"You want to head for Vegas tonight?" Royce asked Amber.

"Vegas is a terrible idea," said Stephanie.

Royce had left the jet under the command of his copilot and dropped into one of the seats in the main passenger cabin.

"Thank you," Amber said to Stephanie from the seat next to him.

They'd picked Stephanie up from a junior jumping show in Denver, and Jared and Melissa were hitching a ride from Chicago to the ranch for the last few days of their honeymoon.

"Well, she'd better come up with something," Royce told his sister. "I don't want her father gunning for me for the next year."

"He likes you," said Amber.

"No, he likes you. He tolerates me because you love me."

"I do love you," she confirmed, giving him a quick kiss on the cheek.

"And I love you," he automatically returned.

"Oh, gag me," Stephanie groaned.

"I thought you were a romantic," Melissa put in, moving up from the back of the cabin where she'd been sitting with Jared.

"I am a romantic. But, yuck, she's kissing my brother."

"Well, I totally get it," said Melissa.

"That's because you kiss my other brother."

Melissa got a gleam in her eyes. "You know what else I do to your other brother?"

Stephanie clapped her hands over her ears. "Pink fuzzy bunnies. Pink fuzzy bunnies."

"What the hell?" asked Royce.

"She's obliterating the image from her brain," Amber informed him.

Royce shook his head at the nonsense. "You," he said to Amber. "Come up with a wedding plan, or we *are* heading for Vegas." Then he exited his seat and moved to the back with his brother.

"Hey." Jared nodded to him, looking up from a table full of reports.

Royce sat down, lowering his voice. "You met with Alec Creighton?"

"I did."

"What did you think?"

Jared glanced to the front of the plane where the three women were chatting. "Seems like a good guy. Smart. On the ball."

"Did you talk to the VPs?"

Jared nodded. "They were shocked about Barry Brewster. It's got them looking over their shoulders. But I think in a good way."

"What about Konrad?"

Jared grinned. "Oh, he really hates you."

"Yeah. I kinda got that."

"He's demanded to deal directly with me from now on. Threatened to quit if you're involved in the construction division."

Royce clamped his jaw, while a burning anger roiled up in his stomach.

"Told him no," Jared said mildly. "Told him you

were taking over the construction division, and if he didn't like it, he should have his letter of resignation on your desk Monday morning."

Royce gaped at his brother. Konrad might be a jerk, but he was an incredibly valuable employee.

"Family is family," said Jared. "It's your company, too, and you did one hell of a job while I was away. Well, except for ticking off David Hutton."

"I'm working on that," said Royce, glancing to Amber, struck as always by how much he adored her.

"That's what counts, bro. Everybody's working hard at head office, looking to streamline, reallocating cash flow. We've survived trouble before."

Royce's attention shifted to his sister, and he lowered his voice. "After that, there's Stephanie."

"Yeah," Jared agreed. "We need to talk about that one."

"Does Melissa know?" asked Royce.

"That Frank Stanton is Stephanie's father?" Jared shook his head. "I'm keeping the club as small as possible for now."

Royce nodded. He was glad Amber already knew; he wouldn't want to have to make the choice to keep a secret from her.

"It was hard enough on me," said Jared. "Finding out what I did the way I did."

Royce nodded his agreement with that, too.

"Stephanie can *never* find out," Jared vowed.

"She won't." Royce had had most of his life to come to terms with his parents' secret, and it had still colored him in ways he hadn't even realized. It had almost cost him the love of his life.

He caught Amber's gaze.

She sobered at the sight of his expression, eyes

narrowing. Then she unobtrusively stood from her seat to move toward him.

He smiled and snagged her wrist, pulling her into his lap to wrap his arms around her.

"What's wrong?" she asked.

"Nothing."

She raised her brows to Jared.

Jared shook his head. "It's all good." His smile was back, and it was easy. "Except *you* can't seem to decide on a wedding."

Royce knew Amber wasn't buying their jovial mood, but she played along. "This is not a decision to take lightly. I'm only getting married once."

"In Vegas," said Royce.

Amber socked him in the arm.

"Tahiti, maybe." Melissa joined in. "On a beach, just family?"

"I vote for Tuscany," Stephanie called out. "Or Paris in the spring."

"She'll be pregnant by spring," said Royce, and Amber gave him a wide-eyed look of surprise.

"And we'd better damned well be married by then," he growled low.

"Babies?" she mused.

"I want babies," he confirmed.

"Good," she whispered and hugged him tightly, pressing her face into the crook of his neck, sighing in contentment, while the rest of his family joked about wedding plans.

& *Desire*™

2 in 1
GREAT
VALUE

THE MILLIONAIRE MEETS HIS MATCH by Kate Carlisle

Adam Duke's mother plans to marry him off. And when his desirable assistant, Trish James, hints she wants more than just a business relationship, alarm bells go off...

DANTE'S TEMPORARY FIANCÉE by Day Leclaire

Rafe Dante's family paraded women in front of him. Until Rafe hired sweet Larkin Thatcher to be his fake fiancée...

HIS CONVENIENT VIRGIN BRIDE by Barbara Dunlop

Just weeks after their roll in the hay, virgin Stephanie Ryder was expecting his baby. Now millionaire Alec Creighton's proposing...

SEDUCTION ON THE CEO'S TERMS by Charlene Sands

Frustrated that her boss was judging her by her looks, Ali had a reverse makeover. Ironically, as a plain-Jane, she *really* caught the wealthy bachelor's eye.

VIRGIN PRINCESS, TYCOON'S TEMPTATION by Michelle Celmer

Garrett Sutherland wanted his biggest claim to fame to be the seduction of Princess Louisa—the infamous virgin princess.

THE SECRET CHILD & THE COWBOY CEO by Janice Maynard

Trent Sinclair had never forgiven Bryn Matthews and her lies. But Bryn had returned...with a child he could not deny was pure Sinclair.

On sale from 17th June 2011
Don't miss out!

*Available at WHSmith, Tesco, ASDA, Eason
and all good bookshops*

www.millsandboon.co.uk

are proud to present

June 2011
Ordinary Girl in a Tiara
by Jessica Hart
from Mills & Boon® Riva™

Caro Cartwright's had enough of romance – she's after a quiet life. Until an old school friend begs her to stage a gossip-worthy royal diversion! Reluctantly, Caro prepares to masquerade as a European prince's latest squeeze…

Available 3rd June 2011

July 2011
Lady Drusilla's Road to Ruin
by Christine Merrill
from Mills & Boon® Historical

Considered a spinster, Lady Drusilla Rudney has only one role in life: to chaperon her sister. So when her flighty sibling elopes, Dru employs the help of a fellow travelling companion, ex-army captain John Hendricks, who looks harmless enough…

Available 1st July 2011

Tell us what you think!

millsandboon.co.uk/community
facebook.com/romancehq
twitter.com/millsandboonuk

BAD BLOOD

A POWERFUL
DYNASTY,
WHERE SECRETS
AND SCANDAL
NEVER SLEEP!

VOLUME 1 – 15th April 2011
TORTURED RAKE
by Sarah Morgan

VOLUME 2 – 6th May 2011
SHAMELESS PLAYBOY
by Caitlin Crews

VOLUME 3 – 20th May 2011
RESTLESS BILLIONAIRE
by Abby Green

VOLUME 4 – 3rd June 2011
FEARLESS MAVERICK
by Robyn Grady

8 VOLUMES IN ALL TO COLLECT!

MILLS
BOON

www.millsandboon.co.uk

BAD BLOOD

A POWERFUL
DYNASTY,
WHERE SECRETS
AND SCANDAL
NEVER SLEEP!

VOLUME 5 – 17th June 2011
HEARTLESS REBEL
by Lynn Raye Harris

VOLUME 6 – 1st July 2011
ILLEGITIMATE TYCOON
by Janette Kenny

VOLUME 7 – 15th July 2011
FORGOTTEN DAUGHTER
by Jennie Lucas

VOLUME 8 – 5th August 2011
LONE WOLFE
by Kate Hewitt

8 VOLUMES IN ALL TO COLLECT!

www.millsandboon.co.uk

MODERN

THE MARRIAGE BETRAYAL
by Lynne Graham
Sander Volakis has no intention of marrying—until he sees Tally Spencer. He can't resist her…little knowing that one night with the innocent Tally could end his playboy existence…

Doukakis's Apprentice
by Sarah Morgan
Wanted: willing apprentice to handle incorrigible, womanising (but incredibly sexy) tycoon! Polly Prince is determined to make a lasting success of the position, but soon learns that her workaholic boss *can* put pleasure before business!

Heart of the Desert
by Carol Marinelli
One kiss is all it takes for Georgie to know Sheikh Ibrahim is trouble, Trapped in the swirling sands, she surrenders to the rebel Prince—yet the law of his land decrees that she can never really be his…

Her Impossible Boss
by Cathy Williams
Successful New Yorker Matt Strickland's sexiness is off the scale, but new employee, feisty nanny Tess Kelly, thinks his capacity for fun definitely shows room for improvement! Although he's *determined* to keep things professional…

On sale from 17th June 2011
Don't miss out!
Available at WHSmith, Tesco, ASDA, Eason and all good bookshops
www.millsandboon.co.uk

THE ICE PRINCE
by Sandra Marton

No opponent can penetrate Prince Draco Valenti's icy exterior…except high-flying, straight-talking lawyer Anna Orsini! They're at odds in business, but in the bedroom Draco's desire for Anna has the power to melt *all* his defences!

SURRENDER TO THE PAST
by Carole Mortimer

Mia Burton thinks she's seen the last of Ethan Black—the man who haunts her heart. But Ethan's returned in all his very real glory, and it's clear he'll do *whatever* it takes to win her back!

RECKLESS NIGHT IN RIO
by Jennie Lucas

Gabriel Santos offers Laura Parker a million dollars to pretend she loves him. But they've already shared one unforgettable night in Rio, and Gabriel's not aware he's the father of Laura's baby…

THE REPLACEMENT WIFE
by Caitlin Crews

Theo Markou Garcia needs a wife—or someone who looks like his infamous fiancée—so offers disowned Becca Whitney a deal: masquerade as the Whitney heiress in exchange for her own true fortune…but don't fall for her husband!

On sale from 1st July 2011
Don't miss out!

Available at WHSmith, Tesco, ASDA, Eason and all good bookshops

www.millsandboon.co.uk

Dating and Other Dangers
by Natalie Anderson

After being trashed on Nadia Keenan's dating website, Ethan Rush faces three dates with her! *He's* determined to clear his name. *She's* determined to prove him for the cad he is…

The S Before Ex
by Mira Lyn Kelly

World famous celebrity Ryan Brady's secret wife is filing for divorce! Unfortunately for Claire Brady, her soon-to-be-ex is *still* the only man her body wants…

Girl in a Vintage Dress
by Nicola Marsh

Lola Lombard, 1950s style siren, is petrified: she's got to organise a terrifyingly glam hen do! Worse still, the bride's gorgeous brother seems interested in the shy woman behind the red lipstick…

Rapunzel in New York
by Nikki Logan

When a knight in pinstripe rushed to the aid of this damsel, she declared she didn't want saving, even by a billionaire! *Yet sometimes even modern Maidens secretly need rescuing…*

On sale from 1st July 2011
Don't miss out!

Available at WHSmith, Tesco, ASDA, Eason and all good bookshops

www.millsandboon.co.uk

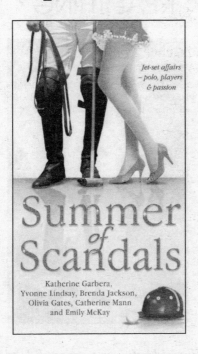

711/25/MB345

SIZZLING HOLIDAY FLING…OR THE REAL THING?

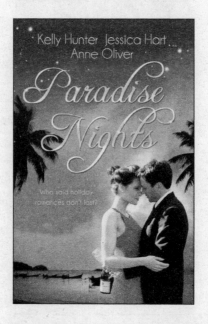

Who said holiday romances didn't last?
As the sun sets the seduction begins…
Who can resist the baddest of boys?

Royal Affairs – luxurious and bound by duty yet still captive to desire!

Royal Affairs: Desert Princes & Defiant Virgins

Available 3rd June 2011

Royal Affairs: Princesses & Protectors

Available 1st July 2011

Royal Affairs: Mistresses & Marriages

Available 5th August 2011

Royal Affairs: Revenge Secrets & Seduction

Available 2nd September 2011

Intense passion and glamour from our bestselling stars of international romance

Available 20th May 2011

Available 17th June 2011

Available 15th July 2011

Available 19th August 2011

FREE BOOK
AND A SURPRISE GIFT

We would like to take this opportunity to thank you for reading this Mills & Boon® book by offering you the chance to take a specially selected book from the Desire™ 2-in-1 series absolutely FREE! We're also making this offer to introduce you to the benefits of the Mills & Boon® Book Club™—

- **FREE home delivery**
- **FREE gifts and competitions**
- **FREE monthly Newsletter**
- **Exclusive Mills & Boon Book Club offers**
- **Books available before they're in the shops**

Accepting this FREE book and gift places you under no obligation to buy, you may cancel at any time, even after receiving your free book. Simply complete your details below and return the entire page to the address below. You don't even need a stamp!

YES Please send me a free Desire 2-in-1 book and a surprise gift. I understand that unless you hear from me, I will receive 2 superb new 2-in-1 books every month for just £5.30 each, postage and packing free. I am under no obligation to purchase any books and may cancel my subscription at any time. The free book and gift will be mine to keep in any case.

Ms/Mrs/Miss/Mr _____ Initials _____

_____

Surname _____

Address _____

_____

_____ Postcode _____

E-mail_____

Send this whole page to: Mills & Boon Book Club, Free Book Offer, FREEPOST NAT 10298, Richmond, TW9 1BR